Kindergarten Baby

A School Days-Grimm Nights Novel
Book One

by
Cricket Rohman

Publisher's Note

This is a work of fiction. Names, characters, places, and incidents are the products of the author's imagination or are used fictitiously. Any resemblance to actual persons, living or dead, business establishments, events, or locales is entirely coincidental.

This book is dedicated:

To my mom, MaryLee Rohmann,
who read to me often.

In memory of my dad, Edward J. Rohmann,
who taught me the value of hard work.

To caring, creative, and talented teachers everywhere.

Acknowledgments

I would like to thank:

My very first reader, Sharon Erb, and the feedback readers Adrienne Magee, Beth Pearson, Wendy Parks, and Colleen Roh who read every single word before 15,000 words were cut from the manuscript.

My talented and delightful editor at Writing Wildly Editorial Services who kept me laughing through most of the editing process.

Doug Aghassi for his creative website designing.

Guido Henkel for his speed and patience (with me) in formatting the ebook versions.

Jaycee DeLorenzo at Sweet 'N Spicy Designs for my beautiful cover.

My three sons, Doug, Jeff, and Justin for providing inspiration—each in their own way.

Jerry Gallegos for his everlasting love, unwavering moral support, and genuine encouragement.

School Days-Grimm Nights Books by Cricket Rohman
Kindergarten Baby: a novel
A Break in the Clouds
The Road Trip

Once Upon A Time ...

A lonely little girl sat on the shore and stared vacantly at the advancing waves, waiting for a miracle.

"Come on. Time to go," a woman's voice called. "Your new foster family is expecting you."

The little girl sighed, her small shoulders slumping with resignation. No miracle today. But she would survive, safe inside a world she'd created in her mind. She'd cope with the loneliness and endure the fears that reached beyond the realm of her understanding by cultivating a powerful belief in myths—fairy tales and happily ever afters. And, for her own protection, she'd learn to bury her sorrows between the pages of Snow White, Rapunzel, and Briar Rose.

Fall

Chapter One

Lindsey Sommerfield smiled into the wide-open faces of her kindergarten students, all of whom waited impatiently for her next word. She had begun their day—as she always did—with a story. A fairy tale.

"She gently washed the cinders from her face, then dressed in the most beautiful, shimmering gown in all the kingdom, for she was about to marry the brave and charming prince," she declared, her voice ringing with the magical tone of a true storyteller.

Lindsey no longer read from the pages of the books she loved. She embellished the sometimes lackluster text with more description and enticing enchantment, and threw in an occasional kindergarten vocabulary word, using the book's illustrations to assist her young students' imaginations.

A small hand went up, waving wildly.

"Yes, Harley?"

"What are those things? The … the … sidders she washed?" he asked.

"They are cinders," Emma told him. She was the brainiest girl in the class.

"I know. I know," interrupted Willy, chest puffed with pride. "They're people that do bad, bad things."

Lindsey smiled at each child. "I'm glad you are all paying attention. Good question, Harley. Willy, you were very close, but I think you were thinking of 'sinners.' Sinners are people who do bad things. Emma, you are right. Cinders are leftover coals or dirt from a fireplace or wood stove," she explained as she flipped back to an illustration of Cinderella sweeping up around the fireplace.

"Shall I go on?" she asked. She continued after unanimous agreement from the group. "Kind as always, Cinderella invited her stepmother and stepsisters to live in the palace after the royal wedding. They didn't stay long, though. They couldn't be their grumpy old selves among all the joyful noises that could be heard throughout the cheerful kingdom. So, Cinderella and the Prince really did get to live happily ever after."

"Hurray! Read it again," the children pleaded.

Lindsey Sommerfield was a lucky woman. She loved her job almost as much as she loved her husband, who she absolutely adored. She usually arrived at the school early and left late, not so much out of duty or contract time, but out of true dedication and love for her students and their successes. She thrived in this environment, finding joy in the complex challenges she and other teachers faced on a daily basis.

Today, however, Lindsey had fallen prey to one of the numerous, marauding germs in her classroom. They took hold like an ornery pitbull and wouldn't let go. Before long, the agonizing headache, the more-than-scratchy throat, and her total lack of energy became increasingly difficult to ignore. It was only when she nearly passed out in the middle of snack time that she surrendered to the infection and went home early.

Lindsey hesitated at her front door, though she wasn't overly concerned when she heard muffled noises coming from inside. Her first thought was that either she or her husband, Anthony, had accidentally left the television on. It wasn't until she stepped into the echoing, terra-cotta tiled hallway that a tingling sensation of apprehension swept through her weakened body. Something wasn't right.

The noise seemed to trickle down from upstairs, which was strange, because there was no television up there. She had seen to that, insisting that upstairs was for love, rest, and rejuvenation. That was their private nest, their soothing refuge from the outside world. It was also the place where they kept heirloom jewelry, Anthony's designer clothing, state-of-the-art computers storing years of personal and work-related data, and their combined collection of rare books. Add to that the priceless, original artwork painted by her mother, and it amounted to a treasure trove for a thief.

Thieves. Panic shot through her. Fight or flight? Dabbing at the fever-induced perspiration beading across her forehead, she wondered vaguely why the air conditioning wasn't blowing full-force on this hot September afternoon. Then she realized it was.

She cocked her head, hearing the muffled sounds again. A voice? Voices? She bristled. How dare any intruders enter their home? She'd transformed the tiny old house into a charming, cozy, southwest home, and she loved it. Without another thought, she grabbed the banister and ascended the wooden stairs, meaning to confront the intruders.

The noises were coming from her bedroom. The thickening congestion in her head brought new pain with each weary step, and her fever soared. When she touched the door handle, she wished she could just lie down between the cool crisp sheets and breathe in the subtle scent of her husband, still lingering from their romantic night before. Oh, to sip some chamomile tea and drift off into a fuzzy, numbing sleep. Soon, she promised herself. Soon.

The curtains were drawn; the bedroom was dark. The sounds that had lured her quieted to an eerie, sudden silence, as if someone had flipped the master switch on the fuse box.

"Lindsey? What are you doing home?"

She'd been expecting intruders. Nothing could have prepared her for this.

"I ... I live here," she managed. "And ... and I'm sick. Oh, God. I am so sick," she groaned, then stumbled to the bathroom.

She reached the toilet just in time to vomit far more than her lunch. Her dream come true life, her happily ever after, and everything about her steadfast world spewed from her throat, leaving her empty.

Chapter Two

Three Years Earlier

Lindsey Lark met Anthony Sommerfield literally by accident. She'd reached up for the crate of percussion instruments, lost her balance, and pulled the entire heavy wooden bookshelf—including all its contents—down on her head. There she lay next to the rectangular-shaped rug resembling a small town, surrounded by tambourines, shakers, and *Dr. Seuss*, *Cinderella*, *Franklin the Turtle*, and *Clifford the Big Red Dog* picture books.

In a helpless daze, a dancing collage of fanciful, classroom apparitions appeared before her like a weird, disconnected cartoon.

I'll make breakfast for the prince, giggled Cinderella, yes, green eggs and ham would be nice, no . . . no ham, just eggs, green eggs, green eggs and . . . yams, and I'll give some to that dog, the big red dog, but there won't be enough for a dog that big, why is that dog so darned large, something must have gone wrong, but the turtle will fix that, he's a very nice turtle and Franklin wants a pet, I know he does, but it's . . .

Get a grip, Lindsey, came a voice from within. *This is your life, not some fractured fairy tale.*

"Lily, go get the principal," she managed to say as the swirling room and the distorted sounds around her faded to black—just like in the movies.

When she awoke in the hospital, Anthony was the gorgeous white-coated doctor taking her pulse.

"Your vital signs are stable," he told her, "and you don't appear to have broken or sprained anything. Your head and your knee are going to be sore for a while, though. If you promise to go straight home and take it easy for two or three days, I think Dr. Hapner will release you," he said. She'd thought it odd that he deferred to another doctor, but what did she know of hospital procedures? "Can we call your husband to come pick you up?" he asked.

She blinked, momentarily mute. "Oh, uh, I'm not married," she stammered, mortified at the blush that burned her cheeks. "I ... I don't mean that I'd never get married, but I'm not just yet. I mean, uh ... what I mean is ... I'm not married now—not that I've been married before. I'm just ... well ..." She shrugged, feeling idiotic. "I'm single."

The doctor leaned in to examine her pupils, then expertly re-examined her delicate jaw and neck. *Mmmm. He smelled good.* Lindsey was thankful he wasn't checking her heart rate right then, or he'd have a different comment to make about her vital signs. He might have even whisked her away to the cardiac wing.

"Perhaps, Miss Lark, it is too soon to release you after all," he said with a wink and a smile. That was the moment in which Lindsey, the no-nonsense, career-minded teacher, fell head over heels in love.

Anthony spent almost every weekend at her place. She loved the attention and companionship, and tried to overlook the fact that his presence kept her from getting routine things like laundry, cleaning, and shopping done. She simply added those tasks to her already busy weekdays. When he asked for her assistance in making arrangements for the opening of his first office, she was flattered. She began to type letters for him, write advertisements, and fill out loan papers till she was utterly exhausted. She was a little confused when she discovered he was a chiropractor, as opposed to a medical doctor, but the fact that he'd kept that from her seemed inconsequential after a while. Maybe he hadn't meant to deceive her at all. It just hadn't crossed his mind to tell her that little detail.

Lindsey was aware that her best friend Laura viewed all this as a warning. Laura didn't trust Anthony one bit. But Lindsey cherished every moment with him and dreamed of the day when he would officially become her family, filling the emptiness she'd lived with for so many years.

Their courtship was brief, their passion fiery. Anthony radiated a vitality that drew her to him like a magnet, and he seemed both intrigued and challenged by her innocence and delicate beauty. Within a matter of weeks, their physical bond was driving them both crazy, and they decided they couldn't wait. So, a mere three months after they'd met, she and Anthony started to plan their wedding.

She'd done it. She'd met Prince Charming, and now she was being swept away in waves of Happily Ever After.

That was then. This is now.

Moving in slow motion, Lindsey grabbed a pillow and a spare blanket, then she stumbled downstairs and collapsed on the sofa. She wasn't about to lie down in their bed. Couldn't even look at it. Not now, not ever. How could he do this? Had their marriage vows meant nothing to him? They'd had a good marriage—or at least she'd thought so. Maybe it hadn't been perfect, but it was good. Even better than good at times. Her mind swirled, trying to make sense of it all. She wanted to run away, but she had no strength. She wanted to scream at him with blistering anger, but her voice was raspy from being sick.

Most of all, she wanted everything to be the way it was—or at least the way she thought it had been when she'd headed out to work that morning. She let the fever carry her away, let herself melt into foggy memories of that morning, when he'd brought her breakfast in bed, complete with her favorite crunchy wheat toast, sweet cantaloupe, a tall, hot latte—even a red chrysanthemum from their garden, standing in a bud vase. He'd smothered her with cool, tickling kisses and told her to have a wonderful day in kinderland. It had all seemed so romantic ... and so unreal. Could all the extra attention he'd given her lately merely have been a cover up? Had he hoped just to keep her happy so she wouldn't suspect him of this destructive, sordid affair?

She was startled when a wet nose nuzzled her fevered cheek. "Oh, hello, Wendell," she said sadly. "You've been a good boy today, right?"

He sat by her side, cocking his head as if he were trying to understand her mood.

"You don't want to know, Wendell. Believe me, you really don't."

"I've got to get back to the clinic," Anthony announced, sweeping into the room. His voice carried about as much warmth as a corpse.

"Really?" she croaked, giving him a taste of her own bitter coolness. "It wasn't so important to be there earlier today, was it?"

He sat on the coffee table in front of her, propped his elbows on his knees, and met her eyes. "Look, Lindsey, I know you're upset. We need to talk."

We need to talk? "It seems a little late for that," she said dryly.

The combination of illness and shock blanketed her with an oddly numb, empty sensation, but she knew it was only a matter of time before her intense pain and justifiable anger arrived.

"I never meant for you to see that."

Her eyes narrowed. "Well, that's probably true. That's probably the only truth I've had from you in quite a while." She made an attempt at a shrug. "Of course you wouldn't want me to see that. It's much more difficult to pull off an affair when the wife knows about it."

He stared at her, his strong jaw set, and she thought she'd never seen such cold, distant eyes before. "We'll talk," he told her. "I've got to go."

Without another word, without any attempt to comfort his ill and traumatized wife, he left.

Wendell kept vigil by her side as she stared at the ceiling, detaching herself to the best of her ability from the unfathomable situation at hand. So this was her new reality, she mused, waiting for the Nyquil to take affect. Why did they always seem to call things a "reality" when the outcome looked dreadful or dim? All she'd wanted was a little happiness, a little love.

The clock on the mantel ticked, and Wendell's warm, damp, rhythmic breathing puffed on her face as he waited for an explanation.

I was a good wife, she thought, just before her eyes closed. *I was.*

When she awoke, the clock still ticked, but darkness had crept over the interior of their tiny home. Lindsey rose from the sofa like a feeble old woman, searching for Wendell, Anthony, and something cool to drink. The drink was easy to find. The fridge was full of not-so-healthy soda, fruit and vegetable juices, and sparkling water. She chose a soda and drank it straight out of the can, enjoying the cool shock of the bubbles against her rough throat. Locating Wendell took a bit more effort. He wasn't in his well-worn, jumbo-sized, dog bed, and he wasn't in the backyard, which was his favorite place to be when left to his own devices. When she finally found him, he was sitting stiffly by the front door, as if on guard. Then she noticed the clock. Not the sound, but the time—3:45 a.m.

Wearily, she climbed upstairs, expecting to find her sleeping husband. She would forgive him, she decided. They would start over. She toyed with the idea that the whole ugly scene had been a hallucination, just a figment of her fevered imagination. Deep down, though, she knew that wasn't the case. Still … there might be a reasonable explanation—or perhaps not reasonable, but at least an explanation of some kind. No matter what, she would save her marriage. Anthony was everything to her. He was her only family.

She poked her head into their bedroom. "Honey? Anthony?" she called in her softest, sweetest voice.

He wasn't there. He hadn't come home. She walked to the side of the bed, stroked her fingers over his pillow. Then she pulled her hand away and examined the long strands of hair that had attached themselves to her fingers. The other woman was a redhead.

Out of habit, she glanced at the upstairs answering machine, and her mood lifted when she saw the red light blinking. Only one message. With anticipation, she pressed Play, expecting to hear him apologizing with the utmost sincerity, begging for forgiveness. Instead, she heard Laura's perky voice, inquiring about her health.

"Hey Linds, you're not answering your phone. Good! You must be sleeping. Rest up. You don't often get the chance to lie in bed all day. They called a sub for you tomorrow, so don't even think about coming to school. And don't stay up all night writing lesson plans. I put a video on your desk for the sub to use. It's educational … or it's *somewhat* educational." She hesitated. "Well, okay. It's entertaining, and the kids will like it. I'll say a tiny prayer that the principal doesn't do a walk through while it's on. And I borrowed some fun worksheets from the Ditto Queen. Your students will survive one day of less than perfect instruction. Don't worry about a thing. Sweet dreams. Call me if you need anything your hunky hubby can't provide."

Lindsey dropped onto the side of their king-sized bed and stared despondently ahead. Her friend and colleague cared more about her than her own husband did. Her thoughts drifted to memories of her first true friend, Cindy, a little girl she'd met at the group home after her parents died. Cindy was the one who had introduced her to fairy tales. Together they read from a collection of fairy tales for hours. Often, in their own way, they acted them out.

"All right," she remembered Cindy saying, "you can be Sleeping Beauty first, and I'll be the old granny at the spinning wheel. But next time, I get to be the pretty girl."

Just as little Lindsey pricked her small finger on the imaginary spindle, the home's supervisor walked in, grabbed Lindsey, and marched her down the hall. Then she handed the little girl off to her first foster family. Funny, she'd forgotten all about that day until just now.

Where is my husband? As if she didn't know. She bit her lower lip, forcing herself to think straight. That wasn't fair. Maybe he was just at a friend's house—a *male* friend's house—trying to figure out how to make things right, win Lindsey back.

Who am I kidding? He was probably with *her*, she admitted to herself.

Who was this mystery woman who had seduced Anthony, singlehandedly destroying their marriage? Lindsey scowled. She was probably tall and gorgeous, with long red hair—no matter how she tried, Lindsey just couldn't get her hair to grow quite as long as Anthony wanted—and most likely the other woman was far more voluptuous than Lindsey would ever be. *Damn it!* she thought, springing off the bed. That woman had been right there in her bed, doing God knows what with her husband.

Lindsey's life had become a soap opera, and she was the most pitiful character of all.

She couldn't stay in that room, but she couldn't physically stand up any longer. Wrapping her arms around her stomach, Lindsey dragged herself back downstairs to the sofa. She held her breath against the strong, medicinal smell, then took an extra large swig of the stop-the-aching-coughing-sneezing-fever-so-you-can-rest medicine, hoping to escape.

Wendell stared at her, his big brown eyes confused. She reached over and scratched behind one ear. "Wendell, you might as well lie down," she said. "He's not coming back tonight."

Her faithful friend gave her a sympathetic nuzzle, then circled three times and lay down with a grunt. Lindsey briefly hoped she'd fall asleep first, but Wendell won. He began to snore, making a sound that only a one hundred and sixty pound, overtired mastiff can make. It was going to be a long, long night.

"Lindsey? Are you okay?"
Anthony!
"Have you been sleeping all day?"

She battled her heavy eyelids and looked up, still groggy. "What? Huh? What time is it?"

Anthony stood beside her, as handsome as ever, and the look in his eyes was tender. He sat beside her and placed a cool, strong hand against her forehead, then shook his head. Just like that, he began to take care of her, with all the usual attention. He took her temperature, brought her an extra pillow, then placed her favorite books and DVDs so she could reach them without getting up. After that, he set out some aspirin and made a phone call to a friend from the hospital for a prescription that he couldn't legally write.

After last night, all this wonderful attention made little sense, unless … Wait. Could it have all been a dream? A nightmare? Maybe. Yes. She blinked slowly, watching Anthony when he brought her toast and a cup of tea then set it gently by her. *He must still care if he's able to do all this and still smile at me so tenderly.* That meant it had all been a nightmare. It *had* to mean that. *Oh, thank you God,* she thought, fleetingly happy, despite her aches, fever, sore throat, and cough. She couldn't imagine her life without him.

"Honey," he said softly, sitting by her. "I'm sorry that you have to go through all this."

She smiled, trying to sound like her usual perky self through the congestion. "Oh, I'll be all right. This darned thing will run its course, and I'll be back on my feet in a few days."

He swallowed. "I'm not talking about the flu, Lindsey."

"All right," she said sleepily. "What do you want to call it? A bad cold? Sinus? Overwork? Poor alignment?" She gave him a lopsided grin. "With a few of your super spinal adjustments, maybe a cranial adjustment or two, I'll be back on my feet even sooner."

He jumped to his feet. "Lindsey!" he said sternly. "Stop it!"

The walls she'd built around her began to crumble. So it hadn't been a hallucination. *No, no, no!* But he kept talking, saying things she couldn't stand to hear.

"Listen. I never wanted to hurt you. I didn't mean for any of this to happen. I wish it hadn't, but it did, and now I'm in love with someone else."

She tried to speak, tried to scream, but nothing came out. He shook his head violently, then turned away. She stared at his back as he walked out the front door.

"No!" she whimpered. "No, you don't. You love *me!*"

Life swirled in slow motion around her, out of reach, out of control. Her head buzzed, throbbed, and she felt a deep, enveloping numbness close around her as if she were submerged in murky water. She was nothing but a pawn now, she realized, waiting for Anthony's next move.

Chapter Three

When Lindsey woke to the pounding, ringing, and shouting, still hazy from her trauma-plus-Nyquil induced sleep, it took a moment to put it all together. Fighting gravity, she managed to sit up on the sofa, though even that made her dizzy.

"Lindsey?" she heard. "Anthony? Wendell? Is *anybody* home?"

Wendell bounded in from the backyard, barking loudly, ready to defend his territory, but he backed off when he recognized Laura. The barking turned to wagging as she let herself in.

Laura narrowed her eyes at her friend. "You really ought to lock your door, you know. Even with the world's greatest—well, at least the world's *largest* watchdog."

"Oh. Hi, Laura. How are the kids?"

"Your kids are fine. But how are you? You don't look so good, Linds."

Lindsey made a brave attempt at a smile. "You know me. I'll find some way to pull it together by Monday. I've got all weekend to get over this."

"Oh, I have no doubt that you'll be back at school on Monday," she said, frowning, "but I'm worried about you." She sat beside her friend, looking concerned. "I've never seen an illness get a hold of you like this. Are you sure you're all right?"

No, she thought, feeling miserable. *No, I'm not all right.*

She hesitated at first, not wanting to tell her friend what had happened. What if Laura saw her as a loser? But deep down Lindsey knew better. Laura was the closest thing she had to family besides Anthony. So she confided in her friend. She told her how it had been, coming home to a not-so-empty house.

"What am I supposed to do?" she cried.

"What *did* you do?" Laura asked, eyes wide with shock.

She felt her body give in, and the tears started up again. "I fell apart."

Laura gathered her friend in her arms, rubbing her back and speaking gently. "Oh, honey. Maybe he just made a mistake. Granted, it's a big one, but it doesn't mean it's the end. She might have caught him in a vulnerable moment and seduced him. Maybe she—"

"His last words were, 'I'm in love with another woman,' and I assume that meant her. You have to admit, that doesn't sound like a momentary lack of judgment."

Laura wiped tears from her own eyes. "Oh Linds. Don't give up. This other woman, who is she?"

"I don't know. In my book she's the wicked witch, the cruel stepmother, the evil fairy all rolled into one," blurted Lindsey. "All I know is that she's got long red hair. And I seriously doubt she's ugly."

"Ah, now that's where you're wrong, my friend. In my opinion, any woman who would do what she did—sleep with another woman's husband, and *especially* in the other woman's bed—well, she *is* ugly."

Lindsey sniffed, then silently nodded. "What do I do now?"

"Take a shower," Laura advised. "You're a mess. I'll whip up something for dinner."

It felt surreal, stepping into the familiar shower, and her mind couldn't help but flash back on intimate moments she and Anthony had shared there. As the steam rose around her, Lindsey yielded to the pain roaring through her mind, body, and soul. She slid down the wall until she sat on the cool tiles, then rocked back and forth, sobbing convulsively, and her tears mingled with the drops of water raining down from the shower.

Awhile later, clean and dressed, she made her way back downstairs.

"All right, much better," Laura said with approval. "I think I might even recognize you now if we passed on the street. First a little food, then we'll make a plan. I, for one, want to find out just who this woman is."

Lindsey was too weak to argue. Besides, as much as it hurt to think about the other woman, she, too, wanted to know who she was. What was so special about that woman that had made him want to leave their marriage?

"I can't believe he'd do this to you—or even to himself, for that matter," said Laura. "You two were the perfect couple."

"You know it wasn't perfect," corrected Lindsey

Laura shrugged. "Okay, but it was better than most. He at least could have had the decency to take her someplace else, though. I mean, right here in your own home? That's … that's not right. That's beyond hurtful. Almost vicious."

A car pulled up, the tires crunching gravel as it parked. "Speak of the devil," muttered Lindsey.

Anthony didn't seem bothered by the cold looks aimed at him. Instead, he swaggered into the kitchen and regarded them both as if they were the ones who had done something wrong.

"Let me guess," he began, his tone thick with sarcasm. "You're talking about me, right? Me, the bad guy." He crossed his arms. "Well, gossip all you want, but I did what I had to do. A man needs a woman who has time for him. I did you a favor, Lindsey." His voice rose in volume. "Now you can write in your precious little plan book all you want. You can call as many kids' parents as often as you want. You can go to PTA meetings and Math Nights and In-services twenty-four hours a day for all I care," he shouted angrily.

He paced the kitchen one more time, then dashed up the stairs. Within moments he was back, a bulging duffle bag slung over his shoulder, ready to make his second grand exit. Grabbing a bottle of wine from the counter, he turned toward the two women and spoke his parting words.

"At least Shawna has time to make dinner for me."

The door slammed, and Lindsey and Laura turned toward each other.

"Shawna?" was all they could say.

On Monday morning Lindsey took a deep breath, put on a happy face, and stood at the classroom door, welcoming her students as they entered. Her legs still trembled with weakness as she fought the residual symptoms of the flu. At least the worst was over. If only she could say that for the rest of her life. She was completely unable to shake the haunting vision of her husband in their bed with that woman only four days before.

Twenty-six happy children sang brightly as they gathered on the rug area around her, completely oblivious to the nightmare her life had become. "Good morning to the sun, good morning to the ..."

When the song was over, Emma was the first to ask. "Where were you?"

"We got to watch Garfield," Marvin shared.

"Yeah, but the sub was kinda mean," Harley said quietly.

Questions and comments came fast and furious, and she wasn't surprised. She had never missed a full day of school before, let alone two. And since this was kindergarten, Lindsey was the first teacher most of them had ever known. With her gone, the students had discovered that not all teachers possessed the patience or kindness that came so naturally to Lindsey.

"She yelled at us," whined Bobby. "And she made Joseph sit in the corner by himself." Bobby was a perpetual whiner. Even when things were going well. Today, however, his tone seemed more grating than usual.

Teaching kindergarten was not for everyone. Being around one or two five-year-olds for a day can be difficult; being in a room with twenty-six of them can be impossible. It can push a normal person right over the edge, and Lindsey could attest to that. Even for her, there were days when she would have liked to send Joseph to the moon. But she never let it show.

Lindsey explained all about her bad cold then read the story, *Teddy Bears Cure A Cold* by Suzanna Gretz. Needing a little time to herself, she suggested they all sit and make pictures of their own experiences with sneezing, sore throats, or runny noses. Out came the pencils, crayons, and paper, and away to the tables went the eager young artists. Lindsey went to her desk to blow her own nose and take another dose of Tylenol.

From her desk she observed Willy demonstrating his ability to blow snot bubbles out of his slightly runny nose. His table partners displayed varying reactions. Emma politely tried to ignore him; Maggie's face showed disgust at his grossness; Harley giggled; and competitive Joseph tried his best, with no luck, to make something, anything come out of his nose.

Lindsey's classroom was cheerful and tidy—or at least it was tidy compared to most kindergarten classrooms. Martha Stewart might not approve, but students, parents, and other teachers did. Lindsey was a master organizer with color coordinated tubs, all labeled appropriately and housing things like writing folders, individual book bags, thematic folders, and music folders.

"Can I shut off the lights?" Alexa asked about twenty minutes later.

"Yes please," Lindsey said with a small smile. "It's time to clean up." Turning off the lights was part of a routine she was teaching the children, and it made her happy to see them learning.

When the lights went out, everyone froze.

"When the lights go back on," Lindsey said quietly, "Please put everything away and join me on the rug."

A few minutes later, the little group crowded around her, eager to see what she had planned.

"All right," Lindsey said, holding up a pile of the students' 'illness' pictures. "Who would like to share?"

Many hands went up, and Lindsey called on Emma first. She was a great role model and always showed the other students what was expected of them.

"This is a picture of me lying on the couch," Emma explained. "I'm watching TV and drinking lots of juice to make me better."

"What's all the white stuff all around you?" asked Armando.

"That's all my Kleenexes. I had a very, very, very bad cold."

"What's that thing that looks like a pig?" Willy asked with a sneer. He was expecting to get a laugh out of the other kids, and he did.

"That's my dog Sally," snapped Emma. "Sally always stays with me when I'm sick. She's the best dog in the whole wide world."

Emma's words brought Lindsey's thoughts back to her own home, her own very, very, very bad cold, and her own best-in-the-whole-wide-world dog. And, of course, these thoughts segued her thinking to Anthony. She puffed out a breath, feeling as if a ton of shapeless bricks had suddenly crushed the life from her petite body. She silently gave thanks that the end of the school day was near. She could hang on for another thirty minutes. She had to.

"Miss Lindsey!" whined Bobby.

Lindsey shook her head for the millionth time. "Bobby, you know I don't call on students that are being noisy." Maybe by the end of the year he would finally get the idea.

He sat quietly while the next student shared his picture, then she did call on him.

"Um, um," he said in his shrill voice, "I worked really hard on my picture, and I like it. It's me. I'm sick, and I'm wearing my favorite Rug Rats pj's. I had to stay home from school."

Bobby's art was always a little on the bizarre side, and this picture was no exception. He definitely had a style: chaotic. He could make a picture of a flower look like a monster. If he drew a cat, it became a devil-cat, with daggers for claws and spikes for teeth. In her opinion, Bobby's pictures were far more appropriate for a Steven King movie than a kindergarten classroom.

"Thank you, Bobby," she said sweetly. "We have time for one more. Who else would like to share?"

"Miss Lindsey, who is that the man in Bobby's picture?"

Without hesitation, Bobby answered. "That's my dad."

"Wow! Your dad gets to stay home with you when you're sick?" asked Connie. She sounded slightly envious.

"Just when he's sick, too."

"What's he holding?" Joseph asked.

"His medicine and the big stick. He carries it because he's the big dog at our house," said Bobby, pleased to share.

"That's a pretty big thermometer, Bobby. I'm sure your dad took good care of you."

"Oh no, Miss Lindsey. It's not a thermo ... nomo ... momometer. It's his power stick. It gives him power, and it makes mom be good and—"

The buzzer rang, and the kids jumped to their feet, forgetting all about the power stick. Saved by the bell. Lindsey said 'goodbye' and 'see you tomorrow' to each of her students as they left, and she made sure that Bobby received a giant-sized smile. Lindsey was suddenly concerned that, any day now, he would tell her something that could not go unreported.

He'd never mentioned his dad before, and the man had never come to school. Not even for Open House Night. And now she had to wonder about this 'power stick.' Was it a sign of violence at home? Lindsey hoped it wouldn't turn out to be a CPS (Child Protective Services) case, but on the other hand, Bobby was a strange kid. Maybe it was nothing more than that, she tried to convince herself. Maybe she was just overreacting because her own life was so unbearably awful.

If only she had her own power stick. A little superhero talent, maybe some Pokémon energy ... something! With supernatural powers she could right all the wrongs she witnessed at school. She could spin the earth around backwards like Superman had done in the movie, undo the catastrophic event that had plagued her since childhood, and go back to the happy days when her marriage was new, fresh, and alive. When Anthony had loved her, and only her.

Chapter Four

They'd been married in a setting perfect for Snow White, complete with woodland creatures chattering all around them and the Big Thompson River gurgling just a few feet away. Beside Lindsey stood the handsome prince. *Her* handsome prince. They exchanged simple gold bands and spoke traditional wedding words, pledging to always be faithful to one another. Everything had been perfect.

Now he stood before her, a completely different man. A man she didn't know. He'd taken most of her heart, and today he'd come back for the rest of it.

"No, Anthony. You can't take him," she pleaded. "Please don't take him. He's all I've got."

He'd run off with another woman then come back to take the dog, too? *Who stooped that low?* But how could she stop him? Call the police? No, they wouldn't come for something like that. And though she was sorely tempted to punch him, getting physical or using any kind of force was out of the question.

"I'll be completely alone without Wendell. How can you do this to me? Besides, when couples split up, the child stays with the mother," she begged, knowing she sounded desperate. She didn't care. He *had* to give in!

But Anthony just rolled his eyes. "If you're done traveling down memory lane and taking your little fantasy trip back into the '50s, I'll just take Wendell and go," he snipped. "Shawna and I have a large house and an even bigger yard. Several acres, actually. He'll be much happ—"

Her sadness suddenly took a backseat to anger. "What do you mean you have a big house and yard?" She couldn't stop her upper lip from curling into a sneer. "Don't you mean *Shawna* has all this?"

He looked down his nose at her, affronted. "No, *I* do. And I don't like what you're implying."

"Well, if the shoe fits—"

"Shawna is too young to have earned much money yet. It's mine. And I worked hard to get it."

"And just how can that be?" she demanded. "We were broke! We've lived in this tiny house because you said you needed every penny of your income to set up and support your fledgling practice. We've lived off my teaching income, so that you—we—could accomplish that. Now you're telling me that you have a large house on several acres of land a mere two weeks after you walked out on me?"

Pieces of the puzzle were coming together. The life she'd so longed for, so needed to recapture, had all been a lie. A façade. He'd used her as a stepping stone, which meant she was nothing more than a means to an end.

"Shawna is 'too young' to earn that much money? Well, at least you're not after her money. I feel *so* much better knowing that," she snapped sarcastically. "Tell me. Just how young is 'too young' to earn a decent living, Anthony? I'm only twenty-six, and I apparently made enough money for you. How old is Shawna, anyway?"

"That's not important."

"You're the one that brought it up. How old is she?"

"Lindsey, come on. Don't be so unreasonable."

"*Unreasonable?!*" She stepped as close to him as she dared, counting out his sins on her fingers. "You walked out on me. You made love in our bed with another woman. You concealed your financial assets from me." Her breath quickened, her volume increase. "You concealed an affair that you've probably been having for a long time. Now you want to take Wendell, the only thing I have left to care about, and you think *I'm* unreasonable? You *bastard!*" she yelled.

He took a breath, seeming unsure. "You're losing it, Lindsey," he said.

She laughed, a short, cold sound that hardly sounded like her own voice. She definitely wasn't sounding like a kindergarten teacher at the moment. "You're damn right I'm losing it. And I've only just begun. How old is she? I want to know."

"You really don't want to know. It's not important. It's not relevant."

"I want to know."

Anthony strode past her, then picked up the dog's jumbo dish, leash, and rawhide bone. He gave a whistle and headed angrily toward the door. Wendell's tail wag was low and confused. He looked at Anthony, then at Lindsey, questions in his eyes.

"Get over here, Wendell!" Anthony yelled.

Tail between his legs, Wendell ran to Anthony and looked up. Anthony nudged the dog's hip so he moved out of the house, then slammed the door behind them.

A second later, the door opened again, and Anthony poked his head inside. "Twenty," he said. "She's twenty and she's hot! There! Are you happy now?"

It took a moment before she could speak. When she did, it was through her teeth. "I hope you end up just like … just like *The Money Pig*!" she screamed back at him.

He frowned, confused by her strange reply, then shut the door and was gone.

After school, Lindsey drove down Speedway Boulevard, past the post office and the western wear store, on her way to the small, fragrant coffee shop where she and Laura met almost every Monday. They began each conversation with the statement, "Let's not talk about school," but they always did.

After a few moments of school talk, Laura leaned forward, a devilish twinkle in her eye. "All right," she said confidentially. "How about this? I think I know where little Miss Shawna works."

Dropping her head to the table, Lindsey moaned. "You're making my bad day worse. Who cares where she works?"

"You will, I think."

Lindsey lifted her head and put her chin on her hand, then regarded her friend through narrowed eyes. "Well? Are you going to tell me, or do I have to play Twenty Questions to pry the information out of you?"

"She works at the office," Laura said with a smirk.

Lindsey rolled her eyes. "The office. Great. Okay. I can see we *are* going to play Twenty Questions."

Laura's grin widened. "No, Lindsey," she said slowly. "She works at *The Office*."

Lindsey stared at her, stunned. The Office was one of the town's best known strip clubs. "No. I don't believe it." She paused. "How do you know, anyway?"

Laura shifted slightly, looking uncomfortable. "I had to get my tires rotated the other day, so I took the car to Big Daddy's Tires, which is just across the street from the club. While I was waiting I ... well, I'm sorry, Lindsey, but I saw Anthony."

"What?"

"He was ... walking with a leggy redhead, and they were holding hands."

Lindsey closed her eyes, trying to keep her breathing calm. She didn't want to see that image in her head.

"Anyway, he went into the club with her. I was staring—if he'd looked across the street he would have seen me for sure. When they were inside I ran across the street to look at a poster outside The Office's entrance," she said. "It showed—and I do mean *showed*—all their regular dancers. There was the tall, good-looking—sorry, honey, but she is—redheaded young woman I'd seen with Anthony, and the poster said her name was Shawna. It has to be her."

Fifteen days had passed since Anthony had walked out, though it seemed more like fifteen years to Lindsey. She was beginning to believe her unbelievable situation. The reality of losing her husband had sunk in like a rough-edged blade, and it hurt just as much today as it had that first day. Maybe more. She told herself that she was better off without him, saying he was no good for her, and she deserved more. All the clichés about shattered love seemed to apply. But her own lectures didn't ease the loneliness one tiny bit. The days were tolerable. It was fortunate that she loved her job, and the kids kept her busy. School was like a safe little pocket of existence. But she dreaded the abysmal nights and the long, dreary weekends.

And it wasn't just loneliness. Outside of the safety of her school's campus, she was jumpy. Even the smallest sound gave her system a jolt, whether it was a tire screeching, a baby crying, a dog barking—oh, her heart ached for Wendell—or even a tree branch brushing against the wall of her adobe house. Everything startled her, sent adrenalin rushing through her system. She had no idea when she'd become so paranoid.

With cooler weather due any day, she threw herself into planning for a winter garden in a corner of her tiny backyard. Sure, the mental health professionals all labeled what she was doing "avoidance" or "denial," but she was the one who had to cope, who had to get past the loneliness and the all too familiar sense of abandonment. She decided her medicine and therapy of choice would be gardening.

She knew very little about gardening in the southwest except that it could be tricky. A little research was absolutely necessary. She stepped outside, heading to the bookstore, then took a deep breath and smiled. Just taking this simple action felt good. The darkness lifted, if only for a moment.

The exquisite aroma of delicious, premium coffee hovered among the colorful shelves of books and the comfy, snuggle-down chairs. Everyone in the bookstore—shoppers and clerks alike—was a book lover, and she felt a kinship with them all. Lindsey loved this place. She liked to fantasize that anything was possible here. The only sorrows suffered within these walls were those a reader chose to feel while empathizing—or fantasizing—along with a fictional character. That's what she told herself, anyway. It helped her get through another day.

The gardening theme spilled quite nicely into Lindsey's classroom. The students learned to chant part of a poem called "Crops on the Farm."

It takes lots of help from the farmer,

The rain and the sunshine, too.

To grow all the crops that are yummy to eat,

Good food for me, and good food for you.

"Miss Lindsey?"

"Yes, Harley. Thank you for raising your hand."

"What are crops?"

Aha! A teachable moment. "You have great questions, Harley. Class, any volunteers? Does any one think they know or would like to take a guess?"

There were no volunteers. They all simply stared, waiting for her to tell them. But she wanted them to think for themselves. Lindsey kept waiting for an answer, then she asked the question again.

"What are crops?"

Finally, Marvin's hand went up. "Crops ... are a lot like alligators," he stated with conviction.

She drove west, heading to The Desert Grows Nursery, until a red traffic light forced her to come to a stop. This was not a good place to stop. She stared steadfastly ahead, refusing to look to her left. She was not going to look. *Don't ... look.* But of course she looked, and she saw the familiar signage in front of The Office. Could it really be possible that her husband was dating a twenty-year-old stripper? Could Laura have been joking? She grinned. Sure. Laura was probably just trying to make her laugh. But still ... that would be an awfully cruel joke for her friend to play.

Lindsey reached into the glove box to retrieve her digital camera, which had a powerful zoom lens. She aimed the camera at the flesh-revealing poster by the entrance then zoomed in. She focused, shot, and turned the car around. She wanted to see the photo on her television so she'd know what she was up against. The Desert Grows Nursery would have to wait.

Autumn coolness permeated the house, so before plugging the memory card into the viewer, Lindsey wrapped herself in the old coyote-covered quilt her mom had made for her long ago. When she thought she was ready, she brought the image up on her TV and stared mournfully at the photo. How could she compete with someone—a young someone—who looked like *that*? The girl was scantily dressed in a red sequined bikini bottom. A long, sheer red scarf draped strategically across her perfect—and large—breasts. Everything about the woman looked so flawless she seemed unreal. Like a sexy superhero. She made magazine centerfolds look like the average girl next door.

Lindsey had assumed Anthony would get over his immature, foolish fling. Now she wasn't so sure. Why would he come back to a cute little kindergarten teacher when he could have Shawna, the stunningly beautiful, exotic goddess? Somehow, the hurt she'd felt after the initial betrayal seemed minuscule compared to this hopeless feeling of permanent loss settling over her.

Anthony had filled the emptiness she'd felt ever since her parents had died. Now that void felt larger than ever. Anthony would never come back, she realized. Why should he? He had what he wanted: his fantasy life.

Chapter Five

Rehearsals for the school's annual Winter Performance were underway, and as usual, the schoolwide project was time consuming. But if it was done right, it could be one of the educational highlights of the year. So far the performance was shaping up nicely. Lindsey's kindergarten class had teamed up with Judy Lopez's first grade class, and they were writing and performing an acceptable version of *The Twelve Days of Christmas*. "Acceptable" in this public school district meant that it included no mention of Christmas. If Christmas was mentioned, then Hanukkah, Kwanza, and every other December holiday that anyone might think of would have to be mentioned as well.

On the first day of winter
My true love gave to me,
A quail in a Palo Verde tree.
On the second day of winter

My true love gave to me,
Two javelinas
And a quail in a Palo Verde tree ...

The children sang so sweetly—that is, some of the children sang sweetly. Others were too busy wiggling, poking, or pushing their neighbors. Then there was Bobby, hunched under a table scowling. Lindsey didn't dare acknowledge him or try to entice him back into the activity. She knew from experience that she'd only get into a power struggle that way. So she pretended not to notice. Instead, she made good use of those 'eyes in the back of the head' that teachers are given upon receipt of their teaching certificates, making sure nothing bad happened.

On the third day of winter
My true love gave to me,
Three western geckos ...

"What do you think?" Lindsey asked Judy.

"Well, the lyrics are coming along nicely. Only nine more verses to go. Getting these little guys to stand still long enough to get through the song ... now *that's* going to take some work."

Judy was a round, energetic, Back-to-Basics teacher, and the two of them had little in common. This was the first real opportunity they'd had to get to know each other. After school, Lindsey stopped by Judy's classroom to talk over a few editorial changes, and just walking in to the classroom made her smile. The atmosphere was homey, warm, and inviting.

"Oh, my gosh! What is that smell?" blurted Lindsey.

Judy beamed. "Green corn tamales. You want one?"

"Yes! I'm starving!"

"Then by all means, take two."

Lindsey bit into one, then closed her eyes, moaning with pleasure. "Mmmm. Where did you get these? They are delicious."

Judy's smile was proud. "We made them today."

"We? You had a visitor? A cooking visitor?"

She shook her head. "No. No such luck. Just me and the kids. We made them. We ate them, too. We were reading the book, *Too Many Tamales* by Gary Soto and Ed Martinez, and I just happened to have the ingredients on hand to make them. One thing led to another. You know how that happens. I love to cook with the kids, and this was a perfect opportunity for me to integrate a literature lesson, a math lesson, a history lesson, a health lesson, with a whole lot of good food."

Not at all what Lindsey had expected from the Back-to-Basics teacher. Her eyes scanned the room, taking in every nook and cranny, every bulletin board, and every shelf and display around her room.

"What were you expecting?" Judy asked wryly. "Stacks of flash cards? Piles of worksheets? Shelves of textbooks? Rows of desks?"

"Well, yes," Lindsey sheepishly replied. "I heard you were the Back—"

"—to Basics teacher. Yes, I know. That's what they say. But have they ever come into my classroom to check it out? Nope. I like to think of myself as a Back-to-*Balance* teacher. I use whatever methodology fits the moment or the student. People assume a lot. I think my age has something to do with it. Plus, I'm Hispanic. People think I'm a traditional kind of person in every way." She chuckled. "They couldn't be further from the truth. Except maybe in the kitchen … and the bedroom," she added with a wink.

With a chuckle, Lindsey veered back to the subject of the song. "I can live with the verse about four laughing cows," she said, "but I don't know about the five dancing girls. It just leaves itself open for a variety of odd interpretations. How about five dancing deer? We have some mule deer in the area."

Judy agreed, and they wrapped up their little meeting. Lindsey thanked her for her time, then turned to go. "Next week in my class," she said over her shoulder, "I think we might read *The Tortilla Factory* by Gary Paulsen. Do you know how to make tortillas?"

Judy laughed. "Does a *chupacabra* suck blood?"

Not sure how to reply, Lindsey nodded, then left the room with a smile on her face.

Cooking had never been Lindsey's claim to fame, but she'd managed to create special, tasty meals for Anthony. But now, with only herself to feed, meals were less than pitiful. Even calling them "meals" was a misnomer. She couldn't bear to sit at the table alone. Most of her nourishment was taken in the form of a snack while she read, graded papers, or doodled in her plan book.

Tonight was no different, except that her cupboards were so bare she couldn't even whip up a snack. And it was too late to go shopping. She decided to call China Village and order take-out, something she hadn't done since Anthony had left. While she waited for the delivery, she watched *The Christmas Story,* chuckling at the part where the neighbor's dogs come in and eat the entire Christmas turkey right off the table. Unfortunately, that reminded her of Wendell, and the turkey reminded her of how hungry she was. Lately, it seemed she was always hungry.

The doorbell chimed, and since it was beginning to rain, she invited the handsome young delivery driver in while she searched her purse for her debit card.

"Your kids will eat Chinese food?" the driver asked. "I thought it was totally gross until I got to college. That's when I developed a taste for it."

She gave him an awkward smile. "I, uh, I don't have any kids."

"Oh!" he exclaimed. "I'm sorry, ma'am. It's just that I saw *Alexander and the Terrible, Horrible, No Good, Very Bad Day* and *How The Grinch Stole Christmas* lying there on the table, and I assumed—"

"Oh, that's all right. I'm a teacher, so I have lots of children's books around. Do you go to the U?"

"Yes, ma'am. I'm studying psychology."

Before Lindsey knew it, they were deep in conversation about children's cognitive development. Finally, the delivery guy lifted one hand.

"Hey, I'm sorry. I've distracted you. Your food is going get cold. I should go."

Lindsey looked at the bags of food with horror, realizing for the first time what she'd done: ordered enough for both her and Anthony. The realization was like a physical pain in her gut.

"That's not a problem. I really needed a distraction," she said. "When I was in college, I was often hungry from lack of a decent meal. Do you ever feel that way?"

He smiled. "Oh yes, ma'am."

She chuckled, enjoying his enthusiasm. "Well, if you'll agree to stop calling me ma'am, I'll share some of this delicious food with you. Can you stay?"

The moment the words left her mouth, she wished she could take them back. Inviting a total stranger to have dinner with her? Here, in her home? What was she thinking?

"Yes, ma'am." He stopped himself. "I mean ... what *is* your name?"

"Lindsey," she said, slightly apprehensive. "Lindsey Sommerfield. What's yours?"

"Jake Lee. And, no, I'm not Chinese."

They both laughed, and he told her that she was his last delivery, so it really was okay for him to stay and eat. He wouldn't have to go back in as long as he called in.

"I do have one problem, though," he said, hesitating. "It's getting really cold out, and my dog—well, he's not exactly *my* dog, but the dog is in my Jeep, and I'm afraid he is going to get too cold and scared if I leave him there much longer. He seems so sad and—"

"Don't say another word," said Lindsey. "I completely understand. Your dog is very welcome. I even have some dog food that's going to waste."

He headed back outside, and within seconds he returned with a huge, somewhat damp dog at his side.

Lindsey stared in disbelief. "Wendell? Is that you?"

The dog's tail waved madly, and he leaped inside. He did a powerful tailspin and made full circles, knocking objects off the table and Lindsey off her feet. Then he jumped up and gave her the sloppiest dog kisses a dog could give.

Jake tried in vain to control the dog. "Whoa, sorry! I had no idea he'd act like that. Here boy, come here."

The next few hours passed by quickly, and Wendell never left Lindsey's side—not even during one quick trip to the tiny downstairs bathroom. She set places at the table, complete with woven mats and cloth napkins, while this total stranger, this young, cute, male college student lit a fire in the fireplace. For a brief moment, she forgot her sorrows.

Lindsey brought Wendell a dish from the kitchen and mixed in a little white rice, then all three of them ate ravenously. Lindsey and her unexpected guest discussed movies they'd seen and books they'd read, and she was impressed by his knowledge and interest in literature.

Finally, Jake stood and grinned. "I'd better get going. It's late, and I've got an eight o'clock class." He rubbed Wendell's back. "Let's go big guy."

Lindsey tried not to panic. "You're not taking that dog anywhere. He belongs with me, can't you see that?"

Jake smiled apologetically. "I can tell he really likes you, but I kind of ... well, to be honest, I dognapped him from his owner's yard. I've got to get him back before they notice he's missing. I only took him tonight because I felt bad that he'd been left out in the rain and all. Sorry. Thanks again for dinner. We gotta go."

Tears welled in her eyes as Jake led Wendell to the door. Wendell was usually picky with strangers, but he didn't seem to mind going with this young man. She found that very interesting.

"Jake?" Lindsey called softly. "Do you think you could steal him again sometime?"

After a long pause, Jake and Wendell turned. They looked at each other then back at Lindsey, and it was as if they both were smiling. It almost looked rehearsed. Like something from a movie or the seal show at Sea World. If she hadn't been so sad about their departure, she'd have laughed. Instead, she waited. She knew what Wendell's answer would be, but he didn't seem to be the one in charge.

Jake nodded. "Now that I can do," he promised, giving her a boyish smile.

Lindsey stood by the door, dazed, and watched them go. Then the house was empty once again. The methodical ticking of the clock, the far away creaking of the ever-settling walls, and the lonesome drumming of rain echoed through her body. Numb inside, she cleaned up the clutter and went to bed.

Chapter Six

Judy's class was already singing when Lindsey arrived.

"Sorry we're late," voiced Lindsey, slightly out of breath. "We had a bloody nose emergency."

Judy smiled and nodded. She knew those things happened.

Eight canteens of water,

Seven rattle snakes,

Six spadefoot toads,

Five dancing deer,

Four laughing cows,

Three western geckos,

Two javelinas,

And a quail in a Palo Verde tree.

They sang the song three more times then added two more verses. The kids came up with nine kangaroo rats and ten cactus wrens, and both teachers were relieved that they were two appropriate and usable verses. They'd let the laughing cow verse remain, but they'd had to exclude a few, like eight bottles of booze, seven roadkill rabbits, and six dirty diapers.

As the students filed back to their classrooms, Judy called out, "Good luck with your official observation this afternoon."

Lindsey groaned. Typically she didn't panic over these things. On the other hand, she didn't usually forget about them, either. As the kids gathered on the rug, waiting eagerly to hear what they would be doing next, Lindsey glanced at her plan book to make sure she had something planned that was fit for a principal's careful scrutiny. Fortunately, she did. She was glad she had a few minutes to talk with the children about the principal's impending visit.

Lindsey started the reading lesson by guiding the students through a "picture walk" of the book. "What do you notice about the cover of this book?" she asked. "Alexa?"

"There's a lady cooking something."

"Good! How do you know that?"

Alexa answered, but she sounded annoyed at being asked to explain what she considered to be so obvious. "She's got a pot and a spoon. Duh!"

Ignoring the sarcasm, Lindsey went on. "What else? Armando?"

"I see kids. They look like they want what's in the pot."

"Good! Let's turn to the title page and—"

"Mrs. Wilson is here! Mrs. Wilson is here!" shouted the children.

Lindsey smiled. "Welcome to our classroom, Mrs. Wilson. We were just about to read this book. Make yourself at home."

The principal sat just behind the children, looking very serious and gripping an official-looking green notepad in one hand. Lindsey proceeded through the lesson, confident that she knew what she was doing, and that she could do it well. They discussed all the pictures then stopped just before she showed the last page, and she asked for predictions concerning how the story might end. Then she turned back to the beginning and read the words, touching each one as she spoke, simultaneously teaching the young children about one-to-one word correspondence and directionality.

"*The Kitchen Kettle* by Janine Cowlee," read Lindsey.

A maniacal grin spread across Bobby's plotting face. *Oh, no,* thought Lindsey. *Here it comes.*

"She's 'cow'-lee 'cause she looks like a cow," teased Bobby.

"She does?" Harley asked, looking sincere. "I don't think so."

"I never seen a lady that looked like a cow," added Marvin.

And away they went. Every child put in his or her two cents, and all at once. So much for raising hands or talking one at a time.

"Ladies don't look anything like cows," Joseph said in a rare attempt to be helpful.

Emma's little fists were on her hips. She was not impressed. "We never even saw the lady," she reasoned.

"You're mean, Bobby!" said Armando.

"Well, you're stupid!" Bobby shot back.

"You are 'cow'-lee, too!" Connie threw in.

Bobby scowled, closing in on tears. "Am not."

"You guys! The principal is here!" shouted Emma, clearly uncomfortable.

The bickering stopped, but Lindsey could see that some of the students didn't know whether to be upset about Bobby's "cow"-lee business, or if they should be more worried about the school principal witnessing the chaos.

Lindsey wasn't upset. She actually found the whole situation rather amusing and tried not to let the children see her smile, but she wasn't so sure that Mrs. Wilson shared her point of view. So she quickly showed her disappointment in the children's behavior and asked them to return to their regular table seats. When they showed her they were ready to come to the rug and act like students, she said she would invite them back.

Had the principal not been there, she would have used this opportunity to stop, seat the children in a circle, and conduct a class meeting to work through the situation with guided problem solving. In retrospect, she wished she'd done that. But it was hard to think on the spot when she was being observed.

After Laura and Lindsey ordered their latté and mocha, they sat at a round table in the corner, enjoying a good view of the coffee house. They sipped in silence for a few minutes, winding down from the day.

Suddenly Lindsey blurted out, "I can't believe he hasn't called or come by to talk. Don't most couples that split up at least fight for a while? He owes me at least that. And some kind of an explanation, too."

Laura lifted one eyebrow. "I have to admit, it's all pretty weird. Have you tried to call him?"

"I don't even know where he lives," she said, taking another sip.

Laura shook her head, disappointed. "Lame. Really lame, Lindsey. You know where he works. He's got a cell phone. Call him. You need more information so you can get on with your life. What's it been, three months?"

Lindsey stared off into nowhere with few thoughts coming to mind. Laura was right. She wasn't doing very well. Not at home, anyway; not at night.

"Lindsey? Hello, Lindsey? Are you in there? Have you heard anything I've said?" asked Laura.

Lindsey blushed. "Oh, sorry. Bits and pieces. You're absolutely right. I do need to get on with my life." She nudged her friend. "Hey, it's Friday night. Let's go check out that new place. What's it called?"

"Coyote Café, I think," replied Laura, looking inquisitive.

Lindsey grinned. "But we are definitely not wearing our school clothes. We've got to change."

"All righty. Sounds good. How about we meet there at eight-thirty?"

"You're on."

On the drive home, Lindsey did a lot of thinking. Her initial thoughts were full of anger directed at Anthony. She'd show him. She'd have a good time without him. She didn't need him to be happy, she told herself. Then she slumped. Who was she kidding? Not even herself. She still needed him, still wanted him, and she desperately held onto the hope he'd return.

But damn it, she was going to have a good time tonight without him. She deserved it!

Convinced—at least for the moment—that she could do it, a new set of unfamiliar concerns cropped up. What would she wear? All her clothes were teacher clothes. Even the ones she didn't wear to school made her look like a teacher. She had no choice but to make a quick detour to the mall.

She found the perfect black dress: a little too short and a little too tight. No one would suspect she was an elementary school teacher. She wore the dress out of the store after the clerk snipped off all the tags, then touched up her makeup as soon as she was in the car—only this time, she left the delicate hand at home. After all, it was Friday night. It wasn't a crime to look a little made up. There. Ready. She could stroll into the Coyote Café with confidence.

The minute she walked in, a man two stools from the door let out a whistle and an, "Ooh, baby!"

"Hey, buddy. That's a teacher you're whistling at. A kindergarten teacher."

Lindsey blinked in the dim interior of the bar, recognizing Laura's voice. Her friend's words were just the slightest bit slurred, she noticed. She carefully—because of the shortness and tightness of her dress—positioned herself on the high stool next to Laura, and the vocal male spoke up again.

"Ooooh baby. Kindergarten baby!"

Somewhat shocked, Lindsey turned away from him and gave Laura a tell-me-what's-going-on glare.

Laura shrugged. "Don't mind him. He's had a few too many."

"Well," said Lindsey, lifting one eyebrow. "I don't think he's the only one. How did he know I was a kindergarten teacher?" She frowned at her friend's drink. "And what's with the scotch? You don't drink scotch."

Laura fanned a dismissive hand at her friend. "Relax. It's the hunky bartender's fault. He made me drink the scotch."

Lindsey's antennae sprang to attention. Only a couple of times had she heard anyone use the word "hunky" and it had been Laura, describing Dr. Anthony Sommerfield in the hospital the day he and Lindsey had met. A vision of that moment replayed as a burning flashback, and Lindsey was furious with herself that she allowed one word to trigger her thoughts full speed ahead on an "Anthony" crash course. On impulse, she ordered a scotch, too, and Laura began her bartender story.

"He even guessed what drink I would order," she said, giving her a half smile.

Lindsey glanced skeptically at Laura's glass. "He guessed you'd order scotch?"

"No, silly. He guessed I'd order a glass of white zin, which, of course, is what I would have ordered, but I didn't want him to think he could take one look at me and know that. So I had to order scotch."

"I see. And then you had to order a second one?"

"Well, no. He just brought it. Said it was on the house." She batted her eyelashes. "I think it was really on him."

Lindsey peered across the bar, then looked back at her. "I don't think he's either cute or clever," she said.

"Oh, that's not him. He had to leave at 8:30. Something about studying. He's a student. Said he was sorry he wouldn't get to meet you."

"If he's a student, he's probably way too young," Lindsey scolded. "What's going on with you? You're usually way more discriminating." But she was curious. "What's his name?"

"I don't even know."

"Good. Fate stepped in and is handling this for you."

Laura didn't appear to hear her. Her jaw was set. "But I'll find out. He said he'd like to talk with me some more, and I think he really meant it. He wasn't just looking for a big tip."

The girls relocated to a quiet corner table, ordered some sizzling chicken fajitas and a carafe of coffee, and changed the subject to their Winter Break plans.

"You and I should get away," Laura coaxed.

"I don't know. I mean … I really would like to have some fun, and I know I need to get away, but I keep hoping Anthony will call. A little voice keeps telling me that if I'm gone for the holidays, that's when he'll call, and I'll miss what might be my only chance to talk with him—"

"Good. That's exactly what he needs and deserves. You don't want him thinking that you're sitting around waiting for him."

"—and the other not-so-little voice is you, telling me to get real."

"Well," Laura said smugly, "someone has to keep things balanced."

After four hours of people watching, coffee drinking, and trip planning, they were semi-ready to embark on a Grand Canyon winter adventure. Lindsey agreed to make arrangements for their accommodations, and Laura's job would be to put together a list of possible activities. There would be no time left open for sadness or loneliness, and no need for Anthony.

Chapter Seven

The week before Winter Break was always a little hectic, with last minute assessments, semester progress reports and grades, class parties, kid-gifts for parents, and the Winter Performance. Completing the usual academic routines was a struggle, because the students were either excited about their upcoming vacations and holiday celebrations or depressed and frustrated at their lack of festivities.

"What have you got planned for these last two weeks before Break?" Judy asked. "You always come up with some clever way to celebrate without breaking any of those annoying separation of church and state policies."

"Well," Lindsey said with a sigh, "I'm not much in the mood for festivities right now. We'll be doing a thematic unit on trees."

Judy frowned. "That does not sound like you."

She was right. That was not at all the Lindsey the staff was used to, and she knew some of her co-workers were concerned about her diminishing energy and enthusiasm. Today, as she gathered books, videos, pictures, games, art activities, and puzzles for the Tree Unit, she regained a little of the old—but not too old—and innovative Lindsey. The tree unit evolved into the Pine Tree Unit. And because she believed so strongly in hands-on, authentic learning, she felt compelled, even obligated to purchase a living pine tree for her classroom. From there, one thematic unit idea led to another. Since many pine trees grew in cold climates, that led to learning about the animals living in those pine trees—the ones that neither migrate nor hibernate—and to their persistent search for food so they could survive the winter. And what could those birds and rodents eat off their classroom tree? Why, strings of red cranberries and popcorn, of course!

"One for the tree and one for me," chanted Marvin as he worked on a popcorn string.

Lindsey smiled. Sampling the goods was part of the procedure.

"One popcorn, one cranberry, one popcorn, one cranberry," said Emma, creating a mathematical pattern on her piece of string.

Some of the students sang their version of the "Twelve Days" song as they loaded up their string, munching at the same time.

"Beautiful!" Lindsey exclaimed, clapping. "Just remember, it's eight bottles of *water*, not beer. There is no mention of beer in this song. Okay? And there are six what?"

"Six spadefoot frogs!" the children announced.

"That's very close, but here in the desert we have spadefoot *toads*."

Lindsey kept a watchful eye on Willy, Bobby, and Joseph. The thought of giving them needles, even blunt embroidery needles, made her nervous. But so far, they were engaged and acting appropriately. They'd soon want to move on from this fine-motor activity anyway.

The joy she saw on the children's faces, the New Age instrumental, hint-of-Christmas music that tickled all their ears, and the fragrant aroma of fresh pine hovering throughout the classroom urged a little cheer in her. Real feelings. Not pretend or forced. She'd almost forgotten what it was like to feel good. And though a lonely, sorrowful feeling still gnawed deep within her, she felt a glimmer of hope that reached out beyond the day.

That optimistic mood continued as Lindsey made her way home from work, still, however, avoiding Speedway Boulevard and the sick feeling that surged through her body whenever she was near The Office—even though that route would have made the trip a bit shorter.

The Arizona sunset's tangerine rays faded behind the low hills, and Lindsey detected a hint of crispness in the air. The desert winter was just around the corner.

Struggling to get her key in the door, her arms full of grocery bags and book bags, Lindsey glanced down and noticed a folded piece of paper wedged between the door jam and the door. Her heart flipped at the thought that it could be from Anthony, then she thought better of that. Perhaps it's from … Still hugging the bags to her, she knelt and picked up the note.

My friend and I are waiting in the backyard for you, it read. It was not signed, but a large, dusty smudge at the bottom of the paper gave Lindsey a pretty good idea of who her visitors might be.

"Wendell!" she shouted with delight. "I'm so glad to see you!" The big dog spread enthusiastic, slobbery kisses all over her flushed cheeks, and she laughed so hard she didn't notice the other visitor at first.

"Hey, Lindsey." She glanced up, still smiling, and saw Jake standing there, wearing a sheepish, but charming smile. "I'm officially dog sitting tonight, so I didn't even have to steal him. Hope you don't mind the intrusion."

"Mind? I'm thrilled. Really," she said, still grinning.

He nodded at her hands. "If you'll stop clutching a few of those bags so tightly, I'll help you carry them in." He hesitated. "Uh, should I have called first? I just thought you'd be so glad to see Wendell again, and I came rushing right over."

"Oh no," she assured him, handing over a few bags. "It's all right. I'm really glad to see Wendell—and you, of course. You have the night off?"

He nodded. "I worked the lunch shift today."

"Well then, why don't you stay for dinner? Grilled orange roughy is on the menu for tonight."

"Wow! My mouth is watering already."

Lindsey made a quick detour to the bathroom to check her make-up after a long day in kindergarten and numerous dog kisses. When she came out, Jake was curiously perusing the bookshelves in the living room. She wondered what he thought, and her own eyes passed over some of her favorite titles: *Memoirs of a Geisha*, *Sir Gawain and the Green Knight*, *Like Water for Chocolate*, *The Claiming of Sleeping Beauty* ...

"Wow!" he exclaimed. "You've got Alistair MacLeod's book? Did you like it?"

"*No Great Mischief?* I'll let you know. I haven't even opened the cover yet."

Jake stayed by the bookshelf while Lindsey went out to start the coals—with Wendell's help. He never left her side, and she almost tripped over him several times. It was as if the dog were trying to make up for lost time.

"I miss you, too, Wendell," she said, scratching behind his floppy ears. His big, brown, loving, dog eyes held hers, and her heart pulsed with joy. She needed the closeness, too.

Was it possible that she missed Wendell more than she missed Anthony? She grinned and felt a bit of her own mischief rising to the surface. Of course a man and a dog fill different areas of the heart, but dogs sure were easier to love. And apparently a dog's level of loyalty far exceeded that of certain men.

"One delicious doggy dinner, coming up!" she said, filling a mixing bowl with his food.

Lindsey outdid herself in the dinner preparation and felt good while she was doing it.

"That smells really good," Jake said, wandering outside.

She smiled. "Thanks. I'm trying something new. Hope you don't mind being part of my experiment."

They talked, exchanging ordinary questions and answers about Jake's job and school, though deep down she wanted to know more about his relationship with Anthony and Shawna. She told herself she'd work that in later. In the meantime, she was glad to have Jake's company, to be sharing dinner with someone, and to spend time with Wendell.

"It must be difficult, supporting yourself and your home all on your own," he said at one point. "I've heard all the stuff about teacher salaries."

She shrugged. "It's hard, but I get by." She grinned. "I can still afford Chinese food once in a while. Would you like some wine with dinner?"

"I would love some wine," Jake said with an infectious smile.

For a moment she was caught in the twinkle of his blazing blue eyes, then she shook her head, clearing her thoughts, and went inside to select a bottle. On her way she started wondering ... was he even old enough to drink? What if she was supplying alcohol to a minor? That would be a crime. She could just imagine the headlines: Kindergarten Teacher Arrested for Giving a Student Alcohol.

Other than the underage alcohol issue, she found she really didn't care how old he was. She had started to really enjoy his company. He might just be a college student, a fast food delivery driver, and a dog sitter, but most of all he was a really nice guy with shiny, dark blond hair that always looked just a bit windblown. His compelling blue eyes seemed to probe into her soul. There was something about him, some mysterious, attractive aura she couldn't define.

Oh dear, she thought.

She didn't realize she'd mentally drifted off until Jake called from the patio. "Lindsey? Are you all right?"

"Just fine," she said, coming back outside to the grill. "Jake, I have to be honest with you." That was true, she reasoned. It's just that she was only going to be partially honest—at least for now. "And right this minute, I have two things on my mind. First of all, it just occurred to me that I barely know you, or anything about you, and here you are in my house, with my dog, about to drink wine with me and—"

"I think I get it," he interrupted. "I assure you I'm harmless."

She blushed. "Oh, I didn't mean that I was afraid in any way. Not really. It's just that ... well, I'm a teacher and you're a student. You called me 'ma'am' on several occasions, and here we are, about to drink wine together."

Jake's eyes brightened, and he laughed out loud. "I assure you, Miss Lindsey, you are not corrupting a minor. I'm old enough to drink wine without anyone going to jail. No front page scandal here."

Lindsey laughed, too, relieved, though somewhat embarrassed. One question answered, dozens more to go.

While she carried the grilled delights into the kitchen, Jake poured the wine, and they dined on orange roughy topped with a green cilantro salsa, alongside a grilled mix of zucchini, small purple-skinned potatoes, corn, bell peppers, and onions. For a while they were both so involved in devouring the meal that they didn't speak. Before long, the conversation picked up again.

"How long will my dog be with you?" she asked.

He frowned. "Good question. I'm not sure. The lady said just tonight, but I never really count on what she says, so maybe more."

Lindsey set her elbow on the table and rested her chin in her hand. "He *is* my dog, you know."

After a sip of wine, he chuckled warmly. "I don't know what's going on here with regard to Wendell, but he sure knows you well. Do you want to tell me about it?"

She surprised herself. "Yes," she said. "Yes, I do."

They sat on the sofa and talked until dawn. Lindsey opened up, describing how it had felt to come home sick and find her husband in bed with another woman. She managed not to cry when she described how he'd left that same day and planned never to return.

"But he did return—to take Wendell."

And that left me with absolutely nothing to truly care about.

The morning sun blushed through a layer of thin clouds, but Jake hardly noticed it. Most days he would have lingered until this spectacular, pastel vision had faded, but he'd been out all night. He had no time for that. He returned to his small apartment, quickly gulped his first mug of coffee, and opened his laptop.

It took a moment before he could type anything. He was feeling overwhelmed by the amount of information he'd been given over the last ten hours. Information he hadn't even asked for. He'd interviewed many women before, read stacks of similar research, thought he'd heard it all. Actually, he *had* heard it all, but this woman was different. She was still in shock, still numb, and he could feel her pain, her anger, her loneliness. He had to write about her; he wanted to write about her.

Objectivity would be a challenge. Nevertheless, he began to type: *Subject D is an attractive, twenty-six year old kindergarten teacher; separated for approximately three months; reason for being alone—husband left her for another woman. Classic, textbook scenario* ... He typed what he knew of her, and soon the words came faster than his fingers could tap.

Chapter Eight

"I hate dress rehearsals. They're so darned nerve wracking. They always go badly. And there's no way to get the kids—every kid in the whole school, all at once—to sit quietly in the cafeteria until it's their turn. They're too excited. Why do we do this?" demanded Lindsey, addressing no one in particular, though Judy was close enough to hear her.

"Rhetorical question?" asked Judy peering over her reading glasses. "Or would you like an answer?"

"Definitely rhetorical. No, it's actually a stupid question. We do this because this is what we do." She took a deep breath and let it out. "It's what everybody does, and the final performance will be just fine. I know that. It's just all this commotion and confusion is so unsettling." She wrung her hands. "And I don't have my kids' report cards done yet. I've barely just begun."

"Oh, well, that would make any teacher a bit anxious. You are doing the district computer version, right?"

"You know, I thought about it, but it seemed easier to do them by hand, so I could do most of the work at home. The time just got away from me and—"

"Do you have all your on-going assessment notes?"

"Sure. I'm very organized when it comes to assessment."

"Do you want to get it done today?"

Lindsey raised her face to the ceiling and laughed. "Oh, right! Like that's possible."

Judy winked. "Be in my room at 3:15 with your assessment notes, student journals, a blank disc, and chocolate. Lots of chocolate. You will be done today."

"Thanks, Judy!" It seemed too good to be true. "You're a life saver ... or should I say a Hershey's Kiss?"

As the rest of the classes clamored in for the rehearsal, the noise level rose considerably. One of the fifth grade classes sat up front, which was a definite no-no. Kinder classes always sat in front, then first grade, then second grade, and so on. Everyone knew this. But for some reason, one class was way out of order today, and it was seated in Lindsey's spot. To make matters worse, Lindsey had forgotten to have her students bring their own chairs. Kinder classes always brought their own little chairs.

"Excuse me," Lindsey said, attempting to get some of the fifth graders' attention. "Why are you sitting up front today?"

At first the children completely ignored her. After all, she was just a kindergarten teacher. What could she know? How to color? Take naps? Finger paint? Play with sand and water? What power could she have?

"Where is your teacher?" she tried again.

Still no response. Either they were deaf or she was invisible.

She set one hand on her hip. "Who here likes Katy Perry?"

Hands shot up as all the girls and a few of the boys suddenly noticed her. Amazing.

"I like her, too," she said. "And I like to sit up close during a concert or any performance just like you are doing right now."

"We hate having to sit in the back all the time. We can't see," a small fifth grader whined.

"I know just how you feel," Lindsey replied, and since she was only 5'3" she knew what she was talking about. "But look how little these students are compared to you."

The kinder kids were masters of pouting and donning sad dog-eyes. Now the entire class used their powers at full blast, looking pitiful and forlorn as they blinked at the fifth graders.

"Okay! Geez! Make them stop!"

"We can't take the pressure," another agreed.

One boy started to walk back, and he signaled for his friends to follow. "Come on, guys. Let's go get their stupid little chairs for them."

When everyone was ready, Lindsey played a simple chord on her electric keyboard and Judy conducted while the little angels sang. Behind the scenes, Emma tried to organize the other children. Joseph jumped toward the front of the stage and started some sort of gyrating, tap dancing, break dancing routine that had absolutely nothing to do with the performance. Bobby sulked in the dark, far corner of the stage behind the backdrop, and Willy ... well, Willy, for reasons unknown, took off his belt and whirled it above his head as fast as he could, his eyes crazed and intense. The students around him ducked out of the way to avoid getting hit. It actually got a little dangerous.

From experience, Lindsey knew that asking Willy to stop would not work. Demanding that he stop would merely begin a power struggle that couldn't be won by anyone of authority. Physically forcing him to stop could have dire consequences. When this child became enraged, his strength seemed to quadruple. But she had other strategies to try.

Lindsey halted her piano playing, leaving a sudden vacuum in the room. She stood and placed a finger over her lips, giving the "quiet" sign to everyone, then moved her palms toward the floor several times, signaling for the rest of the choir to sit down. A curious hush settled over the once squirming, wiggling audience.

The entire school, including over three hundred pairs of eyes, focused on the tiny, impulsive kindergarten boy. The silence finally grabbed Willy's attention, and Lindsey saw the moment when he made the connection between the whirling object over his head and his own arm attached to it. The belt fell to the stage floor, and Laura quickly retrieved it.

Willy scowled at the rows of wide-eyed students and shouted, "What are you lookin' at?"

"Take it from the top," instructed Lindsey. "One, two, ready, sing." The singers got back to their song, the audience resumed its wiggling, and Willy stood perfectly still.

The temperature had dropped far below normal for Tucson, though it still wasn't winter weather, according to outsiders. Nevertheless, old pueblo residents got out their winter clothing, taking advantage of the rare cold spell.

Shawna came slinking down the hallway in a fur coat. "Finally, I can wear this," she said. "Come on. Let's take the doggy for a walk."

Anthony, still easily aroused by her flamboyant, sexual ways, grinned. "Should I ask what you're wearing under that fur coat?"

"Only if you want to know."

He chuckled. "Oh, I already know. Just how far did you want to walk the dog?"

"It's more of a 'how long?' question really," she replied, ramping up her seductive tone a notch or two.

"All right, then. I'll play along. How long of a dog walk does my baby want to take?" he asked, lowering his own voice.

She shrugged. "Just long enough to be seen by a few people and to cool off. I'm getting hot in this coat already."

"So take it off," Anthony suggested, going along with the provocative game of the hour.

Shawna pouted, batting her long eyelashes. "Not yet. I've just put it on. Come on. I'll make it worth your while," she teased.

"You always do."

She jangled the leash and called, "Here, Rover."

That was one thing Anthony didn't like about Shawna. She always called Wendell another name, like Rover or just plain Dog, and she gave him attention only when it suited her needs. Her lack of affection or even appreciation for his lovable dog baffled him. Wendell was a great dog.

They ventured into the cold night air, the doctor, the dog, and the stripper. Anthony stared at her feet as they walked.

"How can you walk in those shoes?" he asked. "You know how hard they are on your back. After all the treatments you've been through for back and leg pain, you amaze me."

She smiled sweetly. "And I hope to keep amazing you for a very long time, darling." She flapped a dismissive hand at him. "You know I like to look good, love. High heels are a woman's legs' best friend. You'd complain even worse if I went out in Birkenstocks. Besides," she said, stroking his arm, "I rather like all those adjustments you give me."

Only the clicking of the stilettos and the jingle of Wendell's collar broke the quiet of the night, though a discriminating listener might hear other noises of the desert around them: a neighbor's horse whinnying, the hoot of an owl announcing its location, or a distant coyote yipping. Anthony took Shawna's hand while they walked. He wanted to talk—to *really* talk, like he had in the past with Lindsey.

"You know," he said gently, "I don't feel good about what we're doing to Lindsey. Maybe we're rushing things."

Her reply was snide. "Ah, yes. Your little fairy tale princess has come up in conversation once again. You do know that she doesn't have a monopoly on the 'happily ever after' thing, right? Every woman wants that. You're *my* handsome prince now, and you know what they say: 'You snooze, you lose.' Well, I don't intend to lose. So why don't you come over here, baby, and feel good about this," she purred. She leaned against the nearest tree trunk and let the coat fall open, exposing just enough naked skin to avert Anthony's emerging conscience.

Wendell, who had been sitting up straight, his gaze shifting eagerly back and forth as each of them spoke, now sighed a long, disgusted sigh. He laid down, set his head on his paws, then waited, and waited, and waited. Again, he was a mere prop: the watchdog used to facilitate tonight's little fantasy.

Chapter Nine

The school hallways buzzed with excitement, brimming over with parents and students, all dressed in their Sunday best. Little girls still wore pretty dresses, but most of the older girls wore skinny-legged pants, glittery tops, and sparkly shoes with high heels they could barely walk in. To Lindsey's eyes, far too much skin could be seen. Ignoring the dress code and feeling like rock stars, they looked ready to put on a show. No one mentioned that they looked like ten-year-olds playing dress-up.

"Thirty minutes till show time!" came the announcement over the intercom.

Lindsey's classroom phone rang, and she picked it up.

"Mrs. Sommerfield? Sorry to bother you, but there's a gentleman in the office that needs to see you for a minute. He said it was very important."

Lindsey glanced at the restless children. "I'll be right there," she said, somewhat annoyed. This was bad timing.

She stepped into the office, curious. A man stepped toward her. "Mrs. Sommerfield?"

"Yes?"

"I have some important documents for you. Good evening."

Then he was gone. A dark, nauseating sensation spread over her, like black storm clouds taking over a blue sky. She peeked into the manila envelope until she saw official looking seals and the word "Divorce" in the title, then she closed it again.

She was barely aware of what she was doing as she placed one foot in front of the other, heading toward the cafeteria. Young, high pitched squeals of "Miss Lindsey! Miss Lindsey!" went unnoticed. Then the house lights went out, the stage lights went up, and the principal began her opening speech. When she was done, the audience clapped, school children resumed their chatter, babies squealed and cried, and parents tried to quiet the younger children around them.

Lindsey withdrew into the depths of her personal suffering, and that was not a good place to be. Her head swam, her ears seemed to be stuffed with something, and her eyes blurred with unbearable visions of Anthony and Shawna together. Then Laura was there, holding her hand, leading her from the school. The five-mile drive home was quiet. Lindsey vaguely heard Laura's voice, but she could make nothing of what her friend was saying. Without a word, she handed Laura the divorce papers.

So it really was over. Anthony was gone for good. Shawna, the young, beautiful stripper, had won.

Laura brought Lindsey inside, helped her get into a comfy set of sweats, then lit the fireplace. Once her friend was settled in, she brought her a glass of wine.

"Lindsey, talk to me. I can't leave you like this."

"Why not? Anthony did."

Laura jerked back, and Lindsey wished she hadn't said that. But it was out, and she couldn't do anything about it.

"Hey friend, don't start comparing me to that … Anthony."

Lindsey shook her head. "Please go, Laura. I just want to sleep right now."

"Are you sure?"

"I'm sure."

"Judy's going to come by as soon as she can leave the students."

"Tell her not to bother. I'll be all right."

Laura stood, resigned. "Well, if you say so. But call me if you need anything. Otherwise, I'll call you first thing tomorrow. We've got some final vacation details to work out, you know."

Under normal circumstances, Lindsey would have enjoyed the mild buzz she was getting from the wine and the warmth of the fire, but not tonight. She didn't want to be comfortable. She grabbed the bottle of wine and unsteadily, almost catatonically, shuffled out to her backyard, out into the chilly night. She slid onto one of the cushioned patio loungers and stared up at the twinkling, distant stars. They were just another enemy in her life tonight. They, too, had betrayed her. How many times has she wished upon a star?

The mere thought of Anthony and Shawna together made Lindsey feel hollow, worthless, and sick to her stomach. Depression spread through her entire being like anesthesia before a surgical procedure. Except this time, when she awoke, nothing would be better. Nothing would be fixed. She'd be just another lonely, unneeded, unwanted woman, soon to be divorced.

Her thoughts sank lower, to a darker, disjointed place where the present entwined with the past. Frightening scenes from her second foster home drifted in, and she saw her twelve-year-old self sitting at the top of the stairs, watching the men. Her foster dad's friends had always shown up for a "boys' night in" whenever her foster mom left for a "girls' night out." The little girl had wondered what all the commotion was about—the laughing, the whistling—since they were just watching the TV, so she'd snuck downstairs to take a peek, then gasped in shock when she saw the images of women—naked women doing nasty things: spreading their legs, touching themselves, shaking their tops and their bottoms. She stared in disbelief until one of the men noticed her.

He took a step toward her, leering. "Bet your new girl's almost ready to dance with a pole," he told her foster father. Lindsey fled to her room and vowed never to sneak out again.

The remembered images brought Shawna to mind, and against her will she pictured the tall, shapely redhead from the poster wrapped around a pole.

Sleep was her only sanctuary, but it eluded her. She reached for an apple she'd set on the patio table, left over from her school lunch. The bright, shiny apple triggered Lindsey's fairy tale button, pushed her into once-upon-a-time mode. She picked up the apple, declared it to be poison, and transformed herself into Snow White by taking a deep, satisfying bite. Another bite, and another, but the effects of the imaginary poison never set in.

She chased the apple with another swig of wine. Tonight the wine would replace her poison apple.

The unusual and extreme cold front was perfect for the night of the Winter Performance, but it wasn't great for sitting in the backyard without the benefit of a sweater, let alone any winter wear. The temperature dropped rapidly, but Lindsey barely felt it. In fact, she welcomed the anesthetic quality of the bitter, cold air, and her mind gently toyed with the irony that she felt as cold and numb on the outside as she did on the inside. Her eyelids had become so heavy they wouldn't open, and her body was still.

Winter clouds quickly covered the starlight, and within an hour the temperature had dropped from 49 degrees to about 33 degrees. Lindsey didn't feel the tiny, wet snowflakes as they touched her face, though she would have loved that. Snow was a rare treat in the desert. The sight of it usually brought indescribable delight to her heart. Not tonight. Tonight the flakes propelled Lindsey toward the darkest corners of her mind, and she drifted into a deeper level of sleep. The temperature dropped a few more degrees.

An odd whistling sound broke through the coldness of her mind, coming closer, growing louder. *What was that?* It sounded like a young child trying to learn to whistle. Over and over the child tried, and she smiled in her sleep, admiring the dedication. The sound changed again, becoming a wolf whistle, the strong, masculine sound she associated with construction workers admiring women in tight, short skirts.

She burst into consciousness, chilled to the bone, then panicked when she sensed the thin film of ice on her face. When she opened her eyes, it cracked like a facial mask left on too long. Disoriented and shaking with cold, she clawed the ice from her face, then stopped when she heard the whistling sound again. It was coming from under the lounge chair, she realized, but it was too dark for her to see. She tried to move, but her body was stiff from the cold. The noise changed back to sounding like a child's voice, and Lindsey wondered vaguely if it were a dream. Nothing felt real.

The source of the mysterious noise suddenly hopped up on the end of the patio lounge chair and flapped its wings, singing with great vigor.

"Who are you?" Lindsey asked, staring at the beautiful white bird.

She'd never seen such an exotic bird before, and had a feeling it wasn't a desert native. It wouldn't do well in the snow. Lindsey sat straight up, suddenly alert. Snow? She wrapped her arms around herself, shivering convulsively.

"You must be f-f-freezing," she said through chattering teeth. "We'd b-better get inside."

The strange little bird climbed onto Lindsey's outstretched hand, and it didn't object at all to being carried into the warm house. The last few embers of the fire were still flickering faintly, and Lindsey went directly to its delicious heat. She had no idea what to do with the bird, which kept up with its enthusiastic singing. The little yellow head cocked to the side, and she noticed its tiny crown and orange cheeks. It gave another wolf whistle, then declared "Pretty bird!"

"I don't have any bird seed," she told her visitor, "if that's what you want. I could get you some tomorrow. How about a drink of water?" The bird scooped the water up with its curved beak then tipped back its head, obviously thirsty. "How about some banana?" He pecked at it a bit, but Lindsey wasn't sure he actually ate any of it.

As the bird warmed up, so did its singing. It gave her a comical sampling of little bird songs, trills, whistles, chirps, and squawks.

"Take a breath, little guy!" Lindsey said, laughing, and it seemed to understand. For the next thirty minutes or so, her feathered friend ceased talking whenever she spoke, then resumed its twittering when she was quiet. Lindsey freshened her wine and refilled the bird's saucer of water.

"You know, bird, if I am going to tell you my life's woes, you'll need a name. How about Tweety? Nah. Already taken.

Polly? Nope, too old fashioned." She narrowed her eyes, thinking. "How about Malcolm? I like the sound of that. So, Malcolm, here's the story. Just before you flew into my life, I didn't much care if I lived or died. I actually felt like I had died already in a way."

The bird reacted with a shrill litany of chirps.

"I know. Pitiful, huh? But my husband is divorcing me. He's leaving me so he can be with a stripper."

"Pretty bird. Pretty bird. Pretty bird."

"Oh, sure. She's pretty. So pretty she doesn't look real. But you know what? I can't think about her anymore. I can't think about him anymore, either. I've got to think about myself—and you, of course. Don't worry. I won't send you out in the cold. You don't look like a wild bird. You're probably someone's lost pet. And I'm sure they miss you very, very much. I'll put out some posters in the morning."

Lindsey and Malcolm continued their conversation until midnight, then she found some old newspapers and placed them under the large vase on her coffee table where Malcolm perched. She hadn't seen him fly yet, and he didn't seem to want to go anywhere. He tucked his head to the side, almost laying it on his own shoulder, then drifted off to sleep. Lindsey still couldn't go back to her bed, since it brought back memories of the betrayal, so she laid down on the living room sofa.

Just before she fell asleep, she looked at Malcolm, then whispered to herself, "My very own little white bird. Cinderella would be proud."

Winter

Chapter Ten

When Lindsey and Laura arrived at the Bright Angel Lodge, almost six inches of new fallen snow had accumulated. It was absolutely beautiful. Lindsey was relieved to see that the stone steps they were about to climb had been shoveled. She grinned up at the lodge then grabbed her friend's hand and squeezed it.

"This is fantastic, Laura. So rustic! And I don't think I've seen this much snow in … well, maybe ten years."

Laura frowned at her, looking baffled. "I don't get it, Linds. Two nights ago you were in a miserable catatonic state. Now you're bubbling with joy. Now don't get me wrong. I'm your friend. I want you to be happy. It's just … how'd you get happy so fast?"

"Don't get *me* wrong, my friend. I may seem happy, but I am still hurt and lonely and devastated. A nasty, adulterous divorce will do that and more. It's not that I'm suddenly a happy person again. I'm not. But I can be happy in the moment, and this, well, this is a great moment."

Laura pulled open the lodge door, ushering Lindsey ahead of her.

"I don't really know how I came back to earth," Lindsey mused. "I think it started with the bird. He fluttered my focus off the 'poor me' syndrome and on to ... well, just on. I'm looking forward instead of back. I'm not waiting for Anthony anymore. He's made his choice, and as much as I hate it, I can't change it. Now that I know for sure I have to live my life without him, I can get on with it. And that begins today. This glorious, snow-filled day."

"You're amazing."

They beamed at each other. "So are you," Lindsey assured her.

"Good afternoon ladies. Checking in?" A tall, thin man stood behind the knotty-wood registration desk, smiling at them. He wore wire half-glasses and a gray cardigan sweater with leather patches on the elbows, looking more like a retired college professor than a desk clerk. The only thing missing was the pipe, Lindsey thought, and that was probably tucked away in his pocket, waiting for the moment he entered an area void of any "No Smoking" signs.

"Yes," Lindsey replied. "We reserved a lodge room for two under the name Sommerfield. Lindsey Sommerfield."

The clerk's brow wrinkled with concern as he looked over his book. "Oh dear," he mumbled, shaking his head.

"Is there a problem?"

"It seems so. Did you bring your confirmation number with you?"

Lindsey rummaged through her bag and came up empty-handed. "I give up. I don't know what I did with it. But it began with a 'Y' and there were some threes and sevens in the number. I'm sure of that."

He nodded but maintained his frown. "Well, now. I do believe you. I certainly do. But that's not going to do us much good right now, because I don't have any rooms left anyway."

Lindsey's stomach dropped. But she'd called and confirmed!

"Why don't you take a stroll along the rim while there's still some daylight," the clerk suggested. "I'll make a few phone calls and see what I can come up with. You can leave your luggage here, behind the counter."

It had been a chilly fifty degrees when they'd left Tucson that morning. Fifty degrees sounded warm to them now. A sign outside the lodge entrance read: "High today: 38 degrees. Low tonight: 4 degrees."

"Now that's cold!" said Lindsey slipping on her fur-lined leather gloves.

As he'd suggested, they headed west along the Rim Trail, stopping at every informational sign along the way.

"Look Laura. Can you believe this? It says the Grand Canyon is 277 miles long, between four and ten miles wide, and six thousand feet deep. That's a lot of erosion!"

"It'd be cool to watch the making of the canyon on time-lapse photography. How many millions of rolls of film or memory cards would that take?" They gazed in quiet wonder at the giant canyon, and Laura let out a sigh. "I wish we could go down there, don't you?"

"Get that thought out of your mind," Lindsey said quickly. "We are here to relax, eat lots of good food, take nice, short walks in the snow, and maybe drink one or two too many Grand Marniers in the El Tovar bar. We are not here to exhaust ourselves."

"Okay, I see your point. But you left out 'flirt with all the good-looking men.' "

"You're kidding, right?"

"About the hiking or the flirting?" Laura asked with a beguiling smile.

They came upon a quaint old bookstore nestled among the pines on the south rim of the Grand Canyon, and Lindsey read "Kolb Studio" on the carved, wooden sign mounted over the door. Inside, they read another information sign, and discovered that Emery and Ellsworth Kolb, who had originally used the structure as their photography studio, had built the place in 1904. The shop was brimming with nostalgic charm, and it had an atmosphere so alluring that Lindsey figured even the most skeptical non-shopper would find it difficult to leave without making a purchase. For two elementary school teachers it wasn't just difficult, it was practically impossible.

"*Who Pooped in the Park?*"

"Geez, Lindsey. Keep it down!"

Lindsey laughed. "It's a book. A picture book. Look! That's the main part of the title. It's by Gary D. Robson."

"So it is," her friend said, smiling over her shoulder. "Your little guys are really going to like that."

Lindsey made her first Grand Canyon purchase—the "poop" book and an Arizona alphabet book—while Laura bought *"Hey Ranger!" Kids Ask Questions About Grand Canyon National Park.* When they returned to the lodge, the clerk was on the phone. By the look on his face, they could tell the news was not good. He hung up then shook his head.

"I don't know how this little mix-up occurred, ladies, but it did, and there simply isn't another room to be had."

"But how can that be?" Laura asked. "We've been walking around for an hour, and we haven't seen many people. How can every room be taken?"

"We're expecting several tour buses to arrive any time now, and all those folks have reservations."

"But we had reservations, too! And we're here! We're here *now*!" Lindsey cried. She wasn't about to let anything rain—or snow—on her parade. She was going to enjoy life. Relax. See the sights. Maybe even hike the canyon. Do it all—and that included sleeping in a bed. "There must be something we can do."

"Of course there is. Just drive back out of the park to the little town of Tusayan. They have a few rooms left there," said the clerk.

"We can't. Our car is back in Williams. We took the old Grand Canyon Railway. Why can't you give us one of those rooms that belongs to someone on one of those buses that hasn't yet arrived? Maybe someone won't show up. People do get sick, you know. Plans change."

The clerk shook his head sadly. "Ah, but what if they all arrive as planned, with their exact confirmation numbers. I'd be in trouble so big it would make the canyon seem small."

The women kept on, whining and pleading, looking for a solution, but the clerk was helpless. Eventually, a small man walked up to the desk, shaking his head. "All right, already. Stop your begging. It's not ladylike. George, just give them my room. I can sleep with my son. He won't be thrilled, but what's he gonna do?" He kept shaking his head as he turned from the desk and walked away, still mumbling to himself.

"Thank you, Mr … Mr …"

But he was already gone.

The clerk raised one eyebrow. "Well now. That's a stroke of luck for you."

The room was incredible. It had its own wood-burning fireplace, two large log beds, a sitting area complete with two overstuffed, roomy chairs, and a small kitchen. When Lindsey pulled opened the heavy, azure drapes, an unrestrained squeal of delight filled the room. They were rim-side, and the view was spectacular. The setting sun, glimmering through just enough cloud cover, painted a purple glow on the rust-colored cliffs that already sparkled with a light dusting of snow.

"This must be the best room in the whole place!" she exclaimed, unable to take her eyes from the view. "I wish Anthony was here. He would love this," came tumbling from her lips before she even realized what she'd said. She looked guiltily at Laura. "Oops."

"What? I thought you weren't—"

"Okay! I still miss him. I still love him, Laura. Just because I've decided, mentally, to get on with my life—and I will— that doesn't mean I don't still care. It's going to take a while. I know that. It's ... it's just odd, not having someone to share moments like this with."

Laura huffed good-naturedly. "I'll try not to take that personally," she said.

"Oh, you know what I mean."

"Of course. I know exactly what you mean. This could have been one of life's most romantic moments if I was Anthony, or you were ... Oh, damn. I still don't know his name."

"Whose name?"

Laura tilted her head to one side, smiling wistfully. "That great guy we met at the Coyote Café that night. You know. The bartender."

"He left before I got there, remember? You really like him? Someone actually got to you?"

She shrugged. "Kind of. But he doesn't know it yet. I plan to see him again when we get back."

They unpacked, took long, hot showers, then sat on their beds, staring out the window.

"I'm hungry," Laura said.

"Me, too. Let's try the Arizona Steakhouse. I saw it when we came in."

"You don't eat steak."

Lindsey lifted her chin and gave her friend a haughty look. "Well, I might tonight."

She ended up getting the grilled chicken, since it turned out she wasn't ready to give up Anthony's healthy eating rules just yet.

"This is delicious," she announced.

Laura swallowed a bite of steak. "Speaking of birds, what did you do with your newfound feathered friend?"

"Actually, it was the oddest coincidence. Yesterday I was in the pet store, buying a cage for Malcolm when—"

"Malcolm? You named it?"

"Yeah, well, I couldn't just call him 'Bird.' Anyway, there I was, picking out a bird cage, all the time wondering what I was going to do with him while we were here, and in walks Jake."

"Jake, the Chinese food guy?"

"Yep. To make a long story short, he followed me home, I made him lunch, we talked for a while, then he left, taking Malcolm with him." She smiled. "He's so nice, and he really likes animals."

Laura's eyes widened. "Lindsey, my dear, I think he likes you."

Chapter Eleven

"Malcolm, you're a lucky bird. Rescued by the kindest woman I know. I wish you could talk, buddy."

Malcolm gave him a loud squawk, then reminded him, "Pretty bird!"

"Yes, you are. And you're good at talking, your way. I'll give you that. But I need details, little fella. In English. Where did she find you? What did she tell you? What was she feeling? What does she really look like under those 'teacher clothes?" He chuckled. "Sorry, bud. That just slipped out."

While Malcolm looked on, Jake typed out what he could, based on the conversation he'd had with Lindsey over lunch.

Subject D appears to have found new energy, new hope. She's coping with her loneliness better and sooner than I would have anticipated. Didn't want to talk about anything but the bird and her trip to the Grand Canyon. She was preoccupied with both. Perhaps these factors are distracting her from her own problems, her own pain. Only time will tell.

At a loss for more details about Subject D, he moved on to other research subjects.

> *There is more to Subject C than meets the eye. I am baffled at the coldness and selfishness of this woman. I am also tired of dog sitting, so I may have to resort to hiring a private detective to uncover the missing information on this one. Hiding in shadows, waiting in the wings to talk with her is not my style. I hope I'm not in over my head.*

Jake felt unusually agitated, and he wasn't sure why. He was aware that by getting too close to his subjects he was losing some of his objectivity, and he thought that might contribute to how he was feeling. Or maybe he was just exhausted. After all, he was working two jobs, attending classes, and writing his thesis. And now he was taking care of a chatty bird. All that might be getting the better of him.

He glanced at his watch and quickly closed his laptop. "Damn it! I'm late again."

A light dusting of snow floated down from the dark winter sky and now sparkled under the few lights illuminating the walkway. Only the crunching of their boots and a few distant, cheerful voices broke the blanketed silence as the women walked in the direction of their room.

Laura suddenly slammed on her brakes. "No. Stop! We are *not* going back to our room yet. We only have five days here. We don't have time to do nothing."

Lindsey groaned. She wanted to go back to the room, jump into that huge log bed, and snuggle down with the bag of books she'd brought. She always read nursery rhymes and fairy tales to her students, but this year she'd dedicated the month of January to the implementation of a thematic unit about fairy tales. Many of the books in her bag were newly published versions of fairy tales, and she couldn't wait to read them. She'd even brought a novel length version of Sleeping Beauty that had been sitting on her shelf for years.

"Oh, all right. How about one drink at the El Tovar Bar while we plan tomorrow's activities?"

Laura tightened her lips, obviously disapproving. "Yes, teacher. Did you bring your plan book?"

"Well, if you're going to be that way, let me rephrase my idea. Here goes." She threw her hands up in the air. "Let's drink till we're blind, and during that time we'll think about the grand possibilities and adventures that could take place on the morrow."

"Now you're talking—I think," replied Laura, though she looked dubious.

The temperature dropped, the snowfall thickened, and the women's pace quickened. Fortunately, the El Tovar wasn't far.

"Look at that Christmas tree!" Lindsey exclaimed, gawking. "It must be twenty-five feet tall."

A large fire roared in the mammoth stone fireplace located in El Tovar's lobby, and several couples sat on the leather love-seats, holding hands and warming themselves in front of the flames. The scent of pine, the glow of the crackling fire, the beauty of the tasteful holiday decor, and the company of the joyful patrons was more than enough to lift Lindsey's spirits.

I can do this, she told herself. *I can enjoy all this without Anthony.*

Then she slumped. *Oh, Anthony,* she thought. *How could you leave me? And, why can't I leave you behind?*

Laura glanced at a faltering Lindsey, grabbed her arm, and ushered her into the bar. The cozy room was full, not crowded, but buzzing with park guests who looked as if they'd just come from a photo shoot for an LL Bean catalog. Adirondack barn coats, fleece beanies, quilted parkas, fleece-lined jackets, boots, and hats, all color coordinated as if selected by a winter fashionista. Laura's and Lindsey's closets back in Tucson contained mostly summer wear, along with a few sweaters for those rare, cold, southern Arizona days. The few snow gear items they owned were old, though barely used. Glancing around at the show of fashion, Lindsey felt an urge to shop for more than books, and she knew Laura felt the same.

"What can I get you ladies?" asked the smiling, outdoorsy looking woman behind the bar.

"Two Grand Marniers, heated, in snifters, please," Laura replied.

They sipped the smooth liqueur and settled into the welcoming mood of the place.

"So, I've decided I really would like to hike tomorrow," Lindsey said, though she hoped to avoid a heavy workout. "Maybe follow the rest of the rim?"

Laura shook her head. "I'd like to hike down into the canyon. It's really calling to me."

"A nice bus tour is calling to me."

"We could do that, too," Laura said, but she still sounded determined. "We wouldn't have to go all the way down—"

"Don't even think about going halfway down. It's the middle of winter." The deep, resonating voice came from the table next to them, and both women turned toward it. He smiled through his beard then stuck out his hand. "I'm Brad Silverton," he announced.

"Hi, I'm Lindsey," she said, taking his warm hand. "And this is Laura. You don't think the hike is a good idea?"

"Well now, that depends." He said a few things about the weather, the inherent dangers of the trail—especially in winter—and the women's inexperience.

Laura squinted skeptically at him. She didn't look impressed. "I suppose you're some kind of canyon expert?"

Their new acquaintance was handsome in a teddy bear sort of way. Lindsey could see Laura didn't want him to be right about the hiking, but it wasn't long before her friend started smiling. It was hard to resist Brad's warm smile, and he was both charming and intelligent. By the time their drinks arrived—for which Brad insisted on paying—Laura was totally into her flirting mode. After about an hour of intriguing conversation, including making a plan for a short hike into the canyon the next day if the weather cleared, Lindsey and Laura agreed it was time to call it a night.

As they walked away and were putting on their hats and gloves, Brad called out, "How about dinner tomorrow night in the El Tovar dining room?"

Without a second's hesitation Laura called back, "Sounds great. What time?"

"Dinner at eight. See you then."

"It's eight o'clock," Anthony said, pacing across their dimly lit bedroom.

At first he'd welcomed the fact that Shawna wanted to spend so many hours in bed with him, but now that the newness and the intense, addictive thrill of their high energy sex episodes had diminished, he craved a more typical routine. That kind of routine did not involve his babe sleeping the day away, every day.

"Yes, darling," Shawna drawled. "It is eight o'clock. Eight o'clock in the *morning.*"

"Come on. It's Saturday. You're not expected at The Office today. I'd like to go out and enjoy the sunshine, the crisp air, the people—do something, do *anything.*"

She glared at him in disgust. "This Beauty needs her sleep."

He knew she wasn't about to go out and play in the sun. That wasn't her style. She always had reasons for staying in, laying low in the daylight. After all, this was Tucson, the skin cancer capital of the world. He guessed it seemed reasonable for someone so beautiful to avoid exposing her skin to the treacherous southwest sun. Or did it?

The fact that she was more than willing to make mad, passionate love to him whenever he desired—as long as the event took place in their dark bedroom, or anywhere else that was dimly lit—had clouded Anthony's vision. Her aggressive, dominating style of making love—which had thrilled him in the beginning— was also getting old. In fact, it got downright creepy sometimes.

And strangest of all was that it definitely didn't include the one thing that he'd commonly considered to *be* making love, which was actual … sex. She'd told him right up front that she'd do absolutely anything for him—except for penetration. That was only for her husband, she'd teased.

At first he'd been skeptical. But then she'd shown him a whole new world of sex. And the things she did to him …

But her night owl tendencies were getting old.

"Get up, Shawna. We're going out, sunshine and all, like real people. It's December, for God's sake. A few winter ultra violet rays are not going to hurt you."

"No!" she shouted.

"No?" he shouted back in disbelief. "No? How can you say that? How can you be so unreasonable?" Pulling the edge of the heavy window covering aside, he added, "Look! It's a cloudy day."

She shrunk away from the light as if it burned. Shawna was the most baffling individual he'd ever met. Lindsey had always been so rational, so practical. They would talk things through and compromise, make sense of their disagreements. But this woman was different. Oh, he still loved her sexuality, her hunger for him, and her perfect body. But he missed having a friend and a partner. Second thoughts flickered through his mind.

Chapter Twelve

A fire crackled in the fireplace as the two women snuggled down, each in their own log bed. Lindsey perused her new fairy tale picture books, but soon settled on the Sleeping Beauty novel. She stared at the cover for a while and thought about tomorrow—in particular, tomorrow night. Did the eight o'clock dinner date include her? Sometimes three's a crowd, and he'd spoken mostly with Laura. She'd figure it out later.

Lindsey's novel didn't waste any time. Within the first few paragraphs the prince made his way into the castle and found the young sleeping beauty. Lindsey was surprised by the speed—how in the world was the author going to fill the next two hundred and fifty pages when the only things left to do were kiss the princess awake, marry her, then live happily ever after? Perhaps the happily ever after part would go on forever.

She continued and discovered the famous wake-up kiss was a bit more than a kiss. That was okay, she figured. After all, this was a novel, not a children's picture book. She kept reading, and her mouth fell open with shock. The book grew steamier with every word, each one seductively describing the handsome prince's skillful removal of Beauty's hundred-year-old velvet gown, and the journey his hands, eyes, and mouth took in and around her delicate, young body.

"Lindsey!" Laura said, laughing. "What's going on over there? You're reading with your eyes bulging out, and your jaw looks like it's about to hit the floor."

"It's the book. It's ... let's just say it's not quite what I expected."

"Okay, so what did you expect?"

"Sleeping Beauty. Sleeping Beauty with a lot of detail, and new information about all the characters, and vivid descriptions and—"

"Are you saying there are no details?"

Lindsey let out a long, slow breath. "No. Oh no. There are *plenty* of details."

"Okay, so it's the characters? There's not enough information about the characters?"

She bit her lip. "No. There's more than enough information about the characters, and lots of vivid descriptions, too. It's just that ... well, I didn't think the author would spend so much time vividly describing things like body parts—*private* body parts."

"Let me see that," said Laura, looking curious. She read a few paragraphs silently, then checked the front cover of the book, and grinned. "Linds, you forgot to read the fine print. Oh, it's a book about Sleeping Beauty, all right. Look right there." She pointed to some text at the bottom of the feminine-looking cover.

"'An Erotic Fairy Tale Adventure,'" read Lindsey. "Oh, I can't read this."

"You're absolutely right," agreed Laura, matter-of-factly. "You can't read this. But *we* can!"

Giggling, they wrapped themselves in blankets by the fire. They took turns reading the sexually explicit, bizarre fairy tale out loud, occasionally cringing, sometimes blushing, often laughing, even rereading some of the extra good parts now and then.

Hours later, Lindsey awoke to Laura's screaming. Why? It was too dark to see. She fumbled for the bedside light switch, and saw a man sitting on the side of Laura's bed, topless.

"What the ... *Laura?*" he asked.

"*Brad?*"

"What are you doing here?" they both said at the same time.

"This is our room," Lindsey said, rubbing the sleep from her eyes.

"Huh. Well, all last week and earlier today, this was my father's room," said Brad, one eyebrow lifted.

"That was your father?" both women exclaimed.

"*Who* was my father?"

"Well, we don't know exactly," Laura explained. "But a nice man offered us his room because the front desk mixed up our reservation and they didn't have a room for us. And it was impossible to go back because we had taken the train, and—"

"Whoa, slow down," said Brad. "I think I'm beginning to understand now. I went to my room, discovered Dad there, and I figured he must have crashed in my room by mistake. So I decided to sleep in his room." He grimaced. "He snores terribly."

"So that really was your father," Laura said, frowning. "You seem quite different from each other. He seemed so New Yorkish and you seem so mid-westish."

He chuckled. "Well, it's kind of a long story, so maybe we'll continue this conversation tomorrow. If you're really going

91

hiking tomorrow, you're going to need some rest. And … I'm actually a little uncomfortable sitting here in bed with you, Laura, in my underwear—"

Laura blushed, then squeezed her eyes shut. "Oh, oh, sure. Um—"

"Laura, get in bed with me," Lindsey ordered. "Brad, roll over and go to sleep. We can figure it all out in the morning, and that will arrive sooner than I even want to think about."

They did as she said, and in the morning he was gone.

"He left a note," Lindsey said, padding lazily from the bathroom and climbing back into bed.

"What does it say?" Laura mumbled.

Lindsey blinked. She'd just about fallen asleep all over again. "Huh?"

"Brad's note. What does it say?"

"Oh, that he'd have breakfast sent to our room, and that he'd see us tonight if we still wanted to have dinner with him."

"Do we?" asked Laura.

"Don't we?" Lindsey countered.

A knock at the door interrupted their banter, and Laura opened it. A young man wearing a cowboy hat and a sheepskin coat handed them a tray. Laura reached out for his arm as he began to walk away.

"Wait. We want to tip you," she said.

He gave her a crooked smile and touched the brim of his hat. "No need, ma'am. Everything's been taken care of."

The friends exchanged a glance, grinning at each other. Then they devoured the scrumptious breakfast of scrambled eggs, bacon, sour dough toast, a delicious salsa with pine nuts, and freshly squeezed juice. It was so good, neither of them said a word through the entire meal.

The day proved to be exceptionally beautiful. The grayish-purple snow clouds had vanished completely, and the bright white sun prevailed. By ten o'clock even the wind had ceased, and the decision to take a short hike had been made. The women dressed in their warmest clothing and began the descent down the Bright Angel Trail. Between the physical exertion and the constant sunshine, they were surprisingly comfortable, despite the freezing thirty-degree temperature.

"I can't believe I let you talk me into this," grumbled Lindsey, though deep down she was enjoying their outdoor adventure.

"Isn't it fantastic?" Laura bubbled. "We're hiking the Grand Canyon in the snow! How many people can say that?"

Not many today, that's for sure. In fact, the women had met no other hikers on the trail so far. They'd spotted what they thought might be the footprints of several mules, but it was hard to tell for sure because the early morning dusting of snow had mostly covered them. They noticed newer tracks of smaller animals off to the side of the trail. Rabbits and squirrels for sure, something with a narrow hoof—probably a deer—and a few prints that looked like cat prints, only larger.

The walk downhill was relatively painless. For the most part, the snow was only about six inches deep. Once in a while they came to a drift and had to high step their way through, but that just added to the fun. Fortunately, the drifts were rare and only popped up in the wider areas of the narrow, cliff-like trail. Time passed quickly, and before long they found themselves on a large, flat mesa where most of the snow had melted under the intense sun.

"Let's relax for a minute," said Laura. "Break out the trail mix. I'm starved."

The temperature climbed higher than they or any of the "experts" had anticipated, so Lindsey and Laura removed their outer parkas and sat on them while they rested and enjoyed the view.

Lindsey was the first to notice a large, majestic bird off in the distance. "What do you think that is?"

"I'd have to get closer to know for sure," Laura said, squinting, "but it's either the biggest hawk I've ever seen or it's an eagle. Either way, I don't think it's happy that we're here. He's definitely not smiling."

"I don't think birds smile."

"Oh really? Have you forgotten about all those stories you told me about Milton ... Murray—"

"Malcolm. His name is Malcolm."

"Right. Malcolm. You led me to believe he did a lot of smiling, not to mention talking. And I believe he is a bird."

"That's true," she allowed. "But Malcolm is not a predator. He's not a raptor. He eats seeds and fruit. I don't think birds that eat other animals are ever too smiley or chummy looking."

Laura nodded sagely. "That makes sense. Hey, now that we're sitting still, I'm getting a little cold. What do you say we hike to the edge of this mesa, have a look down, then head back up to the rim?"

"Sounds good."

Estimating mileage in the canyon turned out to be more difficult than they'd imagined. They never reached the mesa's edge after all. Instead, they headed back right after catching a glimpse of the Colorado River in the distance. The air was incredibly still, so quiet and serene it made their ears ring. When the large bird returned, swooping near them, its huge wings created a loud whooshing sound as they pushed against the air.

"Whoa!" they both screamed breathlessly, ducking out of the way.

"That was no hawk or eagle," Laura said.

Lindsey shook her head. "It looked more like a pterodactyl. Wow." She snapped a picture of the great dark bird in flight as it headed toward the cliffs. "There! That alone was worth the effort of this hike."

Laura chuckled. "Let's see if you still feel that way after we hike uphill for a while. I think the 'effort' has only just begun."

By the time they were ready to ascend, it was much later than either of them had thought, and the sun was out of sight. They would need to hurry to make it back to the rim before the pending darkness engulfed them. They huffed and puffed their way up the steep, narrow trail for a while. At first it was simply exhausting. Then other difficulties set in. The warmth of the day that had made the hike down so pleasant had turned the snow to slush. When the air grew cold again, that slush became ice, and the trail became not only challenging, but also dangerous. There was no room for error. One slip in the wrong direction and even the most experienced hiker could fall over the edge. The bottom was a long way down—hundreds, even thousands of feet in some places.

Neither Laura nor Lindsey knew anything about surviving in the wilderness. Especially in a freezing cold wilderness. Lindsey taught her students about safety and survival in the desert, but not much of that applied here. It was getting darker and colder with every step, and they weren't even halfway back. Lindsey's pulse raced as she realized the steepest part of the hike was still ahead of them.

"At least I'm not cold yet," Lindsey said, trying to be positive.

"No, me either. In fact, I'm hot. I'm sweating. Imagine that, sweating when it's most likely below freezing."

But they were both frightened, and neither wanted to admit to it. The trail was a bumpy, jagged, treacherous path of slippery ice—difficult going, to say the least. Eventually, when they were within a mile of the rim, the trail became so steep that forward, upward progress was impossible. They'd take one step forward and slip two steps back.

"We can do this," they said to each other, because they had no other choice.

"I think I can. I think I can. I think I can," Lindsey quietly chanted to herself.

The Little Engine That Could," Laura said, smiling.

"Yep. I always liked that story. That poor little train worked so hard to get up the hill. But I'll admit, I never thought I'd be living it." Just then, her foot slipped and she lost her balance. She pitched forward and came close to tumbling over the edge. "I can't. I can't do this," she cried.

"Yes, you can, Linds. We can and we're going to," Laura assured her. "Look up at the lights. You can see them now. We've just got to make it to those lights. It's not that far. I think we'd better try crawling. We're not getting anywhere trying to walk on this ice, and we can't take the chance of falling again. Besides, we can barely see where we're going anyway. It's so dark."

Both women were strong willed, but crawling on the icy, rocky trail was excruciatingly painful, and it quickly wore them down. Their knees received more bumps and bruises in an hour than they had during their entire childhood. To make matters worse, an icy, cutting wind began to blow, pushing at them. The blowing quickly advanced to howling.

Since they'd rounded the last switchback, the distant, beckoning lights were no longer visible.

"What time is it?" shouted Laura, attempting to be heard above the wind.

Lindsey pushed her glove and jacket cuff away to look at her watch, but it was hard to read in the dark. "I think it says five-thirty, but I'm not positive. Why?"

"Actually, I was hoping it was later," answered Laura. "No one is going to even miss us till we don't show up for our eight o'clock dinner date."

"We might not even be missed then. Brad might think we decided to pass on his offer. Oh, Laura. What are we going to do? I'm so cold. I'm so tired. Every inch of me hurts, and we are making the progress of a snail."

"I know ... Do you think it hurts to freeze to death?" Laura asked softly.

Changing the subject, Lindsey asked, "Well, when we do get back and have our dinner date with Brad, which one of us will take on the role of major flirter, and which one will be the tag-along friend?"

Laura didn't say anything. They sat huddled together in the darkness for a few minutes, working up the strength to move ahead.

"I keep picturing the students' smiling faces, remembering my chat with Malcolm by the fireplace only a few nights ago, and fantasizing about curling up in Anthony's strong arms."

"I'll take your visions any day," Laura said quietly. "I see my stubborn, independent self, still all alone. I could die and no one would miss me."

Chapter Thirteen

With all but one of his subjects out of town, Jake's only choice—if he wished to continue his work over Christmas vacation—was to connect with Shawna. Usually she called him at the restaurant for a delivery, or at his apartment if she needed a dog sitter. But he hadn't heard from her in a while, and some critical data was needed for her file. Actually, critical data was needed for each subject's file, but today it was Shawna or nothing. He thought about going with nothing, taking the day for himself, but his driving work ethic and sense of urgency soon returned, and he was back on track.

He had to admit that a complication now existed. He was personally involved, making it harder to be objective. Was he still objective at all? But it was too late to turn back. He'd gone too far, and time was running out. So he dialed, initiating the contact, breaking all the rules.

"Hello," answered a sleepy voice.

"Shawna?"

"Anthony?" she replied.

"No. No, it's Jake. Remember me?"

"Of course. Hello, Jake. What time is it?"

"Almost six. Sounds like you hit the hay early tonight. I'm sorry I disturbed you, I just thought—"

There was a rustle in the background, as if she were getting out of bed. "Six o'clock? Damn! I've got to get up. Anthony will be here any minute. In fact, he should already be here. I've got to go, Jake."

"Okay, sure," said Jake. "It's just that some friends and I had a huge cookout and we've got lots of great steak bones left. I thought Wendell might want them. I'd hate to see them go to waste. I could drop them by on my way to work."

"I don't know, Jake," she stammered. "Anthony is angry with me, and now he's an hour later than usual. I want to plan something special for him. It's almost Christmas, and I can't have my lover mad at me over the holidays. That simply wouldn't do. Can I call you later?"

She hung up without waiting for an answer, and Jake stared at his phone. Was he losing his touch? He'd always gotten what he wanted from women before—with the exception of his first love—at least in the work-a-day or academic world. Now what should he do? Perhaps today was a day to forget about school, work, lost loves, and new loves. Maybe he'd just go out and relax.

"Pretty bird. Pretty bird," squawked Malcolm.

Jake sighed. "All right, Malcolm. I'll stay. But I'm opening that bottle of vodka that's been in the freezer for three months." He mixed a vodka and grape juice, then a vodka and 7-Up, and finally a vodka with coke. Except for the occasional glass of wine, Jake didn't usually drink, so three vodkas in a relatively short period of time was more than he could handle.

Malcolm kept the conversation going as the vodka dwindled. The little bird reminded Jake of Lindsey every time it opened its little beak. And tonight its beak was wide open.

"Damn it, Malcolm," he said, his words sloppy. "I know. She's so likable. She's so … so … everything. I like everything about her."

He scribbled some handwritten notes in Lindsey's file, though they took on a less professional, less objective tone as the evening progressed.

> *Lindsey: Her loneliness took a turn for the worse as the pending divorce slugged her in the face. She still hopes Anthony will come back someday. Hope has faded and her reaction was to withdraw. She's hit a new low, a dangerous low, which could have resulted in serious, physical damage. Example: falling asleep outside in snowy, sub-freezing temperatures. Was she conscious of this danger? Don't know. Was she attempting to end her life? Don't know—yet. But a bird saved her—why couldn't it have been me?*

"I would have saved her," he told Malcolm, feeling miserable. "I *should* have saved her. I still want to save her. I want to rescue her from her loneliness. Instead, I was outdone by a bird. I should be her hero, her knight in … khaki shorts—"

The phone rang, bringing him back. "Hello?"

"Now look who sounds sleepy," taunted Shawna, fully awake. "I need your help. I don't have time to explain it all now 'cause I've got work to do, but I need your dog sitting services for about twenty-four hours. Can you do it? Can you pick up Wendell and keep him at your place?"

"Uh, sure. I guess so," he replied.

"Good. The key is under the mat. See you tomorrow."

When Jake arrived at Shawna's house, Wendell was obviously glad to see him. His tail drew huge circles in the air, and his smiling face was all Jake needed to remember how much he really did like this dog. Not just because he was the gimmick to get close to Shawna, or because he was the second love of Lindsey's life. He was a great dog, and he had won a place in Jake's heart on his own merits.

"Hey, buddy. How ya doing? Ready to go for a ride?"

They were about to leave when it occurred to him that he might as well do some research while he was there. Just a little. He wouldn't touch anything; he'd just have a look around. A bit unethical, yes, but only a little. He wandered through the house looking for clues, information, signs—anything that might help him understand Shawna's life a little better.

He needed details, which included more information than she'd been willing to reveal. She'd been such an enthusiastic, talkative subject at first, but during the past few months her comments had become calculated and controlling. He hadn't been able to crack the code with this one. The other women in his research made sense. Their profiles supported, for the most part, his hypothesis. But Shawna, well, she was different. On the surface she seemed like your everyday, gorgeous nymphomaniac, looking for love, attention, and money. Strangely though, she appeared to already have plenty of money, which he assumed was family money, and was receiving plenty of love and attention. Jake sensed a dark side, and it was this unknown factor that kept him wandering through the house with Wendell by his side.

"I wish you could talk," he told the dog.

The living area was darkly decorated—black, overstuffed leather furniture, dark blue velvet drapes, and dark wood floors covered with much darker rugs. Even with all the lights turned on, the place felt dark—and creepy. Totally out of place here in sunny Tucson. He couldn't picture Anthony as a "dark" kind of guy, but looks could be and often were deceiving. Maybe they couldn't stand the heat—he laughed at the irony of that—and the décor simply kept them cooler on scorching hot days.

At first glance, Jake noticed that the kitchen appeared to be more typical than the rest of the house. There were several large windows covered by nothing more than sheer burgundy curtains, a large teak table that could seat six comfortably, and a wooden breakfast nook, as well as the usual kitchen appliances. He broke his own rule of not touching anything and opened the refrigerator, startled to find that both the fridge and freezer were almost empty. The stovetop and the oven were spotless—like new. He got the distinct impression there wasn't much cooking or eating going on around there.

Having spent far longer in Shawna's and Anthony's home than he'd intended, and still riding his vodka buzz, Jake began to enjoy his sleuthing. He headed down the hall toward the bedroom, but when he reached for the door knob of the first door, Wendell began to bark.

"What is it, boy?" asked Jake. *Good grief,* he thought. This was beginning to feel like a twisted scene from *Lassie*. That would make him … Timmy. *I've hit an all time low.* "You're right, Wendell. I shouldn't be snooping around. Let's go."

Jake, now regretting his rash decision to play detective, hurried toward the back door where he knew he'd find Wendell's leash and dish. He gathered the items with such haste that the leash got caught on the door knob, and the dish fell to the cold hard floor with a jolting clatter, landing on its edge and rolling across the room. Wendell whimpered, as if he wanted to leave, and Jake couldn't disagree. He didn't know where Shawna and Anthony had gone or when they might return, but an air of urgency was upon him. He didn't feel guilty—he hadn't done anything illegal, after all—but it felt wrong.

The dog dish had ended up under a bench in the breakfast nook area, so he stooped to pick it up. While he was there, he noticed a dusty, old envelope on the floor, just barely visible.

He picked it up and was going to place it on the table when he read the word, DAD, scribbled in orange crayon across the front of the envelope. Strange. He knew for sure there were no kids living here. Curiosity got the better of him, and he shoved the envelope into his pocket before finally locking up the house, putting the key back under the mat, and heading for the car.

They drove around for a while, needing some time and space away from Shawna's dark, dim house before they got to Jake's bright and airy apartment. Eventually they ended up at the Jack-in-the-Box drive-up window on Grant Road, where they sat quietly in the car and gulped down cheeseburgers. Wendell finished first, Jake was a close second.

Both seemed satisfied, though the dog began to drool, and Jake reached into his pocket, hoping to find a handkerchief to soak up some of the slobber. Instead, he found the envelope. *Stupid.* By impulsively taking it, he had done something illegal. That made him a thief. Fortunately, he was fairly sure his accomplice wouldn't talk.

He decided he'd take a look and put it back another day. Obviously, neither Shawna nor Anthony gave it much value or importance, since it had been dropped carelessly on the floor. Maybe it didn't even belong to either of them. Maybe it had been there for years. He opened the envelope and discovered a faded, cracked photograph of a very tall man and a very small boy. The man looked a little like Shawna—maybe her father. But who was the little boy?

Chapter Fourteen

Huddling on the icy, narrow trail made them feel even colder. The women knew they should keep going, keep moving, but they crouched in the darkness instead, holding each other tightly as the velocity of the wind increased and the temperature fell.

"Did you hear that?" Lindsey whispered.

"Hear what? All I can hear is the howling of the wind whipping around the canyon walls. That, and my heart beating inside my head."

"No. Come on, Laura. Listen. I think I hear something. It sounds like singing."

They paused and listened hard, then Laura nodded slowly. "You know, I think I hear it, too. Either we've lost our sanity, or we're dead. We must be dead. We couldn't be insane. Not us."

"No," Lindsey agreed. "But I don't want to be dead. Not yet. I saw 'Our Town,' and the dead were lifeless. Pain-free, but lifeless."

Laura snorted. "Brilliant deduction, Linds."

"But I don't want to be insane, either."

"I'll take insane over dead any day," said Laura. "They have medication for insanity. There's no pill for the dead."

"Well, we may not have a choice," Lindsey said, sitting taller. "I hear Christmas carols. Maybe we're dead and that's our angel."

They sat silently for a few moments, getting colder by the second, listening for their angel. Yes, they both heard a voice, and it was definitely singing. Then the blustering, wintry gale suddenly stopped, producing a vacuum of stillness. Delicate snowflakes danced down from the sky, weaving a soothing, white blanket to cover the women up, tuck them in for the night.

The singing came again. Their angel's footsteps crunched on the ice and snow as he approached, and the voice grew louder.

"Now the ground is white. Go it while you're young. Take the girls tonight and sing this sleighing song."

But an angel would not have crunching footsteps or be singing Jingle Bells, especially the second verse.

"Someone's coming," Lindsey exclaimed, shaking Laura. "We're not dead. Wake up!"

They both began to shout, and within minutes a man appeared, shining his large flashlight toward the shouting.

"What the—" he began to say, taken back.

"Can you help us to the top?" Laura cried.

"Sure, but ... why are you just sitting there? You're going to freeze to death. You've got to keep moving."

"Please, no lectures," Lindsey begged. "The slush turned to ice, we kept slipping ..."

The stocky, heaven sent stranger got right to work. He crouched down to them, then gave each a sip or two of brandy. The women started to come around, mentally returning to their old selves, though physically their bodies were still dangerously cold.

"Well, no wonder you can't get up the hill," he muttered. "You're not wearing crampons. You should always take crampons when hiking the canyon in the winter. Always! Here, I've got an extra pair. That will help one of you get up the trail, anyway. Ladies, on your feet. March in place for a minute."

He took charge like an army sergeant: no humor, and all business. Lindsey was grateful for that. She didn't feel the least bit like laughing.

"You, the taller one," he said, pointing to Laura. "Let's get the crampons on your feet. You'll make it to the top. It's really not that far. Just go one step at a time. Plant your foot firmly, making sure it has a good grip before lifting your other leg. You can do it."

He handed her an extra flashlight and explained that they'd be just a few steps behind her. Lindsey was smaller and weaker, and therefore more affected by the elements. Without crampons, she'd continue to slip and slide on this steep, dangerous part of the trail, so he placed her in front of him to keep her from slipping backwards.

"We're going to have to synchronize our steps," he told her. "Don't worry. This will work. Left foot first," he instructed.

They headed up the path like a very short centipede, with Lindsey about a foot ahead of him, his hands on her waist. This arrangement worked for about ten paces. Lindsey warmed up a little, which caused her hands and feet to tingle and sting as the circulation crept through her shivering body. Then she stepped on an icy patch and skidded back into the stranger, nearly knocking him down. His strength, the gripping crampons, and his determination to get her up the trail all held fast. He quickly and carefully put both strong arms around her waist, held her tightly to him, and spoke firmly.

"It's okay. You're all right. The trail's slicker than I thought. So let's try it this way for a while."

"Thanks," was all she could say. She felt suddenly safe and even a little warm, wrapped in his arms, pressed firmly against the full length of his sturdy body. As they worked their way up the trail as one, Lindsey wondered if this experience was real or if it might be a dream. Either way, she liked it. Who was this helpful stranger, this mysterious angel? It didn't matter. Dream or not, for the moment he was her very own knight in shining armor, the prince saving her from a fate far worse than sleeping for a hundred years.

Brad grew impatient, waiting for his dad. They'd agreed to meet for drinks before his dinner date with Lindsey and Laura, but he was late. He tapped a steady beat on the heavy wooden table with the swizzle stick from his second cognac.

"Been waiting long?"

"Hell, yes, Dad. As a matter of fact I have."

"Well, sorry. I needed a few things that I'd left in my old room, but I didn't want to bother the girls. As it turned out, they weren't there anyway."

"They weren't in the room? That's funny. I'd have thought they'd be showering, doing their hair or whatever other stuff women do before going out. They're meeting me here in about thirty minutes."

"No. No sign of them, so I was able to get what I needed. I forgot to ask how long they were staying. Maybe I should go back and get all my things out of the room." He put up one hand, gesturing to the waitress. "So tell me. Have you come up with any good ideas for our new catalog? I assume that's why you wanted to meet me tonight."

"Sure I have, Dad. I'm always thinking about the catalog. But that's not why I wanted this meeting." He frowned. "I know what you're up to."

"Up to? My dear son, how can you think such a thing? I'm not up to anything."

"I think you are. I ended up in bed with Laura last night."

"*Mazel Tov!*" declared his happy father. "You're not wasting any time, for a change. You've moved too slowly in the past, son. Life's too short, and you're not getting any younger. You need a wife. You need children. You need—"

"Don't you mean *you* need a daughter-in-law, and *you* need grandchildren?" Brad asked, feeling heat rise in his face. "Besides, *aleyn iz di neshome reyn*[1]."

"*Oy, vey.* You're breaking my heart. I'm only thinking of you. I just want you to settle down and be happy. So you slept with Laura. Was that the feisty redhead, or the sensible brunette?"

"Laura has red hair."

"Oh, good. Good choice, son. I, myself, wasn't sure. They each had something special about them. I couldn't choose."

Brad scowled at his father. "I didn't choose Laura, Dad. I was set up, and you know it. I stumbled into the room in the dark and fell into the bed closest to the door. It just happened to be the bed Laura was sleeping in. She screamed; we all screamed. It wasn't good, Dad."

His father held his hands up, shaking them and grinning. "Ah, but this *was* good. This was better than good. God has chosen for you. Don't you see that?"

---

[1]   Being single has its advantages/Literally: Alone, one's soul is pure.

Brad sighed. "Oh, please. Spare me the religion. It was just one of your calculated pranks that went awry. I'm just worried that after they thought about the awkward event of last night, they might have decided to forgo having dinner with me. And I really was looking forward to their company. I was looking forward to seeing both of them. They're fun to be with, and they're intelligent. They're both teachers."

Brad's father sat quietly, then looked his son in the eye. "*Shtil vasser grobt tif.*[2]"

"What the hell does that have to do with anything?"

Shrugging, he replied, "Oh, nothing. I just like to say it."

A commotion arose in the hotel lobby, and a noisy, inquisitive crowd gathered in front of the massive stone fireplace.

"Should we call a doctor?"

"How long were they down there?"

"That one doesn't look so good."

Brad's eyes widened when he heard Laura's weak voice. "I'm fine. I'm fine," she said. "I just need to warm up a little."

Lindsey stood beside Laura in silence, shivering uncontrollably as other guests helped her out of the sweat-soaked coat and sweaters, then covered her with their coats and offered sips of warm drinks. Brad and his father worked their way close to the women just in time to hear Lindsey say weakly, "I'm going to be sick."

Her hero scooped her up and carried her off to the ladies room, where he continued his princely activities by carefully holding her hair back from her face as she vomited. His voice

---

[2]   Still waters run deep.

soothed her, told her everything would be all right, even said this awkward cleansing was, in fact, a good thing.

After the retching had ceased, the déjà vu set in. This was her second experience vomiting in the presence of a man, but the only other time it had been Anthony. The thought of that fateful day brought forth more bile, and the heaving continued. When she was done, Lindsey was overwhelmed again, this time with embarrassment. Here she was, in a compromising situation with a nice looking, obviously kind and strong stranger—in the ladies room!

"I'm so sorry," she managed. She struggled to her feet, and he helped her reach the sink, where she rinsed her mouth out and splashed water on her face. "I don't know what happened today. Everything went wrong."

"No problem," said the stranger. He gently dabbed at her face with a warm, damp towel. "Probably a good night's sleep is all you need, but I do think you ought to be seen by a doctor."

She smiled weakly. "Oh, I'm fine now. Really. In fact I'm supposed to have dinner in the El Tovar dining room with friends, so I should try to find them. Why don't you join us?"

He looked slightly startled by her request, but she smiled, trying to persuade him.

"All right," he said a bit reluctantly. "Thanks. But first, there's one thing I need to know. And there's one thing you need to know."

"What do you need to know?"

"Your name. I insist on knowing the names of all the women I rescue."

It was hard to read him, to figure out if he was being serious or just joking. "Lindsey," she told him. "Lindsey Sommerfield. From Tucson. And what do I need to know?"

"My name," he said, smiling. "Most people call me Emmett. Now, with introductions out of the way, and since you say you're up to it, let's have some dinner."

But as soon as Lindsey took her first step, the ladies room went dark, as if she were falling down a deep, narrow rabbit hole. The circle of light at the end shrank as she slipped into an oblivious state of unconsciousness.

She awoke hours later, and the first thing she saw was Laura's frowning expression. "You gave us quite a scare last night, Linds," she said.

"I'm sorry."

"Oh, don't be sorry. None of it was your fault." She grinned. "Besides, things turned out pretty good. Even great, don't you think?"

"What are you talking about?" Lindsey asked. "What turned out great? All I remember is almost freezing to death, then throwing up in front of a perfect stranger."

Laura filled in all the missing pieces, telling her how she'd gone off for dinner with Brad and his father while Lindsey had been carried to her room. She smiled.

"Emmett—your knight in sheepskin armor—kept vigil over you all night."

Lindsey gasped. "He was here in our room?"

"He sure was, and he was wonderful. First he sent for a doctor, just to make sure you were all right. Then he got you tucked into bed—"

"Oh my gosh. How did he ... I mean, I'm wearing pajamas now, so—"

"Lindsey, you're blushing!" She chuckled. "I assure you, he was a total gentleman, and I helped. A lot, actually. Anyway, then he built a fire and sat next to you the whole time. He was still here when I got back from dinner. It doesn't get much better than that, Lindsey, not even in one of your fairy tales."

Lindsey shook her head, confused. "I must have really been out of it, because the only thing I remember between the throwing up and right now is a dream oddly similar to the story of *Emmett Otter's Jug-Band Christmas*."

"Well, Emmett's definitely not an otter," said Laura, and they both laughed. "He is a writer. A travel writer. He goes all over the world visiting and writing about tourist attractions."

"So he's here working?"

"Yep. That's why he was on the trail. He was going to stay at and write about a Phantom Ranch winter, got halfway there and realized he'd grabbed the wrong pack before getting on the mule. Without his notebooks, pens, pencils, mini-recorder, and all that stuff, he felt it was a waste of time. So he headed back up the trail on foot to return another day. You know the rest. It was fate that brought the two of you together."

"Maybe," Lindsey thought out loud. "And was it fate that placed Brad in your bed the night before?"

"Definitely not! It was his dad."

"What?"

"Yeah. It was his dad's doing. And I have to admit, I don't mind the old man's meddling one bit. Brad's terrific. A perfect vacation fling."

Breakfast was the first order of the day, so they headed down to the Bright Angel dining room to feast upon golden pancakes and fluffy scrambled eggs. They decided to spend a leisurely day sightseeing the easy way, so Lindsey got her bus tour after all. They took the forty-six mile roundtrip tour to Desert View, and with not a cloud in the sky, they were able to see San Francisco Peaks, Painted Desert, and the Colorado

River, complete with a covering of sparkling snow, enhanced by the bright sunlight.

"It all seems too fantastic to be real," Lindsey said softly, staring at the vastness. "I feel like I'm at Disneyland, looking at some manmade creation designed to trick my eyes. To think that this is all real is too, too awesome."

It was a pleasant, laid back day, with no rushing, no snowstorms, no men, and no rescues. Just a relaxing day of sightseeing and book buying at every gift shop they came upon. It was difficult to pass up a good book of just about any kind.

"You know," Laura said as they came out of one store, laden with books, "we could probably buy these books right in Tucson."

"Yes, I know. But it wouldn't be the same. Besides, these are for my class. After we're done with the fairy tale unit, I think we'll study geology." She shrugged. "Okay. Rocks and dirt. But what study of rocks and dirt would be complete without some information about our breathtaking Grand Canyon?"

When they got back to the room, there was a note from Brad taped to the door. He requested the pleasure of their company for dinner in the Arizona Steakhouse.

"It says to leave a message at the desk if we can't make it. Otherwise he'll see us at eight," read Lindsey. "It also says that he took the liberty of inviting our new friend, Emmett. He hopes we don't mind. Do we mind?"

"I don't if you don't," Laura replied.

"No. As a matter of fact, I'd like him to see me with my head out of the toilet. Our initial meeting was ... well, let's just say it left a lot to be desired."

The women arrived right on time, and the men were waiting to pull out the ladies' chairs for them. Once they were all settled, Brad poured them each a glass of wine, then raised his own.

"A toast," he announced. "To new friends … and safe hikes."

"Hear, hear!" his dinner companions answered.

Dinner went without a hitch. Brad orchestrated the evening beautifully, with just the right amount of conversation and wine. Justin, the waiter, was more like entertainment than food service, and he kept them all laughing. Emmett, the hero of the day, spoke very little, but he was polite and obviously still concerned about Lindsey's well-being.

Lindsey liked what she saw. Emmett was a good-looking, mature man who flirted subtly with her. If he'd come on strong, she'd have run, but he didn't, so she didn't. She was curious about him, and all she could come up with was that he was different. Almost old-fashioned. A rare kind of man—the type that would have asked her father for permission to marry her.

Her father had been dead for sixteen years. Her mother, too, for that matter. She tried never to think about her parentless childhood, because it opened up a floodgate of sadness. *No! Not tonight!* She was finally having a good time, and she was determined to fight those sad memories so she could live in this delightful moment.

"Can I get you anything else?" asked Justin. "We've got dessert specials that no human has ever been able to turn down."

"Well, I'm afraid I'm going to be the first to ruin your persuasive dessert record, because I'm on the wagon. The dessert wagon, that is. No dessert for me," Laura said matter-of-factly.

"Don't look now, my dear friend, but that infamous dessert wagon is fast approaching," Lindsey said, laughing.

The waiter definitely had a gift when it came to "gab." He made chocolate pudding sound fit for a king, and the vanilla ice cream worthy of presidential gatherings. He was so entertaining; they didn't want him to stop. "I know you lovely ladies are probably watching your ... health, and you guys, well, you aren't into fancy desserts."

"You got that right," said Brad and Emmett together.

Four slices of Grand Canyon Cheesecake later, Justin returned with the bill.

"Here, let me get that," Emmett said softly.

"Sorry, pal." Brad intervened, grabbing the check. "This dinner was my invention; therefore, I demand the honor of impressing the women."

Emmett's laughter twinkled in his eyes. "Well, I wouldn't want to deprive you of that opportunity. The next one's on me."

"Hey, you guys like to dance?" Justin asked when he returned with the credit card receipt. "There's gonna to be a kick-ass band over in the vehicle maintenance building, and it should be starting up any minute. It's sort of an underground event. Just 'Park' people—the cool ones—and invited guests. Just say 'The Frog sent us' to the guy at the door, and he'll let you right in."

Brad grabbed Laura's hand and pulled her to her feet. "We're in. Let's go cut a rug with the 'cool' people." They dashed out into the cold, snowy night, leaving Lindsey and Emmett alone together.

Lindsey felt a twinge of anxiety. She was alone, in unfamiliar surroundings, with a man she barely knew. No longer could she tell herself this was just a group of people having dinner. Was this a date? She didn't know. Brad had set up the whole thing, which meant Emmett might have simply come along for the ride because he had nothing better to do, or even worse, because he was merely hungry. Or had Emmett asked Brad to help him set up the evening so he could get to know Lindsey better? Perhaps he was pursuing her. She had no idea. He seemed nice, but he was at least ten years older than she was. She'd never dated an older man before.

Emmett broke the silence. "Well, I have some writing to do, an article I need to finish so I can email—"

"And I have some reading to do," interrupted Lindsey. All at once she was relieved, and yet she was disappointed at the same time. "There's so much reading and planning involved in creating a thematic unit that it's not possible to do it all during official work hours. And I've learned never to read something to the kids unless I have read it first, since something inappropriate could come up," Lindsey rambled, feeling like an awkward, inexperienced teenager.

"May I walk you to your room?"

Lindsey nodded, and they headed back.

As Lindsey unlocked the huge, hand carved wooden door, she thanked him for seeing her home. "It was a nice dinner, don't you think?"

He hesitated, then reached for her hand. "You know, Lindsey, it was a very nice dinner. And I've been thinking, well, that a sweet lady like you deserves more attention. Sorry I've been so out of it tonight. I was just preoccupied with my article. But I want to make it up to you. Join me for a nightcap at the El Tovar Bar? I promise I'll escort you right back here whenever you wish. What do you say?"

She couldn't hold back her smile, and she gladly let him lead her to the bar. She enjoyed every minute of her time with Emmett, and it wasn't just the two glasses of wine at dinner and the snifter of warm Grand Marnier that followed. When it was time for the bar to close up, Emmett and Lindsey were the last two people to leave. Emmett escorted her home as promised, but the desk clerk stopped her on the way through the lodge.

"I've got a message from your friend," he told her, holding out a piece of paper. "She said it was important."

The note was from Laura, though the handwriting was barely recognizable, let alone readable. Apparently, she'd had a few cocktails.

"Is everything all right?" Emmett asked. "What did she say?"

"Well, I *think* the note says, *'Don't wait up. I hope you are having as much fun as I am. See you in the morning. Laura.'"*

"I'd say she and Brad hit it off very nicely. Looks like you don't have a cabin mate this evening," Emmett said, chuckling.

She knew exactly what Laura's note meant. She'd gotten lucky. She liked Brad and he liked her, and they were going to engage in mad, passionate sex all night long. It got her thinking. *I wonder how much Emmett likes me.* She liked him—of course she didn't love him, since they'd just met. But it had been over three months since the last time she'd … *I bet Anthony has had more sex in the last three months than I've had in my whole damn life.*

"Would you like to come in?" Lindsey asked. "There's a complete kitchen, so I'm sure I can find something for us to eat or drink."

Emmett looked momentarily surprised, but his expression warmed almost immediately. "I'd like that a lot," he said, closing the door behind him.

He built a crackling fire while Lindsey poured wine and sliced some cheese. The setting was perfect, except now she'd really had too much to drink. The room began to spin ever so slightly, and she had difficulty stringing words together. Emmett was a perfect gentleman, though. He sensed her tipsiness, coaxed her into bed—by herself—then gave her a warm, gentle kiss on her forehead.

"I'll stay with you tonight, but I'll sleep in Laura's bed. I think you and I need to take our time and do things right. Good night, Lindsey. Sleep well."

Chapter Fifteen

"Miss Lindsey! I got a computer for Christmas," shouted Emma, her smile bright as the desert sun.

"I got a Katy Perry poster and CD," Willy reported proudly.

"That's nothin'," bragged Joseph. "I got to go to Hawaii, and my parents bought me everything I wanted. I just said, 'I want that' and they bought it. I got way more than eight days of Hanukah presents."

Harley was listening closely. "We don't get to do Christmas or hakan ... kanhac ... what is it that you do, Joseph? We don't even do birthdays. My mom says those things are bad for people, or that bad people do them. I forget which. It's something bad, I know that."

"Oh, Harley, I don't think that's what your mom really meant," Lindsey said gently. His mother probably *had* said that celebrations like Christmas were bad for people, she thought, since she had raised her five kids according to Jehovah's Witnesses beliefs.

"Since we are all so excited about what we did during the two week winter break, let's write or draw about our experiences," she suggested, moving away from Harley's confusion. "Emma, do you want to write about your new computer?"

"Oh, yes! It's so cool, and I can write and draw on it, too."

Lindsey began a brainstorming list to assist other students in formulating their own ideas. At the top of the white board she wrote, 'I might write about …' and under this heading she began to write Emma's idea.

"I might write about … " she reiterated, pointing at each word as she read it, " … my computer. I hear *mmmmm* at the beginning of 'my'. What letter makes that sound?"

"M," many of the students said together.

"Good," said Lindsey. She wrote the letter 'm' and added the 'y' without any discussion. "Okay. We've written the word 'my.' Now we need to write the word 'computer.' *Computer*—what sound do you hear at the beginning of the word? Let's all say it together."

"Computer."

"I hear *ca-ca-ca*," Armando said. He was still learning to speak English and was often hesitant to answer, so Lindsey beamed with joy at his participation and risk-taking.

"You hear ca-ca?" Bobby said with a sneer. "Then I hear doo-doo."

Some of the students laughed out loud while others turned and stared at Bobby, shaking their heads with disapproval. Lindsey ignored him.

"Thank you, Armando. You are absolutely correct. What letter might make the 'ca' sound?"

"The letter 'k'," said Connie. Others nodded in agreement, but a few looked puzzled.

"You're so close, *Connie*," said Lindsey, exaggerating the beginning sound of Connie's name. "The letter 'k' does make that sound, but it's not a 'k' this time. What other letter makes that sound?"

There was silence. She waited.

"I'll give you a clue. The word *cat* has the same beginning sound, and begins with the same letter as our word *computer*."

Now they all knew the answer and cheerfully offered, 'c.' Lindsey wrote the letter.

"What other sounds do you hear in the word, computer?"

"I hear a ... a ... P," said Willy, hoping to make the other kids laugh.

Lindsey quickly gave Willy and Bobby her rarely used 'teacher look,' just in case they had any intention of using this second opportunity to be a bit disgusting. The boys saw it and wisely chose to let it go.

That first week back at school was difficult for Lindsey. Her mind wandered from the classroom back to the canyon more than she wanted to admit, and she was glad when Friday finally arrived. She wanted to talk with Laura about some of her current concerns during their almost weekly, non-alcoholic, happy hour at the Chocolate Lizard coffee house.

Laura was only a few minutes late, and just as perky and vibrant as usual. Her endless energy amazed Lindsey. She never seemed the least bit tired at the end of the day.

"So what's this big secret you made me wait a whole week to hear about?" asked Laura.

"Well, it's not really a secret, nor is it all that big. I just needed some time to make sure about my answer to Emmett."

"Your answer? What was the question?"

"Well, you remember that he is a travel writer?"

"Yes. Yes. Get to the point."

"Well, he told me he had a choice of taking an assignment in the Seattle area or one in Tucson. If I want to advance our budding relationship, he said he'd take the Tucson assignment.

If not, he'd proceed to Seattle with no hard feelings. He's going to call tonight at ten o'clock for my decision."

"And your decision is?"

"Well, I'm not officially divorced yet, and I still think about Anthony a lot, and I know it's really too soon to get involved with anyone, and—"

"And? And? Your decision? What will you say to him tonight?"

Lindsey gripped her coffee mug, needing something to keep her hands from shaking. "I'll tell him the truth. I'll be honest about my situation, and if that doesn't send him running to the Pacific Northwest, I'll tell him that I'd love to get to know him better."

"Wow!" Laura's mouth gave a mischievous grin. "You must have had a really great time with him that night I danced until dawn."

She smiled, remembering. "Actually, it's not what you think. He was a perfect gentleman; just like the night he rescued us off the trail. Men like that are rare these days." She took a sip, then looked into the mug, considering. "Who knows? Maybe he is the one for me. I don't know that yet, but I'm willing to explore the possibilities if he comes to Tucson for a while." She looked at Laura from the corner of her eye. "What about you? Did you and Brad make any plans? You guys were quite the pair back at the canyon."

Laura looked uncharacteristically serious. "No. I don't think so," she replied. She sipped her latte and stared blankly ahead.

The sudden silence was more than Lindsey could bear. "So, that's it? Goodbye and good luck? Nothing more?"

Laura shrugged. "He's a terrific guy. A terrific and very wealthy, great guy who's into his own work, his family, and his independent lifestyle. He's not interested in changing any of that. It was what it was: a great week. Nothing more, nothing less. As we said goodbye, he said, 'Same time next year?' and I, of course, said 'Sure,' knowing he was just making light conversation. A man like that could have anyone in the world. Why would he want a pixie-haired special education teacher from Tucson?"

This was a whole new Laura she was seeing, deep in thought about herself, her love life—or the lack thereof. Her usual *c'est la vie* attitude seemed suppressed below layers of melancholy. Within a couple of minutes, she snapped out of it, regrouped and was back to her old self.

"Besides, I still want to get to know that cute, young bartender from the Coyote Café."

"Oh, that's right. Ol' what's-his-name. Do you even know his name yet?"

"Well, no, but I will. And soon. In fact, I'll wager that not only will I know his name by next Friday, but he'll ask me out by then, too. If I'm wrong, I'll pay our next coffee tab; if I'm right—"

"I'll pay the next Coyote Café tab," Lindsey said with a laugh, "though I'd expect a special friend or VIP discount."

123

Chapter Sixteen

Lindsey sat on her sofa, pretending to read as she waited for Emmett's call. Her eyes kept straying to the clock. Ten o'clock, ten-fifteen, ten-thirty. She tried to stay positive, but memories of her naivety in the realm of romance bombarded her thoughts. Ten forty-five. *He won't call.* He was never going to call because he'd been toying with her all along. He'd set her up to be hurt, but why? He barely knew her. First Anthony deceived her in the worst way possible and now this. When would she learn?

Then the phone rang, and Lindsey jumped. She stared at the receiver, trying not to grab it on the first ring, then couldn't manage to do it until the eighth ring. Her heart raced.

"Hello?"

"Lindsey?" Emmett asked. "Is that you? You sound different."

"Hi, Emmett. Sorry. It's me. I was … baking cookies and had to run to the phone. I didn't realize it was so late," she lied. She didn't want him to know that she'd been sitting there, counting each overdue minute, and feeling desperately sorry for herself.

"Yes, it is late. *I'm* late. I'm so sorry. I'll be able to explain my lateness better tomorrow. So ... have you thought about my proposal? Should I be packing my rain gear or my sunscreen?"

Lindsey cleared her throat, then performed the speech she'd rehearsed over and over in her head, saying she didn't know if she was ready for a real relationship, that her divorce wasn't final, and that she might still have some feelings for Anthony. None of this seemed to bother Emmett. He said he felt all her concerns were legitimate and normal, and nothing he couldn't live with—at least for the time being.

She couldn't stop smiling. "Then by all means," she said, "head to Tucson, but pack the rain gear, too. We're due for a wet January this year."

"You won't regret your decision, Lindsey. Trust me on this one."

She sat straight, startled to hear a knock on the door. No one ever came to her door at 11:30 at night. Not even on a Friday night.

"Someone's at my door," she whispered into the phone.

"Answer it. I'll stay on the line. You'll be okay," he assured her.

Lindsey might have been naive in the ways of dating and courtship, but she wasn't stupid. There was no way she was going to simply open the door at 11:30 at night. She scooted the leather ottoman over to the door so she could peek out the glass panes at the top of her front door, cursing herself for not insisting on a door with a peephole when she'd been remodeling. She tried to be quiet so the visitor wouldn't know she was standing right behind the door peering out into the darkness. It was definitely a man.

"I'm not opening the door," she whispered. "I don't know who it is."

The dark form looked up, meeting her eyes. "You do now. It's me."

Lindsey flung open the door and into Emmett's waiting arms.

Before Lindsey could even take the mail and memos out of her school mail slot, Laura was at her side, begging for answers.

"Did he call? What did he say? What did you say? You're looking pretty happy."

"Yep. He called Friday," she said smoothly.

"Why didn't you call me after you talked to him? What's going on?"

Lindsey smiled contentedly. "I don't know where to begin. Everything is happening so fast. Why don't you drop by my classroom at lunch, and I'll get you up to speed."

Laura grabbed her friend's arm and squeezed it. "No. Absolutely not! I cannot and *will* not wait until lunch to find out what happened."

Lindsey's students would be entering the classroom in about ten minutes, and there was much to do before they arrived. "Okay, walk me to my classroom."

"Is he coming to Tucson?" Laura asked. "That should hold me till lunch."

"He's here."

"He's *here?* In Tucson? Already?"

Lindsey grinned. "Yes. He was so sure I'd say yes that he took the Tucson assignment. He even rented an apartment, though there seems to be a slight problem with it. Something about a small power or plumbing malfunction, so it won't be available for a few more days. In the meantime, he's staying at my place."

Laura's jaw dropped. "And you're okay with that?"

"He's every bit the perfect gentleman that we met in the canyon," Lindsey assured her.

"What's a canyon, Miss Lindsey?" asked Marvin as he approached the classroom doorway.

By now many of the students were skipping, chatting, and singing their way into the classroom. Laura winked meaningfully, then excused herself, making it very clear that she'd return the second Lindsey's students headed to the cafeteria for lunch. There was some explaining to be done.

Mondays were special in the classroom because that was the day Lindsey displayed the folktale, fairy tale, or fable that she would read on Friday. She showed the cover of the book, read the title of the story, then conducted brief discussions Monday through Thursday as to what the story might be about. Every day one more illustration would be revealed. All week long that story sat on the chalkboard ledge, tantalizing her students' imaginations and building suspense. Rarely was a child absent on Fairy Tale Friday.

"My mom says *Thumbelina* is really good, Miss Lindsey. Is that going to be the new story?" asked Emma.

Other students overheard Emma's comment, and they too had things to say about the potential story selection. Connie wanted a story about a giant, which prompted Joseph to make a snide remark correlating Connie's weight, mentioning the fate that had met the giant in *Jack and the Beanstalk.* Oh well. At least he had comprehended the story. Marvin rooted for a story with a king, Bobby liked the king idea as long as he killed a lot of people, and Willy shouted out, "Fairy tales are for fairies!"

"Isn't there a story about a bean hurting a queen?" whispered Harley, attempting to participate in the discussion.

"I think it was a pea ... nut," contributed Armando.

Bobby grinned slyly. "That's right. It was a pee ... and a poop!"

"Come and join me on the rug, on the rug," Lindsey sang quickly. *"It's time to start our day. So we'll have time to play. Come and join me on the rug, on the rug."*

The students went through all the morning's instructional procedures: lunch count, calendar, attendance, and announcements, until it was finally time to view the cover of this week's Fairy Tale Friday book. Lindsey walked to her closet to withdraw the book, taking her time. There was some whispering and some *shh-shh-ing* as she returned to the comfy chair near the white board. Slowly, she revealed the cover of the book. Hands shot up immediately, and she smiled. She'd taught them well.

"There's a cat."

"He's got clothes on."

"I see a fancy cat!"

"What makes it a 'fancy cat'?" asked Lindsey.

"Well, he's not just wearing clothes, he's got on boots, a hat, and a thing round his neck," answered Marvin.

Lindsey nudged their thinking a little deeper. "You said 'he's' wearing boots. Are you sure the cat is a boy?"

Hands dropped, eyes glanced sideways.

"How many of you think the cat on the cover is a boy or male cat?" All the hands went up again. "Well, why do you think that?" Hands lowered, then Emma hesitantly lifted her hand again. "Yes, Emma?"

"I think it's a boy cat because I'm pretty sure it is not a girl cat. This cat has on a hat, boots, and a scarf. A girl cat would also have on a dress or a skirt. This cat doesn't even have pants on!"

Bobby's hand shot up, but Lindsey pretended not to notice him. "Based upon the cover, what do you think the story might be about?"

"A talking cat."

"A circus cat that does tricks."

"A bad cat that lost its pants."

The morning passed quickly, and now the teachers only had twenty-five minutes to eat and talk before the students returned. Laura watched and waited for Lindsey to fill her in on the Emmett situation but grew impatient. "So he's staying—*sleeping*—at your house? You barely know the man!"

"I know it must look bad, but like I said, he's a perfect gentleman. And it's only for a couple of days. Until his apartment is ready."

Laura narrowed her eyes, looking skeptical. "If he arrived at your door Friday night, then he's already stayed more than a couple of days."

"You're being so negative, Laura. Give the guy a chance. I am. Besides, we both know that sometimes things don't go as planned." She lifted one eyebrow. "Especially on a weekend."

"You're right. That makes sense." She grinned. "So how is he in bed?"

"Laura! I told you, he has been a perfect gentleman."

"Not in my book," Laura said, chuckling. "A perfect gentleman would kiss the back of my neck, the back of my knee …"

Lindsey smacked her friend lightly on the shoulder. "Stop! I know where you're going." She shook her head but couldn't help smiling. She was glad to have any excuse to talk about Emmett.

The first Monday afternoon of every month was set aside for the school staff meeting, which was more like a "social" than a meeting. Today, talk and laughter could be heard in the school library as the staff shared holiday stories and classroom delights—or disasters. After about twenty minutes of socializing, Mrs. Wilson, the principal, clapped her hands to get everyone's attention.

"Teachers, grab some snacks and take a seat please," she requested. "Today we will explore the use of The Five-Step Writing Process as an instruction base for the teaching of writing. I think you'll find it fascinating." As the teachers selected their seats, the principal excused the other members of the staff, then approached Laura and Lindsey. "It looks like you ladies will have some free time today. I've looked over these materials and they wouldn't be appropriate or helpful for Special Education students or kindergarten students. So we'll see you in the morning."

They watched her leave, both of them frowning. "Wow," Laura said grinning oddly. "This is the first time we've gotten out of a meeting. I'm stunned. I don't actually know how to react."

Lindsey folded her arms across her chest, indignant. "Well, I do! I'm angry. It should be our call as to whether we learn new information. She's not a writing expert, let alone a kinder expert. She only taught for three years before becoming a principal, and that was sixth grade social studies," she complained. "It feels like a slap in the face. This is educational information, and I want to learn more about this methodology. I teach my students to write, albeit kindergarten writing."

Since neither woman was in the mood for a confrontation, they walked back to Lindsey's room to pack up. Laura broke the silence. "I've got it. Let's stop by the Coyote Café for a cocktail on our way home."

Lindsey's expression was unimpressed. "It's Monday," she said flatly.

"So? It's Monday. We'll just have one drink to lessen our frustration, and—"

Lindsey interrupted. "And we can begin a discussion about creating our own writing program that uses some of this five-step stuff."

"Ah, the old 'turning lemons into lemonade' adage," said Laura with a mischievous lilt to her voice. "And perhaps we'll run into my bartender friend while we're there. Everything's looking much better now, isn't it? Coyote Café, here we come."

"That would be good," Lindsey admitted, "since you have only four days left to figure out his name." She couldn't help but visualize Laura's nameless bartender as the infamous Rumpelstiltskin. Perhaps that story would appear as next week's fairy tale.

Chapter Seventeen

Emmett had an interesting afternoon, with a couple of intriguing phone calls. He'd hesitated to answer the first one, but he gave in and picked it up, thinking it might be Lindsey.

"Sommerfield residence," he said awkwardly. Silence. "Hello? Is anyone there?"

More silence, then a click as the caller hung up.

The phone rang again almost immediately. "Who is this?" the caller demanded.

"Who wants to know?" Emmett replied, matching his tone.

"Where's Lindsey?"

Emmett stayed calm and cool. In control. "Again I have to ask, 'Who wants to know?'"

The caller dropped his voice to a lower note. More threatening. "This is Lindsey's husband. Who the hell are you?"

"Ah, yes," Emmett said, feeling smug. He'd thought that's who it was. "She did mention that her divorce was not quite final, but I should probably tell you that she never refers to you as her husband. Ex-husband, former husband, maybe, but never husband. Wonder what that means?"

"Where is she?"

"She had a staff meeting after school today. I'll have her give you a call when she gets home," Emmett offered. "Care to leave a number?"

"No. And ... and don't bother telling her I called. I'll catch her another time," stammered Anthony.

Feeling vaguely pleased, Emmett had returned to the living room shelves housing Lindsey's home library. Then, it occurred to him that he might score a few more points with her if dinner was ready to eat when she arrived home from school. Emmett wasn't a kitchen kind of guy, so he was pleased to find a Chinese Take-Out flyer stuck to the refrigerator, and several selections highlighted in yellow. He made the call, ordered the highlighted food, set two forks on the table, and waited for dinner to arrive as he searched the cupboards for a bottle of wine.

The phone rang again. "Sommerfield residence," he said.

"Who is this?" asked a different, huskier male voice. "Oh, never mind. Don't want to know."

"Well, I do. Who are you?"

The caller sighed audibly, sounding annoyed. "Oh, if you must. This is Sean. An acquaintance. Just want to make sure that little Miss Linds knows what a bastard her husband is. The guy doesn't give a damn about her. He's living with the hottest dancer in town—and I don't mean ballet."

That had given Emmett something to think about ... But two hours later, he had grown impatient. Where the hell was she? He'd found some wine and romantic music, then gone over and over the pivotal conversation he'd planned to have with her that night. The staff meeting should have been over by 4:30 at the latest, and she should have been home by 5:00. The clock on the mantle ticked away, reminding him that it was close to 7:00 p.m. and she hadn't even called. The food was cold, and he was getting hot with anger.

The phone rang again when he was in the bathroom. Before he could get to it, the caller began to leave a message. "Me again, your informative pal, Sean. Lindsey, I thought you should know, in case you were hoping for a little alimony, that your soon-to-be-ex-husband will be closing his chiropractic practice in the near future. Apparently he has better things to do."

Hearing the front door open, Emmett quickly erased the message. Nothing, absolutely *nothing*, would distract from the evening he had planned.

"You're home," he said with a smile, resisting the urge to bark, *"Where the hell have you been?"* That would have been counter-productive. He needed to be patient, do the right thing. Frustration turned to optimism when he saw she was in a great mood and happy to see him.

"Oh, look!" she said, beaming. "You've got dinner all ready for us. That is so nice of you!" She wiggled an admonishing finger when he reached for the bottle of wine. "And you can put that right back on the shelf where you found it. I won't be needing it."

He poured the wine anyway, and she picked up her glass and took a sip. She started talking, and he genuinely tried to listen to her ideas about incorporating a program of some sort into her kindergarten curriculum, but it meant nothing to him.

"How was your day, Emmett? Did you do much writing?"

Finally, the opening he'd been waiting for had arrived. Emmett reached across the table and took her hand in his, then he kissed her fingertips ever so lightly. "I had a terrific writing day," he said smoothly. "I finished two of my Southwest articles and faxed them to the publisher. She loved them and said no revisions were necessary. I'm way ahead of schedule now, so—here comes the good part, Lindsey—I've been promoted to Senior Travel Writer."

"Congratulations!"

"Thanks. Well, my next assignment is on the island of Saint Barthelemy, which is more commonly called St. Bart's. I want to take you with me, Linds, spend Spring Break on the island. What do you say?"

She looked puzzled for a moment, intently chewing a mouthful of food as if she were thinking about his proposal. Then she said, "We're eating my favorite Chinese food from my favorite Chinese restaurant. Did the delivery boy say anything?"

He blinked, caught off guard. He scratched his head. "Well, let me think. She said something like, 'that will be twenty-two seventy-five.' Then, 'have a good evening.'"

"That's it? That's all he said?"

Emmett stared at her. What was this about? "*She* said. Yes, I believe so. Why would she want to say more to me?"

"Oh," Lindsey replied weakly. She hesitated, then she smiled at him again. "What were your articles about? You never did tell me. Do you think about using 'voice' in your articles? Or do travel writers not have that same kind of 'voice' I've read about? If you do use it, do you use your own all the time, or do you ..."

She was rambling again. *Oh, hell. This has got to stop*, thought Emmett. Apparently she'd been telling the truth earlier: she really didn't need any more wine. She was a lot more relaxed than he'd hoped she'd be. Emmett cleared away all evidence of their dinner, made some hot coffee, and began again where he'd left off—at the fingertip kissing. He had to get her back to thinking about the trip to St. Bart's.

This time she stayed with his train of thought and stared wide-eyed when he showed her brochures of lavish places to stay and restaurants to try.

"There is one catch, Lindsey," he said. "You'll have to do some work." She looked momentarily concerned, but he gave her what he hoped was a reassuring smile. "Your assignment is to take these brochures and decide where we should stay. There are cottages, villas, or hotels. Then you can begin perusing the restaurants and pick your top three favorites." He rubbed the back of his neck, trying not to show his excitement. "Oh, wait, there's one more assignment I almost forgot. Besides playing at the beach—that's a given—I'll need you to prioritize the following activities: general sightseeing, sailing, scuba diving, jet skis, spas, fitness centers, and shopping. Feel free to add anything else you can think of."

She stared at him, her eyes bright. "Oh my. This seems too good to be true." She narrowed those same eyes. "And it seems too expensive to be possible."

He lifted one eyebrow. "That sounds like the safe and conservative teacher talking," he said with a chuckle. "Well, to put your mind at ease, you should know that except for your portion of the airfare—which I insist on paying—the rest will be picked up by my publisher."

She stared at him, blinking hard, and he held his breath. Sometimes she was hard to read. At least she hadn't said no yet.

"Oh, Emmett," she finally said. "I feel like the luckiest girl in the world!"

Chapter Eighteen

Tension between Anthony and Shawna mounted. After Christmas, Anthony's chiropractic office was busier than he'd ever experienced, probably due to the fact that everyone had managed to injure themselves in the name of fun during the holiday time off. Plus, a lot of adults had made New Year's resolutions to be healthier and take better care of themselves—a resolution he'd seen made and broken far too often. Consequently, he spent extra hours at the office and came home more exhausted than ever before.

Shawna had been somewhat successful at keeping him from talking about Lindsey; she wanted no part of his ex-wife's memory in their home. She'd also managed to prevent him from thinking about leaving her due to her odd, night-owl lifestyle, at least for the time being. Between the long hours at work and extra attention paid to him at home in the evenings, the relationship managed to creep forward.

As soon as he walked in the door, Shawna met him, dressed in a long black dress, slit on the side to her waist. "Darling, come with me," she said seductively. "I promise you won't be disappointed."

He groaned. "Not tonight, Shawna. I'm tired. I just want to eat and go to bed."

"Well, then this is your lucky night, Dr. Sommerfield, because that is exactly what I want, too." She took his hand and led him toward the dining room. Anthony stopped at the entrance to the room, staring. The room had been transformed into an Italian Café, complete with sights, sounds, and smells of Italy. Shawna had outdone herself, and Anthony was thrilled. She was actually doing something that he liked, and they weren't even in the bedroom. That was a first. A step in the right direction. Maybe, just maybe, this relationship could work.

"Everything is amazing, Shawna. Thank you. Thank you for this."

She snuggled up against him. "I'm smarter than you think, Anthony. And I do want you to be happy with me, you know. I want a life with you."

His arms tightened around her. "We'll make it work," he assured them both. "We'll find a way."

They lingered in the dining room, candles flickering, holding hands, and finishing off the second bottle of wine. When they were finally done, Shawna stood and motioned for him to follow her. Happy, tired, and tipsy, he obeyed, completely happy that she was catering to all his needs tonight. That was something she rarely did. Ah, sleep. He soon would be asleep.

Seconds after his head hit the pillow, it began with the snap of handcuffs as she put one on each of his wrists then onto the bedposts. He groaned when she pushed the button on her light machine, painting psychedelic swirling patterns around the walls and ceiling. He knew what was next: the seductive removal of her clothing until she was clad in nothing but her signature black lace panties.

"Shawna, stop it!" he yelled. "Don't do this tonight. I need a normal night just this once. Don't ruin our best evening together."

"*Ruin* it? How dare you? How dare you shout at me after all the trouble I went through to please you tonight. How *dare* you?"

"Take the cuffs off now, or I swear I will leave you."

She set her hands on her hips, giving him a wry grin. "And just how will you leave me if you are cuffed to my bed?"

The yelling went on longer that usual, but Anthony refused to play any games. He hated this ... and yet he loved it.

The following week, Lindsey selected an extra story to read to her class every day, and each story contained explicit examples of one or more of the five steps in the writing process on which she and Laura had worked. She was amazed at how quickly her students were picking up the terminology.

Lindsey checked her email at the end of the day and found the usual, annoying spam, but there was also a message from Laura. It read:

> *It is Friday, and I know something you don't know! AND be sure to keep a week from Saturday unencumbered. We are going to celebrate your birthday! Laura.*

Before Lindsey could log out, her friend was standing right behind her, reading over her shoulder.

"So? What don't I know?" Lindsey asked.

Laura beamed. "The name of our bartender buddy."

"*Your* bartender buddy. I've never even laid eyes on your phantom friend."

"Oh, I am quite sure he's going to be far more than a friend," Laura clarified.

Lindsey puffed out a breath. "Come on. You're kidding, right? You can't be serious about a bartender that you barely know."

"I know him a little better now," Laura assured her. "I've seen him three times since we were at the Coyote Café last Monday."

"What? You've gone to a bar four nights—four *school* nights, in a row?"

"It isn't as bad as you make it sound," Laura said, scowling. "Besides, I went during the day."

"Oh, that's *much* better. You skipped school to visit a bartender? Wow. That is really, *really* not like you."

Laura held up her hands as if to fend off her friend. "Let me explain. It began quite innocently. One of the teachers cancelled my time with her class due to a field trip she forgot to tell me about. I was in the office when the nurse and the principal cornered me. They asked me to drive Enrique home because he was sick, and his mom didn't have a way to pick him up. Coincidently, Enrique lives just three blocks from the Coyote Café."

Lindsey regarded her, unconvinced. "So?"

"So, after I dropped him off I drove by the Café. Well, actually, I drove into the parking lot, not thinking he would be there, since it was only one o'clock in the afternoon. But he was."

"Let me guess. You went in to get a Coke—a low-carb Coke—and one thing led to another, and—"

"That's it exactly! There was hardly anyone there, so we talked for about an hour. That was okay because it was my lunchtime by then. He's so cute and intelligent and really sensitive. He wanted to get to know all about me. Of course he won't always be a bartender. He'll quit that when he's finished with school."

Lindsey couldn't believe her eyes or ears. Her friend was actually going ga-ga over a guy. She'd never seen this happen before. Not even with Brad, a talented, rich, already graduated, has-a-real-job guy.

"I think I'm happy for you, Laura," she said tentatively as she gathered up her book bags, planner, and purse, and edged toward the classroom door. "It's just all so sudden, and you're acting so ... so high school. It's thrown me for a loop. Hey, I've got to go. Emmett and I are going out for dinner. He's so perfect. I couldn't ask for a nicer guy. Sorry to run. Call me tomorrow and we'll talk more about your guy," Lindsey hollered as she dashed down the hall.

It wasn't until she was on her way home that she realized she hadn't stuck around long enough to hear the name of Laura's mysterious boyfriend.

Lindsey tried to be calm, tried to feel sophisticated as she carefully applied more make-up than usual and slipped into the little black dress she had worn only once before. Perhaps if she hadn't been humming *"Whistle While You Work"* she might have pulled it off. Instead, she felt like an awkward teenager preparing for her first real date.

"Oh my," she said to herself. "It's a good thing no one is around to witness this silliness." Then she laughed at her reflection. Not only did her voice sound like Snow White's, she even looked like the fairy tale character after she'd added red lip gloss and tons of mascara. She applied the finishing touches of mineral powder and blush, and was just about to say, *Mirror, Mirror on the wall* ... when she heard the front door open and close.

"I'll be right there," she called out happily, but there was no reply. "Emmett, is that you?"

Puzzled, she peeked down the stairs, but she couldn't see anyone from that vantage point. She cautiously tiptoed far enough to see the entire living room, including the front door.

"Emmett?"

Emmett wasn't there, but she noticed something on the stand next to the door. She felt a pang of delight and hurried toward it.

"A beautiful red rose," she said. "How thoughtful. Ouch!" She stuck a finger into her mouth and tasted blood. "Ooh. A sharp red rose," she corrected herself, then her eyes went to the other item on the stand. An apple. "Interesting," she mused. "A red rose for Rose Red, and an apple for Snow White? A *poison* apple perhaps? Huh. Emmett!"

No reply. Where was he?

Moments later, Emmett casually walked through the front door and gave a slight bow. "Your carriage awaits, my lady."

Lindsey grinned. "Terrible acting, Emmett. Just terrible," she said, giving him a knowing wink.

A tall, slim, hostess pulled open the glass door to the chic Northside Restaurant, and Lindsey smiled reflexively, her eyes scanning the room. She hadn't been there before, but she'd heard all about it and had read about it in the paper. Northside was *the* place to go, apparently, and from the looks of it, Lindsey wasn't going to be disappointed. The walls were mostly glass, providing a splendid view of Tucson's lights, and the rest of the walls were brick. There was an abundance of chrome and wood along with large orange lamps, and the décor was sleek and modern, hip and upbeat—a far cry from a kindergarten classroom. The only commonality was the noise; Northside was noisy, too.

The hostess seated them at a table by the window and handed them menus. Soon after that, their waiter arrived, bearing glasses of ice water. "Good evening folks, my name is—"

"Justin?" asked Lindsey. "Is that you?"

The waiter stepped back, startled. "That would be me. You guys look familiar. Give me a clue so I can catch up."

"The Grand Canyon, just a few weeks ago. You were our waiter at the Arizona Steakhouse, remember?"

His smile warmed. "It's coming back to me now. But weren't there four of you?"

"Yep. That was us. This is so cool," said Lindsey, grinning girlishly at Emmett.

"Hey, Justin, good to see you," he said, then reached over to shake his hand. "Did you quit your job?"

"Oh, no. I always work the Canyon from June through December; then I spend December through May here in Tucson. Works out great. Can I get you guys something to drink?"

While they waited for their drinks, Emmett reached over to take Lindsey's hand. He looked directly into her eyes, and she was immediately captive in his gaze.

"Lindsey," he said softly, "I may be good with words on paper, but in person it's not so easy for me. Especially in matters of the heart. I don't often talk about things like that. What I'm trying to say is that my feelings for you are speeding along much too fast. My gut tells me to slow down, but my heart keeps pushing me forward."

She leaned closer, eager to encourage him. "Emmett, I don't feel like you are pushing too fast or rushing into this relationship." If the truth were known, she thought he was moving far too slowly, playing the perfect gentleman card a little longer than necessary. She hoped tonight might be the night they became lovers.

Justin arrived with the wine, and they drew apart slightly. "Here you go, folks. Have you been here before?" Emmett and Lindsey shook their heads, and Justin launched into his speech. "Well, you've come to one of Tucson's hot spots. The guy over there's the mayor. The man at the table right behind me is the U of A football coach, and he's here with his wife. The ladies at the tall two-top to your right are both news anchors. Well, you get the idea. It's a happening place. You're going to love the food, too. Are you ready to order?"

They were. They started with zucca chips and salads. Lindsey ordered a chopped salad with pine nuts and Gorgonzola vinaigrette, and Emmett went with a classic Caesar. As they ate, his eyes scanned the large, busy room, but they always returned to her. She watched him, curious. She was touched by the fact that he'd noticed her fascination with fairy tales, but she was getting impatient, waiting for him to comment on the trick he'd played back at the house.

She sipped on her water, waiting, but when he didn't say anything, she did. "I thought by now you might have asked what I thought of your joke," she inquired demurely.

He frowned. "Joke? What joke?"

"Oh, come on. I'm not stupid. The red rose from *Rose Red* and the apple from *Snow White*," she said with a twinkle in her eye. "I heard the front door open, but you were pretty fast. I never saw you. Doesn't matter. I figured it all out. And I loved it, thank you."

He slowly shook his head. "It wasn't me."

She scrunched her nose and grinned. "Why are you being so secretive? It's just a little joke, and I actually really liked it."

"Uh, because I didn't do it. I wish I had, but I didn't. Besides, I don't know anything about fairy tales."

"Oh," she replied, vaguely uneasy. She quickly changed the subject, giving him a coy look. "I've finished the assignments you gave me. Do you want see the answers?" He nodded, and she pulled a sheet of paper from her purse. "We will stay in a villa, and I don't care which one as long as it is on a sandy beach." She bit her lip, daring herself. "And I think we should pick a one-bedroom villa, if that is all right with you. Anything larger starts at $4,000 a week. We can get a one-bedroom for a little under that. As far as restaurants go, I think we should go to La Plage, Grand Cul de Sac, and Gustavia, although there are over ..."

She knew she was taking over the conversation, but once she began talking about the trip, there was no stopping her. Just when she could see that he thought she was finished, she brought out a second sheet of paper and grinned. "I took it upon myself to complete a little 'extra credit.' Here is your very own copy of additional information about the island. You know, things like the official language is French, though most speak English, too."

"Wow," he said, sounding a little stunned as he glanced down at her extra work. "That's even more information than I'd hoped for."

Justin showed up with their main courses, and then returned with a shared side of grilled asparagus with Parmesan reggiano. "I heard you talking about Bart's Island," he said. "My uncle goes there every year. It is a tropical paradise, and a playground for the rich and famous. You guys are going to love it!"

Lindsey settled back in her chair, completely content. She'd had two glasses of wine, an exquisite meal, and had made plans for the vacation of a lifetime with this take-charge man that treated her like a lady.

Emmett seemed just as happy. "Ah, Lindsey, you are so beautiful." He kissed her knuckles and watched her eyes. Then he grimaced slightly. "A small problem came up today. I hate to discuss it with you, but I don't want any secrets between us. It seems I need to prepay the airfare and the cost of our villa within the next ten days. Normally, this wouldn't be a problem for me, but then again, they don't usually send me to places like Bart's Island. Neither the Grand Canyon check nor my partial advance for the Bart job will arrive in time to meet this deadline. I'm not sure what to do. With this promotion comes more responsibilities, and I don't want to let down the publisher, nor do I want them to know that I haven't been putting away money for a rainy day or situations like this one."

"How much do you think you will need?"

"Well, it *is* Bart's Island, and you know the price of a small villa, so I'd say around six or seven thousand. Thank God all my expenses are paid by the publisher. It's just the timing of this trip that's causing a temporary problem. Try not to worry, Linds. I'll think of something." He smiled apologetically. "Now tell me more about little kid writing. It is fascinating how you get them to write at such a young age."

Lindsey was a natural planner and problem solver. Using those talents, she began thinking about solutions to Emmett's dilemma. They decided to skip dessert, but they each had a warmed snifter of Grand Marnier. They took their time, sipped their drinks, and anyone glancing their way would have sworn they were in love. Justin brought the check as their glasses emptied, and Emmett excused himself, heading for the men's room.

"Hey, Justin, ol' buddy," called Emmett when he was a good distance from the table. "This is so embarrassing, and such a cliché. I either lost my wallet or left it at home. At any rate, I need your help. Can you cover tonight's bill for me? I'll bring cash by for you tomorrow."

"Well, uh," Justin stammered in disbelief. This was a first. "I suppose I could but I don't work tomorrow. In fact, I am taking three days off. Can you bring the money by next Tuesday?"

"You got it. Thanks, man. I owe you one. A big one! And here's our address and phone number just to make you feel better about this whole thing." Justin didn't feel better. Emmett on the other hand, felt great.

Chapter Nineteen

She had been warned. Laura was trying her best to hide a mischievous smile, and it was driving Lindsey crazy.

"Where are you taking me?" she asked. They were headed west on Speedway Boulevard, past The-10, top down, hair blowing wildly in the wind.

"You'll see," was all her friend would say. "It's your birthday. I'm allowed to surprise you."

They kept heading west as the road narrowed and became steep, meandering through what resembled a forest, except the leafless trees were massive saguaro cactus. To see one or two was a great sight; to see an entire hillside filled with saguaros was out of this world. Especially in this February, late afternoon light.

"We're going to Old Tucson, aren't we?" guessed Lindsey. It had been a long time since she'd been there, and she'd never gone without the task of keeping twenty-five kinder kids safe and accounted for. This would be fun.

Laura was cryptic. "You'll see."

Lindsey sat back and enjoyed the drive, making a conscious effort to keep memories of past birthdays with Anthony from slipping into her thoughts. Laura turned north at the next crossroad, and Lindsey frowned.

"I guess my prediction was wrong. We're not going to Old Tucson, are we? The only other place out here is the Sonora Desert Museum. That's it, isn't it?"

A sideways grin from Laura. "You'll see."

Feeling rather smug, Lindsey settled back, certain she'd figured out her friend's surprise. Her confidence faded as Laura drove the little blue Miata right past the entrance to the museum.

"But now we're heading to … to the middle of nowhere," Lindsey cried, perplexed.

Laura threw up her hands. "Damn! You guessed it! My big surprise is no longer a mystery. Yes, I am taking you to the middle of nowhere for your birthday. A real get-away-from-it-all experience."

Lindsey was a little baffled, and she tried not to let her disappointment show. "Well, that's a surprise all right."

They veered down a dusty dirt road—a road that could have been better navigated in a high clearance vehicle—and Laura did the best she could in her little sports car by jogging around the deepest ruts and largest rocks, giggling and shouting, "Hold on!" Eventually she pulled over by an abandoned, rundown picnic area and turned off the engine.

"Here we are," she declared. From the tiny trunk of her car she produced a bottle of pinot noir, some red and green grapes, a container of spreadable Gourmandise with walnut cheese, a pre-sliced baguette, and a blanket to sit on. Then she handed Lindsey a small boom box and said, "Let's go!"

They walked up a primitive path to higher ground, spread the blanket, opened the wine, and sat down to enjoy the approaching sunset. Lindsey surveyed the picturesque scene, thankful it wasn't rattlesnake season. All rattlers should still be tucked snugly away for the winter. That's what she told her students, anyway. As much as she loved nature and the outdoors, this place was a little wild and wooly for her tastes. It was also, curiously, not typical of a celebration master-minded by her dear friend. Regardless, she was determined to enjoy it.

The Tucson sky transformed into a breathtaking light show. Even the clouds added to the splendor by letting strands of blue, pink, tangerine, and purple pierce through. Good wine with a good friend ... a relaxing birthday for a change, thought Lindsey, trying hard to convince herself that this first birthday without Anthony would be okay.

Laura reached over and pressed Play on the boom box, then grinned at Lindsey as the music started.

"*You say it's your birthday! It's my birthday too, yeah,*" bellowed the Beatles.

"Dance with me!" Laura cried, and Lindsey's eyes lit up.

The women jumped to their feet, singing along with the CD, dancing like kids. As the song played again, a male voice came from the south side of the small hill, adding to the sing-a-long. Laura glanced at Lindsey and nearly laughed out loud at the confusion in her friend's eyes—a confusion that only increased when more singing from another voice—approached from the north.

A bulky shape bounded through the dusky evening light, all legs and wagging tail, and Lindsey shrieked with joy. "Wendell!" She hugged the dog, then leaned back and looked in his big eyes. "What are you doing here?"

Laura tugged her back to her feet. "Lindsey, I'd like you to officially meet the new love of my life!" she bragged, grinning madly. She held out a hand for the man on her right, and he stepped out of the shadows.

"Jake?" Lindsey asked. She frowned with disbelief.

"Lindsey?" he stammered, sounding equally baffled.

Laura put her hands on her hips and glanced between the two of them, looking just as lost as Lindsey felt. "You guys know each other?" she asked.

"Yes," they both said, and then gave Laura their best *what the hell is going on?* look.

"What? Why are you so shocked, Lindsey? I've been talking about my bartender friend at the Coyote Café for weeks."

Lindsey turned to Jake. "You work at the Coyote Café?"

"Well, yes, now and then." He appeared as shocked as Lindsey. "I can always use a few extra bucks to help out with college expenses and things. Hey, I knew I was attending a very cleverly planned birthday party for one of Laura's best friends," he said, glaring at Laura, "but I had no idea that friend was you, Lindsey. And that's the truth."

Turning back toward Laura, he mouthed, *Love of your life?*

"But you … you deliver Chinese food. That's your job," Lindsey said, trying to regroup.

"Hold on, everybody. Let me get this straight. He's your Chinese food guy?" Lindsey nodded, still frowning. "Well, that explains why Wendell is here, anyway. The dog is one guest even I wasn't expecting. I just wanted you to meet my new boyfriend, and when he offered to supply dinner, it seemed like a good idea and—"

"You never told me his name was Jake," Lindsey said.

Laura put her hands on her hips. "Well, I tried to, but you were hurrying off to get ready for your dinner date with Emmett." She blinked through the confusion. The awkward silence was broken by the forgotten voice coming from the north. "You both know me, right?"

"Emmett!"

He chuckled. "And only one of you is claiming to have a relationship with me?"

A low, growling sound rumbled from Wendell's throat.

"Cool it, dog," snapped Emmett.

Jake and Emmett exchanged inquiring, territorial glances, like two more dogs.

"Just how do you fit into this picture?" Jake asked Emmett.

"Oh, Jake, this is Emmett, who I met at the Grand Canyon. I guess I haven't had the chance to tell you about him. We've both been so busy since the holidays—well, especially you, with *two* jobs and all, besides going to college and dog sitting, and bird sitting—" She froze. "Oh my gosh," she whispered, hand over her mouth. "Malcolm. I completely forgot about Malcolm. I am so sorry! You're still bird sitting for me? Why didn't you call?"

Jake's expression held more than a hint of annoyance. "Why didn't *you* call? Oh wait. Stupid question. Now that you have a boyfriend, you can suddenly forget about the others you used to care about, whether they were humans, canines, or birds," he replied hotly.

The air grew thick with tension, and Lindsey stared at Laura. Laura looked panicked and confused. Jake glanced nervously between the ladies, and Wendell continued to growl at Emmett.

The night sky was almost black now. The curve of the full moon silently edging over the surrounding hilltops would soon shed some light.

Emmett walked away from the confusion and lit a fire he'd obviously set up earlier, while the others gazed uncomfortably at each other, not knowing what to do next.

"It's Lindsey's birthday," he said, "and no matter what else is or isn't going on here, her birthday is the most important thing right now. Laura, you've planned a unique experience for your friend, and I suggest we let it continue. We have music, presents, bags of food—Chinese, I presume, Jake?—an interesting location, a fine full moon, a friendly fire ... And hey folks, I didn't lug all these bottles of wine up this hill for nothing. So let's party! What do you say?"

With the help of a little Wild Horse Merlot, they made it through the evening for Lindsey's sake, though conversations were now being restricted to safe topics like the weather and the southwest desert. Everyone knew there would be more questions and—hopefully—explanations forthcoming in the next few days.

Shawna's use of the silent treatment was almost more than Anthony could bear. The air was so thick with stress and strain, he found it difficult to breathe. Something had to give. Something had to change. Today the disturbing silence was abruptly broken when a vase crashed to the floor, shattering into countless pieces.

"I've given you everything you said you wanted. I've done everything little Miss Goody-Goody never would," Shawna shouted.

"True, but I want *love*," insisted Anthony.

"You think I don't? Do you really think I don't?"

"That's exactly what I think. All you wanted was a boy-toy," Anthony said. "Well, I can't play that role if that's my only role. I need more. I need a real relationship that includes love, companionship, friendship, and, yes, the great physical pleasure you give me.

Her eyes were angry slits. "When did you become Mr. Goody-Two-Shoes?" she hissed. "You never seemed to mind my lifestyle until recently. In fact, you craved it!"

"Shawna," he said, shaking his head. "It's too weird. You won't go anywhere with me unless it's at night. You won't make love—let me rephrase that—you won't have kinky sex with me unless we are in a dark place and you completely run the show. The only place I really get to see your body is at The Office, and even there, parts of you are covered up and the lighting is as dim as it is here at home. What's with you?"

"I had a strange childhood, okay?" She crossed her arms and glared at Anthony, saying no more. She reminded him of a stubborn, pouting child.

"That's it? That's all you are going to say?"

He was not about to let it go, but the only thing she'd say in response to his badgering was, "Shut up, you bastard!"

Wendell looked first to Anthony then to Shawna, his tail low. The shouting got louder and angrier until Shawna exploded, slamming Anthony's jaw with a powerful left hook. He stood back a moment, in shock not only from the physical contact, but also by the fact that a girl could throw such a punch. He was still dazed when, seconds later, Wendell lunged at Shawna. She backhanded the dog, who yelped in pain, then stood his ground between the two angry people, growling at Shawna.

"Get the fuck out of my way, dog!" she shouted, moving toward Wendell.

Anthony felt a twinge of concern for the dog's safety. He held out a hand. "Wendell, come on boy. Let's go!"

Anthony ushered him quickly outside, away from this volatile situation, and Wendell seemed more than happy to go. Shawna followed, as enraged as ever, and when Anthony saw her in pursuit of him, he jumped in his car and took off. He wasn't thinking about anything but escape as he screeched away. Deafened by emotion, he didn't hear the "thud" against his car.

Jake cursed, wishing he were anywhere but here. But she'd called, and she'd sounded desperate. When he burst through the door, Shawna stood in her fur coat, sharply pointed heels, and powder blue chiffon scarf, her eyes hidden behind large, dark sunglasses. She looked like a redheaded Jackie O gone wild.

"What took you so long?" she demanded, her voice uncharacteristically low.

"Hey, back off. I did the best I could. Besides, half the time you call me it's for no reason whatsoever. This time, you called me while I was in class. You should have given me a bit more information, you know. You left out a key component: location. I went to three other 24-hour clinics before I found this one. So how did it happen?"

She flapped her hands, trying to quiet him. "Look, Jake. The details don't matter. What matters is that I need to hire you to do a few more things for me. Here's the deal. I don't care if he lives or dies, but I can't let Anthony know that I screwed up. Oh, he's definitely earned a portion of the villain status this time, but he's already upset with me. This inconvenience could be the end of us. You know, that straw and the camel thing? And I need him in my life. He *must* stay with me. If the truth were ever discovered—which it never will be, Jake, *never* will be—he'll know this accident was kind of my fault."

Jake was seeing another side of Shawna, though this didn't particularly surprise him. She was the strangest woman he'd ever encountered. Tonight she wasn't using any of her feminine wiles to get what she wanted. She was nervous, calculating, and almost threatening. He wanted no part of this—whatever *this* was.

"You can come in now," said a sympathetic voice coming from the doorway of the harshly lit surgical suite.

Shawna was visibly upset by the man's words. Agitated, she signed and gave Jake a blank personal check. She instructed him to "just handle it," then call her on her cell phone in a few days. With that, she hurried out the door into the darkness, still wearing her sunglasses. She turned back with one last, chilling order.

"No one is to know about this."

Jake ventured beyond the swinging doors and was welcomed in by a kind, old doctor. It was obvious the gentleman truly cared for his patients, and he seemed especially fond of this one with the sad brown eyes, lying helpless and attached to an IV.

"Hey, Wendell," Jake said softly, stroking the broad neck. "You're gonna be all right. Hang in there, big buddy. What happened, Doc?"

"He's been here a couple of days. Looks like he got hit by a car—more than once, I think. Some of his injuries look older than others. Lucky someone found him and brought him in. He lost a lot of blood."

"Who found him?"

"Nice guy. Didn't give me a name. Just said he found him laying near a bush over by 4ᵗʰ and Oak."

That wasn't far from Lindsey's place, Jake thought, struggling to unravel what had really happened.

"The prognosis?"

"Too soon to know."

"Can you at least estimate when he might be able to go home?"

The doctor regarded him somberly. "Well now, that depends on what kind of care awaits him at home. Who does this dog belong to? Surely not that fancy lady that arrived before you tonight." He peered critically over the tops of his half-glasses. "Those two are not a good match. A dog and owner need to be a good match for both their sakes."

Jake nodded. He stayed by Wendell's side till midnight, talking in a calm, soothing voice, patting the suffering dog's head. Every now and then Wendell opened one eye and gave a small whimper, letting Jake know he was glad he had come.

Chapter Twenty

"Ms. Lindsey?" came the call over the intercom.

"Yes?"

"Please send Bobby to the office. He has a visitor."

"He'll be right there."

Lindsey used her cell phone to call Laura's office and see if she could walk with Bobby. Fortunately, he was having a good day, but he was a kid with whom she never took chances. He was too unpredictable.

"Hey, Linds," Laura said. "Glad you called. Let's get together after school today."

"Let's make it lunch break. I have an important meeting at the bank after school. Can you swing by and walk Bobby to the office?"

As it turned out, an investigator from Child Protective Services was there to interview Bobby. Both Laura and Lindsey had had numerous discussions about the little boy, and while they sensed something was wrong, they'd never had specific information that would warrant a formal call to CPS. They knew that without seeing a suspicious injury on the child or without the child stating that someone had hurt him, CPS would merely make note of the call, but no action would be taken. Apparently someone had finally made the call.

"Ms. Lindsey," came another intercom call from the office just moments after Bobby returned.

"Can you take a call? I'm so sorry to bother you again. I offered to take a message, but he says it's urgent. I could put it through to the classroom."

All sorts of thoughts raced through Lindsey's mind. It could be about Bobby. Or Anthony … or Emmett … or …? "Yes, please put it through."

"Hello?"

"Ah, finally. If you had a cell phone I could text you. That would be so much more efficient."

"I have a cell phone. Who is this?"

"Not important," said the caller. "But I did leave my name with your new boyfriend. He and I had a nice chat. Didn't he tell you? Oh, well. We men are not great at taking or delivering messages. Just to keep you informed, here's the latest of Anthony's dastardly deeds. He hit your big dog with his sleek car. How could you ever care about a man like that? You were wise to break your ties with him. Such a shame about the dog. Hope he lives."

"What? When? Where? Who are you?"

The phone went dead, and Lindsey turned to face twenty-five curious kindergarten students. They knew something was wrong.

"Who was it, Ms. Lindsey?" asked Emma.

Armando had another idea. "Can we see your cell phone?"

"Does your phone have the Talking Cat or the Angry Birds?" asked Joseph.

Lindsey took a quick breath to compose herself, but her heart was racing. Wendell? Anthony had hit Wendell?

"Let's finish up our Art Journals," she said.

Why had this person called her at school? Why had he called her at all? And he'd already spoken with Emmett? Emmett hadn't said anything about that. Nothing made sense, and she wanted answers.

A little while later, Laura appeared. "Hey, Teach. Get off the phone. I've brought lunch and we've only got twenty minutes to gobble it down," she said, sporting an unusually happy face.

Lindsey did hang up, but only because neither Anthony nor Jake answered their phones. "Yum," she said, distracted. "Leftover pizza. One of my favorites. What's the occasion?"

"Oh, nothing really. I just wanted a chance to talk about our Jake."

That got Lindsey's attention. "*Our* Jake?"

"Yes. *Our* Jake. He's been delivering food to you for quite some time, he takes care of your dog and your bird, and I thought I detected a hint of jealousy at your birthday celebration. You seem to like him a lot."

"Jealousy?" replied Lindsey defensively. "Well, I do like him. He's a nice guy, and he's been a big help to me, but I don't like him like a boyfriend. He's way too young for me. And besides, I now have the perfect person to spend time with, and to get me over the hump—"

"The hump being Anthony?"

She shrugged. "More like the lack thereof."

"And this perfect person wouldn't happen to be your Grand Canyon squeeze, would it?"

"You know it is. Emmett has been wonderful. He's just what I need right now: sensible and mature."

Laura cocked her head to one side. "Then you're okay with me moving forward in developing a relationship with Jake? And I do mean the part about *me* moving forward, because if the truth be known, Jake has never even asked me to go out with him. Perhaps he's playing hard to get. One thing I know for certain about him is that he's selfless—unlike most men—and he seems very interested in me, my life, my hopes and dreams, always asking how I feel about just about anything and everything. What a breath of fresh air—pardon the cliché."

"As long as you can live with the robbing the cradle aspect and being the older woman, how could I object? I've got Emmett now," Lindsey tried to say with conviction. It bothered her that something in her gut was uncomfortable with this arrangement. "Go for it!"

"Emmett, I'm home," called Lindsey. "Are you here?" She found Emmett in the spare room, packing his clothes.

"Lindsey! You're home a little earlier than I'd expected. I, uh ... guess we should talk," he said sheepishly.

"Okay, but me first. Close your eyes. No peeking," she ordered, though her words sounded almost like a song. "I have a surprise for you, but I think you'd better sit down."

He sat, eyes closed.

"Open your eyes," she commanded with glee.

He blinked and stared, open-mouthed. "Oh my God, Lindsey. What is this? Where did you get it? *How* did you get it? What is it for?"

Lindsey held up a check for $8,000 and smiled at him like she'd just won the lottery. Emmett beamed at her, looking incredulous.

"Well, when you explained the timing glitch for all the pre-payments, I knew I wanted to help out. After all, if it wasn't for you, I would never have the opportunity to go on this dream vacation. On a teacher's salary, I pretty much live month to month, and don't have a nest egg or a golden goose. But I did have some equity in my home, so I got a Home Equity line of credit. It was far easier to get than I thought it would be."

"Oh Lindsey, you shouldn't have. You are an angel. You truly are."

"Everything is going to work out, Emmett. And this whole process will even help me. That's what the banker said. She said that I will be able to demonstrate that I can pay back the loan, and my good credit rating will get even better. I didn't tell her that I'd be paying the loan back very, very soon, but that shouldn't matter because there is no penalty for that with this loan. As soon as your advance and expense money arrives, I will pay the whole thing off. See? It's perfect. *And* we get the vacation of a lifetime together!"

Gathering her into his arms, Emmett held her close and brushed a gentle kiss across her forehead. Her body tingled from the sensual contact. *He's the one,* she thought. *He might really be that knight in shining armor I've wanted all my life. He might be everything Anthony could not, or would not be.*

"Oh," he said, smiling down at her. "I have good news, too. My apartment is finally fixed and ready for occupancy, hence the duffle bag and the packing. Give me twenty-four hours to get it set up and finalize our travel arrangements, then we will have a celebration like never before. Just you and me, really getting to know each other. I'll call you with the address." He hesitated, frowning slightly. "On second thought, let's make it forty-eight hours. That will be Saturday, and you won't be distracted by celebrating on a school night. We can even sleep in … if you know what I mean."

A warm flush rolled through her chest, and she grinned. "You are so thoughtful, Emmett. I'm counting the hours."

He stepped back, and she felt briefly abandoned. "I'd better go," he said. "Lots to do before Saturday night."

"Oh, Emmett? Before I forget, I got the strangest phone call at work today. A stranger said that Wendell had been hit by Anthony's car, then he hung up. He also said he'd spoken to you. Did anyone call here?"

"Oh, um, yeah. Some rude guy called, but it wasn't today. He didn't really say anything. I think his name was Sam—no, maybe Sean. Said you were acquaintances and hung up. Don't know if that's the same guy or not. Did seem odd, though."

"Okay," she said, no closer to the truth.

"I'll see you later, okay?" he said.

He gave Lindsey a peck on the cheek then hurried out the door with the duffle bag over his shoulder and the check in his hand.

Waiting for Saturday was like waiting for Christmas. She had thought she'd hear from Emmett before then, along with the promised address and directions to his new place, but the phone never rang. Saturday eventually arrived, and she settled in, waiting for his call. She distracted herself by cleaning her kitchen, including scrubbing the grout in the countertop tile with a toothbrush and pouring boiling water and some citrus peels down her disposal. Oh, and she also took everything out of her refrigerator and washed every rack, tray, and container, including those sticky with old ketchup and jelly.

The dinner hour was fast approaching, and Lindsey's impatience turned to worry. What could she do? She knew nothing more than his apartment was someplace on the north side of Tucson with a view of the city's lights. Not much to go on. She never knew his cell number, since she'd always called him at her own house. She considered calling hospitals and police stations then decided to wait a little longer. It was only six o'clock. Maybe he'd had a family emergency. Trying to be optimistic, Lindsey decided to prepare for their date. She wanted to look great, because tonight would finally be *the* night. Tonight would be the beginning of the rest of her life.

Once she was dressed and ready to go, Lindsey turned on some Pachelbel to help her relax, but she shot out of her chair like a rocket when the phone rang. She nearly tripped over the coffee table as she ran to reach it.

"Hello?" she said, using her most cheerful voice.

"Lindsey? You're home? I thought you'd be at Emmett's by now," said a confused Laura. "I was going to leave you a message saying to call me as soon as you got home, no matter what time or day it was."

"No, I'm still here. The evening has been delayed."

"What the heck does that mean?"

"I … I don't know."

Laura hesitated. "What do you mean, you don't know? What is going on? You must know something."

Lindsey had no idea how to answer.

"I'm coming over," Laura said.

"No, don't do that," Lindsey insisted. "I figure he had a family emergency, or maybe I misunderstood the details of the plans. I'll be fine. I'll give him a few more days to call. Everything will be fine. I'm sure. In fact, I am so tired right now, I think I will just go to bed."

"All right, if you're sure that's what you want to do. But promise to call me tomorrow."

Lindsey overloaded herself with schoolwork the following week, creating several new integrated Art Journal Lessons and aligning them with the Writing and Language Arts Core Standards while also keeping with Tucson's current rodeo festivities, making cows, horses, and cowboys part of the learning fun. She also managed to set up a Child Study meeting with Bobby's mother and grandmother. The goal of the meeting was to share with his family their concerns about Bobby's social and emotional difficulties at school, learn more about his behavior at home, and obtain permission to test the child. The team suspected the tests would show that he was emotionally disabled or ED; they had reams of observational data pointing in that direction. While no one wished the child to be ED, they hoped he would qualify for additional special services.

This time, his mother and grandmother not only agreed to attend, they actually showed up. The meeting took place at the end of the school day on Friday, and it went well, though both Lindsey and Laura were confused by Bobby's mother's total lack of reaction. Fortunately, his grandmother had been open and willing to sign the permission form. They decided to check Bobby's guardianship later on, after they got started on the testing.

Laura paused at the doorway. "What's going on with Emmett? It's been six days since the night of all nights was to take place, and you haven't mentioned him this entire week."

"I've been busy."

"Yeah, Linds. I know that. You've had a long and busy week. So here's the deal. You go home tonight and relax with your bird, or your cleaning, or your music, or whatever. I am coming over tomorrow, and I'm not taking no for an answer. I will see you around ten o'clock. Be there, my friend."

Laura was right on schedule the next morning, smiling. She held a hot mocha in one hand, a latte in the other. "Let's get to work and figure this thing out," she said.

Lindsey stepped aside, welcoming Laura in. "All we need to figure out is what happened to Emmett. We've got to find him. He could be sick or hurt ... or worse!"

They settled in at the kitchen table and Laura dug into her voluminous purse and pulled out a notebook and pen. She nodded. "Well, I've given your situation a lot of thought, and I've made a list of questions just for that purpose. Did he ever use your landline?"

"Of course he did. He had to contact his publishers and make other business arrangements. He was on my house phone a lot—at least when I was home. I don't know what he did when I was at school."

"Okay. Let's look at your most recent phone bill. Almost two of the weeks he lived here should show up."

Lindsey shrugged, then reluctantly went into the office where she kept her financial files. "I don't see how this will help."

"Well, we should be able to see some phone numbers that he called often. Maybe someone has heard from him. It's worth a try."

Lindsey walked slowly back into the kitchen, eyes on her paperwork. She shook her head. "Nothing here. Just long distance calls I know that I made myself. All of his calls must have been local calls. See, Laura? He's so considerate he didn't want any charges to go on my phone."

Something in Laura's expression changed. "Sure," she said. "Maybe. Did he have a cell phone?"

"Of course," Lindsey said defensively.

"Did you ever see him use it?"

"Maybe a time or two when he first got here, but I'm not really sure. I don't think it worked very well. One afternoon my landline wasn't working for a while, and I'd left my cell in the car, so I used Emmett's, but it didn't work. It was completely dead. I guess it served me right, using his cell without asking permission."

Laura scribbled a few words, then tapped her pen against her chin, thinking. "Let's move on. Did he ever get any mail delivered here? He was here for a whole month."

"No, I don't think so," she replied, slightly annoyed. "What are you getting at, Laura?"

Laura exhaled a frustrated breath. "Lindsey, do you remember when we—well, okay, mostly I—saw red flags waving all around Anthony? I'm sorry, but there are infinitely more flags flying over Emmett. Don't you get that?"

Blood surged into Lindsey's cheeks at her friend's suggestion. Laura had just crossed the line, and she seemed to sense that, because she raised her hands defensively.

"Okay, okay. I'm leaving." Laura grabbed her purse and headed for the door. Just before she stepped outside, she turned back. "Come on, Lindsey. Be smart. The man conned you out of $8,000, and now he has a ten day head start on anyone who tries to track him down."

Lindsey slowly closed the front door, her pulse hammering in her head. How could her friend have even suggested that kind of thing? Emmett, she knew very well, was a perfect gentleman. He never could have masterminded an evil plot to hurt her.

Chapter Twenty-One

Jake planned to devote the next twelve hours to his "Woman Alone" research. He was behind schedule and desperately needed some catch-up time. He gathered together all the materials he needed: subject files, related research files, notes to be transcribed, and his laptop, determined to work.

He stared at all five subject files, and he knew he was in trouble in more ways than one. Technically, the big issue was the fact that only three of the five were aware that they were his research subjects. The other two had no idea.

Subject A, Carla, was a never married, young mother of eight-year-old twins, a result of a brief college romance. She had responded to Jake's ad in the campus newspaper. Subject B, Marjorie, was a forty-five-year-old widow Jake had met in the Whole Foods Market in the produce section when they'd struck up a conversation about foods and herbs with cancer preventing or fighting qualities. Her husband of twenty-four years had died of cancer two years earlier.

Jake had met Subject C, Shawna, in May of last year. She'd agreed to be one of his subjects and signed the permission form provided by the U of A. She loved the idea of being "written up" in a university student's thesis—it was all about the attention for her. But the woman grew stranger every time they were together, and she wasn't exactly a "Woman Alone" ever since Anthony had entered her life. In retrospect, Jake guessed she'd been having a relationship with Anthony right from the start, but he didn't know for sure.

Fortunately, Subjects A and B fell into and remained in what he considered the "typical" category for women who conducted their lives without the partnership of a man. His intension had been to avoid any extremes in lifestyles or personalities, since his research would include only five women.

Jake glanced first at Subject D's file, then to Subject E's. Neither woman had any idea about the existence of the files or the specifics of his research.

Where to begin? he wondered, looking at Lindsey's file. Visions of the birthday party took over his brain, and he tried desperately to push them away. Something nagged at him, and he knew it was Emmett. Something was amiss with that guy. Could Lindsey be in danger? His intuition kept yelling at him, warning him that Emmett was dangerous. Or was Jake just jealous?

He realized he couldn't settle down until the nagging, unexplained negativity he felt for the man had either been uncovered or dismissed. He navigated every search engine he knew of and managed to find several entries for an Emmett Anton, journalist. It seemed a guy with that name had written two short articles for a hunting magazine three years before, but Jake couldn't find the actual articles anywhere. Certainly, those articles would not sustain even a single guy for more than a few weeks, if that. Nothing else came up. It is as if he didn't exist.

Out of curiosity, Jake googled his own name, and dozens of entries appeared. *If a nobody like me comes up,* he pondered, *why is there nothing more for this guy?* Emmett had been around longer than Jake had, and according to Lindsey, he was busy with a lot of writing, traveling, and relocating. Who *was* Emmett Anton?

"I've got to get to work," he repeated out loud for the umpteenth time.

It was a relief when the phone rang.

"She called in sick!" the caller cried. "She never does that. I tried her landline and her cell phone. No answer on either."

"Whoa. Slow down, Laura. What's going on?"

Laura told him what had happened between Lindsey and Emmett on Saturday, gave him Lindsey's answers to her questions about Emmett, then admitted the assumptions she'd made so far. Jake, grateful for the information but more worried than ever, agreed to pay Lindsey a visit. If she wasn't at home, he would find her.

As Laura had said, Lindsey didn't answer her phone, but Jake refused to give up that easily. He walked to the door—leading a limping Wendell and carrying Malcolm's cage—and rang the bell. No answer. He peeked in the window and spotted her lying on the sofa, probably sleeping.

He rapped on the window. "Lindsey, it's Jake. Let me in."

No response.

Wendell's pitiful cross between a howl and a moan got her attention. Rubbing her eyes, she rose and slumped toward the door. Jake tried not to show his surprise when he saw her. Her hair was a mess, her smudged make-up was obviously left over from a day or two before, and she was dressed in old sweats. And her expression was ... immeasurably sad.

"Hey, girl. Can we come in?"

Her eyes flew open. "Oh, my God! What's wrong with Wendell? Why is he limping? Why is he bandaged?"

Jake wanted to go inside, get her to settle on the couch and talk with him, but she wasn't moving out of the doorway. "There was an accident," he told her, "but he's going to be all right … eventually. Can he stay with you for a while? He needs to be somewhere he will be loved and cared for. He doesn't need exercise yet, just rest. He's on a fairly heavy dose of Rimadyl for the pain, so he'll be fine all day while you are at school." He frowned, feigning innocence. "Hey, why aren't you at school? Was it an early release day?"

Lindsey held out her hand, welcoming Wendell. "Of course he can stay here," she said softly. "Come on in, boy."

Malcolm tweeted as if to say, what about me? Jake handed the cage to Lindsey; their fingers touched briefly as she took hold of the handle. Then she shut the door, and Jake was left standing there, wondering what had just happened.

Spring

Chapter Twenty-Two

With less than three months until summer vacation, Lindsey decided to create a desert play her students would perform for the student body as well as for their families and friends. By devoting all her waking hours to creating fun and effective lessons for her students, Lindsey not only met the high expectations she always had for herself as a teacher, she exceeded them. Her talents in the classroom were amazing. Her students, even the tough ones, made huge academic gains. In a twisted sense, the students benefited from her pain. Her personal life, other than her love for Malcolm and Wendell, was on hold. She kept any adult co-workers and friends at a distance, avoiding contact, even with Laura. She couldn't face anyone that knew of her troubles with Anthony or Emmett, and that was everyone except for strangers or mere acquaintances.

"I can get it done, Dr. Barston," Jake said. "I've completed all the research and most of the writing. I just want to revise the document; my original thesis statement needs modification. If I could have about forty-five more days, I'm sure you'll be pleased with the outcome."

The extension was granted, but that did little to alleviate Jake's anxiety. He'd never experienced anxiety before, but he knew this was it. His heart was racing, his breathing was labored, and oh boy, did he feel like he was losing control. He had made so many critical mistakes. And now his ability to concentrate eluded him. He didn't know if he could pull it all together, even with the new, extended deadline.

All he could think about lately was the issues beyond his project. First there was Anthony and Shawna. Where were they? He needed to find them and figure out what the hell was going on.

Then there was Emmett. Emmett the jerk, the scoundrel, the con man … the list was long. Jake wanted answers, both for himself and for Lindsey. If he could expose Emmett for the thief he was, maybe he could recover the money that had been stolen from Lindsey. That way she could move forward, get on with her life.

He took out two new files and labeled one *Anthony & Shawna,* and the other *Emmett.* Taking this small step lessened the anxiety symptoms somewhat. Now it was time to get some research done. He headed out in the direction of Anthony's chiropractic office.

"Hi there. How can I help you?" asked the woman when she met Jake at the door. She regarded him with dreamy, flirtatious—and experienced eyes.

Her presence and demeanor threw Jake off for a moment. She was not what he'd been expecting. He doubted that she was what anyone would expect to find in a chiropractic office.

"Well ... ma'am, I'm looking for Anthony. I need to speak with him."

"Well ... sir," she began, giving Jake a taste of his own choice of words, "you've come to the right place, just at the wrong time. He's unavailable, but you can make a payment on your account, or I can schedule an appointment for you after the 15th."

"That's almost two weeks away. I can't wait that long."

She gave him a cheery smile. "Well, you have some options. Dr. Warren is taking Dr. Sommerfield's emergencies. Anthony—I mean *Dr. Sommerfield*, may be back in town as early as the 5th, but he won't be in the office. At least that's what Shaw—that's what I ..." Her smile was apologetic now. "That's all I can tell you. Do you want Dr. Warren's number?"

Jake shook his head, frustrated. "I'm sorry. I'm not here for an appointment, just a phone number where Anthony can be reached. Come on. I'm a family friend," he lied. "Or ... here. Here's my number. You can call him and ask him to call me. Okay?"

"I couldn't call him if I wanted to. It's complicated. Sorry." She winked suggestively. "But thanks for your number." She tucked the small paper deep in her cavernous cleavage and resumed flirting. "We'll all be back in The Office on the 15th," she purred.

"Venice," Anthony sighed, leaning back in their private gondola. The temperature was chilly, but that hardly mattered. They were in Venice! "I can't believe I'm really here. This trip must have cost a fortune. How in the world did you pull it off?"

Shawna watched him, pleased with his reaction. She rarely agreed to daytime excursions, but today was an exception because the weather allowed—no, *demanded* that she wear her full-length fur coat, leather gloves, and her trademark sunglasses. A newly purchased Roberta di Camerino red velvet handbag added to her overall look of wealth, and she caught the eye of many. Anthony had no objections to her extravagant outfit. She knew that he loved the fact that he accompanied the most beautiful woman on the canal, and everyone took notice.

"My darling, don't worry about the cost," she replied. "And before you get all sensible on me, no, I didn't charge any part of the trip. I didn't sell the house or anything crazy like that. I did use some of my nest egg, but you are worth it, darling. *We* are worth it. I want you to be happy. Even more, I want us to be happy together," she explained. "Besides, you love everything Italian, and they say Venice is one of Europe's most romantic cities," she said, running her tongue over her glossy red, pouting lips.

Shawna was determined to make Anthony love her. She needed him to want only her, and she'd do anything to keep him from thinking about or comparing her to Lindsey. It wasn't only because she could never be like Lindsey, but also because she had no intention of ever leading such a boring, conservative life. So far, her extravagant getaway to Venice had accomplished everything she'd wanted. But Shawna always had multiple desires and motives. On this trip she wanted more than a good time. She wanted a commitment from Anthony in the form of a marriage proposal.

"I want us to be happy, too, Shawna, but you know we both have to make some changes for that to happen," he said, taking her gloved hand in his.

She smiled sweetly, knowing exactly what he wanted to hear. "And I have far more to change than you do. I know that.

And believe me, I am working on it. But let's not talk about that now. We're in Venice! It's like an early honeymoon."

Anthony glanced at her, frowning, but she thought it was probably best to ignore his expression, and she quickly changed the subject to dinner plans.

"The second we step onto land, we'll head for Vino Vino or La Zucca. They were the only two restaurants I could find listed that I could actually hope to pronounce correctly," she said, then chuckled before taking a stab at a few more Italian words. "I'm starving for some *risi e bisi* or some *taglietelle* with *gorgonzola*. Mmmm."

"Just as long as it's not *bisato*," added Anthony, minus any attempted accent. They both laughed at their lame efforts to use Italian words. "Of course, we'll have to have a bottle of *prosecco* with dinner, and a few *baicoli* for dessert."

The evening's dining experience was pleasant, with no arguing or negativity at all. Shawna enjoyed herself, but she focused inwardly on the fact that no words of love leading down the matrimonial path were being spoken, or even hinted at. And then ...

"This week, this trip has been the most unforgettable vacation of my life, Shawna," he said, smiling. She leaned forward, hoping to hear the words she'd dreamed of. "But I've got to get back to my patients before they find someone else to keep their spines adjusted. And you know, now that I'm thinking about home, it's strange that I haven't had any calls from my office. Not even one. Mrs. Madera usually calls me about patients or suppliers when I'm out of the office."

Shawna hesitated before responding. "Well, when I said I took care of everything regarding this trip, I meant everything. So Mrs. Madera is also on vacation. She's visiting her grandchildren in Denver. She was very happy to take the time off, and you don't even have to pay her."

Anthony's mouth dropped open. "Oh, my God! What about my office, my patients? Many of them simply drop in every week for an adjustment, or to pay on their accounts, or both."

Shawna shrugged a slender shoulder. "Not to worry, Doctor. Tara, a co-worker of mine, is answering the phones and scheduling appointments for your achy, breaky patients. It works out great, because she is only working weekend nights at The Office this month. She'll handle it all. And she'll refer any emergencies to your friend, Zach Warren. See, love? I've taken care of everything so you can just sit back and relax."

A variety of emotions passed across Anthony's face, though Shawna was pretty confident he was pleased with the news.

"Oh, and we have plenty of time to see everything Venice has to offer," she said sweetly. "Our flight home won't be leaving for another two weeks! Isn't that great?"

"What? No! That's not great at all! Look. This has been amazing, but I have to get back. I can't jeopardize my business just so I can be with you in some exotic location. Find us another flight, Shawna. I mean it."

She leaned even closer, letting her breasts press against him when she put her lips by his ear. "I'll try, darling," she whispered seductively, knowing full well that she wouldn't. Instead, she'd switch to Plan B.

Back in their suite, Shawna could hear Anthony pacing, and the sound of Italian TV chattered through the door. She lit three candles in the bedroom and gazed critically at her own near-naked reflection in the beautiful girandole mirror. Someday she'd look perfect—she'd *be* perfect. If only Anthony would commit to her—and only her—her master plan and lifelong dream would come true.

She slipped into the slinky, slit to the hip, long black dress that she knew Anthony loved. The slick black material plunged to great depths in both the back and the front, revealing skin to her waist and emphasizing her best curvaceous attributes. Tonight she'd seduce him, but she would not undress Anthony or tie his hands, she wouldn't bring out her collection of feathers, and she wouldn't tie the blindfold over his eyes. Tonight, while Anthony was hot and hard, she would play hard-to-get and walk away, leave him begging for more.

Lindsey hurried home every day after school to be with Wendell. Tonight, carrying two heavy book bags that contained this evening's school tasks, she made it home by five o'clock. Unfortunately, the colossal workload she'd self-assigned for the purpose of forgetting her troubles and the emotional rollercoaster she'd been riding this year had taken its toll. She could barely move out of sheer exhaustion. So, after tending to the slow-moving dog and the hyperactive bird, she collapsed on the sofa.

At last, a chance to rest—except her tired eyes would not close. The little scene reminded her of that first dreadful night when Anthony had cheated on her then left her in the living room, sick and alone.

She hadn't heard from Anthony in a while, and she wasn't sure if she wanted to or not. *He might still come back,* she mused. There'd been no word from Emmett, and she had to keep hoping he was all right and not hurt. She'd received no more creepy calls from the mysterious Sean, and she was at least glad of that. She still had no idea who he was. Jake hadn't been in contact since he'd left Wendell and Malcolm with her, and that made her sad. Actually, none of her friends had been in contact, and she knew that was entirely her own fault. That's what she got for saying she needed space. She figured she was a perfect example of 'be careful what you wish for.'

"I guess it's just you, me, and Malcolm," she told Wendell. "But at least you can sleep."

She sat up, postponing any thoughts of drifting off, and picked up her mail. "Trash … trash … electric bill … mortgage statement … more junk mail." She frowned at a second bill from the bank, then opened it. Her stomach dropped when she remembered the home equity loan she'd taken out for Emmett. Now she had a bill for $304, and it was due in three weeks.

Tears surged into her eyes. *There's no way I can pay this, and next month won't be any better.* "I wasn't supposed to have to pay this!" she cried. "Just look what you've done to me, Emmett! I'm not only an emotional wreck, I'm facing financial ruin!"

She jumped to her feet and paced, desperate for ideas. What could she do? Sell her house? No, she'd just taken out the home equity loan on the house, so that wouldn't work. Beg Anthony for help? Definitely not! *Well, maybe …* No!

The phone rang, but Lindsey was too upset to answer it. She glared at the phone, willing it to stop. On the fifth ring, the answering machine picked up.

"Hi, Lindsey!" Mrs. Wilson? That was strange. The principal almost never called her. "So sorry to call you at home, but I wanted to be the first to tell you that *you won the award!* Oh, you don't even know what I'm talking about, but … remember that day we sent you and Laura away from the staff meeting about the 5-Step Writing Process? It was all a ploy so the staff and I could fill in the application." She spoke at such a rapid pace; it was hard to comprehend the information. "Sorry. Too much info for a message machine. I won't be around tonight, so I'll leave the details with Laura. Give her a call ASAP, even if it's late, because there's not much time. Ooh! This is so exciting!"

But sleep overcame her confusion, and she lay back down, too tired even to question the call or phone Laura. That would have to wait.

Chapter Twenty-Three

"Anthony, darling, come to bed." Shawna's sultry voice floated through the closed bedroom door. "I need your help getting out of this dress."

"I'm not in the mood," he replied, keeping his voice sharp.

While she no doubt sulked in the bedroom, Anthony grabbed a "Facts About Venice" pamphlet from the table and sat back to read. He had hoped she'd just fall asleep, but he could practically hear her wide awake frustration.

He spoke first. "Shawna, come out here. I want to show you something."

The bedroom door opened slowly, and she leaned against the door jam, as gorgeous and sexy as ever. "I want to show you something, too," she purred. She dimmed the lights, straddled his lap, and whispered in his ear, "Now, what was it you wanted to show me?"

He faltered a moment, then regained his composure and began reading to her from the booklet. "Did you know that Venice was the setting for the James Bond movies, *From Russia with Love* and *Casino Royal?*" He glanced at her and was surprised that she seemed to be paying attention. "It was also the setting for Madonna's music video, *Like a Virgin.*"

"You're kidding; let me see that," she said lightly, then reached for the pamphlet. "Look here. It also says that Thomas Mann's 1912 novella, *Death in Venice*, was the basis for an opera and a film and—"

"You read *Death in Venice?*" Anthony blurted out.

She rolled her eyes. "Yes, the whole class had to read it, but I don't remember any of it. Maybe I just pretended to read it. Not sure." Her eyes drifted over the page. "Oh look! There is a strawberry flavored vodka martini called 'Death in Venice.' Oh, Anthony. Let's go. I've *got* to try one."

He agreed but did not want to venture out very far, since it was so late. He didn't entirely want to dismiss the opportunity, though, since it had dawned on him that this short conversation was probably the most normal, non-sexual conversation they'd ever had. She disappeared into their bedroom then came out a few moments later in a sleek, one-piece, black outfit that stretched from ankles to barely-there neckline, hugging every curve like a second skin. He watched her slip into her long, fur coat, thinking that tonight the coat made sense. The early March evening was both chilly and humid. What he didn't understand was why, in spite of the darkness of the night, she still wore sunglasses, though this pair had a lighter tint than those she'd worn during the day. *She's eccentric, that's for sure,* he thought.

They strolled arm in arm down the narrow, stone footpaths inquiring in every bar about the desired drink, and while several bartenders said they'd heard of it, some claimed it was merely a myth. Others seemed willing to try and make it, though they hadn't done it before. The happy couple sampled some counterfeit concoctions, but those drinks were disappointing. In the end, they decided to head back to their hotel empty-handed, so to speak. It really was late now, the walkways were almost empty, and the canals were still. Shawna's four-inch spike heels clicked as she walked, sending an eerie, echoing noise into the night.

It was a relief when they finally stumbled into the hotel bar, which was still open. "One nightcap? What do you say, Shawna?"

"You read my mind, darling."

Anthony leaned over the counter and got the bartender's attention. "You wouldn't happen to know how to make a "Death in Venice," would you?"

The man behind the counter grinned. "How many would you like? Just happens to be my specialty."

"Ha!" Anthony cheered, victorious at last. Shawna sidled up to the bar beside him, smiling in anticipation. "Let's start with two."

Two, then two more, on top of what they'd already consumed. They were soon both joyfully tipsy and incredibly horny. They signed the bar tab and tipped the bartender, then they made a dash for the elevator. Unfortunately, the courtyard's uneven stone flooring was not designed to accommodate a tall, tipsy woman in ultra high heels. Shawna screamed when she fell, then rolled into a ball, clutching at her ankle and moaning. Anthony the chiropractor leaped into action, but soon determined she'd need more than an adjustment.

Half a dozen curious hotel employees huddled close, and Anthony called out to them. "I need ice and an ambulance!" he ordered to no one in particular.

The ice arrived within seconds, and soon afterward a couple of men appeared with a gurney. They carried her to a water ambulance that floated both Shawna and Anthony to the nearest medical facility. The ride took about fifteen minutes, and

Anthony held her hand the whole time, trying to comfort her. He'd never seen her in physical pain before, and he noticed right off that she didn't handle it well. She couldn't hold back the moans and sobs. But he was surprisingly pleased to notice his own level of compassion for Shawna. Was that because he was in a healing profession? Or maybe because of the magnificent evening they'd just had? … Or could it be love?

Shawna was carried into the brightly lit emergency room, and two nurses prepared her to be seen by the attending physician. As soon as they touched her, Shawna's groaning turned to hysterical shrieks, and she thrashed her arms about, shoving and punching at anyone trying to help her. Based on her behavior, Anthony and the staff concluded her injuries were far more serious than first anticipated—internal injuries might even be at play. They needed to examine her so they'd know how to treat her. After several unsuccessful attempts to calm her, they got the doctor's permission to sedate her.

The initial injection, helped along by the night's alcoholic contribution, quickly rendered her unconscious.

"Let's get her into a hospital gown," called the nurse. "What color do you think she might like?" she asked Anthony.

He stared at her. "You have different colors?"

She smiled and rolled her eyes. "Of course! This is Venice."

"Uh … she likes red and purple. How about purple?"

"One purple gown coming up," she said, but then frowned. "Oh, boy. It's going to take some talent to get this outfit off. It fits like a glove." She continued to undress Shawna, always careful and respectful. She spoke to Anthony as she worked, giving him a blow-by-blow, so to speak, and Anthony watched with a sort of detached fascination. It occurred to him that he'd never really seen Shawna's body or even her skin, except in very dim light or almost total darkness.

"How cute! Purple panties to match the hospital gown. She can keep the bra and panties on. The doctor won't need to go there, obviously. Your wife sure has had a lot of surgery. Was she in a car accident or something?"

Ignoring the 'wife' reference, Anthony shook his head. "Not that I know of. We haven't been together very long," was his response. "How do you know she's had surgery?"

"Look at the scars around her hairline. And there by her chin. She's even got scars on each of her calves. Those are really bad. Somebody did a poor job of putting her back together."

Anthony was suddenly sober. Whatever had happened in the past, Shawna obviously hadn't wanted to share. She'd wanted to hide her surgery or injuries or whatever was going on. The doctor came and went, and he ordered x-rays for her knee, foot, and ankle. When the nurse came to check her vitals, Anthony asked if the scars could be from routine cosmetic surgery.

The nurse peered closer, then tilted her head from side to side. "Some, maybe. The hairline scars and the chin could be. And ... her bust line is larger and much perkier than is typical," she added with raised eyebrows.

Anthony grinned. "Oh yes. They are extraordinary," he admitted with a twinkle in his eyes.

But look here," she said, shaking her head and pointing out an odd scar on Shawna's neck then another at her brow line.

When the x-rays returned, the Venetian doctor pulled Anthony into his office and explained that no bones appeared to be broken, but she at least had a torn tendon. She would need medical follow-up and probably surgery as soon as they got back to the States. Under no circumstances was she to put any weight on her ankle for at least two weeks. Otherwise, the damage would be more difficult to correct.

As soon as the sedative wore off, Shawna awoke and became fully aware of the changes in her state of undress, which prompted her to start screaming again. "No! This can't be happening! Get my clothes. Get them now!" she yelled, struggling with the nurse. She pulled out her IV, pounded on the bed rails, and threw whatever she could get her hands on at the poor woman. She was about to receive another sedative when Anthony and the doctor ran in.

Her eyes, dark and naked without the sunglasses, pleaded with him. "Anthony! Help me, darling. Take me out of here. Take me home," she begged, reaching for a reassuring embrace.

Anthony had never seen Shawna so terrified, and it roused his long suppressed, nurturing instincts. The recent doubts he'd had about their future as a couple diminished right there in this Venice Emergency Room. Still, he couldn't understand her extreme reaction. He'd seen all kinds of people in various levels of pain, but nothing like this, and he wondered if it was more than just physical pain. Perhaps it had something to do with her past surgeries. He'd find out on their flight home. Suddenly he was glad it was such a long flight. She'd be forced to stay in her seat and listen to him.

The next few days passed without incident, though it was inconvenient. Shawna was confined to a wheelchair and steadfastly refused to leave their hotel room. Her tolerance for pain was minimal, so she relied heavily on the pain prescription she'd been given, and her resultant naps gave Anthony time to enjoy long, contemplative walks around Venice. The more he thought about it, the more he worried about her mental state rather than her ankle. He needed to know about her past. It seemed incredibly strange that they'd been together so long—and done so many intimate things—and yet they knew so little about each other.

Who was this woman for whom he'd cast away his beautiful, sweet, loving wife? He'd gotten caught up in the kinky, wild sex Shawna offered, and he understood why. He'd already known he was a borderline sex addict—something he'd convinced himself was a positive trait … but was it really?

The trip to Marco Polo Airport was uneventful and quiet, albeit challenging. Water taxis and wheelchairs were a precarious pair. They made their flight without any issues, and finally settled into their seats. Once they reached their cruising altitude, Anthony took a deep breath, ready for a difficult conversation. Shawna, on the other hand, was ready for another pain pill, and some wine to wash it down. Anthony reluctantly gave in to her wishes.

"How does your ankle feel today?" he asked.

"With each pill I get a couple of hours of tolerable pain. But then the stabbing pain starts up again. The ache in my hip throbs all the time. Oh, I just want to sleep, Anthony, just sleep till the pain is all gone."

Sometimes the drama was hard to take, but he bit his tongue. It wouldn't do to get her going again. "You know that's not possible," he said gently. "These things take time. Besides, you have surgery on that ankle ahead of you. We'll find the right combination of medication and distractions to get you through this."

He saw her long lashes blink behind the sunglasses. "You're a good man, Anthony," she replied, rendering him momentarily speechless. She'd never said anything like that to him before. Even the tone in her voice was different—straightforward, friendly, almost kind, and it lacked even a hint of her normally seductive, ulterior motives. Maybe *now* was the time.

"Hey," he said, starting slow. "During this entire vacation you never mentioned Wendell. Where is he?"

Shawna explained with little detail that Jake, their Chinese Food delivery guy was watching him, assuring Anthony that he barely charged her anything. Anthony thought briefly that he should have left the dog with Lindsey, but he knew he couldn't bring that up with Shawna. He took another deep breath and decided to move on to the difficult topic while Shawna still seemed willing to talk to him.

"Shawna, we need to discuss your scars and—"

Her face went white. "What? You saw my scars? You were there when they undressed me? Oh my God. Venice hospitals don't believe in privacy? In a patient's dignity? How *could* they?" She narrowed her eyes and focused her rage on him. Fortunately, she didn't want to create a scene any more than he did, so she managed to keep her ranting to a seething, snake-like whisper. "How could *you*? Don't you care about me?"

"I do care about you, Shawna, but yes, I did see scars. Lots of scars. Why do you hide them from me? Why the deception? Don't you trust me enough to share this with me? I am shocked that you'd go to all that trouble just to keep the world and me in the dark. It explains the sunglasses and your refusal to be in bright light ... but Shawna, you're still beautiful. You're the most beautiful woman I've ever seen. Lots of women undergo surgery to improve their appearance, though I can't imagine you needed it."

She blinked at him, not committing to anything, so he continued. "The ER nurse said something that concerns me, though. She thought some of your scars looked more like someone had 'put you back together after an accident.' What else should I know about you? I really want to know *you*, not some false image you've created."

This was a new, subdued woman beside him. She bit her lip, looking much younger all of a sudden. When she spoke, her voice was soft and tentative. "Oh, Anthony. You're okay with all of this? You still want me?"

She still hadn't answered his question, but he could see how difficult this was for her, how much reassurance she needed. He'd find out her secrets eventually, he assumed. "Of course. More than ever. And right now, for the first time, I feel like we are beginning a real relationship," he admitted. "Whatever comes along, we'll work it out. And, Shawna, you are fine. You are beautiful just the way you are. As far as I'm concerned, you don't need any more surgery."

The pain pill began to take over, and Shawna's speech slowed. "This is what I've been waiting for: a commitment from you, Anthony. That is all I ever wanted. As soon as the ankle is fixed, I will have one last surgery, and I promise that will be the end of it." Her eyelids drooped closed, but she forced them open. "You'll stick around, right? Like you said, we'll work it out."

Chapter Twenty-Four

Today is the beginning of the rest of my life, Lindsey told herself, staring out the airplane window. She couldn't stop grinning. Three days ago her world had seemed bleak and unbearable—especially after she'd received the bill for the loan, thanks to Emmett. But she'd left her worries behind for now.

Today she was flying to Rugby, North Dakota. When she'd called Laura the morning after their principal's late night phone message, she'd been given the best surprise of her life—she'd won *Arizona's Innovative Teacher of the Year Award.* Of course that had meant extra work, since she had to write the guest teacher plans for the three school days she would miss, then plan an oral presentation to deliver to an audience of other "Innovative Teachers," but that was hardly anything to complain about. She'd hid her key under the mat then left a message for Jake to come and pick up the animals, confident he wouldn't mind.

She was thrilled with this amazing opportunity to be recognized for her work with kinder students in the area of writing, but nervous about giving a presentation. She'd never spoken in front of an audience of educators before—or any audience, for that matter. She took out her presentation and read it over and over to herself, then studied the samples of student work she'd brought to share. She knew she was prepared. After all, she was merely showing other teachers what she did every day. Simple, right?

I'd feel far more confident if my audience was made up of five and six-year-olds, she said to herself.

The plane touched down in Denver, and she waited for the usual announcement for passengers to remain in their seats until the plane came to a complete stop. When it was done, it was followed up by, "Due to strong headwinds today, this flight is running about fifteen minutes behind schedule. If you have a connecting flight, check the screens to your right as you deplane, and proceed quickly to your next flight. Thank you for flying with us, and welcome to Denver."

Lindsey disembarked, then spotted an airport employee before she'd reached the screens. She asked where she should go, and he told her, "It leaves every day out of Gate 4 on Concourse E." He glanced at his watch and then shook his head. "And it leaves in twelve minutes. I hope you've got your running shoes on. You're going to have to sprint to make it."

"Thanks," hollered Lindsey as she began to run, dragging her carry-on behind her. She was confident she'd make it, though she wished she'd had time to stop in the ladies room. When she reached the end of the long hallway that connected the various concourses, she looked around, confused. There was no Concourse E in sight. Had she missed the sign? She circled around, looking up at the few signs above her, but she couldn't see anything that said "Concourse E."

"Hey, can I help you?" asked a young, handsome man. He looked like he was in a hurry, too.

"I'm supposed to catch a flight to Rugby on—"

He grinned. "Say no more. I'm headed to that same plane. Follow me," he said with an exaggerated flair, as if he were an actor.

She looked more closely at him but refused to believe her eyes. The guy looked just like the actor, Matthew McConaughey. Could it be him? Could a star like that be going to Rugby? Trying not to stare, she followed him right through an unmarked door, down two flights of stairs, and out into the cold Denver air.

"There's your plane," he said, gesturing dramatically toward the smallest airplane Lindsey had ever seen. "Just remember to hold on to the railing as you walk up the stairs. They tend to be a little slick now and then."

"Uh, sure. Thanks," she said, staring wide-eyed at the plane.

The stairs were so narrow she had a hard time holding the railing with one hand and lifting her rolling carry-on with the other, all the while trying not to fall. Her handsome rescuer followed, and she kept worrying she'd slip and tumble back on top of him. When she finally made it to the cabin door, she let out a breath, thinking she was home free. That's when she smacked her head on the low doorframe. The good-looking guy, today's knight in shining armor, was right there to catch her.

"Sorry," he said, helping her into her seat. "I forgot to mention that you needed to duck." He frowned at her forehead, and rearranged a strand of her hair to cover the spot where a lump was likely to appear. "There. Doesn't look too bad."

Lindsey stared at him in wonder. He still looked amazingly like Matthew McConaughey, even close up.

Once she was settled, he stood as straight as he could in the low-ceilinged space and addressed the eight passengers. "You know the drill. Fasten your seatbelts." Then he turned and pulled back a curtain before entering the small cockpit. Her knight was the pilot?

Lindsey stifled the urge to giggle. *I'm flying to a tiny town in a miniature plane flown by an actor. What's next?*

On cue, he poked his head out from behind the curtain. "Everybody ready? Hold on tight—we've got a bit of weather ahead of us. Rugby, ready or not, here we come!"

Lindsey's flying experience was fairly limited, but even so, she was pretty sure this flight would redefine the word "flying." The engine noise inside the cabin was so loud she wished she had brought earplugs, like two of the other passengers. They'd obviously done this before.

Suddenly realizing how thirsty she'd become, she turned to the Native American woman sitting directly behind her and asked if she knew when drinks might be served. The woman laughed out loud.

"No drinks, no eats on this plane. Here." With a sympathetic smile, she offered Lindsey a cookie from a package of peanut butter cookies.

Lindsey tried to settle in, get comfortable, but it was difficult. She couldn't concentrate. One man in the back of the plane—the back being only a few steps away—began singing *Don't Worry, Be Happy,* and before long two other passengers chimed in. Everyone was having fun, and they actually sounded pretty good. One added some harmony and another started whistling. She didn't want to interrupt by walking past them on her way to the dreaded airplane lavatory, but she had to. She couldn't wait any longer.

"Goin' for a walk, lady?" one of the men asked. "It'll be a short one. You can't get in shape on this putt-putt."

"Oh, I'm not trying to … uh … I'm just going to powder my nose."

A quiet looking older woman glanced up and motioned for Lindsey to bend down so she could whisper in her ear. "Honey, there's no bathroom on a plane like this. Didn't anyone tell you?"

Now Lindsey had a new predicament to deal with. Panic set in. It was going to be a very long, uncomfortable flight.

They finally landed, and with the challenges of the plane ride behind her, Lindsey searched for a bathroom in the tiny Rugby airport—there had to be one. She was desperate to empty the container she'd used as a tiny emergency toilet, given to her by the kind and well-traveled lady on the plane who had also assisted her through the awkward process. With relief she spotted a nondescript door marked Restroom, and she grabbed the door knob, but the door was locked. No problem. She'd waited this long, she could wait a little longer. She heard the flush, the water, and the hand dryer before the door opened.

A tall, stocky man with a friendly smile emerged from the small bathroom. He tipped his cowboy hat in her direction. "Hi, there. Just land?"

"Hi, to you, too. Yes, I flew in from Tucson." It seemed a little odd, having a conversation with a stranger at the entrance of a bathroom while she held a container of urine; she tried to keep it out of view.

"Tucson?" he bellowed. "I love Tucson. I went to grade school there, and my business takes me there now and then, though I spend a lot more time in Phoenix. Well, you have yourself a good time while you're here. See you around," he said, then he turned and headed toward the door leading out of the terminal.

While he walked away, she pondered who he was. He looked comfortable here, as if he'd been here before. Then she wondered what elementary school he'd attended in Tucson, and what line of work might have brought him to Rugby.

Bathroom duties accomplished, Lindsey was at last ready to pursue her purpose for being in Rugby. She approached the only remaining person in the terminal—a strong, stocky woman at the counter, who was probably the ticket agent, baggage handler, custodian, and security agent all wrapped into one—and inquired about a hotel.

The woman shook her head. "Nothin' here that I'd call a hotel," she said with a chuckle. "We've got several rustic cabins for the hunters that come up each year, though. Don't think you'd like 'em."

Butterflies swooped through Lindsey's stomach. What had she gotten herself into? "I am here for a conference, and it was my understanding that we'd all be staying in one place."

Light dawned in the woman's eyes. "Oh, you're one of the teachers," she said, smiling with confidence. "I don't see many of them 'cause most fly into Bismarck and hitch a ride over to Rugby. I do know that everyone attending that meeting is staying at the Mackelroy place. It's about five miles from here," she said. "They converted their old barn into a pretty interesting meeting location. Most folks really enjoy it."

"Oh, good. Thank you. Can you call a cab for me?"

The laughter was back in her eyes. "No, can't do that," she said apologetically. "The folks that fly in to this airport usually have family or friends that pick 'em up—no need for cabs. But I can call my sister if you'd like. She'll be happy to drive you out there."

Lindsey enjoyed the company and hospitality of the woman's sister, but she was shocked when she laid eyes on the accommodations: a small house beside a huge barn, both of which looked as if they might fall apart if the wind even thought about blowing.

"Looks can be deceiving," was all the woman said.

In contrast, all Lindsey could think was *What you see is what you get*.

A young man in his late teens ran out from the small, old house and helped Lindsey with her bags. He led her into the barn, then stood back, obviously enjoying her expression of relief. Inside, the barn had a north woods motif that included a mixture of hidden high tech and luscious comfort, nothing like a typical convention center meeting area. Instead of rows of tables and chairs, an assortment of comfortable leather chairs, loveseats, and sofas arranged in semi-circles took up about two thirds of the room. Western-styled lamps lit the room, which was a welcome change from the normal fluorescent ceiling lights in many meeting areas. Several dozen laptop computers were set out on a long, narrow pine table by the west wall of the barn, and a slightly raised and carpeted presentation area was located at the northern end. The front third of the barn, just inside the massive barn door entryway, contained six large, round wooden tables. The area was separated from the rest of the room by potted pine trees. The young man who had carried her bags informed her that all meals and snacks would be served in this area, family-style.

"I know this must sound like a silly question," asked Lindsey, "but where do we sleep?"

"Sleep? There's no time for sleeping here," the young man said with a straight face. He winked. "Just kidding. Follow me. Every barn needs a place to store the hay."

He led her upstairs and showed her four bunk rooms, each large enough to hold a dozen sleepers. "This room is yours," he said. "Enjoy your night."

About half of the bunks appeared already taken, and their absent occupants had unpacked and organized their belongings. Lindsey did the same. A few minutes later, another woman was escorted up and assigned a bunk. She and Lindsey quickly became acquainted and went to explore the rest of the second floor. They were pleased to discover a very nice bathroom, complete with five stalls, five sinks, five showers, five private dressing areas, and one large hot tub. It was almost like being at camp—all modern, yet artistically rustic. Lindsey had never seen an interior with so much wood. A great deal of creative and unusual thought had gone into the design and décor of this facility.

When they were done exploring, they sat by the upstairs fireplace, sharing school stories and a few misadventures with men when the announcement came, seemingly out of nowhere.

"Welcome, everyone. Please begin making your way to the dining area and look for your name cards. Dinner will be served in about ten minutes."

Chapter Twenty-Five

Jake knocked on the door and got no response. He rang the doorbell several times and still heard nothing. Good. That's what he'd hoped for. But he'd also hoped the front door would be unlocked or at least that the usual hiding place for the key would still be holding a key. He walked around to the side kitchen door, looking guiltily over his shoulder every step of the way.

This door was unlocked. Anthony would have locked it, but Shawna? Well, she might have forgotten. Her mind rarely dwelt on mundane, domestic things. Jake stepped inside.

"I wish you were with me, Wendell," he said out loud, but the dog wasn't up to sleuthing yet. He still moved very slowly and with a limp. He'd picked him up as Lindsey had requested; the poor dog was sleeping in his apartment once again.

Jake had brought his camera this time. He'd decided to take photos of anything and everything that he thought might shed some light on Shawna. It wasn't just for his thesis, though he told himself that was the prime reason for his being there. He figured that in the long run, more knowledge of this woman—this *couple*—might be helpful to Lindsey.

Today his curiosity overpowered his common sense. He began his snooping at the far end of the house, in the master bedroom, making a mental note to meticulously set everything he touched back to its exact location so no suspicions would be raised. He came up empty in the master bedroom, finding nothing out of the ordinary except for an abundance of dark-colored satin bras and panties. No thongs, though. That surprised him a little. He assumed she'd be the thong type.

Just across the hall he saw a door to another bedroom. Probably a guest room, he thought, though somehow he couldn't imagine this couple ever having guests. He peeked in, saw nothing at first, but he stopped before skipping the room entirely. Something made him hesitate, and his hand still rested on the door knob. He entered the room to take a closer look around and noticed that the only furniture was a queen-size bed draped with a shiny purple coverlet. There were no drawers to open, no shelves to peruse, just one small door. He presumed that led to an equally small closet.

The closet door was locked, which made Jake more curious than ever. Fortunately for Jake, it was an old, outdated key lock, and he opened it easily with a credit card and the pick on his all-purpose utility knife. He pulled a chord he hoped would illuminate the space, and *voila!* Light ... and lots of relatively new men's clothing. Not Anthony's style, though. Perhaps it belonged to a previous boyfriend or a relative. That might make sense. Jake snapped a few photos then carefully relocked the door.

Jake conducted a mental inventory of his findings as he moved through the house. He had seen a lot of photos of an older man—presumably her father—and of a young boy that he assumed was her brother. He only found recent photos of Shawna, none of her as a child. A variety of lawyers' business cards were stacked in one of the desk drawers, and several paid receipts from a clinic in Trinidad, Colorado were in the bottom drawer, but they were too vague to decipher much more than the amount paid. The oddest papers were some letters held together with a purple ribbon, addressed to a guy named Sean. Uncomfortable about reading private notes, he quickly snapped a photo of two of the envelopes before leaving the house.

Now, as he drove away from the scene of his crime, he regretted not having read at least a few of the letters. His investigative work had raised more questions than answers.

"Did you enjoy your Rock Cornish game hen?" asked the woman at the podium. Participants responded enthusiastically with cheers and applause. "Excellent," she said. "My name is Elisabeth Meriwether. To my right is Frank Bartlett, and to my left is Cheryl Thompson. The three of us organize and oversee this conference every year. This is the fourth annual gathering of *The Innovative Teacher of the Year Award* recipients. We select one winner from each state, and I am delighted to inform you that this year, every winner was able to attend. That is a first!"

Everyone applauded politely, and the participants smiled at each other.

When they were quiet, Elisabeth continued. "We gather here in Rugby every year, right here in this barn. Some of you asked, why Rugby? That's Frank's story, so we'll let him tell it before the conference is over. Between now and then, think about your own answer for the question, 'why Rugby?'"

Excitement and anticipation grew as Cheryl explained the general schedule and specific events that would take place over the next two days. "Each morning you will awaken to a recorded medley sung by cheerful, local birds—eastern wooded pee wees, horned larks, black-capped chickadees, and house wrens—at approximately 6:30, followed by breakfast at 7:30, then introductions and announcements at 8:30. Four oral presentations will commence right after that. Everyone will share, ask questions, build upon the presented information, and be able to apply the new learning to their own teaching situations. After lunch there will be a group excursion lasting two to three hours, followed by ninety minutes of free time before dinner at 6:00 p.m. Immediately after dinner, we will continue our learning, featuring some of the written presentations."

"Shelley Brown, Ronda Mitchell, Frances Garcia, and Lindsey Sommerfield will be our morning presentation speakers tomorrow. I would like you four ladies to come and see me as soon as we finish here tonight. There is a list of those sharing tomorrow evening's written reports over by the computers. Do take a packet—they are on the table by the stairs—and read through it before breakfast. It should answer most of your questions about the presentations as well as about the follow-up opportunities available throughout the year.

"Enjoy the rest of your evening. Oh, just one more, quick item: because of our dormitory-style sleeping arrangements, lights out is at 10:30. We have clip-on book lights available if you care to continue your reading after lights out."

No one wanted or needed a book light that first night. Almost everyone had been traveling since the wee hours of the morning, so many were asleep long before lights out. Lindsey wasn't one of them. Not that she wasn't exhausted—she was—but the reality of speaking in front of this group of educators in the morning had begun to set in. She had to admit, she was nervous. What if she couldn't remember what to say? What if the pages of her presentation fell onto the floor and ended up out of order? What if her power point malfunctioned? *What if? What if? What if?*

After breakfast, Shelley Brown, the Ohio winner, spoke first. She had developed a Supplemental Saturday Program for 4th and 5th grade students who struggled academically due to their inability to succeed in a typical classroom environment. Through her program, the town she and her students lived in—the parks, the museums, the businesses, the post office, everything—had become their Saturday classroom.

Next up was Ronda Mitchell from California. Ronda worked at a school where all classrooms were multi-age. She shared several thematic units that she created and currently used with her 1st, 2nd, and 3rd grade students. With these specially crafted units, she could teach the whole group similar concepts and information, but with enough differentiation that all students could participate at their instructional level.

After a quick break, the third presenter of the day, Frances Garcia, from Texas, was up. Because most of the mandated teaching materials didn't meet the needs of all her students, she wrote adaptations. For example, Frances wrote an adaptation of the social studies textbook so that it contained the same information but at a lower reading level, and she translated the most important facts to Spanish to ensure all her English Language Learners were successful, too.

As Lindsey watched these imaginative and noteworthy presenters, she became increasingly nervous. The other women were so polished and well rehearsed—so *professional*. The more she thought about her presentation, the more she worried.

"Our next presenter is Lindsey Sommerfield. Come on up, Ms. Sommerfield," announced Elisabeth.

Lindsey stood slowly and approached the presentation platform, trying to disguise her terror. She felt wobbly both in her stomach and in her knees, her palms were slick with sweat, and the inside of her mouth felt as if it was packed with cotton balls. How would she be able to talk? *What have I gotten myself into? Please, please don't let me make a total fool of myself,* she prayed.

Elisabeth was waiting for her at the microphone. Lindsey pressed her notes against her body, trying to make them stop shaking.

Elisabeth smiled warmly, then addressed the audience. "Teachers, I'd like to tell you a little inside information about Lindsey. You all had over three months to prepare for your participation in this program, including arranging your travel and guest teachers." Her smile grew. "Poor Lindsey knew nothing of this award or conference—let alone the prospect of making a presentation—until just three days ago."

There was an appreciative gasp from the audience, and Lindsey managed to give them a weak smile.

Elisabeth went on. "Not only that, but due to the last minute travel arrangements, Lindsey had to fly in directly to Rugby. Some of you know what that means." She turned to Lindsey, a twinkle in her eye. "How was your flight, Lindsey?"

With no idea of how to answer, Lindsey decided to stick with the truth. "It was a lot like a nightmare," she tried to say, certain her words came out sounding like she was holding her own tongue as she spoke. To her delighted surprise, her brief response roused smiles and laughter from the audience.

"Today Lindsey will tell us all about teaching kindergarten children to write through the use of her own innovation which she calls Art Journals. Let's get her started. You know what to do," encouraged Elisabeth.

As the audience applauded, Lindsey centered herself in front of the microphone and began to speak. The first few minutes seemed to last forever, as she struggled to regain normal levels of moisture in her mouth and recover her full voice. Her knees still shook, and she wondered how she would make it through her presentation without falling down. She'd barely begun when a hand went up from the audience. It was her new friend, Shelley, wearing a questioning frown.

"I always thought an art journal was simply a book where an individual drew, painted, or whatever. Anything they felt like making, without any rules," stated Shelley. "Am I wrong?"

After a brief second of worry—*are they turning on me already?*—the teacher in Lindsey jumped into action. After all, she knew her topic inside and out.

"Absolutely not, Shelley. You are not wrong. You have described a common type of art journal. My art journal is slightly different. It's a vehicle that produces enjoyable writing practice for very young students. In a nutshell, my art journal is an individual student's collection of art—that is often created during a guided drawing lesson—and a specific type of writing to accompany that art. The writing often reflects recent learning. This will all become clear by the end of my forty-five minutes. And thanks, Shelley, for your comment, because it has brought to my attention that my art journal, my innovation, is unique and needs a more descriptive or definitive name. Perhaps you all can help me with that."

The ice was broken, or at least cracked a little, and Lindsey forgot all about the nervous state of her mouth and knees. She was on her way, discussing her innovation and sharing specific lessons and student work resulting from those lessons. The time flew by.

A hand went up, and Lindsey smiled, encouraging the other teacher. "Like you, Lindsey, I teach kinder, and after seeing your student samples I have to say that I really doubt my kids could do what your kids have done." Her statement was backed by numerous nodding heads.

Lindsey disagreed. "I guarantee your students will be successful at some level. Here. Look at these three drawings of a pig. The first little pig looks just like a pig; the second little pig looks like a pig that an average five-year-old might draw; the third little pig, well, he cried *wee-wee-wee* all the way home." The group laughed, and Lindsey paused enjoying the moment. "Each student took part in the same lesson and participated at their current ability level. All the pigs had two ears, two eyes, a nose, a mouth, and they were all pink. Each child was successful in his or her own way. I also guarantee they will be so proud of their work they will want to do more. And, come parent conference time, or portfolio conference time, each student's art journal will be a treasured piece of work in the eyes of both students and parents. Each child's growth and maturity will be obvious as the year progresses."

Questions and comments kept coming. "I can't draw," one teacher said. "I could never lead students in a guided art lesson."

Lindsey thought for a moment, then asked, "Elisabeth, can I take fifteen minutes more?" She got the nod and proceeded to lead the entire group, step-by-step, through one of the lessons she had already completed with her students called, *The Frog's Story*.

At the end of the fifteen minutes, Elisabeth returned to the microphone. "It seems you've captured everyone's interest, but we need to move on now."

The room echoed with applause, and Lindsey smiled at everyone, drinking in the first positive energy she'd felt in a long, long time.

Chapter Twenty-Six

The group excursion after lunch was to the Prairie Village Museum. The bus pulled up outside the barn and, since the ground was still a bit icy, the driver gave each woman a hand up.

"Hi, there," the bus driver said to Lindsey as he took her hand. "I thought you might be in Rugby for this conference.

She stared at him, startled. Then she smiled. "Hey, bathroom guy!"

She settled into her seat beside her new friend. "You know him?" Shelley asked.

"Not really." Lindsey shrugged lightly. "We kind of met by the bathroom at the Rugby airport. I guess he's my bathroom/bus driver buddy."

Shelley raised one dark eyebrow. "He's a tall, good-looking, friendly, cowboy kind of guy, don't you think?"

"Yes, I suppose."

"And? You're single, aren't you? I'm married, so I don't—"

Lindsey laughed out loud. "No way! I've had it with men, at least for now. Besides, he drives a bus in Rugby. That's a heck of a long way from Tucson."

They both looked up as the bus pulled into the museum parking area. The main building of the complex housed wildlife displays, antique guns, items that pioneers used to make their homes, and many Native American and Eskimo artifacts. Lindsey thought the bus driver might also guide them through the various buildings at the Prairie Village Museum, but he was nowhere to be seen. Lindsey and Shelley, who were becoming great friends, stuck together, visiting the old-time dress shop, the Old Norwegian house, every building and display, the jail, the livery, and the blacksmith shop. By four o'clock everyone was back on the bus. The temperature had dropped from the midday forty-seven degrees down to thirty-five, according to their driver.

"Be sure to dress even warmer tomorrow," he suggested to the ladies. "We'll be outside for much of the time, and the weather will be cold."

The next day the bus took them to a place called the Northern Lights Tower, but they had no idea what that was about. As they exited the bus, the driver instructed them to gather around the tall steel structure that stood before them.

"Not much to it," Shelley whispered.

"There must be something to it, or we wouldn't be here," replied Lindsey. "The colorful metallic paint looks nice."

Their driver stepped forward with a clipboard and began to read information about the structure—in a flat monotone. It did little to grasp the interest of most of the onlookers.

"This is the Northern Lights Tower. It is 88 feet tall, and as you can see, it is painted with many colors. It lights up at night, and it is supposed to replicate the actual Northern Lights, otherwise known as the Aurora Borealis. Any questions?"

The silence stretched until he spoke again. "March and September are the best months to see the Aurora Borealis in this area because of mild weather and dark skies. Also because the Earth's orbit is in a zone of maximum solar activity during March and September."

No one said anything. The driver cleared his throat. "The old St. Paul's Episcopal Church is something you might like to see. It's over a hundred years old." The group was still fairly quiet and unresponsive. "It was closed in 1978, deconsecrated in 1991, and today it is a Victorian Dress Museum." Suddenly they were listening enthusiastically.

Lindsey was the last person in their group to leave the old church and the last person to board the bus. As she was getting in, the bathroom/bus driver/tour guide guy stopped her. "Have you ever seen the Northern Lights? I mean, *really* seen them, in person?"

"No, I don't think so. Tucson skies are anything but dark," she said.

"Well, here's a little tip. Go out tonight between 10:30 and 11:30 and stand about halfway between the barn and the house. There will be just a sliver of a moon. The skies should be as clear as a vitreous column and as dark as a hardwood plank painted with creosote. If you look up, there's a great chance of seeing the Aurora Borealis." He smiled. "Just thought you might enjoy that experience."

"Oh," she replied, not entirely sure of what he'd just said. "Thanks for the tip. I just might do that."

After a splendid dinner of pumpkin and sausage pasta, Waldorf salad with cabbage, and mocha brownies topped with hazelnut cream, everyone gathered in the meeting area. The room's ceiling lights were dimmed, the potted evergreens were adorned with shimmering white lights, and the fireplace crackled and glowed a brilliant orange. A hush fell over the group as each participant found a comfortable spot on one of the sofas or chairs, which had been rearranged into several circles rather than half circles.

Elisabeth, Frank, and Cheryl were part of the circles tonight. From her seat, Elisabeth shared her appreciation for everyone's participation, for each and every innovation, and for the improved and hopeful future of elementary education. Frank spoke briefly about the wide variety of innovations this year and encouraged everyone to take their ideas to the next level, and find ways to share them with their schools, their districts, and even their states. Cheryl handed out the state award plaques, along with envelopes containing certificates of participation that included the number of hours spent at the conference. Teachers would use these hours when it came time to renew their teaching certificates. Lindsey waited, but no one gave her an envelope.

"What's all the excitement about?" she asked the person sitting beside her.

The smiling woman said nothing but showed her a check for $500.

"We hope these gifts will help you in your quest to share your innovations with others," Elisabeth said, smiling.

Frank, the only man in the place, put up his hand to get their attention. "Why Rugby? Why is Rugby the meeting place for this conference? Anyone willing to take a guess, share their thoughts?"

One hand went up. "Because there aren't many distractions here?"

"That is true and also a great reason, but it's not the one I'm thinking of."

Another hand. "Because you knew this unique barn/conference center was here?"

Frank glanced around, smiling contentedly. "It is remarkable, isn't it? But no. It wasn't here when we first selected this location. I mean, the barn was here, but it was just a barn then, nothing more."

Three more brave souls took a stab at answering Frank's question, but no one got it right. He finally took pity on the group.

"Rugby was chosen as the location of our *Innovative Teacher Awards Conference* because ... it is the Geographical Center of North America." He paused, then added, "You can decide for yourself what that means to you."

No one dared to break the silence that followed.

"Isn't silence wonderful for the act of contemplation?" Elisabeth whispered. "But now, forward we must go. Would all eight participants who gave full, oral presentations please come forward?"

Lindsey bit the inside of her cheek, not wanting anyone to see her hopeful smile. Maybe now she'd receive her certificate and $500 check. She could really use that to start paying off her line of credit loan, thanks to Emmett. While she stood waiting at the front, Frank and Cheryl passed out pieces of paper to everyone still sitting. Then the eight presenters were asked to state their name and the title of their presentation.

"Those of you with ballots, please vote for your three favorite presentations," instructed Elisabeth.

When the voting was complete, Elisabeth thanked the presenters, and invited them to return to their seats. Lindsey and Shelley exchanged looks of disappointment. Surely they would receive *something*. Or had they already received their reward by being given the honor of making a presentation? An intrinsic reward? How many times had she and the other teachers asked children to be grateful for such a thing?

Frank explained that in the morning they'd have a nice, early continental breakfast to ensure everyone boarded the buses and made it to the appropriate airport in time to catch their flights. Lindsey glanced at her watch, slightly disappointed. She'd hoped to take advantage of the tip she'd received about the Northern Lights earlier, but it was already 10:45 p.m. and the meeting was not quite over.

Elisabeth Meriwether walked with measured steps toward the top of the circle. "There is just one more announcement to make before we all retire for the evening." She paused as if she were searching her mind for the right words. "We haven't yet spoken of the top award. You've all won the state award for *Innovative Teacher of the Year*, but we also give out a national award. One of the eight presenters will receive that award, so I want you all to know just what that means.

"The winner of the *National Innovative Teacher of the Year* Award will have the opportunity to publish her work and present a minimum of four times at different educational conferences over the coming school year. The team will determine which presentation is most marketable, and we will also take into consideration your three favorites, based upon tonight's ballots. The national winner will be notified on or before June 1st. Good luck, everyone."

Lindsey found it difficult to listen during those last few minutes. She knew she had no hope of winning since she was so new to education and public speaking. All she really wanted was to get out and see the Lights. This could be the only time in her life she might see them.

When they finally were dismissed, she and the other seven presenters were handed their envelopes, and Lindsey breathed a sigh of relief. That $500 would come in handy. She folded the unopened envelope into her coat pocket and headed out into the chilly, dark night, looking for the spot halfway between the barn and the small house. Time to view this curious phenomenon of nature was running out.

When she was in position, she hugged her arms around herself and gazed into the heavens. "Hello, World," she whispered to the night sky, "I'm here. I'm ready for the show." Then it happened, filling the sky with dancing swaths of color, and she couldn't hold in a squeal. "Oh, my God! I see it!"

She stood paralyzed, mesmerized by the display of green, red, and blue light, sparkling, shooting, shimmering across the sky. It was brilliantly powerful, yet made no sound. But suddenly there was a sound. She tensed at the unexpected noise: footsteps coming slowly from behind her. She spun around to face the danger.

"I hoped you'd come," the cowboy's voice was low and smooth. "The Aurora Borealis is spectacular tonight, don't you think?"

At first, Lindsey was relieved that it was him, then she wondered if that was the right reaction. After all, she didn't know this bathroom/bus driver/tour guide guy. It was possible he'd set her up to harm her—she'd seen weirder things than that in the movies. She backed away from him, but he stood firm between her and the warmth and safety of the barn.

The cowboy froze. "You're shaking," he said. "Here, let me warm you up." He shrugged out of his large, fleece-lined barn coat, then gently set it on her shoulders, over her own jacket.

She felt the warmth of it almost immediately, but instead of bringing comfort, it shot her adrenaline through the roof. In the past, she might have fallen for this move, but not anymore. Her distrust of men jumped to the forefront of her mind, and she added his ploy to bring her out here alone, in the dark, to that list. She was going to be smarter with men from now on, she promised herself. She was never going to be that naïve young woman ever again. This was her first chance to prove she had made progress in this area. She shoved the coat off her shoulders and dashed for the barn door, not looking back to see if he followed.

"Oh, Lindsey!" She heard a voice and spotted Elisabeth standing at the open barn door. "There you are, dear. I looked for you after the meeting ... but I see you've been out enjoying the cold night air—"

"And the Aurora Borealis," she added breathlessly.

Elisabeth gave her a knowing smile, catching sight of the bus driver's profile. "Well, anyway, I'm glad we met up, because here is your new ticket for your flight home. It leaves out of Bismarck—on a jet! Thought you'd enjoy a real plane, taking off from a real airport with more than one small runway. So be sure to board the bus to Bismarck tomorrow right after breakfast."

"Wow! That's terrific! Thanks so much, Elisabeth."

"I'm happy to do it, Lindsey. Good night, and have a comfortable flight home."

Chapter Twenty-Seven

The piped-in bird songs the center used as an alarm clock came early, and they were much louder than they had been the previous two mornings. Everyone was up and about, packing and putting on make-up, since today they would reenter civilization.

"Sleep well?" Shelley asked, rolling out of her bunk.

"Yes, thank you. I did," Lindsey replied, folding a shirt into her bag.

"Me, too." She watched Lindsey expectantly. "So … you came to bed later than most of us. What exciting activity did you find to do?"

Lindsey decided not to tell her about the happenings of the night before, other than the good news. "Oh, Elisabeth gave me a different ticket for my return trip. No more miniature planes and tiny airports. I get to take a bus ride to Bismarck like most of the other big kids and hop on a jet complete with flight attendants, head and legroom—and best of all, several bathrooms. I am so happy."

"Oh, good. I'm on the bus to Bismarck, too. Let's sit together. Maybe we'll see that good-looking bus driver one more time. Wouldn't that be fun?" Shelley lifted an eyebrow, waiting, but Lindsey shuddered. "Hey," Shelley said, touching her arm. "What gives?"

Lindsey relived the night's encounter for Shelley, but she couldn't help wondering if she'd been wrong about her interpretation of the man's intentions.

Shelley kept her reaction to herself. "It's better to be safe than sorry," was all she said.

Lindsey frowned. *Whether he's the northern plains version of Jack the Ripper or just a really nice, thoughtful guy, I hope he's not the one driving me to the airport. I don't want to face him either way.*

He wasn't in the driver's seat when she climbed aboard the bus, but once she was seated in the plane, there he was, right across the aisle from her. Her palms went damp with nervous sweat. Was he stalking her? No, that couldn't be ... or could it? She didn't know what to think. She pretended to look for something in her purse to avoid making eye contact with him. Eventually, after the flight attendant asked passengers to store their items, she closed her eyes and feigned sleep. This worked for a while ... until a large, warm hand touched her forearm.

"Hey, you'd better fasten your seatbelt. That flight attendant headed this way seems like a stickler for the rules," the cowboy said, grinning.

"Oh, thanks."

"Are you feeling all right? I thought maybe you were ill last night, after you ran off like that."

"I'm fine. Just needed to get back inside," she replied, though she knew her tone was unconvincing.

The woman occupying the seat on Lindsey's other side noticed the man, and she smiled across at him. "Hi, I'm Christy. I don't remember your name—did you tell us?"

"I can't remember if I did," he admitted, grinning sheepishly. "This whole thing was pretty new to me. I'm not used to driving a busload of women around, let alone giving them talks about the local sights. So I apologize if I left that part out. I'm Martin Mackelroy. My friends call me Marty."

"So what were you doing in Rugby?" Christy asked, her flirting voice sweet as honey. "Surely you weren't flown in just to drive fifty teachers around for a couple of days."

"No, you're right about that. I come up to visit my mother and younger brother at least four times a year. This time I got roped into helping out at the conference since the regular guy had a family emergency and wasn't available. My younger brother works the conferences, but he's not allowed to be a commercial driver until he turns eighteen. So you all got stuck with me."

Lindsey kept her eyes closed, but she listened as Martin answered all of Christy's questions, telling her how he spent most of his time in the Phoenix area running an architectural firm—*his* architectural firm. Apparently his specialty was designing homes, offices—and yes, conference centers for families and businesses desiring western or southwestern architecture.

She opened her eyes. "So you designed the barn?"

He nodded, seeming pleased that she'd joined in the conversation. "That was a special project for my mother and my little brother. They wanted to stay in Rugby and needed to make some money."

"Do your mother and brother live in the small house?" asked Christy.

"Yep, and when I come home to visit, it's crowded," he said. His laugh was easy and relaxed. "The bunk beds worked fine years ago but not now. I stay in the barn when there are no conferences. That works out well."

The more he spoke, the more Lindsey wondered if she'd been all wrong about him the night before. If so, she was awfully embarrassed. How could she explain her actions? Fortunately, her dilemma remained on hold, because Martin closed his eyes for the next hour of the flight. When they arrived at Sky Harbor in Phoenix, they were behind schedule, leaving her little time for boarding her connecting flight to Tucson. In fact, she and several other passengers were allowed to deplane first, due to the short time in which they had to catch their flights.

The airport was bustling with commuters, and it seemed everyone was in her way. To her surprise, Martin waited at her gate and was already leaning casually against a pillar when she dashed up, out of breath. How had he done that? She had no time to ask, since her flight was boarding. Most of the passengers were already on board.

Martin stopped her just before she went through the gate. "Hey, there," he said, sounding a little shy. He handed her a familiar-looking envelope. "You dropped this while you were making your quick getaway. Listen, I don't know your name, but I do know that I like you. I do. At the risk of appearing too forward, I wrote my cell phone number and my email on the back."

"Ma'am?" the airline attendant said, ushering Lindsey forward.

"I'm coming to Tucson in two weeks," Martin called before she disappeared, "and I'd love to take you to dinner. If that sounds good to you, let me know."

Looking over her shoulder at him, Lindsey shoved her conference envelope deep into her jacket pocket and watched him stroll confidently away, cowboy hat and all.

The next morning arrived far too soon, but Lindsey jumped out of bed the instant her alarm rang. She was tired, but she couldn't wait to get to school, talk to Laura, and get ready to face the children. Laura had called her a couple of times when she'd been away, ranting about the kinder kids getting out of hand, and Lindsey wanted to find out what had been going on.

Without much thought to fashion, she threw on a long sleeved white T-shirt, a black corduroy vest, and a long khaki skirt. She called Jake's cell to see if he could bring the animals over, and when he didn't answer she left a message. Then she grabbed her book bags and ran out the front door. She purchased a café mocha from the local Starbucks, figuring that would tide her over till lunch, then she stopped by the office to pick up her mail, and found a note to call Bobby's grandmother. There was also one from Laura, saying she was exhausted and needed a day of rest. She said she would see Lindsey tomorrow. That made Lindsey smile. It confirmed her theory that primary classroom teachers had the most challenging, complex, and sometimes toilsome job in education. And yet no other job offered so many moment-to-moment opportunities to make a difference in so many young lives.

"Ms. Lindsey! Ms. Lindsey! You've been gone forever," lamented a couple of the girls as they entered the classroom.

"We got to watch the TV every day," Armando shared.

"Were you sick?" Emma asked. "You always tell us to stay home if we're sick"

Lindsey shook her head, smiling at her students. She'd missed them. "No, I wasn't sick. I was at a conference."

"Oh," said Joseph, nodding sagely. "A really long parent conference, I bet. Someone's in big trouble."

Lindsey laughed. "No, no. No one's in trouble. Come on in and put your things in your cubbies, then meet me on the rug," she reminded the children as she did every morning.

Lindsey's students loved hearing about her plane ride on the tiny airplane and the chirping bird alarm clock, and they were excited when she told them that other teachers had seen some of their art journal pages. She loved their enthusiasm. But something was missing. Something was different. She frowned at the children, then figured it out. She could hear no inappropriate comments, no rude interruptions. Lindsey scanned the rug area and realized Bobby and Willy weren't there. When she asked if anyone had seen them on the playground or at breakfast, all the students shook their heads.

"I wonder if Bobby and Willy are sick," Lindsey said out loud.

Her question was met by an uncharacteristic silence. That alone was cause for concern.

"What's going on?" she asked. "Did something happen to Bobby and Willy?"

After another second of silence, Harley blurted out, "They were spended."

At that news, Lindsey was more than willing to drop the subject, but the students wanted to tell her everything they knew. Their comments spilled out with urgency.

Emma shook her head, her big eyes solemn. "It was bad, Miss Lindsey. The new teacher yelled at them, but they just yelled back."

"Then Bobby went somewhere and hid in the bushes. It took three grownups to find him."

"Willy said the 'S' word!" Harley blurted out.

Lindsey grimaced, hoping he'd meant something like *stupid* or *sucky* or *silly*. "Oh, dear. I am so sorry that you had to hear that."

"And the 'B' word."

Bad? Butt?

"And even the 'F' word." The rest of the class nodded, their eyes as wide as saucers.

No doubt about that one.

"It was really, really bad."

Then their tone changed. "Yesterday, Ms. Laura stayed with us all afternoon."

"I like her. She let us sing and color and dance."

Emma's expression was still foreboding. "But Bobby and Willy didn't want to, so they were bad again."

"How were they bad?" asked Lindsey. "What happened?"

"You should have seen it," Harley exclaimed. "Bobby kicked Ms. Laura and then spit on her."

"What?!"

But he had even more to share. "Willy laughed and threw all the table baskets on the floor. All the pencils and crayons and scissors went flying."

"And then he stood up on the table and danced around," someone else said.

Joseph put up his hand. "He looked like a bad-dancing, stupid chicken."

Lindsey could definitely picture that.

Armando pointed at the wall. "I got to push the button to call the principal. I never got to do that before."

Back to Harley. "Then they got taken away and spended, and we got to sing and color some more."

"Mr. Tom even helped take them away."

Lindsey stared, horrified. "The custodian helped the principal?"

"And the cafeteria man, too," added Joseph, seeming delighted that he wasn't the one in trouble.

Emma nodded. "Ms. Laura got to go home, and Mrs. Peterson came in from the library to watch us for the rest of the day. She was nice. She read us stories."

Chapter Twenty-Eight

Poor Laura, Lindsey thought. She resolved to check with the office to hear the adult version of what had taken place then arrange to do something special for her friend later in the day. At lunchtime she went to see Sally, the office manager.

"Yes, Ms. Sommerfield," Sally said. "The principal suspended both boys. They won't be returning to school until Monday."

"Can I see the paperwork?" asked Lindsey. "Bobby's grandmother wants a call back, and I want to be prepared for that conversation."

"I don't have it. You'll have to get it from the principal, and she's at the monthly administrators' meeting all day."

"There's no way to pull up the paperwork on the computer? I like to get back to people right away."

"Nope. Not that I know of."

"Well, can you tell me anything about what happened? Did you see the boys?"

Sally's jaw tightened, and she glared at Lindsey. "Oh, I saw them, all right. I had to try to keep them on that couch till their rides showed up. Willy's mom came relatively quickly, which was a good thing. If he'd stayed any longer I would have killed him. He jumped on the couch, he swung his backpack over his head and knocked over the plants on my counter—and that's just the beginning. Bobby's mom and grandmother didn't pick him up until an hour past dismissal time. That was the longest hour of my life. I called for the principal and Laura to restrain him—I'm not trained to do that, and even if I were, I wouldn't try it with that kiddo—but they had already gone. I did my best to corral him in the corner where he couldn't reach anything else to throw at me.

"After that, I had to listen to his mom scream at him for being so bad, for forcing her to get out of bed, and other stuff about how he was nothing but trouble. There isn't enough money in the world to get me to spend an entire day with these guys, let along a whole school year, unless I could use a straightjacket and duct tape. And just for the record, I would demand hazard pay."

Lindsey felt terrible. Yes, the boys were trouble, but she'd never imagined they'd behave so badly. "I am sorry the boys were so … difficult. They don't do well with change," she tried attempting a positive spin. "Well, thank you for all you did."

She couldn't do any more today regarding the boys and their suspensions from school, so Lindsey headed home to see Wendell and Malcolm, to unpack, and to make a plan to get together with Laura. Her friend would need to some additional venting time to purge herself of the horrendous experience with the boys over the past few days.

It felt great to get home and know that they heard her coming. Tails were wagging—including Malcolm's, sort of. "Hi guys. I missed you so much," she exclaimed, taking Wendell's head in her hands.

She rubbed his ears and let him lick her face while Malcolm landed on her shoulder and began to peck at strands of her hair. Her two best friends followed her from room to room as she tried to put away her clothes and materials from the conference, not letting her out of their sight. It made the whole process enjoyable, but slow.

She gave her winter jacket one last look before putting it away. "Guess I won't be needing this till next year."

Wendell left her side to keep watch by the phone message machine. One of his eccentricities—all dogs have them, but this one was pretty unique—was to stare at the machine whenever the message light blinked. The first message was Jake, confirming that he'd picked up the animals. The second and third messages were junk—recorded sales calls. One was about refinancing and the other one started off with, "Congratulations! You've won a trip—" Lindsey pushed the erase button before it went any further.

Then a man's unfamiliar voice delivered the fourth message. "Lindsey? Are you there? Pick up." Pause. "Damn."

Lindsey frowned. It hadn't been Anthony's voice—she'd still recognize it anywhere. Pretty sure it wasn't Emmett, though she wouldn't put it past him. Jake? No. Not unless he was sick with a bad cold that had lowered his voice. And it was too soon for bill collectors to be calling. She wasn't overdue on any payments … yet. She was just about to pick up the receiver and call Laura when the phone rang.

"Hello," she said tentatively, hoping it was Laura.

"Well, thank God you are finally home," said the same mysterious, menacing voice.

"To whom am I speaking?" she asked, trying to sound unconcerned.

"Oh, good grief, girl. Do you always have to sound like such a stuffy teacher? You know perfectly well who this is. We talked before. I have news you need to hear. So just shut up and listen, princess."

Lindsey sat down because her knees felt weak. Her hands shook, and her heart raced. She tried to remember the message Emmett had relayed to her before about a caller, but her memory was a bit cloudy; she'd had other matters on her mind that day. Then there was the strange call she'd received at school, telling her about Anthony hurting Wendell.

"You might as well forget about Anthony," the man muttered. "He and his girlfriend are getting married in August. It's all worked out. So, Little Bo Peep, he's not yours to keep," he said in a singsong rhythm. "Leave him alone, 'cause he's not coming home."

Panicking, she hung up, then stared at the phone. Why would anyone want to scare her? Who was this person who seemed to know all of Anthony's and Shawna's plans? She toyed with the idea of calling Anthony. Perhaps he knew who it was or why he'd chosen to harass Lindsey with the sinister phone calls.

When the phone rang again, Lindsey jerked away and almost fell off the chair. She couldn't take another call right now. She decided to let the machine pick it up.

"Hey, Linds. Laura. I was wondering if we—"

She grabbed the phone. "Laura! I am so glad it's you! I was just going to call you, but then this other call came in, and I am still trying to recover from the creepy way it made me feel."

"What creepy way?"

Lindsey began to explain about the calls, the man, and the weirdness of it all, when Laura interrupted. "Lock all your doors. I'm coming over."

Lindsey had never been happier to see another person than she did when Laura arrived. They double-locked all the doors, checked that the windows were closed and locked, then took inventory of all their defense possibilities. Laura had brought two pepper spray canisters and a hunting knife. Lindsey produced a large flashlight and a small gun.

Laura stared at it. "You have a gun? Since when?"

"Since Anthony lived here. He said we should always have a gun for protection."

"And you know how to shoot it? Is it loaded?"

She nodded. "He taught me how to shoot it when we first got married. It has six bullets in it, and here's a box with more."

"Huh. Okay." She blinked at Lindsey, obviously shocked to see her quiet, unassuming friend handling a gun. "Well, you can be in charge of that. I'll stick with my pepper spray."

They spent the rest of the night throwing themselves an old-fashioned, girly slumber party complete with brushing and styling their hair, doing each other's nails, and eating ice cream right out of the container. And though Lindsey hadn't slept in the master bedroom since that awful afternoon, they used that room tonight for the sleepover. The best friends chatted non-stop for hours, laughing and crying. They talked about the two troublemaking boys in Lindsey's kindergarten class, the men no longer in Lindsey's life, and the strange phone calls. But when Lindsey asked Laura how things were going with Jake, the free-flowing talk stopped.

"Come on, Laura. Spill."

Laura shrugged, reluctant. "We still haven't gone out," she muttered. "Not even for a drink or a hamburger or anything. Oh sure, I see him at the restaurant once in a while, and we talk on the phone occasionally—and he does still seem interested in me, always asking questions about me—but it never goes any further. Nothing comes of it. I'd made up my mind that— come hell or high water—Jake and I would have our first real date the weekend you were gone. I planned it all out, arranged everything."

Lindsey gave her a wry grin. "Why am I not surprised?"

"Yeah, well, it didn't work out. All he had to do was show up, but he never even returned my calls, so I never got to tell him about the fun plans I'd made for us."

"How many phone messages did you leave?"

"Uh ... One."

"One?" She shoved her friend's shoulder playfully. "Gee whiz, Laura. That's not enough. And I'll bet you just said something like, 'give me a call when you get in,' huh?"

Laura nodded. "Yeah, something like that. So? I didn't want to sound pushy."

She rolled her eyes. "Obviously, where Jake is concerned, you need to push. Even I know that. Hey, I'm still hungry. How about you? I'm craving Chinese food."

"You're bad, Lindsey. Brilliant, but bad."

Lindsey smiled. "Get ready to push, my friend."

Chapter Twenty-Nine

The doorbell didn't ring, but they knew someone stood on the doorstep because Wendell hobbled closer, listening. They heard a definite thump, followed by a voice mumbling something like, *Come on. I'm here. Open up.* They'd been expecting to see Jake, loaded down with their Chinese order—they'd even ordered enough for him to join them. Instead, when they opened the door, they saw an overweight woman in her late fifties.

The woman dropped the bag she'd held between her teeth. "Here's the sesame chicken and white rice. And here we've got the lettuce wraps, the veggie egg rolls, and the chef's special." Then she pulled out a basket from under her left arm and handed it to Laura. "That will be $31.27."

Lindsey handed her $35.

"How much was the basket?" asked Laura. "I don't think we ordered anything that comes in a basket."

"Oh, I didn't bring that. It was on your porch when I got here. I just picked it up so I wouldn't trip over it. Do you need change?"

They didn't need change; in fact, they added another dollar to her tip then hurried inside to check the contents of the basket. The purple cloth that lined the old woven basket also covered the items within, and they hesitated, unsure of whether they were more excited or wary.

"Wait," said Lindsey. "Let's try to guess."

"Okay, Ms. Kindergarten Teacher, I'll go along with that idea as long as we can eat while we think."

Lindsey gathered plates and glasses, a bottle of chardonnay, and utensils for Laura—Lindsey preferred to use chopsticks—then set up their feast on the coffee table in the living room.

By the time they were all ready to eat, Wendell, tired of waiting, stuck his head into the basket, revealing what appeared to be a flask and some small cakes or biscuits. Laura unscrewed the flask's top and sniffed.

"Smells like some kind of red wine."

Lindsey examined the food. "These are just little cakes without icing."

They didn't know what to make of this orphaned basket of goodies, and neither of them could make any kind of reasonable guess at who had left it. To be on the safe side, they decided not eat or drink any of the basket's contents, just in case a big, bad wolf was involved.

At midnight they turned the lights out with the intent of falling asleep. After all, the next morning was a school day. After about twenty minutes of lying on their backs, eyes wide open, Laura rolled over to face Lindsey.

"Are you still awake? You never finished telling me about the cowboy."

Lindsey chuckled. "That story is not going to help us get to sleep. Plus, it's kind of long," she replied. Regardless, she managed to tell a condensed version of the events surrounding Martin.

"Are you going to call him?"

"I haven't decided yet. Probably not."

At the end of her long, exhausting week, Lindsey slumped with relief. She sorely needed the weekend to recuperate from the conference, the traveling, the terror she had felt—whether real or imagined—and the havoc Bobby and Willy had caused, not to mention the trouble they were in. Her first course of action began with a soothing cup of chamomile tea along with a plate of cheese and crackers. Then she proceeded to write several To Do lists, hoping to prioritize and relax a bit.

Tonight's list would be short, Saturday's list would be long, and she'd keep Sunday open for now. First she would clean out her traveling bag, then organize her purse. After that, she would play with Malcolm and Wendell for a while. Then they would watch her complete the remaining simple but necessary tasks from her list: cleaning, laundry, and bill paying.

She reached into her purse and sudden flash of panic shot through her veins. Her driver's license wasn't in her wallet where it should have been. She flipped the purse upside down and dumped everything out.

"Oh no. This is not good," she muttered, relieved that at least she hadn't been pulled over by the police during the past couple of days. "This is not good at all."

'Find Driver's License' was added to the top of her Friday night list. She mentally retraced her steps all the way back from Rugby, and it didn't take long for her to remember the last time she'd actually seen her driver's license. Security had required her to present it with her boarding pass at the checkpoint in Bismarck before boarding her flight to Phoenix. She looked in her carry-on bag, wondering if she'd accidentally dropped it in there. It wasn't in any of the zippered pockets.

She put in a load of laundry, dusted the living room, and vacuumed, thinking all the time. The instant she flipped the power switch, Malcolm flew upstairs and Wendell followed slowly. Neither approved of the noisy task. Convinced she'd eliminated enough dust and dirt, she returned the loud monster to its place in the closet, and a realization hit her. Her winter jacket. She'd put her license in the pocket of her jacket as she boarded the plane.

"It's here!" she cried, grinning. "Hey, guys. I found it. My license is right here with ..." Along with the license, she pulled out the envelope Elisabeth had given her. She'd forgotten all about it. She added 'Make Bank Deposit' to Saturday's list, and then opened the envelope, curious to see the certificate for professional development hours. She wondered how many had been awarded for the conference.

She stared at the paper with surprise. They'd given her a generous forty-five PD hours along with ... "Oh my God!" she shrieked. The check wasn't for the expected $500—it was for $1,000. She whooped with delight, exciting the animals, who joined her in a little dance around the kitchen.

This check meant that Lindsey's looming financial woes—courtesy of Emmett's hurtful, criminal actions—would at least be taken care of for the next three months. She carefully attached the envelope to her refrigerator with a cactus magnet made by one of her former students, then noticed Martin's email and phone number written on the back.

Feeling upbeat and optimistic once again, she considered calling him. Going out to dinner would be fun, and she really needed an evening out. "I'll call him tomorrow," she told Malcolm, and he chirped his approval.

The dinner date was set for the following Wednesday evening. Martin had offered to pick her up, but Lindsey requested that he meet her at the Coyote Café instead, since she was making a conscious effort to play it safe where men were concerned. She'd chosen the location because it was close to her house, she knew several of the regulars, and Jake had worked Wednesday nights before, so there was a chance he would be there as well.

On her way in, Lindsey almost bumped into Jake.

"Hey, Lindsey! Good to see you! Are you finally taking a break from all your hard work? Come on over. The drinks are on me."

She smiled. "Thanks, Jake. I've missed you, too." For a moment Lindsey was tempted to ask if he'd been working at the Chinese Restaurant last Thursday and if so, why hadn't he made the delivery, but she didn't. "But actually, I'm meeting someone tonight."

"I haven't seen Laura yet."

"Oh, I'm not meeting Laura this time," she said, feeling awkward. "I'm meeting a gentleman."

Jake tilted his head at the man seated at the bar, and Lindsey nodded when she recognized Martin.

"Hey, there you are, looking as lovely as usual," Martin said, standing to help her onto the barstool.

"Hi, Martin. It's good to see you. What's it been? Nine, ten days?" she teased feeling comfortable around him already.

He chuckled. "The bartender has picked out a special table for us in the dining area."

"Really?" She shot Jake a questioning eye. "The bartender is giving us a special table? That's interesting."

Strangely, she was disappointed that Jake didn't appear to be the least bit jealous about her date with Martin. That was a ridiculous idea, though. Jake was more like a brother to her. Laura was to be Jake's love interest someday—maybe.

They had a good time, and when Martin asked if she would join him on Sunday to visit the Sonora Desert Museum, she didn't hesitate to say yes. In her mind she rationalized the outing easily: her class of kindergarteners was in the midst of rehearsing for their Desert Performance, so perhaps she would gather a few new ideas for the show. Besides, she felt at ease with Martin—though she'd still be cautious.

At the evening's conclusion, Martin walked Lindsey to her car. Once she sat safely in the driver's seat, he reached through the open car window and gently touched her cheek with his fingertips. His fingers slid through a few strands of her long, brown hair, hanging loose by her ear, and she shivered at the sensation. Then he said a simple, quiet goodnight and tipped his cowboy hat as he backed away ... leaving Lindsey speechless.

The students were grouped into four categories: the Kangaroo Rats, the Rattlesnakes, the Coyotes, and the Tortoises. The Kangaroo Rats were enthusiastically chanting, *I'm a Kangaroo Rat, a ratty, tat, tat!* when Sally, the office manager, entered the classroom carrying a large bouquet of flowers.

"We have a special delivery for Ms. Lindsey. Is there anyone here by that name?" she joked.

The kids were thrilled to help. "She's right there. That's her. That's Ms. Lindsey!" they shouted.

"Wow! Look at the flowers!" Emma cried. "So beautiful!"

"Thank you, Ms. Sally. You're right, Emma. They *are* beautiful. Did they just arrive?" Lindsey asked.

"About fifteen minutes ago," Sally replied, leaving the room. Then she poked her head back in to the classroom. "They were delivered by a driver from the Tucson Florist, so none of us knows who they're from. If you want to share that info later, we wouldn't mind."

The arrangement was gorgeous, lush with reddish-orange Indian Blanket flowers, Mexican Gold Poppies, pinkish-purple Desert Penstemons, and a few sprigs of white Arizona Rosewood and purple Desert Sage. Her stare slid toward the attached card.

Dear Lindsey,

Thank you for two incredible dates.

I hope we can have many more.

As it turns out, I will be in town next Saturday.

Let's get together.

Martin

Chapter Thirty

Despite Shawna's objections, Anthony returned to work the day after they landed in Tucson. He thanked Shawna's co-worker, Tara, for her help, then called Mrs. Madera, hoping she'd returned from her trip to Denver. Unfortunately, the call went unanswered. He'd get by—he had to.

No patients were scheduled for the next three days. He planned to spend the time going over the books, patient records, and files, things he hadn't taken the time to do before. Now, since Shawna was homebound due to her ankle injury, Anthony was able to focus on his practice, which was something he'd neglected for several months. Shawna had zero tolerance for pain, and he knew she would continue to ingest pain medication like jellybeans until every last twinge of pain vanished, meaning his time was his own. At least for the duration of her discomfort.

Anthony had paid little attention to bookkeeping in the past, primarily because he had Mrs. Madera. She was magnificent with money, people, and paperwork. But now, as he looked over the books, common sense told him something was very,

very wrong. He could find no evidence of any cash payments having been brought in the entire time he was away, and little evidence of checks arriving by mail or in person. He found only one deposit of $380 in checks sitting in the desk drawer. He called the bank to see what other deposits had been made during his absence, and discovered, to his dismay, that no money had gone in. There had to be an explanation. Clenching his fists, he paced across his office and grabbed the phone.

"Shawna, pick up. Pick up *now*!" he growled. "We've got to talk."

Of course, she didn't answer. Sleeping, probably. He'd try again in a little while. He continued to pace, fueled by a hot anger building deep inside him. He wasn't accustomed to being a victim, and he absolutely refused to be the victim of a thief. He suspected Shawna's friend, Tara, had something to do with the missing funds since she'd been the only one there. All he could do was hope and pray that Shawna was not involved.

Even the office plants had been ignored while he was gone. He headed into the bathroom to fill a watering can but was interrupted by someone pounded on the door. Curious, he poked his head around the corner.

"Mrs. Madera!" he cried, thrilled to see her. "Thank God you're back."

"What do you mean? I've been driving by here every day since I was told to stay away, and I—"

He frowned. "You weren't in Denver visiting your grandchildren?"

She set one hand on her hip, looking impatient. "Dr. Sommerfield, my grandchildren are in San Diego, and, no, I wasn't visiting them. I was worried sick about you. That woman told me you were taking an extended vacation and my services would not be needed for quite a while. I tried to call you the very next day, but no one answered your home phone, and the message machine never came on."

Anthony felt suddenly as thirsty as the plants. He licked his lips, but it didn't help. Since the facts about Mrs. Madera's whereabouts were a complete lie, he had to wonder about other fabrications. Suddenly, his thirst was not for liquid, but for knowledge.

He explained that he had been on a vacation—a surprise vacation—and that he had mistakenly assumed that she would be in the office holding down the fort. It wasn't until he'd confronted Shawna about the details that he'd learned a friend of hers was doing the "holding."

Mrs. Madera scowled with disapproval. "Well, there was a 'lady' in here," she confirmed, stressing the word as if it were difficult to say. "The first few days I knocked on the door, but she just pointed to the 'Closed' sign and went back to her desk—I mean *my* desk."

"Why didn't you use your key?"

Her expression softened with regret. "I don't have it anymore, Dr. Sommerfield. She took it from me when she told me you'd be gone and the office would be closed. I am so sorry. I should have done more. I knew something wasn't right, but I didn't know what to do. That's why I kept driving by, hoping to see you here."

"Mrs. Madera, the lady that took your key and told you to go ... was it Shawna?"

"Oh, no, Dr. Sommerfield. It was the same lady that came here every day. I assumed she was from a Temp Agency," she replied. She pulled a large envelope from her purse, looking slightly nervous. "I did do one thing, though. I hope you're not mad."

Anthony chuckled at her odd smile. "And what might that be?"

"Well, after that first week, I came by every day and intercepted the mail for you. That nice mail lady simply handed it over to me right out there by the curb, and here it is."

Anthony was relieved on two counts. First, more than likely, his only loss was several weeks' worth of cash payments. Second, bringing Tara on board could have been Shawna's only direct involvement.

Note to self: give Mrs. Madera a raise.

With renewed energy, they got right to work. Mrs. Madera looked over the books while Anthony contacted a locksmith—new security measures would be in place before the end of the day. Afterward, he would call Shawna again. If that failed, he'd go home to speak with her in person. He'd get to the bottom of this somehow.

But when he got home, all he came up with were more questions.

"Shawna?" Anthony called as he walked toward their bedroom.

He heard a faint voice responding from across the hall. "Here. I'm over here."

Confused, Anthony walked into the sparsely furnished spare bedroom and spotted her in the purple covered queen bed, her eyes hidden behind a sleep mask. She seemed barely able to speak.

"What's going on, Shawna? Why are you in here? How did you even *get* in here? Come to our bedroom if you need to sleep. I'll help you." He pulled back the comforter, preparing to help her hobble across the hall.

"I'm in so much pain. I can't stand to be up or moving around. I just didn't want to bother you. And … I didn't want you to see me like this."

Okay, he thought. That kind of made sense, knowing her flamboyant ways. But his level of shock quickly increased, seeing her in a pair of men's tailored pajamas. When he'd left earlier she'd been wearing a silky nightgown. The words, "Nice PJs, babe," slipped out before he could stop himself. But he couldn't understand how the pain could possibly have influenced her choice of sleepwear.

She finally agreed to move back to their bedroom. After tucking her in, he went to the kitchen to search for something for them to eat. With her inability to move about the house due to her physical suffering and her use of pain medication, he doubted she had eaten anything. A hint of guilt crept in when he admitted to himself that he shouldn't have left her alone for so long. He'd make it up to her, cater to her every need tonight. Obviously, this wasn't the time to confront her about his office situation. After her ankle repair surgery, she'd feel better. Then he could move forward and find answers to all of the lingering and gnawing questions. Then they could get back on the path of building a future together.

Chapter Thirty-One

An email reminder from Laura went out to Lindsey, Anne, the school psychologist, and Louise, the part-time social worker, with a CC to the principal. It read:

> *Thanks everyone for getting your reports and evals completed (in record time) for the two boys. METs a go for both next Thursday. Willy's mother at 2:00 and Bobby's mother and grandmother at 3:30. It will be a long afternoon. I'll bring treats. See you then.*

The team gathered around an oval table in the psychologist's office, leaving a space for Maggie Waters, Willy's mother. When she walked through the doorway, Lindsey got up, escorted her to the table, and introduced her to the others. She did her best to make the young mother feel comfortable, though these meetings were rarely comforting to parents. No parent likes to hear that their child has problems above and beyond the everyday difficulties life can bring.

The psychologist began. "Thank you Mrs. Waters for—"

"That's Miss Waters," she said defensively.

"I'm sorry. *Miss* Waters. Thank you for coming today. We have gathered information through specific testing, observations, and several checklists, and today we will share the interpretation of all that data with you. Please feel free to ask questions at any time during this meeting. Laura, why don't you begin with the academic achievement portion of the testing?"

Laura reiterated data from Willy's progress reports and kindergarten testing results including the DIBELS data. He fell into the "At High Risk" or "Falling Far Below" categories in every area of school academic performance. The mother agreed with that information, saying she wasn't surprised. Then she put the blame squarely on his teacher, Ms. Lindsey.

"He hates school," Miss Waters said with a shrug. "He doesn't even want to come. We begin every day arguing, because first he won't get up, then he won't eat, then he won't go out the door. Everything is a struggle. If you would make school more interesting and fun—get him to *like* school—we wouldn't have this problem."

Lindsey tried not to take this attack personally, but she couldn't help feeling defensive. She bit back her natural reaction. "I am sorry that you both go through such a difficult ritual every day. Of course we want Willy to like school. Most children love school, especially during the primary grades. I assure you, the students in my class have a joyful day every day. Tell me, Miss Waters—can I call you Maggie?" After receiving the hoped for nod of approval, Lindsey continued. "How does bedtime work at your house?"

Miss Waters rolled her eyes. "Oh, that's even worse. He won't brush his teeth, he won't wash his face, he won't even lie in his bed. I have to wait till he falls asleep on the couch or on the floor, then I pick him up and put him in his bed."

She dropped her head into her hands. "It's awful. *Everything* is awful," she said with frustration.

Moving on, the school psychologist explained the Stanford-Binet Intelligence Scale had been used to acquire a clearer picture of Willy's needs. "These assessments measure a child's intellectual strengths and weaknesses, and they also give information about their abilities as compared to other children of the same age. Other areas like processing speeds and working memory are measured, too. We have some good news in this area, Miss Waters. Willy's IQ score, though below the average range of scores, does fall into the Low Average range, with a score of 86," stated the psychologist.

Moving on to Behavioral/Emotional Ratings, all team members contributed data from their observations and checklists before the psychologist helped Maggie understand what the various T-scores represented, then she summed up the findings. Every team member gave specific examples where aggression, rule breaking, anxiety, or social skill deficits had adverse affects on Willy's educational performance. Maggie nodded throughout as her eyes welled up with tears.

Lindsey leaned over and gave her a tissue and a gentle hug. "We have a plan to help him. That's the last part of today's meeting. I think you will feel better after we put the plan into place," she said kindly.

"Willy qualified for Exceptional Education Services due to his Specific Learning Disability in Reading (SLD) as well as his Emotional Disability (ED)," Laura explained. "The team recommends that he remain in his current general education classroom with Lindsey for the rest of this school year, receiving pull-out services with me every day for forty-five minutes."

Miss Maggie Waters left the meeting with a stack of papers and a bewildered expression on her young face. It would take time to comprehend all she had heard today, and Lindsey certainly didn't envy her.

"Snack time," Laura announced.

The next meeting was due to start in twelve minutes, and everyone needed to regain strength before Bobby's meeting began. Lindsey brought bottled water for everyone, to add to Laura's cookies. But snack time went on a lot longer than planned because Bobby's mom and grandmother were now twenty minutes late. Lindsey called their house and received no answer. Maybe they were on their way. The team waited half hour before they agreed that the pair was going to be a "no show."

"That's odd," said Laura. "I just spoke to the grandmother this morning, and she said they would be here. Was Bobby at school today, Linds?"

"Oh, he was here all right, whining and fussing and complaining about everything from the floor being too hard to the lights being too bright. I couldn't get him to sit down or sit still all day. He had one of his worst days ever."

After a lengthy discussion concerning their dining options, Lindsey and Martin decided on a casual, western restaurant located in Old Town where the wait staff dressed as cowboys and cowgirls, and the bar employees appeared as saloon gals. It was a far cry from romantic, but the mood was festive and family-friendly, and Lindsey had been craving something upbeat and happy.

Martin ordered the largest steak on the menu for himself and the petite version for Lindsey. She hadn't had red meat in a long time, but now that she was here with Martin, she decided it was time for a change. The steak was delicious. At the first available respite from all the cutting, chewing, and drink sipping, she became aware of him reaching for her hand, but they were interrupted by a group of waiters singing a raucous version of Happy Birthday at the table directly behind them. Martin joined in, singing along and clapping at the end.

Their next opportunity to physically connect arrived when they were seated in a dark movie theater, watching previews. That's when he took her hand in his, brought it to his lips, and planted tender kisses on her palm.

His kisses left Lindsey surprised and a little confused. Just the week before, after their visit to the Sonora Desert Museum, he had kissed her for the first time, and she'd felt nothing—no, worse than nothing. They'd been standing just inside the doorway saying their goodbyes, and he'd brushed a gentle kiss across her forehead, then kissed the tip of her nose, and finally found her lips. She was ready. She wanted his mouth on hers. But it was like nothing she'd ever experienced before. It was like ... like ... kissing cardboard. This light touch on her palm was completely different. What had changed? Last week it had been cardboard, and this week tiny, hopeful tingles of heat sparked all through her body.

After the movie ended and the house lights went up, Martin walked her to her car, just as he'd done on their two previous dates. But tonight her car wouldn't start. He lifted the hood and stared at the engine as Lindsey turned the ignition key over and over. No luck. He hooked up the jumper cables in her trunk to the battery in his rental car. Nothing.

"Well, I suppose I'll have to drive you home."

She shrugged. "I guess you will," she agreed, not knowing what else to do. "It's not far. Just a couple of miles."

Other than Lindsey's directions, letting him know where to turn, they drove in silence. She couldn't stop wondering what he was thinking.

"Here we are," she said, getting ready to open the car door and jump out.

He held up a hand. "Hang on there. Don't think for a minute that I'll let you open that door when you're in a car with me, and then let you walk yourself to the front door of your home this late at night. That's my job, and you'd better let me do it," he said, and though he sounded as if he were teasing, she had a feeling he meant it.

She blushed. "Oh, I'm sorry. It's been so long since anyone did those things for me. Yes, please open my door ..." She hesitated. "Uh, make that doors. I would love that."

"Doors? Plural?"

"Uh-huh. Both doors: the car door and my front door. And agree to come in for a drink before you head back to your hotel," she said, letting her guard down. After all, what could happen with Wendell and Malcolm there as her ever-present—though sometimes annoying—chaperones?

"I should warn you," she said, "that a one hundred and sixty pound mastiff is right behind that door, waiting to greet us."

Martin frowned. "Does he bite?"

"Only if I tell him to," Lindsey said with a grin, knowing Wendell probably would never hurt a fly. "Mastiffs are very protective of their castles and their women, you know."

"I see," Martin replied. His eyes opened wide when she opened the door. Wendell stood in the middle of it, wagging his tail madly. "Whoa," he said. "He *is* big. I hope he likes me." He looked around appreciatively. "Your home is very attractive. I don't often compliment architecture and designs, but you've done a good job decorating this small space. It feels cozy but not cramped, light and airy, but not too girly."

"Thank you," she said, feeling somewhat proud. After all, he was an expert on these things. She placed two wine glasses and a bottle of merlot on the coffee table, and Martin poured. "Would you like a tour?"

"Absolutely."

She grinned. "It won't take very long. Bring your wine."

Lindsey led him through the kitchen and out to the backyard where her winter garden was winding down and her spring plants were just beginning to sprout. Even though it was too dark for him to take in the full effect of her garden, she could tell he was impressed. She turned on the lights in the downstairs bathroom, guest bedroom, and makeshift home office to offer a quick peek. Nothing too special there. She hadn't gotten around to adding the "Lindsey touch" to those rooms yet. She was excited to show off the master bedroom and bath, because she'd spent a fair amount of time, effort, and money creating a modern, eclectic, yet southwestern space. She was thankful she'd given the area a thorough scrub and polish after her slumber party with Laura. That might have been difficult to explain.

When they stepped into the room, Martin took Lindsey's wine glass from her and placed it on the nightstand along with his. He took both of her hands and kissed them just before he wrapped his arms around her, pulling her close enough that their bodies touched from top to bottom. With his fingers he pushed her hair back from her face and held it all in a ponytail behind her head exposing the usually hidden part of her neck. Then he bent down and placed a kiss there. Heading just a bit lower, and after a subtle movement of fabric, he kissed her shoulder.

Oh my God, thought Lindsey. *What am I doing?* She'd only known him for a few weeks, and his first and only kiss on her lips had been nothing. Nothing! No flames, no flutters. But now … was she simply just horny? Or was it something more? It had been over seven months since Anthony had left her, and it'd been slightly longer than that since the last time she'd had sex. Now that was all she could think about.

Martin held her face, gazed straight into her eyes with a faraway look, then kissed her forehead, her cheeks, her eyelids, and nibbled at her ears, distracting her from any additional thoughts. She quivered at the sweetness of his kisses, knowing she was lonely and horny, and knowing right then and there that she would give in. Martin knew it, too.

He lifted her easily, his strong arms curling around her as if she were weightless, and gently eased her onto the king-sized bed and began helping her out of her clothes, though he left her pretty blue silk bra and panties in place. Lindsey was relieved she wasn't wearing the plain, unmatching cotton underwear she usually had on. She sat up and helped unbutton his shirt, but he took charge of his pants. For one brief moment Lindsey silently giggled, thinking *this adds a whole new meaning to the phrase 'Cowboy up!'* In spite of his size—everything about Martin was large—his manner and technique were both arousing and soothing.

Their lovemaking was good. Nothing out of the ordinary, but good, nice. Nothing he did made Lindsey uncomfortable, and she appreciated that. Only one aspect of his lovemaking was new to her: he wore a condom. She appreciated that, too, but made a mental note to purchase some lubricant in case there was a next time. Afterward, her body melted against his, and—for now, at least—she felt safe and at peace. She drifted off to sleep in the strong arms of a good man.

When she opened her eyes, she was surprised to see that it was nine o'clock in the morning, and Martin was gone. He'd left a note on the pillow.

Dearest Lindsey,
Thank you for a great evening. You are an incredible woman in every way.
I'm taking care of your car. Hope you don't mind. It will be in your driveway by the time you need to drive to work Monday morning. Enjoy your Sunday at home. I will call you the next time I'm scheduled to be in Tucson. I have only one favor to ask. Do you think you might be able to call me "Marty" now?
- Marty

Lindsey was well aware of her limited experience with men, but even so, she knew Martin wasn't a typical date. It wasn't that he was complex—he wasn't—but he was different somehow. She spent the better part of Sunday trying to figure him out. He was good looking, he seemed intelligent, he had a very good career that included creativity—a definite plus in her mind— he helped his mother and brother, and he treated Lindsey as if she were special. She liked all of that. On paper he was perfect. She'd been comfortable with him in bed, though it had been their first time. That surprised her, even shocked her. But there had been no flames, no heat. Her heart didn't skip any beats.

"Maybe true love takes longer to blossom." she mused. After all, what did she have as a comparison? Her husband, who had run off and left her for a stripper? Emmett, who had used her, lied to her, and stolen money from her? Besides, she and Emmett had never made love. Maybe she wouldn't have felt anything with him, either. She'd give this relationship more time. Martin was so ... nice.

He was also true to his word. Her car was in the driveway when she looked out her window early Monday morning.

"What a good man," she repeated, smiling to herself as she loaded her book bags, purse, snacks for the students, and some props for their desert performance into the back seat. The car was so clean and shiny it practically glowed. It had not only been repaired, it had been washed, waxed, and vacuumed—the works. Then she saw a little something extra. On the passenger seat sat a box supporting a beautiful arrangement of red roses. The card read: *Please set these on your desk at school and think of me. Marty*.

"Oh, my," she said out loud. "I could get used to this."

Chapter Thirty-Two

As they did every morning, the children gathered around Lindsey on the rug, ready to talk. Everyone was present—with the exception of Bobby.

"Has anyone seen Bobby this morning?" Lindsey asked.

Most of the small heads shook, but two children said they thought they'd seen him right before the "going in" bell had rung. Lindsey pressed the intercom switch to speak with the office manager.

"Hi, Ms. Sally. This is Ms. Lindsey. Bobby did not come in, and several students are pretty sure they saw him on the playground. Can you have a monitor look around for him?"

"Will do, Ms. Lindsey. Oh, while we're talking, a giant-sized package arrived for you just a couple of minutes ago. Would you like someone to bring it down?"

Just as Lindsey began to ask Sally to hold it for her till lunch, the children—who had heard the whole conversation—chimed in with their enthusiastic responses.

"Yeah! A package for a giant. Cool!" said Armando excitedly.

"We want the package! We want the package!" chanted several students.

"It could go with our fairy tale," exclaimed Connie.

Harley's head turned from Connie to Lindsey. "Our fairy tale this week is about a giant?"

"Maybe, Harley. Could it be, Ms. Lindsey?" questioned Emma.

Lindsey sighed, smiling. "Okay. Bring it down whenever it is convenient to do so, Ms. Sally. Somehow we will turn the large box into a teachable moment."

Within ten minutes, Mary the monitor had dragged the box into the classroom. She also brought the news that Bobby was nowhere to be found. That was odd.

"Do you know if the office called his home?"

"Yes, Sally tried every phone number we had for his family. None of them were working."

Lindsey's gut told her something was very wrong. But it wasn't as if she could call Child Protective Services based on a funny feeling. Putting those worries on hold, she turned her attention to the other twenty-five students now gathered around the box and guessing its contents.

Marvin supplied the first guess. "I bet it's a flat screen TV."

"No," Emma decided. "It's too light."

Harley's eyes lit up. "Maybe it's filled with new crayons for everybody."

"No," said Emma, narrowing her eyes skeptically. "It's too quiet."

"I think it's a pillow and a blanket so Emma can go take a nap," Joseph said with a smirk.

That brought giggles. Emma turned toward him and put her hands on her hips, and Lindsey held her breath, waiting. "You know, Joseph, I think you might be half right."

With relief, Lindsey clapped her hands and called the troops to order. "Back to the rug everyone. It's time to introduce our fairy tale of the week. Then we will open the box." She had reservations about opening an unknown, unexpected package in front of the children, but she couldn't wait to see what was inside. She decided to try and take a peek before it was unveiled for the students to see.

The children were well versed in this procedure by now and eagerly participated in a discussion concerning the cover of the book.

"What do you notice about the cover?" Lindsey asked. This was always the open-ended first question.

"I see some bears and a little house," stated Harley beginning the conversation.

"A burglar is sneakin' in the door, and the stupid bears don't even see her," mumbled Willy, sounding as if his mouth was full of marbles. It wasn't marbles, though. His words were blocked by a wad of gum large enough to choke him.

"Willy, please wrap that gum in a paper towel and throw it in the trash can under the sink. Marvin, would you please go with him?" asked Lindsey, knowing Willy was more apt to follow directions when there was a witness.

As she'd hoped, Willy followed the directions. Of course, he also added several steps to the process with which Marvin, willingly, participated. But when something lunged at them from the spot under the sink where the trash can should have been, they both screamed. Lindsey was by their sides in seconds, and the rest of the class followed.

"Bobby!" Lindsey cried. "What were you doing in there? Are you all right?"

The little boy wouldn't answer—at least not with words. Staying on hands and knees, he grunted and growled, then crawled around the back of the room. The children watched, making hushed comments or just staring with shock.

"Is that really Bobby?" wondered Connie.

"What's he doing?" Armando asked.

Willy crossed his arms. "What a dumb-ass!" he declared.

"Shut up, Willy," shouted Joseph, seeming to notice there was a real problem going on.

Harley edged toward Lindsey and pressed against her side. "What's wrong with Bobby?" he asked quietly.

Lindsey called Laura, asking her to stop by as soon as possible to help with Bobby. As she and the rest of the children went back to the rug area to wrap up the book cover introduction, he seemed to settle down a little. But something had definitely changed; he was different today. She decided to give him some space, but she'd also keep a constant eye on him.

"Ms. Lindsey! Ms. Lindsey!" several of the children cried, bringing her back to the moment. "The box. You said we could open it after the fairy tale!"

"Thanks for reminding me," she lied sweetly. She'd actually hoped they would forget. No such luck.

They dragged the box to the rug area, and the students sat in a big circle around it—everyone except Bobby. He hung back at the opposite end of the classroom, but his eyes kept moving in the box's direction. Good. Maybe his curiosity would take his mind off whatever was bothering him.

As soon as Lindsey opened one end of the box, she knew—with some relief—exactly what it was. She tugged at the object while four students pulled the box away.

"It's huge!"

"What is it?"

"It's a bed for a dog, silly."

"A giant dog!"

She beamed at them in turn. "You are all correct. It is a dog bed. A very large—yes, even giant—dog bed. My dog Wendell will fit perfectly in this bed!" she said. "Turn to the person next to you and have a discussion about your dog or other pet, or a pet you'd like to have." They did as they were told, giving her a few seconds to read the attached card.

Dear Lindsey,
I hope Wendell enjoys the bed. I thought he could use a little extra comfort while he recuperates from his injuries.
As ever, Marty

A lump rose in her throat. *Such a considerate man,* she thought. He took care of everything. Wendell's old bed was indeed on its last legs, and this new, memory foam bed was better quality than the bed she slept in herself. Martin was such a 'take-charge' kind of man, and she liked that about him. *What's next?* she wondered.

"What's the matter, Ms. Lindsey? You look sad," Joseph said.

"Actually," she said softly, "I am very, very happy."

She asked all the kindergarteners to get their Art Journals from their cubbies then find a seat. She guided them through drawing the giant dog bed and asked each one to draw something or someone in their dog bed. Even Bobby joined in this activity. In fact, he seemed to be highly engaged, even though he could not sit still. He wiggled and jiggled, but he kept on working. Lindsey smiled, observing him. Miraculously, his *terrible, horrible, very bad day* had taken a positive turn. So when Bobby asked if he could lie down on the dog bed when math time arrived, she let him.

Twenty minutes passed, and Bobby still hadn't gotten out of the dog bed. Upon closer examination, she saw that he was asleep. He looked very peaceful—until he began to thrash around in his sleep, clawing at the air and making growling noises. She woke him and insisted that he get out of the bed and sit in a chair. Within seconds, he was back to his typical grumpy, angry, troubled self.

Laura popped in during lunch break, and Lindsey was quick to ask where she'd been when she had needed her.

"In the middle of testing. Can't stop in the middle, you know that. What's up?"

Lindsey ran through the events of the morning as Laura sat wide-eyed, listening intently.

"Your new boyfriend bought Wendell a bed? Wow. He sounds like a keeper. And I suppose that's it over there?" she asked, standing to get a closer look. "What's the red stuff on it?"

"Red stuff?" she frowned, following Laura. "There's nothing red on it. It's solid tan to match Wendell's fur."

"Well, there is now. And I think it might be blood. Did one of your darlings have a bloody nose today? Crusty boogers, maybe?"

Lindsey felt a little ill when she remembered back to the sleeping child. Blood? "No, but Bobby slept in it."

"I'm not even going to ask you how you let that happen. Did you see his journal work? What did he draw? Did he write anything?"

"I haven't had a chance to look yet. We just finished math and the kids went to lunch."

The two women stared in horror at Bobby's journal. He had drawn a boy—probably himself—curled up in a dog bed. Exaggerated tears fell from his eyes, and small sticks poked out from his back and hips. He had scribbled red over the drawing of himself, made the dog bed blue, and the rest of the picture was pure black. The only words he attempted to write were, *BAD DOG BAD DOG BAD DOG.*

"Maybe he used U of A Wildcat colors. You know, red and blue," Lindsey tried, looking desperately for a bright side.

But her friend's expression was anything but encouraging. "Uh … I don't think so. I think we'd better go find him and take him to the nurse. I'm pretty sure you'll be making that CPS call today."

Bobby looked very little, sitting on the cot in the nurse's office. Laura and Lindsey managed to escort him from the cafeteria without incident—at least without anything major. A few kicks to the wall and a spattering of bad words were nothing unusual for Bobby.

"What's everybody starin' at?" he asked the three women. "Am I sick? Do I have to go home?"

"Probably not, Bobby," Lindsey said, her voice gentle. "But after you had your nap on the dog bed, we found some blood on it. We just want to make sure you are okay."

"That's right, Bobby," Lucy, the health assistant added. "Do you have any cuts, bumps, or bruises you could show us?"

"No," said Bobby, then yanked the bottom of his T-shirt tightly over his hips.

Lindsey could see panic building in the little boy's eyes. She had no choice. "We have to look, Bobby. It's our job to check students and make sure they're all right. I won't even touch you. All you need to do is lift up your shirt."

Bobby had gone pale and was shaking his head wildly. "No! No!" he cried. "I can't let anyone see it. Nobody gets to see it but me and dad. If you see it, he'll make another word," he shouted hysterically, scooting under the cot.

Dad? Lindsey had never seen 'Dad,' and Bobby hadn't mentioned him since that one and only time last fall when he'd drawn a picture of his dad staying home with him because they were both sick. Thoughts of calling CPS had nagged at her since then. Was there really a dad in the home? Only the mom and the grandma—mostly grandma, actually—ever had any contact with the school. She made a mental note to recheck the boy's file and birth certificate as soon as her students left for the day.

Mrs. Wilson walked into the health office in time to see and hear enough to justify the next steps. "Well, ladies," she said quietly to the adults, "we are about to break the rules a tiny bit, but I don't see that we have a choice. Lindsey, you have the best relationship with this little boy, so you coax him out from under the cot. Laura, you have the most experience holding or restraining students, so once you can reach him, do your thing, and I will move his clothing just enough so we can see what needs to be done. Lucy, stand by for whatever may happen. Ready?" They all nodded.

Lindsey's heart raced with dread. "Here we go."

Bobby screamed and thrashed at first. Then he stood perfectly, eerily still, stiff as a statue, as if he were bracing himself so he wouldn't fall down. His eyes deadened, becoming glossy as he stared at the wall with a faraway, detached look. Mrs. Wilson lifted the front of his black T-shirt, but they saw nothing unusual there. But when they turned him around and pulled up the back of his shirt, Bobby crumpled to the floor.

The four women gasped in shock, and Lindsey's eyes filled with hot tears.

Words had been carved into the little boy's back; most of the cuts were scabbed over. They weren't deep cuts that would have required sutures, but they were deep enough that they bled, scabbed, scarred, and left bloody spots on a dog bed. Lindsey could only imagine the levels of pain Bobby had gone through, not to mention the fear, confusion, and humiliation he must feel now.

Mrs. Wilson took charge, speaking in a hushed, calm voice. "Call 9-1-1, Lucy. We need a police officer here ASAP." As she spoke, she moved more clothing aside, revealing the lower half of Bobby's body.

"Oh my God," Lindsey and Laura silently mouthed.

More words. The same words, really, but an alternate means of imprinting the words on soft, innocent skin had been used. The words BAD DOG carved into his back were horrific enough. Now they saw the words where they'd been burnt into the skin of his tiny bottom, probably with cigarettes. One side of his bottom said BAD, and the other said DOG.

So many aspects of Bobby's behavior suddenly made sense, and Lindsey's heart broke for the little boy. She had to wonder which was worse: the physical pain or the emotional pain. Both would stay with him for a very long time.

She guided Bobby gently toward her so that he stood by her, next to the cot. She placed loving and gentle hands on his waist. "Bobby, do you know what the words say?"

"Uh-huh. Bad dog," he whispered.

"Why do they say that?"

"'Cause I've been a bad dog all my life," he said, matter-of-fact. His voice had lost all trace of the grumpy, complaining child from her classroom. He was a completely different boy, and Lindsey wanted to gather this new, damaged child in her arms, comfort him. "That's why I sleep in a dog bed in the garage. Your dog has a way better bed than me. He's so lucky. I have my own dog dish, too."

Lindsey looked up at Laura, feeling physically sick with helplessness. She saw tears forming in the heath assistant's eyes just before the girl ran into the bathroom and vomited behind a closed door. Laura and Mrs. Wilson kept watch outside the health office door, waiting for a law enforcement officer to arrive, and Lindsey held Bobby close. He never even cried.

Chapter Thirty-Three

Jake sat with his laptop on his lap and a cup of tea by his side, poised and ready to work. The problem was that not even one intelligent thought or idea came to mind. He needed more information from some of his subjects, since he couldn't squeeze anything more from the data he currently had. He decided to call Shawna.

A man answered her phone, which threw him for a moment. No one but Shawna ever answered there.

"Uh … Hi. This is Jake from—"

"Jake? Hey, I was just thinking about you." Jake recognized Anthony's voice. "You must be psychic."

"I don't think—"

"Hey, man," Anthony interrupted. "I need a favor. Can you deliver some food over here for Shawna? She hasn't been eating well since her fall, and now that she's had the ankle surgery, she's eating even less. Too hard for her to get around, let alone make it to the kitchen. But I'm sure she'd love to have some of her favorite Chinese dishes. And I'd feel a lot less guilty about going to work if I knew you were coming by with food for her.

The thing is, I've got to go. I'm already running late. I can settle up with you later. What do you say?"

Jake couldn't believe his good fortune. Anthony was actually begging him to stop by and see Shawna. Perfect.

"I'll be there by eleven with some of her favorites," Jake promised.

"Fantastic! I'll leave the front door unlocked. She won't be able to get up to answer the door, so just go on in. She'll be so surprised and glad to see you. This will make her day. Uh, but be prepared for a shock, though. She's not her usual self right now, Jake, probably due to the trauma of the fall, the ankle surgery, and the pain meds." He chuckled weakly. "Boy, does she love her pain meds. Thanks, man. I owe you one hell of a tip."

As promised, Jake brought over the food, then slowly, carefully, and quietly—he didn't want to startle Shawna—opened the front door. The situation felt odd, but then ... all of his encounters revolving around Shawna existed outside the boundaries of "ordinary."

"Shawna? Are you here?" Jake asked quietly. He got no reply, so he asked again, a little louder this time, as he walked further into the living room area. "Shawna, it's Jake."

Still no reply. If she felt as bad as Anthony had indicated, she was probably in bed, her sleep aided by a strong dose of pain medication. Jake very quietly made his way down the hallway toward the master bedroom with Chinese food in one hand and his laptop in the other. As soon as he entered the hallway, he heard a voice—or was it voices? Shawna was apparently not alone, and that thought made Jake's skin prickle. He stopped outside the bedroom, wanting to hear what Shawna was saying. Her voice sounded calm, almost sad.

"Sean," she said, "we've been on a long and painful path together. I've loved you, and I've hated you. But today's a big day for both of us. My life will soon be perfect, but yours is about to end. You will no longer exist. I will never see you again or even think about you after today. No one will."

Jake stood frozen outside the bedroom door. *What have I just walked in on?* From what he could hear, Shawna was threatening someone's life. Who the hell was Sean? He hesitated, remembering back to the day he'd snooped around the house. Hadn't he come across some letters addressed to a 'Sean' that day? He seemed to recall ... But why wasn't Sean saying anything? Did she have him tied up and gagged? Jake glanced behind, tempted to run and call 9-1-1. That would be the intelligent thing to do. But someone's life might be in jeopardy at this moment. He needed to help ... he *had* to help, didn't he?

He touched the door with his toe, opening it just enough to catch a glimpse of the setting—except he caught more than a glimpse. Shawna stood across the room from Jake, her hair pulled back into a tight ponytail. She was completely naked other than the bandage on her ankle, and she was staring at herself in a full-length mirror. Jake stared, too. It was impossible not to.

There was no evidence of anyone else being in the room, but that didn't mean anything. The room was dark and large. He should go, Jake realized, his eyes glued on the scene. His hands were slick with nervous sweat, and he made the sensible decision to run out of the house and call her from his cell phone once he was out of sight. But as he turned to go, the laptop slipped from his hand, and he instinctively lunged for it. His forehead slammed against the wrought iron door knob, and he couldn't stop himself from cursing.

She turned instantly from the mirror toward the startling sounds. He watched her fall to the floor, trying to hide from the eyes of her unexpected visitor. Her expression was one of absolute terror, and now that she lacked the advantage of expertly applied make-up, she didn't look anything like the gorgeous, sexy Shawna he was used to.

After a breathless second, Shawna screamed.

Jake dropped the bag of food outside the bedroom's entrance and grabbed his laptop. All he wanted was to run, but he had to say something. Anything.

"Jesus, Shawna," he said, at a loss. Then reality rushed in. "What about Anthony?"

Shawna's expression changed instantly from terror to rage, and Jake ran, going as fast as he could until he was safely in his car, driving away from … what?

What the hell was he running away from?

A few days past before Jake received the inevitable phone call from Shawna. At first his finger didn't want to move across the phone's screen, but curiosity got the best of him.

"Hello, Shawna."

"What did you see, Jake?" she demanded right off. "Be honest with me. Exactly what did you see?"

Jake, still in shock from the events of his visit, took a deep breath. "Everything, Shawna. Come on. You were naked. I saw everything. I am sorry. None of that was supposed to happen. Look, I was only there because Anthony sent me. He asked me to—"

"That bastard!" she blurted. "And I thought he was on my side. I thought he understood me. Now I suppose you're going to go and tell his little princess all about it."

Before Jake had a chance to explain Anthony's concerns about Shawna's need for nourishment, she emitted an ear-splitting noise that sounded like a cross between a growl and a scream, and then hung up.

Except for one interview with the police regarding what she knew of Bobby and his family, the following week went by without incident. Nothing unusual happened either at school or on the home front. Martin had been unable to make a trip to Tucson, but he had emailed several times.

Lindsey used the week to catch up on her housecleaning, her lesson planning, and her sleep. She met Laura for coffee on Saturday—something neither of them had been able to make time for in several weeks. She even went to the mall one evening and bought two new outfits—one for school, and one just right for another outdoor, daytime date with Martin. Life was good.

On Sunday evening, Martin called. "How's my beautiful kindergarten baby?" he asked, the smile in his voice obvious.

"Hi," she replied, smiling back. "I'm fine, and I'm glad you called. I was missing you a little bit."

"Only a little? I'd better step up my courting techniques. Must be losing my touch." They both laughed, and Lindsey felt a familiar warmth rush through her. Being with him made her happy. Maybe not thrilled, but happy nonetheless. "Anyway, the reason I'm calling is that I have some news. It's sort of one of those good news/bad news deals."

"Do I need to sit down?"

He chuckled. "Nothing like that. I have an all day meeting in Tucson this coming Wednesday, but I have an early morning meeting in Flagstaff on Thursday."

Lindsey frowned. "Is that the good news or the bad news?"

"I guess it's kind of both. With my time constraints, I need to fly, not drive, so I will only have about two hours that I can spend with you. Are you willing to go on a mini-date? There's something we need to talk about."

"I'm willing to do better than that," she replied. "I'll come home right after school and begin preparing our dinner. All you have to do is take a taxi from your meeting to my place. When we're done with dinner—and whatever else there's time for—I will drive you to the airport. What do you say?"

"I say I'm the luckiest man in the world. See you Wednesday."

Lindsey had to smile. That was bad news? He obviously didn't know the meaning of bad news. Then she remembered something he'd said and stopped smiling. What did he want to talk about? It sounded important. Was he getting too serious, too fast? What if he wanted to talk about moving in with her? Or …? She liked him a lot, he treated her well, and she always felt safe with him. Plus, he had a real career and seemed to have his finances in order. He was perfect … almost. The only thing holding her back was the physical side. His lovemaking was just … nice. Nice? It seemed to her that it should be far more than nice. If he was going to talk about a serious commitment, how could she turn him down and still keep the relationship going?

It was too much to think about, and she was happy to let herself become distracted when Malcolm popped over for a chat.

Wednesday was busy and exhausting, but that was typical. Lindsey was used to the mental and physical rigors of being with twenty-six young children most of the day. What she wasn't used to was rushing home to create an impressive feast in record time for a man she had decided she wanted to impress.

She'd almost made it out the door to the staff parking lot when an announcement came over the schoolwide PA system.

"Certified Teachers." Mrs. Wilson's voice echoed through the hallway. "ALL certified teachers please meet me in the library as soon as possible."

"Damn," whispered Lindsey. She turned around and headed for the library, hoping whatever this was would be quick.

So much for impressing him with a home cooked feast, Lindsey thought as she drove home a little too fast. On the seat beside her sat a bag of salad and two bottles of Merlot. The pizza would arrive in about fifteen minutes. Hopefully, by the time Martin showed up, she'd have the table set, the salad tossed, the wine breathing, and the pizza warming in the oven. Unfortunately, when she pulled into the driveway, her tall cowboy was already there, crouching by the front door.

"Hi!" she said, hopping out of her car. "Sorry. I was delayed due to an emergency meeting at school."

"Not a problem," he said, walking toward her. She started to loosen her ponytail, but he stopped her. "Your hair looks pretty like that. You should wear it back more often. Here. Let me help with those bags." He put out his hands. "I was a little earlier than I anticipated, but it gave Wendell and me a chance to become better friends ... through the door."

She laughed. "He's a good listener. I will give him that."

After dinner, Martin smiled at her across the table. "We've got almost an hour before we have to head for the airport. I could help you clean up the kitchen."

"Or you could take me upstairs and make mad, passionate love to me," Lindsey suggested, surprising even herself.

He grinned and took her hand. "Well, if you insist. I suppose that's an option. What guy in his right mind would turn down an offer like that?"

Their lovemaking this time was unusually lust-filled and urgent. Every move, every caress intensified the passion. Tonight nothing was slow or gentle. The heat was on and turned up high. There were no words of love, because both of them were too breathless to speak. Lindsey was thrilled with the change.

Their intimate hour flew by far too quickly, and Lindsey, now a bit tousled and tired, found herself at the airport, saying goodbye. There was little time for words, since Martin's flight was already boarding when they arrived at the gate. Lindsey kept waiting for him to drop the bomb, have "the talk." Was he going to propose? Or did he want them to move in together? She knew it was too soon, but their recent time in bed had been headed in a positive direction. Even the kissing had improved … a little.

"Lindsey, I don't know where to start," he said, gripping her hands. "There is so much I want to tell you. Maybe I should call you when I get home."

She gave him a coy look. "Nothing doing, Mr. Mackelroy. I don't need details tonight. Just the summary in twenty-five words or less," she suggested.

He shrugged, but his brow was drawn with concern. "All right. If you're sure … Well, the thing is, I'm a one-woman kind of guy—"

"I thought that might be the case. That is a good trait, Martin. A very good trait," she assured him.

"And I think you are terrific."

"You're not so bad yourself," she replied.

"In fact, you're probably the nicest woman I have ever known—beside my mother. It's just that—"

Lindsey shrugged off the mother comment, though it certainly seemed strange, considering what they'd been doing an hour earlier. "And you are the nicest man I've ever known," she told him. "You are considerate and thoughtful and helpful," she said.

"Yeah, well …" He bit his lip, looking more concerned than ever. He reached over and tucked her hair behind her ears, stared at her intensely, then shook his head. "The thing is, I really like you, and I've tried to make an exception this time, make it work with us—"

"Last call for boarding Flight 275 to Phoenix. Last call."

Lindsey leaned closer, not wanting to miss what he was saying. His words weren't making sense.

"Lindsey, baby, I'm sorry. The truth is, I really prefer blondes. I always have. My woman has to be a blonde."

She stared at him, momentarily speechless. She snapped her mouth shut and swallowed. "You're kidding, right? This is some kind of joke?"

He squeezed her hands. "It's been great but I gotta go. I am so, so sorry."

"Wha—" Lindsey's vision started to get dark around the edges. He had to be joking, didn't he? For a split second she considered coloring her hair. "But I'll call you 'Marty,'" she cried, her voice cracking. Tears welling in her eyes and rolled down her cheeks. "Marty?"

But he didn't even look back as he walked toward his plane.

Lindsey collapsed onto a chair in the waiting area and dropped her head into her hands, not caring if anyone noticed. *What is wrong with me?* She had really misjudged him, been so convinced … just like she had been with Anthony and Emmett. This time she thought she'd been using her head, moving cautiously, weighing the pros and cons. Apparently, not cautiously enough. Dumped by three men in a row, in less than a year. *Three strikes and I am out. I'm done. No more men!*

She drove home, obsessively replaying Martin's words in her head. Had she really just been left at the gate—though that was better than at the altar, she supposed—all because of her hair color? Her hand went to her hair, and she closed her fingers over the long, dark strands, not wanting to follow the memories. Because the truth was that this wasn't the first time she'd been left alone … but back then her hair had played a much different role. Back then her hair had been a life preserver.

The sobbing started up again as her unwanted, half-forgotten memories came flooding back, and she pulled over, parking safely on the side of the road.

It had been at one of her foster homes. They hadn't been bad people; no actual harm had come to her. But they hadn't been really good people, either. They were careless, party people who locked her in her bedroom every week for two or three nights, saying it was "for her own safety." The door slammed behind them, leaving her alone and in the dark.

Little Lindsey had gazed out that second story window, watching and waiting, just like Rapunzel. Waiting for what? A miracle? A savior? A prince? Alone in her little room she began to play the role she'd given herself, and she found some joy emulating the fairy tale princess. She began to let her own hair grow, and by putting herself in her own make-believe world, Lindsey was better able to endure the fear of being locked up and left alone. When her foster parents returned home, drunk and fighting, she attempted to block out their horrible yelling by placing her hands tightly over her ears and chanting repeatedly, *I am Rapunzel, and I do not swear. I am Rapunzel with long, brown hair.* By morning her door would be unlocked, and the adults were going about their day as if nothing had happened.

I am the adult now, thought Lindsey, sucking back her cries. *I should have more control over my life.* And yet ... what had she done wrong this time? No, she hadn't loved Martin, that was true. But she'd thought she might learn to love him. He'd started to grow on her. Still, it hurt. Once again she felt like a loser—an unwanted, undesirable, brunette loser.

Chapter Thirty-Four

The class had worked hard at putting together their desert performance, and tonight was the night. Lindsey's stomach was busy with butterflies. Working toward the show had been more than just a distraction from her miserable personal life; it had been a labor of love, overflowing with joy. She loved watching the students learn, then share their knowledge through drama and music, and she couldn't wait to see the response of all their loved ones.

Laura wandered backstage before the show, looking mischievous. "Guess who came with me to watch the evening performance?"

Lindsey narrowed her eyes and scowled at her friend. "I hope he—I'm assuming it is a 'he'—doesn't mind watching by himself. You, my friend, will be helping with the sound system and lighting."

Laura grinned smugly. "Jake won't mind."

She hadn't expected that. And she hadn't expected the sudden pang of disappointment that flared in her chest. "Jake? So you are finally going on a date with him? I was under the impression you'd kind of lost interest."

"Well, I don't know what he is calling this, but *I'm* calling it a first date." She shrugged. "Could be the last date, too. We'll see. When I ran into him, he asked what you were up to, and I told him about the desert show. He said he'd love to see it. That's probably all there is to it, really."

"How's it looking out there?"

"Come see for yourself. The word is out that you and your kids are terrific," Laura told her.

Lindsey chanced a peek from behind the curtain, past her friend. She could hear the audience in the multipurpose room talking and laughing together, but she didn't spot Jake right away. She kept scanning the room, noting with excitement that it was standing room only. Her eyes stopped when she found him by the wall on the north side of the room. Seeing him there made her smile. It had been too long since she'd seen him. She let her gaze move on, then froze.

Anthony?!

"It's almost show time," Laura said, gently jabbing Lindsey's ribs with her elbow. When Lindsey looked at her, Laura's perky expression wilted. "Hey, what gives? You look like you just saw a ghost."

"I ... did, I think. Anthony's here," she said in a hushed voice. "I saw him. Why would he be here? He never attended school functions before."

Laura squinted past her, and she almost looked away when she saw Anthony right up close. Then she jerked back, spotting another unexpected observer in the crowd. "Lindsey, is Emma still going to use your binoculars as a prop in one of the scenes?"

Lindsey nodded.

"Get them. Quick. Before we begin. I think ..." She hesitated, squinting hard, then turned back to Lindsey. "Oh my God. It's *her. She's* here."

"Who's here?"

"Shawna. Shawna, dressed to kill. See? She's standing in the back on the south side—and she's looking through binoculars of her own. And look! She's not even looking toward the stage. She's watching Anthony."

"Why would she do that? Why wouldn't they sit together?"

The house lights dimmed. The mystery would have to be investigated later.

"Showtime!" Laura said, then gave her friend a warm, encouraging hug.

The audience *ooh'd* and *aah'd* when the curtain pulled back, displaying the beautiful set the students had made. Desert scenes had been painted on paper then projected onto the backdrop, and several papier-mâché cacti decorated the stage.

The principal walked out and waited patiently for the audience to become quiet enough to hear her. "Ladies and gentleman, thank you for coming tonight. You're in for quite a treat, performed by your children and written and directed by our very own kindergarten teacher, Mrs. Lindsey Sommerfield—Ms. Lindsey, to her students. So, Ms. Lindsey, let's get on with the show!"

As the audience applauded, Lindsey took her position on the floor in front of the stage so she could direct the perfor mance without blocking anyone's view, and help any students who forgot what to do or say. With her back to the audience, Lindsey waited for most of her students to make eye contact with her. Once they were ready to begin, she was able to temporarily put the presence of Jake, Anthony, and Shawna on the back burner.

A few lines were forgotten and others were invented. Some of the students danced or moved in the wrong direction, but they kept dancing and smiling anyway, and no one in the audience seemed to notice the errors. If they did, it just didn't matter. When Willy improvised his dance moves with 'jazz hands' during *The Prickly Pear Blues*, he brought the house down with laughter and applause. He beamed with pride, and Lindsey mused that perhaps a star had just been born. Plus, now Lindsey had some new ideas for keeping him engaged in the classroom.

She was sorry Bobby had to miss this experience. She was sure she could have written a part for him that he would be able to do and enjoy doing, but that was not to be. She hadn't seen him since CPS had removed him from his home and moved him to an undisclosed location with the help of the local police. Such a sad situation. But at least he would be safe.

The show ended with the students singing a song about a group of coyotes who spent a week in the desert. When the kids came to the chorus—their favorite part—they let loose, acting like a bunch of coyotes howling at the moon, and the audience spontaneously joined in. A spectacular finish!

At the conclusion of the song, the students took a dramatic, unsynchronized bow, and Lindsey had Laura and the other parent volunteers come on stage to take their bows. They all began to clap and chant, *Ms. Lindsey! Ms. Lindsey! Ms. Lindsey!* And several of the little girls brought bouquets of flowers out from backstage to give to her. Then Lindsey spotted a beautiful, voluptuous woman from the audience bringing another bouquet forward, her exaggerated, hip-swiveling walk toward Lindsey demanded attention. All heads turned to watch, and the thundering applause faded to near silence. Lindsey stared at Shawna's approach, paralyzed.

Suddenly Jake was at Lindsey's side. Laura appeared at her other side, and both of them moved protectively as they escorted her away from the stage.

"Wave and smile. Wave and smile," instructed Jake, moving Lindsey out to the parking lot. "Lindsey, go with Laura and stay at her place until you hear from me. Don't even answer your door. Got it? Promise?"

Lindsey felt dizzy with confusion. After all the adrenaline and emotion brought on by the show, she felt overwhelmed by this new threat. "What's going on?"

"I'm not sure," Jake said, "but Shawna's been very, very odd lately. I don't trust her or anything she might do or say. She had no business being there tonight, let alone approaching the stage. I'm going back in, and I will take care of whatever comes up. Once you're home, stay put, okay? I'll let you know what's going on as soon as I know."

"If you need help," Laura said, "Anthony might still be there."

"*Anthony* was there? Damn. What the hell...?" he said before he dashed back inside.

"But the kids—" Lindsey started.

"—are all being collected by their parents. Everyone's too happy to have noticed anything. Let's just go."

Once they were inside Laura's house, the girls turned off all the lights and sat together in the living room, wondering what Jake would discover. To get their minds off Shawna, they went over the play, reliving the wonderful moments the children had created. The doorbell rang, and they froze. Neither said a word. Someone knocked on the door, then knocked louder.

Laura crept to the door. "Who is it?" she whispered.

"It's Jake. Look out your peep hole."

Laura flipped the lock and let Jake in, and all three moved back to the living room.

"I missed them both," Jake said. "It seems once you were gone, neither of them had any reason to stick around. I have a hunch that Anthony was there to talk to you, Lindsey, and Shawna was there to keep an eye on Anthony and cause a scene. I'm not sure what other motives she had, but like I said before, she's been acting very strange lately." He shook his head, looking confused, then smiled up at Lindsey. "On the lighter side, you'll be happy to know that all is well at school. By the time I left, only the night custodian was there. He wasn't sure what to do with the stuff on the stage, so I told him just to leave everything where it was. Hope that was okay. Oh…" He stood up again and went to grab something he'd forgotten outside the door. "Except for this. I almost forgot. He handed me more flowers for the famous writer-director. It was kind of funny. He said something like 'Make sure this gets to Snow White and Rose Red,' if that makes any sense."

Lindsey shrugged and took the unusual arrangement of red roses and sprigs of jasmine from him. "Not really, though he might have meant me and Laura. I do have a fairy tale reputation, and she's my best friend, and she does have reddish-colored hair. In the story *Snow White and Rose Red*, Snow White marries the prince, and her sister, Rose Red, marries his brother. Interesting, huh? Still, you're right. Considering who the comment came from, it was kind of … odd. Maybe somebody put him up to it."

She opened the attached card then almost dropped it. All the blood in her head raced to her feet.

"What's the matter, Linds?" asked Laura. "You went all pale."

Jake grabbed the card and read it out loud.

> *Breathe deeply now these jasmine blooms,*
> *For in their scent, great magic looms.*
> *I'm keeping the man all for myself.*
> *Stay away! Find your fate in the tale, The Rose Elf.*

"A poem. It's just a weird poem, right?" asked Jake.

"It's from Shawna, isn't it?" Lindsey said in a monotone. "But why? She's got everything."

Laura put an arm around her friend. "She apparently still sees you as some kind of barrier to what she wants."

"Didn't she want Anthony? She's got Anthony. I don't get it. What else have I got that she could possibly want?" Lindsey asked, then she reread the card. "Apparently, she knows her fairy tales. And—"

"The Rose Elf is a fairy tale?" Jake asked. "I never heard of that one. Snow White, Little Red Riding Hood, sure, but The Rose Elf?"

She nodded. "Yeah. Disney never did a version of that one, so it's not well known. It's a complicated tale by Hans Christian Andersen. The nutshell version: the leading lady's boyfriend is murdered, and she ends up dying herself from breathing in the scent of jasmine. It's a little dark. Not sure what the lesson is in that one."

"Geez," Jake said, scowling. "This is beyond strange. This is a threat. You can't go home alone tonight. And I need some time to check out a few things."

"Stay here with me, Lindsey," Laura begged.

"But it's a school night," Lindsey protested weakly

"Good grief, woman," Jake said, exasperated. "Can't you see you might be in real danger? Shawna is in a very weird place right now. You can't trust her. And I don't know what's up with Anthony, either. None of us knows why they showed up at the kindergarten performance, but I'm fairly sure they didn't come to see six-year-olds howling like coyotes." He frowned at the flowers. "Just, uh, don't smell the flowers."

Nothing more happened that night, or on any day in the days to follow, so life went on as usual. Lindsey kept planning and teaching right up to the end of school. When the last school day came to a close, and the last child hugged goodbye, Lindsey headed home for a quiet night on the patio. She was looking forward to taking advantage of the cool mister Anthony had installed a year before, sip a glass of chilled chardonnay, and enjoy the simple companionship of Malcolm and Wendell.

The desert night air was almost stifling, even though only a glimmer of pink and purple lingered in the thin gossamer layer of clouds on the horizon. Lindsey leaned back and sipped her wine, then reached down to rub Wendell's neck. Malcolm chirped quietly to himself.

"Well, guys," she said, interrupting Malcolm's song. "This has been one heck of a year." Wendell put his head on her knees, gazed up at her with loving dog eyes, and sighed deeply. "What would I do without you both? You're the best. And right now, I need to appreciate the good things in my life."

She began to make two mental lists: The Good Things in My Life and The Not-So-Good Things in My Life, but tonight, as much as she fought it, the Not-So-Good list was winning. So much for living the fairy tale and the happily ever after. Slightly discouraged, she began a To Do list for the next day. She'd start by dressing comfortably for the long day of packing up the classroom, then she'd pick up a latte and a café mocha for her and Laura. By four o'clock the packing would be complete and she'd treat Laura to a margarita, check on Malcolm and Wendell ... and, last but not least, pay a visit to the only man on earth she trusted.

Summer

Chapter Thirty-Five

Anthony sped home, constantly checking his rearview mirror for police. He was late and he knew Shawna would be pacing. They had only two hours to catch their flight to Colorado, and he still had to pack.

"Where have you been?" she bellowed from the bedroom the moment she heard him open the front door.

Anthony took some deep breaths to calm himself, needing his reply to be supportive rather than combative. He needed to be the rock—Shawna's strong, other half—as she faced her last cosmetic surgery, though he still didn't understand what that was all about. It made no sense to him that she needed any additional improvements; she was already drop-dead gorgeous. But she was adamant about having the surgery, and she was just as adamant that he be by her side.

It was essential that Anthony demonstrate an infinite amount of patience and selflessness today or their future together would be doomed. He knew his own difficulties needed to be placed on hold for now, since Shawna had no concept or understanding of the stress and responsibilities a chiropractor faced every day—let alone a chiropractor that had to leave his patients in the care of a competitor so he could once again go out of town.

"I'll be packed in five," he assured her. He peeked through the slightly open bathroom door and saw her standing naked at the mirror, applying a bit more foundation and lip color. *That's my babe*, he thought with a smile.

"Well, darling, *I'll* be ready in *four* minutes," she countered.

Anthony grabbed a few shirts and threw a few days worth of socks and underwear into a carry-on bag. Shawna's bag was right beside his on the bed, and a couple of photos poked out of one of the many compartments. Curiosity got the better of him, and he took a look.

He stared, not comprehending … then something inside him snapped. "What the hell is this?! Shawna! What the hell am I looking at?"

Shawna stepped into the bedroom, looking impatient. "What?" she snapped.

He whirled toward her, clutching the photos in one hand and shaking them near her face. This couldn't be happening. It *couldn't*. "These … these photos are of you … right?"

Shawna had gone very still beside him, and very pale.

In contrast, Anthony's face was a furious red. "How the hell … Damn! How did I not … How could you have deceived me all this time? How could you live such a fucking lie and suck me into it with you? How could I have been so fucking stupid? This can't be! *It just can't be*," he hissed through his teeth. He brought his face close to hers. "Tell me, Shawna. What the hell *are* you?"

Her voice was very small. "But … but I thought you knew. You know, after Venice and all. You said you were in the hospital and you saw the scars. Back then you promised to stay with me and said that you were okay with … everything," she said, her tone softening to desperation. "You love me, Anthony. You want me. You *know* you do. Everything will be fine soon. You'll see! Oh, Anthony. Please don't leave me—not now, when I'm just days away from perfection!"

He wanted to shake her, slap her, do something, but for the first time he couldn't bring himself to touch her. The thought of any type of contact between them made his skin crawl.

She reached for his arm, but he stepped back. Shawna swallowed hard again, then tried to give him a pleading smile. "Let's just catch our plane, darling. We'll work it out."

"Are you fucking *kidding* me? No way! No way in hell," he shouted. He grabbed his bag and several shirts, slacks, and jackets, thinking vaguely how good he was getting at packing and running. "I want no part of this. I can't even … Oh God. How *could* you? How could *I?*" Both hands went to his head and he grasped handfuls of his hair. "I'm living a nightmare—a fucking nightmare! Don't touch me. Don't even look at me. Oh my God. I … I hate you!"

He slammed the door behind him and threw his things in the car. *But I hate myself even more,* he thought as he roared down the street. *I've been an idiot on so many levels.* Deeply dazed but no longer confused, he knew exactly where he had to go now and what he had to do.

Jake stared blankly at the two files in front of him. It didn't matter how much he rationalized that any action he'd taken involving his subjects was "research," deep down, he knew better. The first extension for his thesis had expired, and time was running out on the second extension he'd been granted after some serious petitioning. It wasn't like him to miss deadlines. Never in his educational career had he felt this stressed about any project.

When the phone rang, Dr. Barston, head of his thesis committee, explained that because Jake had not followed the university's policies regarding the use of human subjects, he had put himself and the university at risk of legal action. Therefore, Jake would have to start the entire process over. Surprisingly, in spite of the time he had invested in this thesis, he felt an odd sense of relief. With the immediate pressure off, Jake's thoughts shifted to personal soul-searching. Now he had the opportunity to question his own motives with regard to the topic of his thesis. Why had he studied and researched 'women alone and how they coped'? Was it to help understand himself better? That wasn't exactly a *manly* thing to do, but it could be true. After all, he was alone, and he was trying to cope after his first love had dumped him back in Texas. In fact, it could be that he'd overreacted to his own break up, then used the thesis as therapy-by-his-own design—a psychologist's version of "Physician Heal Thyself." It was ironic, really. How had he managed to spend so much time and effort on his research without truly understanding what this endeavor was all about?

Maybe it was time to think about something other than himself, his losses, his mistakes, and his future. Needing a change of direction, he took another look at the files on the table. Actually, they weren't restricted to the table. His research was scattered around his apartment—on the table, on the futon, and in file boxes on the floor. The files were filled with notes, personal thoughts, and conclusions … many about Lindsey. Thesis or no thesis, he really cared about her—both her happiness and her safety. He decided to help her in any way possible, starting tonight. He'd see what he could find out about Anthony and Shawna and their odd appearance at

Lindsey's kindergarten concert. After that, he'd pay Lindsey, Malcolm, and Wendell a visit … and surprise her with a dinner of her favorite Chinese dishes.

He answered the phone without thinking, then wished he hadn't.

"Jake! You've got to come over right away. It's an emergency!"

"Shawna? Is that you? What's going on?"

"Just get over here now! I can't say much on the phone. Something terrible has happened. Hurry!"

I need to stay away from her, thought Jake, but at the same time, he wanted some answers, and this might be the perfect opportunity to get them. He dashed out the door with his notebook and camera, leaving his apartment a mess. He'd be back soon to clean it all up.

He was just about to press the bell when the door suddenly opened. Shawna stood before him, her eye make-up smeared down her cheeks. She'd obviously been crying a lot, which was out of character for her. Sucking in sobs, Shawna stepped back to let Jake in. Once he was inside, she hauled off and slugged Jake in the face with her clenched fist.

"You should've kept your mouth shut!" she roared as Jake fell to the floor.

Another school year had come to an end; another chapter in her life complete. Lindsey always enjoyed the feeling of closure and the sense of relief this time of year brought with it. Only one last entry lingered on today's To Do List: the visit. *I deserve a quiet evening with someone I really trust, someone who*

likes me for who I am, someone who has never judged me. She patted Wendell on the head and gave his ears a tickle, then she looked Malcolm directly in the eyes as they exchanged a few words and chirps. After they were done, she locked up and headed out her door feeling positive, refreshed, and ready for new beginnings.

She'd driven by his apartment building before with Laura, but they'd never been inside. When she reached his door she looked for a bell, but there wasn't one. She knocked softly at first and got no results, so she pounded on the door—which prompted the door to swing open.

"Jake?" she called. "Jake? Are you in here? It's me, Lindsey."

He didn't answer, so she decided to go in and make sure he was all right. After all, he would do the same for her. She walked into the apartment and had to fight the immediate urge to straighten up for him. She was surprised to see such a mess. Papers and files had been strewn everywhere. She sorted through the nearest pile, looking for a blank scrap of paper so she could write him a note, and out of the corner of her eye she spotted her name written on a file. When she looked again, she noticed her name was actually on several files, as well as on a spiral notebook on Jake's kitchen table.

She picked up the notebook, intrigued, and read until she could take no more. She lifted her gaze and stared straight ahead at nothing, unaware that she'd even dropped the book. How could he have … She shuddered inwardly at the idea of Jake— the only man she'd *thought* she could trust—writing about her this way. Why? Why had he written down her thoughts and choices, her problems, and her sorrows?

When she looked again, she noticed more folders—this time bearing Laura's name. She whimpered, feeling entirely betrayed. He'd been using them both all this time. How dare he? He'd used them, invaded their privacy, and written intimate thoughts and feelings down on paper—not to mention the data his laptop might contain—for the world to read some day.

He'd been the one man she'd trusted. Was there a decent man anywhere on earth? She sincerely doubted it.

"I'm done," she said out loud. "Done with them all."

When Lindsey didn't answer the door after much knocking and bell ringing, Anthony put his key in the lock and attempted to let himself in. It didn't work, which meant she'd changed the lock. *Good girl,* he thought. *She's getting smarter all the time.* How long had she waited to do that? He'd ask her sometime in the very near future.

After a moment of pacing by the front door, he decided to check the back door. He found Wendell asleep in a shady, not-too-hot corner of the back yard and felt immediately guilty. Wendell. He hadn't even thought about the dog in so long. Wendell rose to his feet, and at first he growled at Anthony. Then he moved toward him, his tail in full wag as if Anthony had never left.

"Hi, boy. I heard you'd been spending time over here now and then. That's good. Where's Lindsey?"

Wendell walked up to the back door with him, but none of his keys worked in that lock, either. He wasn't about to crawl through the doggie door; he was in no mood to stoop that low. That's when he noticed Malcolm in his cage by the kitchen window.

"When did she get that?" he asked the dog. He watched the bird for a while, and the bird watched him, tipping its head from side to side and chirping loudly. The little thing was *so Lindsey,* he thought with a hint of a smile.

He peered through the window, seeing the kitchen and the hallway from where he stood. The house looked different. There was no trace of him anywhere, no hint that he'd ever existed. One wall of the kitchen had recently been painted a bright yellow and adorned with new artwork of desert plants and herbs. He wondered vaguely what she'd done with the rest of the house. He smiled when he spied one thing that hadn't changed. Boxes filled with of end-of-the-year school materials were stacked in the hall, not yet unpacked or put away.

Where was she? *I need to talk to her now!* For the first time in his life, Anthony felt unsteady, out of control, and he didn't know how to react to being alone and afraid. He returned to his car and waited a nervous half hour for Lindsey to return, but she didn't. When he could wait no longer—patience had never been one of his virtues—he wrote Lindsey a note, placed it in an envelope, then wedged it between the front door and the door jam and drove away. He had no idea where to go.

"Hey, Lindsey," said Laura. "This is a nice surprise, seeing you again so soon. Come on in."

"I couldn't go home. It's all too weird, Laura. It is so *wrong*. What I saw was—"

"Slow down. Come on in and sit. I don't have the slightest idea what are you talking about."

Lindsey told her everything she'd stumbled upon at Jake's apartment, explaining that he had files—many files—which contained notes about both of them, including notes about conversations they'd had with him, and notes about their lives and their backgrounds—followed up by his own comments, judgments, and evaluations of their lives and how they'd lived them.

Laura dropped her head into her hands, looking annoyed with herself. "Good grief. How did I not see that? I *knew* he was writing his thesis about single women. He even told me a little bit about his research. That explains why he was always so attentive and such a great listener. So ... wow. I was one of his research subjects. How could I have been so naive?"

"Well, I feel betrayed. Aren't you angry?"

Laura tilted her head to one side, considering the question. "Oh, well, I'm not happy about it. As a woman, I feel like I've been used, but only in the 'research' aspect. He never led me on about having a relationship; we didn't have one. He just let me talk about myself, and he listened. And ... apparently, he wrote down everything I said."

Her reaction wasn't what Lindsey had expected at all. "You're taking this much better than I am," she told her friend. "I could scream. I want to scream and throw things ... and run away. I feel like such a fool."

"Lindsey, don't be so hard on yourself. You had the year from hell at school as well as on the home front, and your stress levels have taken you on a roller coaster ride. This was just the proverbial straw that broke the camel's back for you. It's totally understandable." She leaned in and gave Lindsey a quick hug. "You know, maybe the running away part would be a good idea. Get away from it all for a week or so. Didn't your doctor say something similar to you last week when you had your annual check-up? And look at you. You're practically hyperventilating just talking to me tonight. Hang on. I'll make us some tea."

Lindsey drooped, relieved to have everything out in the open. Talking with Laura always helped. "Okay. It's just that I feel so powerless. So many memories are marching through my head—like soldiers going off to war. Damn memories. Even the good ones hurt now, because all the good is gone."

A few minutes later, Laura returned with the tea. Lindsey flinched when she reached up to take it. "Ow!"

"What's wrong?" asked Laura.

"Oh, probably nothing. I think I must have gotten a few bug bites yesterday or the day before. Sometimes when my belt or waistband rubs against them, it's uncomfortable. I'll put some ointment on them when I get home." She held Laura's hand. "Listen, I'm sorry to bother you about Jake. I just didn't know where else to go. I feel like I'm really losing it lately. I can't even think straight anymore. You're right. I've got to get far away from everyone and everything. Thanks again, Laura. You truly are a dear friend."

"You should head out of town. Go somewhere completely different. Remember the Zuni Mountains trip we went on with the teacher group? That'd be a perfect place to get away from it all. I don't know. Up to you. Just think about it and call me in a day or two, okay?" Laura said, watching nervously as Lindsey opened the front door and stepped outside. "Promise me. Check in with me, and let me know what you decide to do."

Within the next couple of days, Lindsey's small Saturn was packed and her map to the Zuni Mountains unfolded in the passenger seat. The trunk carried most of her camping equipment, including tent, cooking utensils, sleeping bag, blankets, and pet supplies. Her clothes, some of the food, and a small cooler filled the front seat and floor areas. She purposefully kept the backseat clear, open for Wendell and Malcolm. Even then, Wendell was a little cramped, but he seemed happy to be included in the adventure.

"Ready?" she asked, and they were off—one large dog, one small bird, and one very determined young woman—to a remote wilderness area in the Zuni Mountains, seven hours away. Their mission was to relax, rejuvenate, and start fresh. This trip was the beginning of the rest of Lindsey's life—a new life in which she would be smart, plan carefully, think things through before acting, and focus on the good in even the most negative of situations.

Early June in the canyon brought hot and dry weather, and though the river still flowed, much of the vegetation looked brown and crunchy. Even the saguaros appeared a bit shriveled, in need of the monsoon rain that was still at least four weeks away. The rock formations she passed were diverse, changing from white boulders on either side of the roadway to steep, red-ribboned cliffs as far as the eye could see. At one point she almost wished she could be a passenger so she could better admire the natural beauty all around her, but she was forced to focus on the road, following one sharp curve after another. Once in awhile she indulged, though, and it was during one of these moments of appreciation of the canyon's beauty that the commotion began.

Malcolm's birdcage had a seatbelt around it, but the last series of curves caused it to slip and loosen, setting the cage free from its hold. It rolled noisily from one side of the back seat to the other, and the battered bird squawked from inside of it. The dog yelped, the cage clanked, and Lindsey tried to be reassuring while still keeping her hands on the wheel and her eyes on the road.

"Hang in there, guys," she said, frowning at the road. "I'll pull over just as soon as I can. You'll be fine."

But the curves kept coming, and the birdcage rolled, slamming into Wendell, then into the door. The cage door jammed against the car's door handle, pushing it up and open, and freeing Malcolm from his noisy confinement. Terrified and agitated from the experience, he flapped from the front of the car to the back, looking for a way out, until he finally landed on Lindsey's head. Unfortunately, he quickly became entangled in her hair.

"I've got to stop," Lindsey said, trying to keep her voice calm. "Got to stop now."

As Malcolm pranced on her head, she brushed the hair from her eyes, but she couldn't see any place where she could pull over. The highway along this stretch of the canyon had only two lanes and little visibility for passing. But she obviously couldn't go on; driving under these conditions was too dangerous. Then she saw a runaway truck ramp, and she swerved onto it. That was better than nothing—as long as no runaway trucks came barreling down the hill. She figured the odds were in her favor. The car rolled to a stop, and Malcolm hopped off Lindsey's head. She turned to the animals, taking in their ruffled state.

"You poor things," she said, giving them each a gentle pat on the head. "That must have been very scary for you. I know it was for me. Let's get you all set up again. I promise we'll take a real rest at the next safe parking place." After securing Malcolm's cage by weaving one end of the seatbelt through the bars of the cage, they drove off in search of a rest stop where she could walk Wendell and give them each a cool drink and a snack.

Chapter Thirty-Six

About twenty miles east of the Zuni pueblo, Lindsey began to look for the dirt road that would lead them into the Cibola National Forest, where wilderness camping was allowed. She doubted she'd find the exact spot where she and Laura had camped for a week with a group of teachers on the summer after her first year of teaching, but that didn't matter. Anywhere would do.

"There it is—at least I think that's it. All right guys, our camping adventure is about to begin."

She turned off the highway and onto the narrow dirt road. The first several miles were bumpy, but not bad. Then the road's condition became far worse than she remembered. The dirt road deteriorated until it was little more than ruts. Brush and branches scratched the sides and bottom of her car, and she had to grip the wheel tightly just to keep it from lurching out of her hands. Soon she was battling not only the ruts, the roots, and the branches in her low clearance vehicle, but also a much steeper incline. The car's wheels sputtered and spun on the dry, powdery dirt which, she soon learned, was easier to navigate than the few steep, slippery, muddy spots where she got stuck several times. Fortunately, she was too busy learning new and demanding driving skills on the spot to think about the ramifications of the car getting stuck in this steep, remote area.

Always the kindergarten teacher, she went into '*I think I can, I think I can, I think I can*' mode while Wendell and Malcolm went uncharacteristically silent. After almost thirty long minutes, the terrain leveled off and she came upon a perfect spot for the three of them to set up camp. When she opened the door, Wendell bounded from the car with pure joy. Malcolm began to squawk for attention and a little freedom of his own, but she shook her head.

"Sorry, buddy. I can't take the chance of losing you this far from home," she explained. But she did set the birdcage on a sturdy, level tree stump so he had a 360 degree view of Wendell, the trees, other birds, the bees ... Then she began the chore of setting up the tent—another task she'd never attempted by herself.

The four-man tent raising took longer that she'd anticipated, and by the time it was ready for occupancy the sun had slipped below the horizon. Lindsey was completely exhausted. There would be no cozy campfire or cooking tonight. She fed Wendell his food and she ate a granola bar, then brought nothing but water into the tent. There were still some seeds in Malcolm's cage but she figured they were safe—she didn't think they would attract wild animals.

Wendell stretched out beside Lindsey's sleeping bag, and Malcolm sat quietly in his cage in the corner. A slight, unexpected, and soothing drizzle tapped on the top of the tent as the temperature steadily dropped. The air felt damp and fresh, which was a welcome change after the hot, dry day.

Lindsey lit her small, battery-operated lantern then stared at the envelope she'd brought with her from Tucson. She knew it was from Anthony.

"I can do this," she told her camping companions. "After all, what can he possibly have to say to me now? He cheated on me, moved out, then filed for a divorce, and not once did he show me the slightest consideration."

Their marriage had been over for a long time, she realized. Maybe the note was just letting her know that he wanted to stop by and pick up any remaining possessions. With a deep breath, she tucked her finger into the envelope, slit it open, and unfolded the plain white piece of paper inside.

Dear Lindsey,
I have been an idiot and a fool. And I've made so many mistakes. I realize now that you are the only one for me. I never should have left you. Call me at the office. Love, Anthony

She couldn't believe her eyes, so she read it out loud, needing to hear it. Was it some kind of a joke? Or could she be so tired that she was dreaming? All year she'd longed for him to come back to her. All year she'd pined for him and what they'd had together. But ...

Just what *had* they had together? That was debatable. If their relationship had been so good, if he'd truly loved her, he never would have had sex with that woman. Especially not in their house, in their bed.

Take him back? She snorted, trying not to laugh. Did he think she was that stupid? That desperate? She would never take him back, and she would never trust him again. There had been a time when she would have tried, but not now. She was stronger and smarter than before, and she deserved better. And how insensitive of him, telling her to 'call him at the office.' He still didn't get it. He had no idea how selfish he'd been. Not once had he attempted to be helpful as she struggled with being suddenly single and alone. No, she would not be calling him, and she would not be taking him back.

This revelation surprised Lindsey. She was rejecting Anthony—the love of her life—and it felt good. She drifted off to sleep wearing a confident smile and feeling somewhat at peace with herself and her world.

Malcolm was up with the sun, ready to start his day. The wild birds' songs were being sung from a pleasant distance, but Malcolm chirped and squawked incessantly within the confines of the tent.

"Well, good morning to you, too, Malcolm."

Lindsey stood slowly, rubbing the sleep from her eyes. She was achy and still wearing yesterday's clothes, which were neither soft nor made for sleeping. The durable fabric had rubbed against her sore bug bites all night long; she hadn't brought any ointment because she'd been so sure the sores would have been better today. Unfortunately, they were worse.

"Oh, well," she said with a sigh. She was determined to follow her personal pact of staying positive. "I'll just make some tea and a cold compress, and I will be fine."

She finished setting up camp, then she and Wendell went in search of kindling and wood for the fire. Since she couldn't carry much—and Wendell was no help when it came to carrying—they were back at the site every few minutes, stacking wood.

Lindsey munched on apples and walnuts, her lunch for the day, then sat in the sun on her beach chair with her brand new journal. Her plan was to write about what she saw, experienced, thought, or felt during this getaway, including everything for which she was thankful.

First Full Day of Camping in the Zuni Mountains
I can't believe I'm really here by myself. I never would have done this any other time in my life. Why did I do it now? Lots of reasons. Some I'm proud of, some I'm not proud of.

The weather today is perfect. Not too hot, not too cool. I feel no breeze, but I can hear it high up in the tops of the tall ponderosa pines. Malcolm seems quite content in his cage. Sometimes it looks like he is communicating with the wild birds. Who am I to say he's not? A few have come quite close to him. It's like he has friends—birds of a feather. Wendell is Wendell. He goes with the flow. If I had to describe him right now, I'd say he's working, doing dog work, and he feels important. He is ultra alert—not anxious or nervous, just very alert. That's good.

I appreciate my two lovable companions, the warmth of the sun, the lulling sounds of nature, the solitude of this location, and the opportunity ... just to be.

She shifted her position and groaned. "Damn! I do not appreciate these stupid bites or whatever they are." She hesitated, wondering if she should include them in her journal. "It's not a positive thought," she said to herself, then decided. "But this is something I feel, and it's very real. I'll write about it the next time I add to the journal."

Lindsey lit a fire late in the afternoon so there would be good cooking coals when she was ready to cook hotdogs for herself and Wendell. In the meantime, she splurged and ate potato chips with a soda, figuring she might as well drink it while it was still cold. By tomorrow, the ice in the cooler would probably be gone.

Fortunately, they would likely sleep well tonight since the tent was now better organized. Lindsey put on soft, cozy pajamas and snuggled into her sleeping bag, then relaxed her head onto a pillow. Wendell preferred to sleep on top of the extra bag she'd brought for him. The sky still held light, but all three were ready for bed. Tomorrow they would explore.

But Lindsey awoke during the night, dizzy, nauseated, and groaning with pain, aware that the pain was from the nagging bug bites. All she could think was that they had become infected. She tried to go back to sleep—the moon was still high in the coal black sky—but she couldn't. As the black finally lightened to dark grey, Lindsey felt a powerful urge to pee. Unable to find the flashlight, she stumbled out anyway, hoping to reach the trench she'd dug for this purpose.

"Come on, Wendell. You might as well come, too. We'll be right back, Malcolm."

Chapter Thirty-Seven

The mountain air was chilly, and still relatively free of bird-song. Lindsey crouched next to a tall tree, clutching it when her dizziness intensified. At about the time she was pulling up her pajama bottoms, Wendell barked, which wasn't something he usually did. He stared urgently in the direction of the tent then back at Lindsey, as if to say, *Come on! Do something!* Concerned, Lindsey hurried back toward the campsite, thinking only of getting back to the tent. Her foot caught on a tree root, and she went flying. She broke her fall with her right wrist, which slammed hard against a rough-edged rock, causing a new, greater pain. One that made her scabbed-over bites pale in comparison.

Wendell walked to her side where she lay sprawled on the ground and licked the tears from her face, making a soft, whining sound.

"Oh, Wendell. You are the best dog in the world," she said, sobbing. "I thought this trip was a good idea, but now I'm not sure. We're in the middle of nowhere, and nobody even knows we're here." She stroked his neck, seeking strength. "We're on our own, Wendell, and everything is so much harder for me than I'm letting on. I don't know what I'm doing, and now I have only the use of one hand—my left." Fear began to overwhelm the pain she was feeling. "Oh, geez. We could be in real trouble."

She soaked her swollen hand and wrist in the remaining pieces of ice and cold water, then wrapped it with the gauze and tape she had in her first aid kit. As long as she didn't attempt to use the hand, and as long as she kept it somewhat elevated, it felt okay. If she could build a fire, cook the food, dress and undress, use the trench—oh my, the list was long—they would all be fine.

Easier said than done.

By late afternoon, Lindsey had accomplished little more than trading pajamas for sweats. After attempting to tie her hiking books, she gave up and slipped her feet back into the crocs she'd worn earlier. Malcolm was banished to the tent for his own safety while Lindsey and Wendell went for a short and very careful walk to explore a little further than they'd been before. She couldn't manage buckling the dog pack onto Wendell's back, so the dog willingly donned a fabric grocery bag around his neck. He would be the keeper of any treasures they might find.

They came to a small knoll paved with smooth, sparkling stones the shade of orange sherbet, and Lindsey had to smile despite everything. "My gosh, that's beautiful." She'd never seen glittering rocks like these, let alone an entire hill of them. She collected a few samples and placed them in Wendell's bag, planning to research and learn about these geological treasures when they returned to Tucson.

She decided to stay on or near the road, or at least within sight of the tent, since she couldn't risk getting lost. So they made a wide circle around the camp, gathering pine needles and a few cones that would later become tea or kindling. She saw a patch of wild strawberry plants, but it was far too early in the season for berries, though a few of the leaves could be added to her tea. Wendell discovered a bone from a deer or a small cow, and he carried it proudly in his mouth for the duration of their walk.

Their excursion took less than an hour, but by the time they arrived back at the tent, Lindsey was exhausted. Her body ached, her stomach felt queasy, her head pounded, and her hand throbbed. She needed to lie down. There would be no journaling today, since she couldn't write with her left hand. They ducked into the tent, and Malcolm chirped softly to show he was glad for the company. Wendell rolled on his side and snuggled up with the bone. Lindsey leaned back and closed her eyes, relaxing to the sound of a gentle breeze drifting through the treetops above them.

Suddenly, Wendell sat up abruptly and stared to the west, out the tent's screen door flap. He was alert, focused, and in guard dog mode. Lindsey straightened, panicked and dizzy, and listened hard. She heard the sound of an engine, and adrenaline surged through her body. Fight or flight? Hell, she couldn't fight. She searched through her duffle bag for the car keys, thinking the car would be a safer place to be. She could lock the doors and drive away, if necessary. But she couldn't find the keys.

The engine sound grew closer and closer, until it was too late to make a run for the car even if she did magically find what she was looking for. At least she had Wendell. His presence alone was formidable, and when he barked he'd certainly make any potential enemies think twice.

But he didn't bark. He remained still, watching out the door of the tent as the approaching vehicle came to a halt. Its door slammed shut, and footsteps crunched on the dry ground, headed steadily toward the tent. Lindsey cowered behind Wendell, trying to convince herself it was probably just another camper. Or maybe a forest official.

Wendell whined, then he wagged. In fact, his whole body wagged. That was unexpected. It meant that either the intruder was someone Wendell knew and loved, or whoever it was had a T-bone steak to share.

"Hey, boy. Where's Lindsey?" asked a male voice.

It sounded like ... Jake.

"Jake?" she asked quietly. "Is that you?"

"Yours truly, at your service." Lindsey sagged with relief, fighting back tears. "Should I come in or are you coming out?" he asked.

"We're coming out. We are all coming out."

Despite her joy at seeing a friendly face, Lindsey had mixed feelings. She was still furious with Jake for using her and Laura the way he had, and for all the lying he'd done. She assumed that she didn't even know the half of it. Jake's betrayal had been the last straw for her, the main reason she'd taken off on this wilderness adventure. On the other hand, she had to admit that she desperately needed his help right now, and she was glad to see him. She could no longer pretend that she was fine. Her side hurt from the scabs, her stomach had felt unsettled for days, her whole body seemed feverish and weak, and now her wrist throbbed, making even the simplest tasks nearly impossible. Yes, she needed help.

Lindsey opened the tent flap, and Wendell bounded out. It was slow going as Lindsey got herself and Malcolm's cage out with the use of only one hand, and when they finally did make it out, she got tripped up where the tent's floor met the tent's side. Jake stepped in immediately to set the birdcage upright and give Lindsey a helping hand. Their eyes met for the first time since the night of the Desert Performance, and both pairs of eyes conveyed looks of surprise and disbelief.

"What happened to you?" they asked simultaneously.

"You first," Lindsey said.

One corner of Jake's mouth lifted, and it looked as if the movement was quite painful. His appearance was shocking. She didn't tell him his left eye and cheek area looked like a rotten red potato, but if he happened to read her mind at that very moment, she'd assure him that there was no unpleasant odor at all.

"It's a very, very long story."

"The nutshell version then."

"Shawna slugged me."

She tilted her head, skeptical. "One punch did all that damage?"

"I don't know. Maybe there were two punches, or I might have done some damage when I fell. I'm not sure about all the details, since I was knocked out for a while. She's strong. Your turn."

"Oh, well," she said, glancing at her elevated wrist. "I tripped on a tree root or something and fell on my wrist. It's not doing too well." She hesitated … and then decided to let Jake have it. "Actually, I look like this because you betrayed me, Jake. I'm angry, and this is what anger looks like on me. How could you have used me as a guinea pig for your research without even telling me? How could you pretend to be my friend all the while you were spying on me and my problems and my feelings and—"

"I don't blame you for being angry. I was going to tell you. That's one of the main reasons I'm here—"

"Speaking of which, how in the world did you find us here?" Lindsey had so many questions that even just thinking about them was overwhelming.

Jake shook his head. "Listen. I have so much to tell you—far too much for you to digest or for me to tell in one night. Please, Lindsey, hear me out. Right now, let me build a fire and cook our dinner while you rest and drink the tea I'll make for you. Tonight I will do my best to explain my research project, tell you all the mistakes I made, and the fiasco it evolved into. Then I'll share the story of how I came to find you. If you're willing, I'd like to stay here with you, and over the next three days, we can heal ourselves physically and mentally. Each night I'll tell you another story that will help us both make sense out of this past year."

Lindsey was too weak to argue, but she wasn't sure this was a good idea. It meant three more nights in the Zuni Mountains, and three more stories that would likely take her down the memory lane from Hell. She wasn't at all sure she could do it, but ... she could manage tonight. She wanted to know the scope of Jake's research and find out the role her miserable life had played on the pages of his work. And she was hungry and tired. At least she would eat and sleep. And maybe, for the evening, she'd feel safe.

The fire's hypnotic flames crackled and popped, sending sparks dancing toward the silent treetops. If there were any onlookers of the two-legged variety, the sight of Wendell, Lindsey, and Jake sitting around the fire together might be viewed as a perfect, little family on a camping vacation. The presence of Malcolm added an odd, if not special, touch. But, of course, looks could be deceiving. Jake's storytelling—*his confession, really*—had not yet begun, so an invisible tension permeated the smoke and pine scented air.

"Jake, I think I would like to hear the part about how you found me here first. That way we can kind of 'warm up' before getting into the hard stuff—the stuff that's going to make me want to hit you, too … though I doubt my punch would do even a fraction of the damage that Shawna's did. Why did she hit you, anyway?"

"First of all, I'd prefer that no punching takes place. This face can't stand another blow just yet. As far as 'why she hit me,' well, that's a story for another night. Here. Eat your ramen."

Jake made them each another mug of his special herb tea and put a towel over Malcolm's cage to protect the bird from the rapidly falling temperature, but he left an opening so the bird could still see them. He gave Wendell a store-bought bone and a scratch behind his ears, then scooted his low beach-type chair over so that he sat facing Lindsey, almost knee to knee.

"Once upon a time—"

"You don't have to do that," Lindsey said, not sure if she was annoyed or enamored.

"Okay. I just wasn't sure how to start. I'm more of a writer or a listener than a talker."

Jake did his best, trying to stick to facts. He explained to Lindsey that the morning after Shawna's right hook had met his jaw, he'd gone over to her place. He wanted to make sure she was all right and, in all honesty, he said he was hoping for a little sympathy.

"I was on your porch, ringing the bell, just as the mail lady walked up your sidewalk. I told her I was just about to go in, so she let me take the mail—two envelopes and an educational journal. But after several minutes went by and you didn't answer the door, I looked in the back and didn't see any sign of you, Wendell, or Malcolm. That's when I got worried. So I went by Laura's, figuring that if anyone knew your whereabouts, it would be Laura."

"I didn't tell her where I was going."

"That's what she said."

"Go on."

"When I mentioned to Laura that Malcolm and Wendell were gone too, she was sure all three of you were headed out of Tucson. At first she had no idea where, then she said that maybe you had retreated to the Zuni Mountains. She said she'd mentioned it to you, and she gave me the basic directions. I had no trouble finding the Zuni pueblo, but finding you was another matter. I've been driving around these hills and plateaus on dirt trails for about eight hours." He shook his head. "I've got to tell you, Linds, you chose *the* worst road in the entire Cibola National Forest."

"I'll agree with you on that. I had some ... trouble in spots," Lindsey admitted. "But I don't understand why you drove all the way from Tucson when you didn't even know for sure that I was here."

"I was willing to take a chance. You see, as I was leaving Laura's, she mentioned your 'bug bites' and the discomfort you were having. Based upon what she told me, plus a little of my own research, I arrived at the conclusion that your sores had nothing to do with insects. If my educated hunch was correct, you were going to feel much worse over the next several days. I wanted to help you, Lindsey." He smiled. "And of course I didn't want to break any federal laws, so I needed to deliver your mail, too. So I had to come."

"Well, doctor, what's the diagnosis?"

"Can I take a look?"

Even Lindsey hadn't looked in a few days, though she knew the sores were still there, alive and raging with pain. She lifted her loosely fitting sweatshirt just enough for Jake to shine his flashlight on her midsection, and she didn't like the look on his face.

He sighed and switched off the flashlight. "This is one of those good news-bad news moments, I'm afraid."

She'd heard that before. Oh, well. "Bad news first," demanded Lindsey.

"You have shingles, and they are too far along for medication or natural remedies to slow the disease. It will run its full course. But the good news is that I just happen to have some natural remedies that will ease your pain and soreness a little."

Shingles? She'd heard of that but knew nothing about it. "How did I catch it? From a student?"

"No, from yourself. When adults get shingles it is mostly due to the combination of two factors. The first is that you had chickenpox at some time in your life, and the second is that you are under either unusual physical or mental stress, or both."

She dropped her chin to her chest. "Oh. I guess I fit the bill."

"So can I spray my magic potion on you?" he asked, stoking the fire gently.

"What's in it?"

"Basil tea and apple cider vinegar. No poison apples, I promise."

She stared at the radiant flames of the fire, looking hypnotized, and he passed her a couple of capsules. "Here, Lindsey. Take two of these," he said.

She swallowed them without asking what they were. Was she starting to trust him again? Without further conversation, Jake led her into the tent, sprayed the vinegar and tea mixture on her sores, and sat with her while she drank the rest of her basil tea. Her last memory before she fell asleep was of Jake tucking her and Malcolm in, then returning to the flickering fire with Wendell.

Chapter Thirty-Eight

When she awoke to the aroma of bacon and eggs and coffee cooking over the fire, she became convinced that it was the most delicious smell in the whole world. And she was starving.

She poked her head out of the tent. "Good morning," she said to Jake, who was sitting by the fire with both Wendell and Malcolm. "I will be right there."

"Good, 'cause breakfast is now being served."

After breakfast, following Jake's instructions, Lindsey drank more of the basil tea, swallowed two more of the cat's claw capsules—this time she did ask what they were, out of curiosity—and sprayed her sores again. Jake said she needed to follow this routine for several days, and only stop if there were any ill effects from his remedies. Lindsey agreed willingly, but insisted he get back to all his explanations.

"Okay. Here goes," he began. "My major is psychology—"

"I think I knew that part."

"And I am nearing the end of my program. All that's left to do is my thesis. My topic was "Women Alone and Their Coping Strategies." I obtained my first three research subjects and got signed permission forms, and I began. But between bartending and food delivering, time began to slip away from me. Before long, I was running behind schedule. Then, just by chance, I met you."

She scowled. "I'm sure there were plenty of women in Tucson that would have welcomed the opportunity to be part of a research project. So why me?"

"I had no intention of including you in my research at first. That idea just kind of snuck up on me as I began to think about you more and more. You got to me, Linds, from the moment I met you. In fact, thinking about you, your life, and your problems, even your happiness began to cloud my judgment and my research."

She cocked an eyebrow, not buying a word. "So this is all my fault?"

"No, that's not what I meant at all. Just listen. Please. When I think, I write. And before I knew it, I was writing about you—a sweet, talented, beautiful woman—who happened to be a woman alone. I didn't consider you one of my 'subjects.' Not really, anyway." He took a sip of coffee, watching her all the time. "By the time I met Laura, I was feeling a little—okay, very desperate. I needed another subject or two, and I needed them in a hurry because the clock was ticking. She practically threw herself at me. It was like a gift. Suddenly, there she was, talking up a storm. That woman can talk! After that, I was back on track, almost seeing the light at the end of the thesis tunnel. Soon I'd be done, and I'd have the degree I'd wanted for so long."

"So now you've got your degree, right?"

"No, actually. I don't." They sat in awkward silence, then he started up again. "Do you want me to go on?"

"Yes."

"I planned to tell you all about me and my research, then ask if you would do me the honor of participating in my project. I was going to do that right after I finished helping Laura with her big surprise—" He tilted his head and smiled. "A unique birthday party she was throwing for a friend. I was a mere two days away from telling you everything. As you know, the party turned out to be a surprise for everyone. I had no idea that you and Laura knew each other, and then to discover that you were best friends? Wow. I was shocked. And I didn't know what to do. The situation began to take on a life of its own. Selfishly, I just wanted to finish the project, earn the degree and get on with my life."

Lindsey was confused. "I had no idea that anyone was required to write a thesis for a bachelor's degree." She shrugged. "But then again, my only college experience was in the College of Education."

He grinned. "What? All this time you thought I was an undergrad working on a bachelor's degree?"

"You're not?"

His chuckle was warm. "Hey, girl. You think I'm twenty-one or something? I'll have you know I received my bachelor's degree seven years ago and my master's four years ago. I was going to be 'Dr. Jake' shortly after defending my thesis, which, of course, is not happening now because I screwed up by not having five legal subjects. I now have to start over, if I want to continue down this same path." He shrugged. "But that's my problem, not yours."

Lindsey fought back a blush, embarrassed. "Oh dear. I assumed so much—and so incorrectly."

He shrugged again. "And I guess I let you." His eyes softened, becoming the beautiful blue she remembered. "Lindsey, I am so sorry. I never meant to use you or upset you."

She took a deep breath, willing herself to speak. No longer was Jake just the young delivery boy in khaki pants or the college student in baggie shorts. Before her sat a man in gloriously tight jeans and a white T-shirt, looking good enough to be on the cover of *Cowboys and Indians* magazine.

"I don't know much about you," she admitted slowly. "The truth is that I've been so absorbed with myself, my problems, and my love life that now I'm the one who is sorry."

He cocked his head slightly, gave her a little smile. "Let's take a walk," he suggested, gathering a water bottle, two apples, and two granola bars. "You okay with a walk?"

"Uh, sure. Sure. Let's go."

Malcolm was relocated to the tent, and Wendell followed the two humans. They didn't stray far from the dirt road, but they walked lazily for several hours, speaking about inconsequential things: the trees, the birds, the weather, and the delicious, fragrant scents of nature that surrounded them. They watched squirrels scamper up and down trees and saw a rabbit dash by in a zigzag pattern—they even saw a cow amble slowly along, keeping her wary eyes on the three of them. When they stopped on a small rise under several pine trees to eat their snacks and drink water, Wendell suddenly got distracted and began to dig frantically. Dirt and rocks flew through the air as he focused on his work. Lindsey had never seen him this intense before.

"Stop that, Wendell!" called Lindsey. What are you doing?"

Jake walked over to the deepening hole in the ground. "Hey, buddy. Whatcha got there?" Wendell looked at Jake then back at his hole, obviously pleased about something. "Just looks like dirt and rocks to me. Lindsey, we need your expert opinion. Come take a closer look."

"Yep. Dirt and rocks ... wait ... rocks with fossils in them. Look at this, Jake. The fossils look like shells and maybe snails.

See that? They're all over the place. This area must have been under the ocean at one time in history. Good job, Wendell. Wendell, the four-legged archeologist!"

The smiling moon hung high and bright in the sky, already casting well-defined shadows over the campsite. Lindsey and Wendell settled in the tent while Jake attempted to transform the small back seat in his Jeep into an area conducive to sleep.

Lindsey couldn't sleep. Physically, she felt encouraging signs of improvement, but her brain and its constant stream of thoughts kept her awake. She remembered the first night they'd met, could practically smell the rain in the air on the night Jake had delivered Chinese food to her door with Wendell in tow. When she put her mind to it, she remembered almost everything that had happened between that night and the night of the Desert Performance, when he'd jumped into action, showing concern for her safety. He'd always been so good to her, a real friend—except for the research. But all of a sudden, that didn't seem quite so awful.

Tonight she didn't count sheep; she counted Jake's kindness and the many blessings to which she'd been so blind over the past year. She needed to learn more about this amazing young man—except he wasn't that young after all! He was a full-grown man, weeks away from having his doctoral degree, and that discovery allowed her to look at Jake with new eyes. For the first time she let herself think about how incredibly handsome he was, how his hair gleamed in the firelight when he ran his hand through it, guiding it away from his compelling blue eyes.

He'd asked for two more nights in which to tell his stories. Tomorrow Lindsey would request an additional night, during which she could ask her questions.

By midday the next day, Jake still hadn't mentioned anything about his next story. It wasn't a big deal to her anymore, since she'd heard everything she'd really wanted to hear. What else could there be? But she was curious. Keeping her eyes on Jake, she drank more tea, swallowed more cat's claw, and sprayed the potion on her fading sores. She was feeling much better—even her wrist had improved, though it still hurt if she tried to lift anything.

"Jake, are you okay? You're kind of quiet today."

"I'm fine. Didn't sleep too great, but I'm fine. Just thinking about stuff."

"Stuff? Come on, Mr. Almost-got-my-doctoral-degree. Your vocabulary repertoire has got to have more than that," she teased.

"Well then, Ms. Teacher. I'll tell you what, you and I will engage in a 'happy hour' tale later this afternoon as we dine on a little red wine and cheddar cheese, and you can rate my vocabulary then. How does that sound?"

"Perfect."

"Great. Hey, I was thinking about another hike."

Lindsey quickly took stock. She'd really enjoyed the walk the day before, but she was still a little sore. Besides, she wouldn't mind a little quiet time to write in her journal. "You know, I think I'd rather just stay here. But you can go."

"You wouldn't mind? I thought I could take Wendell for a real hike, for a couple of hours. We're both a little antsy."

"I wouldn't mind at all, and he'd love it. Go. Really."

"You're sure?"

"I'm sure."

She pulled out her journal as Jake and Wendell walked away, disappearing up the dusty, rutted road. The dog still had a stiff, plodding gate—he hadn't completely healed from the injuries caused by the accident—and a contented, wagging tail. The man wore cowboy boots, a baseball cap with the word 'Austin' on it, and a sky blue T-shirt that clung to his muscular arms and firm core. Jake wasn't overly muscular, but he was a strong, lean guy who obviously took good care of his body and possessed great genes ... *and great jeans,* she thought. Why had she not noticed these things before? She didn't dare write her current thoughts as she journaled. Those she'd keep to herself.

> *Still Camping in Zuni Mountains—Jake & Wendell are hiking. Life is strange. Life is ... I don't know. Life changes moment to moment. This moment is good, except for my wrist pain. Sure is slowing me down with my writing. But at least today I can write a little, no matter how messy. I'm not mad at Jake anymore. Not really. How could I be? He's tried so hard to help me in so many ways.*

A soft thump came from the road, and she stopped writing. She put down her journal to listen with a serious ear. Did she hear footsteps? As the sound got louder she wondered if it might be a deer, since they'd seen deer tracks just yesterday, but she didn't think a deer would have such a heavy step. A cow maybe?

Stepping out of the tent after putting her journal away she came face to face with the source of the noise. Not a deer or a cow, she discovered, but a horse. A horse with a rider who looked a lot like a Zuni warrior from long ago.

"Hey," said the warrior. "Who are you?"

"I'm ... I'm Lindsey," she stammered. "From Tucson."

He frowned. "Where is the dog? You're supposed to have a giant dog with you."

How does he know that? "Who are you and what do you want?" she asked, using her toughest teacher voice.

"I'm one of the Zuni Pueblo's police officers," he informed her, chin lifted proudly. "We got a call from a woman in Tucson asking about you. She said you might be in trouble or sick or missing." He scratched his cheek, thinking. "But I can see you're not missing."

That had to have been Laura worrying about her. The thought made her smile. "I am fine. Thank you for checking. And so's the dog. He's just out for a hike with a friend of mine." She softened her tone, relieved. "May I ask why you are riding a horse and dressed like that?"

"Oh, today is one of the days we put on a show for the tourists. It just ended, and I'm one of the dancers. And the horse, well, lady, I wouldn't even think of driving my car up this dirt trail. A horse is the only way to go. What do you want me to tell your friend?"

"Please tell her I'm alive and well, and that Jake is here."

"Will do, though you might not want to stay. Storm's gonna hit tonight. If you're gonna stay, I'd dig a trench around your tent and add more tent stakes."

With that, the horse and rider turned and trotted back down the primitive road, leaving a small but lingering cloud of dust. The temperature had become oppressively hot and still. She walked to Jake's Jeep, pretty sure she'd find a soda in his cooler on the back seat. It might even be cool, if not cold.

Just as she'd guessed, she found a variety of drinks bobbing in the cold water, so she picked one and popped the top.

"Ah, this is living," she said, enjoying the cool bubbles as they washed down her throat.

When she reached in to replace the lid of the cooler, she noticed a topless cardboard box on the floor, filled with files.

She frowned. That was an odd thing to bring camping. Just before she shut the car door, her eyes drifted back to the box and paused on the file on top of the pile. It was labeled: SHAWNA. Shawna? Jake was involved with *Shawna*? How? Why?

She stood paralyzed for a moment as her body filled with the now familiar sense of panic, then she turned and started to run. Vaguely, she heard Malcolm squawking as loudly as he could, but she didn't stop. She ran until her body gave out under a ponderosa pine. Then she leaned over, hands on her knees. Sweat dripped from her face as she tried to catch her breath.

"What am I doing?" she shouted. "What is *he* doing? What is he doing with *Shawna*?"

Just when she thought the shattered pieces of her puzzling life were beginning to come together, they'd fallen apart again. She'd taken a positive step forward, and then had been shoved back.

"I can't win," she sobbed. "I want Shawna out of my life once and for all!"

She didn't hear them approaching, so when the wet tongue licked her hands and face, her body jerked away. She glanced up and met Wendell's happy face. Just past him stood Jake, holding a bouquet of wild flowers.

"Look what we found. Aren't they beautiful?" he asked, but when she didn't answer he stepped closer. "You scared us, Lindsey. When we got back to camp and you weren't there, we worried. Fortunately, Wendell sniffed around and picked up your trail right away. Is there something wrong? Do you feel all right?"

"No, I feel all wrong. I want to go home. I want to go home and be by myself."

He set one hand on his hip, looking confused. "What? Lindsey, you aren't making sense. Talk to me."

"I drank one of your sodas from the cooler on the back seat of your car."

"Yeah, so? Lindsey? Come on. We are getting nowhere playing Twenty Questions," he said, clearly frustrated.

Lindsey glared at him. "You … You lied to me."

He held up his hands, looking helpless. "Geez, Lindsey. I'm just trying to help you. What did I screw up now?"

"What's going on between you and Shawna?" she demanded. "First I lose my husband to that woman, and now I sense I'm losing someone—you—that … that … "

She burst into tears, and he stared at her, his expression shocked. "Oh, for Pete's sake," he said.

She didn't pull away when he wrapped his hand around hers and led her back to the campsite. Then he gestured for her to sit by the fire ring, and he sank down across from her again.

"I didn't lie to you, Lindsey. Shawna was one of my first three official and legal study subjects. She loved the idea at first …" He narrowed his eyes, studying her. "This is a really long story. Are you sure you want to hear it?"

"Go on. I'm listening," Lindsey replied coolly.

Chapter Thirty-Nine

"Right. Well, I got a call. It was Shawna, begging me to come over because there was an emergency. When I got there, she slugged me in the face. She calmed down a little when she realized I was hurt and bleeding, then she helped me up, and we ended up talking till dawn." He chuckled softly. "You know, I knew she was an odd one from the first interview we had almost a year ago, and the more time that passed, the stranger it all got.

"She started off as the woman who stole Anthony away from you, then turned into someone who was a real threat to your safety as well as your happiness. That's when my desire for information about her took a completely different path. I needed to know what was going on with Anthony and Shawna, because their actions did not make sense. But none of my detective work made sense either. Not until that night. I sat there with a swollen and bloody face, and Shawna cried all her mascara off, and she talked. She let it all out, and the puzzle began to take an even more bizarre shape."

Jake pulled out one of Shawna's files and handed Lindsey an old photo. Lindsey stared at it, not knowing what she was looking at.

"What do you see?" asked Jake.

"A tall man and a small boy."

"Right. Does the tall man look at all familiar?"

She stared harder. "You know, he looks a little like Anthony." Her eyes widened. "Is it Anthony's father?"

"No, but you're on the right track. It's Shawna's father, and he really does look a little like Anthony. I'm pretty sure that resemblance was one of the reasons Shawna was so obsessively determined to have him. But I'm getting ahead of myself."

That didn't seem to make much more sense than anything else so far. "So the little boy is her brother?"

"That's what I thought at first." He let out a breath. "Here's the shocker. The little boy is Shawna."

"They dressed her like a boy?"

"Yes. Her mother dressed her like a boy ... because she *was* a boy."

She blinked. "Huh?"

Jake nodded slowly. "Shawna grew up in Benson, Arizona, living there from birth to high school graduation. Her father was an angry, twisted son of a bitch who verbally abused her mother for producing a son instead of the daughter he'd wanted." He watched her eyes. "A son named Sean."

Lindsey gasped. "Sean? He ... could he be the man who's been calling me? Leaving odd messages? But if he ... if he was Shawna, why would he go back to being Sean when he called me? Is she ... is he ... schizophrenic or something? Oh my God. This is unbelievable."

"I know," said Jake. "And trust me, it's about to get even stranger. When Sean was about four years old, his father lost his job with the railroad and became the stay-at-home dad, before that was a cool thing to be. Sean's mom went to work at the local movie theater four days a week from mid-afternoon to about eleven o'clock. It wasn't much, but they got by. That was supposed to be a temporary situation until he found another job, but unfortunately for little Sean, his dad's period of unemployment went on for years."

Jake sighed, then looked down at his feet for a moment before meeting her gaze again. "There's more, but it's really hard core stuff. I don't know if you need to know all the details."

"I've been around a lot of troubled kids, Jake. I can handle it."

"That's exactly why I'm hesitant to tell you everything."

"It's okay. Just continue."

He stood, apparently needing movement, because he started to pace a little, his eyes on his feet again. "Sean's mom felt bad about having to leave her little boy, and she made up for her absence by obsessively reading her favorite stories to Sean when she wasn't at work. And get this, Lindsey—her favorite stories were fairy tales."

That part of the story brought a wistful smile to Lindsey's face. She stood as well, and without a word, the two of them walked quietly away from the campsite. "Like I said when I got those flowers from her, Shawna knows her fairy tales."

He nodded. "And those stories became Sean's mental safe haven, his escape from reality, as his father's abuse took another turn. Before long, while Mom was at work, Dad began to dress little Sean in girl's clothing, transforming him into the daughter he wanted so badly, and treating him like a little princess. When Sean was dressed like a girl, his dad treated him well. When they were not playing this sick dress-up game, his dad treated him badly, shouting at him and locking him in his room just for doing ordinary things that children do.

"Sometimes any kind of attention is welcome, I guess, because Sean began to look forward to the hours Mom was away and Dad took out the hidden clothing: frilly dresses, pink socks with ruffled edges, purple panties, and white patent leather shoes that clicked when he walked on the tile floor. Dad played music on the radio and they danced, then dad made popcorn and pretty, little Sean sat on his lap, watching TV and munching. Pleasing Dad made Sean's life more tolerable, almost pleasant."

"I know where this is heading," Lindsey said, breaking her silence. "He began to sexually abuse her—him, didn't he?"

"Yeah. Shawna wasn't sure exactly when it started, but it was sometime during her first year of school."

"Kindergarten?"

"Probably."

Lindsey stopped walking and sat on a fallen tree trunk. Jake sat beside her.

"That poor baby," she said. "He was just a kindergarten baby."

Jake put his arm around her shoulders, and she welcomed his comfort. Her mind swam with so many thoughts and emotions, landing finally on anger. She drew away and faced Jake.

"How long did this go on? Didn't the mother know? Of course she did. Mothers always know. Did she call the police? Was he arrested? Is he labeled as a sex offender at least?"

He shrugged. "I don't have all the answers. Even Shawna doesn't. She thinks the playing dress up and the sexual abuse went on all the way through elementary school and into middle school. By then he was terribly confused about his own sexuality and who he really was. He'd spent the majority of his life trying to please his dad, and that meant being a girl.

"By middle school, the other kids were certain that Sean was gay. He became an outcast, and his peers constantly ridiculed him. That's incredibly difficult to live with anywhere, but it's worse in a small, rural town. He dressed as a boy at school, but the kids saw through that. And every day when he arrived home, his boyish appearance enraged his dad."

Jake chewed his bottom lip briefly, looking as if he wished he could skip over the next part, but he changed his mind. "One night, Sean's dad sat him across the kitchen table from him, saying they needed to talk. Sean sat, but all his dad said was, *"Goodbye, my princess"* before he lifted the firearm from his lap. He pointed the barrel of the gun right at Sean's head and cocked the hammer. Sean closed his eyes, knowing he was going to die, but he didn't care. Life was too painful to live anyway. The sound of the single gunshot was deafening, but he felt no pain. Death must have come instantly. But he didn't die; he opened his eyes again. That's when he saw his dad slumped over the table, a portion of his head gone. His dad's blood had splattered Sean's face, his shirt, his hands, and throughout the kitchen. Sean cried in his room for over a month then vowed he would never, ever shed a tear again."

Jake, Lindsey, and Wendell walked silently back to camp. It was dinnertime, but only the dog was hungry. Jake and Lindsey brewed and drank some white tea using Jake's tiny one-burner backpacking stove.

"Sean had a difficult time all through high school," Jake continued. "He never thought he was gay, but he did think he wanted to be a girl. His only happy childhood memories occurred either when his mom read fairy tales or when his dad dressed him like a girl and treated him like a princess. He blocked out most of the horrific trauma and began to fantasize about becoming a female and living happily ever after. After high school he moved to Phoenix and found jobs at posh beauty salons and spas, learning about the 'ways of women' while sweeping up and go-fering for hair stylists and make-up artists. That's when he began his six-year physical transformation, letting the world think he was simply a gay man. He took female hormones and had numerous cosmetic surgeries, including lots of face work, some leg reshaping, and nips and tucks to establish a smaller waistline. Apparently, some of these surgeries were botched and there was a problem with unusual scarring, so he was awarded about $250,000 in an out of court settlement. With this money, Sean decided to go the next step by getting breast implants—big ones! He moved from Phoenix to Tucson soon after to begin his new life as the gorgeous Shawna that we all know. Shawna came into your life and destroyed your marriage about three years after moving to Tucson."

Lindsey frowned. "Your timeline doesn't make sense. If all that's right, then how could she have been only twenty when Anthony moved in with her?"

"Twenty? She'll turn thirty in a couple of weeks. What made you think she was only twenty?"

Lindsey couldn't hide a smug smile. "That's what Anthony told me back when this whole thing started. Do you think he was lying, or he just didn't know?"

"Well, I think it's safe to assume that he didn't know about a lot of things."

"So … when she met Anthony, she wanted him, and she had to have him—in part—because he reminded her of her father?"

"I think so. She was relentless in her pursuit of him, from what she said. He didn't stand a chance. She still had money, she looked fabulous, and she was hot and kinky—and all those ingredients were the perfect recipe for Anthony's addictions."

Anthony. She'd been so shocked about all this she'd forgotten about him. "And Anthony didn't know she was a guy?"

Jake shook his head.

"But ... but I don't get how that all worked out ... you know, sexually, I mean."

"I didn't ask, so I don't have details, though I can imagine ... no, I don't even want to go there. She did say they never did anything with the lights on. I know that she needed to be certain that Anthony would love her, marry her, and stay with her forever, supporting her through the last and most difficult part of her transformation: the sexual reassignment surgery, because there was no going back after that."

Lindsey shook her head, speechless. How on earth could all this have been going on around her?

"But Anthony knows now," Jake said.

Her mind flashed on his note to her: *I have been an idiot and a fool.*

She couldn't help smiling. *You can say that again,* she thought. "How did he find out?"

"She was packing for their trip to Trinidad, Colorado for that final step when Anthony stumbled upon some photos, probably taken by the surgeon, that included a completely naked—with the lights on—frontal view of Shawna. The sight of the sexy woman standing naked in the photos with her rather robust male sex organ pointing right at him was, I imagine, fairly shocking."

She let out a long breath, trying not to smile. "I can only imagine."

"There isn't much more to tell," continued Jake. "I assume Anthony was sickened by the sight, because he didn't stick around to ask any questions. He ran as fast as he could, and he headed to your house."

She hesitated, torn between feeling gratified at the change in Anthony's fate and feeling sympathy. "What will Anthony do now?"

"Oh, I imagine his knuckles are pretty raw from slugging the punching bag at the gym. And he's probably putting quite a few miles on the treadmill waiting for you to come home."

Chapter Forty

Gentle raindrops drifted in a mist from the darkening sky, and the dust settled under its pressure. The air was filled with a damp, piney scent, and the temperature dropped along with the rain, just enough to be perfect—not too warm, not too cool. After asking her permission, Jake set his cardboard box of folders inside the tent until the shower had passed.

"Lindsey," he called from inside the tent. "Could you come in here for a second?"

She popped her head in, then settled on the ground beside him when he invited her just to "listen." Rain tapped against the top of the tent in a soothing rhythm.

"Let's stay in here for a while," she suggested. "We can hear the rain on the tent, we can see the rain through the screen door flap, but we won't have to get wet."

"I like the way you think. I'll just get Malcolm and be right back."

Wendell followed the other two into the tent, and for the first time, the whole crew sat cozily in the nylon, outdoor home.

Lindsey glanced at the box in the corner of the tent. "Any more stories? Any more shocking information you want to share with me? Now is as good a time as any."

He tilted his head, looking a little guilty. "Well, I did do a little extra research when I had the time. You have interesting people passing through your life, Linds. I didn't even try to learn anything about that last guy, Martin. That situation seemed to have worked itself out, run its course, and there really wasn't time. Did you want me to do some digging?"

She pictured Martin's warm smile, remembered the well-meant, though cardboard kisses. "No. He was a nice guy. Basically, he was good to me. It just wasn't meant to be. But Emmett, well, that's another story."

"You're right about that. Since I'm not in law enforcement, I couldn't access many details, but there is no doubt that he was—sorry, that he *is*—a professional con man. We know he conned women for their money, but I think he also conned business owners. It wasn't just you he took advantage of. Apparently he's pretty talented."

"I guess I'm a poor judge of character."

"No, Lindsey. You're missing my point. He's conned the best of them. And to be fair, I actually don't believe that was his initial intention when he met you on the trail in the Grand Canyon. Those actions were probably genuine, since he didn't know you or that you would be on the trail that evening. He was merely helping you because you needed help."

The rain began to come down more heavily, and Jake raised his voice to be heard. "I don't think he switched into con man mode until he saw that you were staying in the most expensive dwelling in the entire national park. What I did learn is that he has used at least four aliases in the past—probably more.

And there was evidence that arrests had been made for forgery and extortion in the past, but oddly enough, I could find no evidence of any convictions, which is another testament to his talents. It seems that, as of now, he's off the radar, vanished into thin air. That's all I've got so far, but I'm not done checking him out."

The pleasant rain shower from before had evolved into a real storm and was now bombarding the small dwelling with buckets of water. The tent leaned to the left, then to the right as a strong wind whipped around them. Lindsey smacked her forehead with her hand.

"Ugh! The Indian! He was right. He warned me, but I completely forgot," she cried.

Now Jake looked confused. "The Indian?"

He leaned closer so he could hear her brief story about the unexpected encounter with the Native American man from the Zuni pueblo, including his suggestions that they either leave or prepare for the pending storm. Too late for either option; they were in the midst of it now. The storm intensified with each passing minute.

Rivulets of rain teamed up to form deep puddles that overflowed onto the dirt road, turning it into a river. The river, affected by the downhill slope and the whipping of the wind, carried the illusion of miniature, white-capped waves on its surface and seemed to have a hypnotic effect on Lindsey. A deafening crack of thunder propelled Jake into action. He grabbed a dazed Lindsey with one hand, the birdcage with the other, and made a dash to her car with Wendell right behind.

"Get in and stay put," he shouted over the raging noises of the storm. "I'll be right back."

She watched him throw everything he could find—camp chairs, cooler, and several large rocks—inside the tent to keep it from blowing away, then he grabbed the pillows and hurried back to the cars. There wasn't enough room for both Jake and Wendell in Lindsey's car, so after giving her a pillow, a blanket, and one of his walkie-talkies, he and the dog jumped into his Jeep to wait out the storm.

Through the window she saw Wendell shake, leaving less rainwater on the dog but a whole lot more on Jake and the interior of his Jeep. Jake's walkie-talkie clicked on. "Ah, yes," Jake said. "Nothing like the smell of a wet dog confined in a small area. Good thing I like you, Wendell."

It felt good to laugh. They both managed to sleep a little, and it was reassuring to hear Jake's voice over the walkie-talkie every now and then.

"Lindsey, are you still awake? Over," whispered Jake at one point.

"Yes, Jake. I'm awake. You don't have to whisper. Malcolm is awake, too."

"I just wanted to make sure you were, well, all right. You seemed really bothered by the storm. Over."

"I'm okay now," she assured him. "Are *you* all right? And must you say 'over' each time?"

"That's walkie-talkie talk, woman. You copy?"

She giggled, thoroughly enjoying how he could make her smile. "Okay, then. Copy that, and a big 10-4 back at you," she replied.

He chuckled. "Try to get some sleep, Linds. I just wish that we ... I wanted to ... Oh, never mind. I'll talk with you in the morning. Good night."

"Good night, Jake. And thank you ... for everything.

When the sun rose, the storm was gone, and so was the tent. The campsite was unrecognizable, littered by broken branches. The actual tent site was now a small pond, the fire pit a mound of mud, and the tent and its contents were nowhere to be seen. The morning air smelled fresh and fragrant, and the trees sparkled with tiny raindrops still clinging to the leaves and pine needles. But the ground was thick with sloppy, slippery, red mud that stuck like glue to everything that came in contact with it. The clean up would be challenging.

Lindsey jumped onto a large rock and folded her arms over her chest. "I declare this area to be an official disaster zone," she announced, then dropped her arms. "Where do we begin?"

Jake scratched his matted and mussed hair. "I'm wondering if we should begin at all. Maybe we should just cut our losses and go back to Tucson."

An unexpected wave of desperation and panic overcame Lindsey. "No! We can't end this—whatever this is—like this. Does that make any sense?"

"Yeah," he said vaguely, sounding both tired and sore. Then he muttered, "No, not really."

"Let's at least try to find the tent," she insisted. "We don't want to litter the Zuni Mountains."

After walking the hillside in a search and rescue formation of two, they discovered the battered and torn tent about a hundred yards to the south, trapped in a deep ravine. Some of their things were still in the tent, including clothing, sleeping bags, a flashlight, and the filing box. All were soggy and in poor condition, but at least they hadn't been strewn throughout the forest. The cooler and the camp chairs had dropped out of the tent about fifty yards before it landed, and they'd stayed tucked and tangled in a grove of thorny bushes. Lindsey made one trip up the hill, dragging the empty and ripped tent, while Jake made several trips to carry its former contents and any other items he came across between the tent's final destination and the old campsite.

Attempting to ignore the reawakened pain in her wrist, Lindsey began hanging the recovered items out to dry in the sun. During a brief break she watched Jake set the chairs and the cooler on a flat, sunny, not too muddy spot, then drag away some of the branches that had fallen, saving the best ones for firewood. Starting a fire would be a greater challenge today.

"Jake, I think we should try to set the tent back up. It'll dry faster that way. But I only found two tent stakes, and we really need at least four. Eight would be even better."

"I'm on it, Linds," Jake said, then retrieved his all-purpose knife from the glove box in his vehicle and took a crack at carving a few wooden tent stakes.

By mid afternoon, the tent was almost dry. Except for the rips on the floor and around the door, it was actually usable. Once the sleeping bags were dry, they could be brought in to cover the holes on the floor, and Jake had some double-sided tape that would temporarily help with the door.

"You carry double-sided tape in your car?" Lindsey asked with a hint of a smile.

"Sure. You never know when you might need it. It's handy stuff."

"Uh, huh."

By sundown, the tent was ready for occupancy, a fire was burning, and the exhausted campers sat by it, sipping red wine and eating spaghetti from a can—part of Jake's emergency rations. Fortunately, Lindsey had kept the dog food and the bird food in the trunk of her car, so the pets' meals went unchanged. Jake's warped and sagging box of files sat beside him, near the fire. She had to wonder if its placement was in preparation for destruction by fire, or if it was merely to accelerate the drying process. Or was there more to learn?

Still staring at the box, Lindsey said, "I know you told me a little bit about the topic of your thesis, Jake, but I'm not sure I understand your hypothesis. What exactly were you trying to prove?"

He took a sip, looking thoughtful. "At first the big question was whether women who were alone—without a life partner, regardless of the cause—grew or regressed."

"And the answer is …?"

"Well, I botched up my research in so many ways, but if I was forced to put an answer into words—which I guess is what you are asking me to do—I'd have to say that some women alone grow and become stronger, wiser, and eventually even happier human beings, but others regress and shrink away from the world around them. Most women alone journey back and forth, spending periods of time growing and periods of time regressing."

Lindsey scowled at him, unimpressed. "You had to conduct all that research to come up with that answer? All humans, women and men, alone or with partners, go back and forth like you mentioned."

"Leave it to a kindergarten teacher to tell it like it is, with simplicity and clarity."

They both smiled and went back to their wine, gazing at the stars in the recently darkened sky. A silent but profound and undefined sadness hovered around their campsite like early morning fog, and she knew they both felt it. This would be their last night in the Zuni Mountains. Tomorrow they would head back to Tucson in their separate vehicles, back to their own lives—lives that would be different now after all that had transpired. So when a brilliant, falling star arced across the jet-black sky, she silently and secretly, wished upon that star. She wondered if he did, too.

"Hey, Jake," Lindsey asked gently, breaking the stillness. "Ever since you told me about Shawna's life, I've been thinking about her. What do you think she will do now?"

"Oh, I didn't tell you?"

"I don't think so. Not that I recall."

"Well, after the infamous assault and night-long conversation, I went home and called my sister, Julie. She's a psychiatrist up in Oregon. I told her about Shawna, and Julie thinks Shawna, with some serious, lengthy therapy, might be a candidate for turning the clock back, reversing some of her physical changes, then spending some time investigating and relearning how to be a man. Her desire to become a woman might be due, primarily, to her father's influence rather than her own wishes. It's a complicated long shot for sure, but Julie thinks it's worth exploring. She called Shawna and easily convinced her to postpone the sexual reassignment surgery for a while, and Shawna seemed willing to talk with her again. So we'll see."

"Now *that* would be one heck of a story!"

"I agree, and so does my sister. Shawna's life story has Hollywood written all over it."

As the evening progressed, sounds of the night emerged with great vigor. Insects, owls, and distant coyotes sang their songs as Lindsey and Jake sat quietly, appreciating all nature had to offer.

Lindsey suddenly blurted out, "Hey! Where's my mail?"

"What?"

"My mail. You know, one of your main reasons for coming to find me."

"Oh, right." He flashed a sideways smile. "I guess I almost forgot about that."

"Well, I doubt the United States Postal Service will forget that you forgot."

"Yeah. Sorry. Where did I put your mail? Hmm. There wasn't much, really. But I remember moving it to somewhere it would be safe. Oh, sure. I placed it in the last and empty file at the back of this box," he said, gently sliding the damp and misshapen box closer. He frowned into it and came up empty-handed. "I don't understand. It was right here. It was. I guess we could send out a search party in the morning."

On that note, they both turned toward Wendell's pile of stuff. He'd started up his own search and rescue, and had quite a variety of saliva dampened items in his collection. Lindsey jumped to her feet and headed to his pile.

The first thing she found was a dead squirrel. "Ooh, yuck." She dug a little deeper, then stood up. "Wait! Wait! This could be it—or at least some of it." She brought everything that resembled a paper product back to the fire to take a closer look. "Like you said, not much here: a piece of what used to be a bag of Cheetos, someone's water bill, pages from a magazine—I think they might be from *Teaching Today*."

A twinge of excitement shivered within her as she spotted the last two items—two envelopes addressed to her. One was a bill—no surprise there. The other, a damp, wrinkled, and slightly chewed envelope, was from Elisabeth Meriwether.

"Who's that?" asked Jake.

"She's the head of that awards conference I attended. It's probably just a follow-up letter about future events," she said, happy simply to have received something that was neither a bill nor junk mail.

She carefully uncrumpled and attempted to flatten the damaged goods, hoping to decipher the somewhat smeared or missing words by the light of the campfire.

"What does it say?"

She squinted hard at the typing. "The first line is all in caps. It says—Oh, my gosh!"

"It says oh my gosh?"

She jabbed him with her elbow. "Oh Jake, you're so funny. No, it says ... I don't believe this. Here, look." She passed it to him, and he read it out loud.

"CONGRATULATIONS, LINDSEY. YOU HAVE BEEN NAMED THE NATIONAL INNOVATIVE TEACHER OF THE YEAR."

Lindsey shrieked with joy and amazement. "Do you know what this means, Jake? Do you?"

"Nope, I don't," he said with a charming grin. "But I bet you're gonna tell me."

Lindsey'd had her share of ups and downs, and this was definitely an up. "Actually, I don't know all the details, and most of the middle of this letter is unreadable due to, well, teeth marks," she said, glancing at the dog, "but at the conference I think Elisabeth said the national winner would present her innovations next school year and would be paid for doing that. Let me see if I can make out anything else from what's left of this letter."

"You do that, and I will pour us each another plastic cup of wine, because no matter what else the letter says or doesn't say, this calls for a celebration."

She barely heard him as she sank into her chair. "Oh, this is difficult to read, but I definitely see some words. Oh wow. I can see sabbatical ... arranged with your district ... regular salary ... royalties? ... expenses ... summer pay ... begin work now ... *now?* ... advance of $200 next week ... call soon!"

"Let me see that. Maybe I can piece together a few more words." He peered closely at it. "So far it all sounds great, though. Huh. The only thing I can add to what you already read is a zero."

"A zero?"

"Yep. Your advance is not $200, it's $2,000! Cheers!" toasted Jake. "I think you are going to have an incredibly interesting and lucrative year, my dear."

Lindsey's plastic cup did not rise to join the toast; it didn't move at all.

"Cheers?" Jake tried again.

But she was no longer floating on air, sporting a smile that could melt the hardest of hearts. Tears tumbled down her cheeks, and sobs rendered her breathless. It was too much. She couldn't handle all the emotions roaring through her. She stood up, ready to run into the night—but from what? And to where?

But tonight, Jake was ready. He caught up to her just as she struggled to open her car door, took her into his arms, held her close, and let her cry.

"Let it out, girl," he said gently into her ear. "Let it all out. It's okay."

Lindsey slumped weakly, willingly against his strong body, and Jake leaned against the car. Sensing something was wrong, Wendell cautiously stepped close to the couple and sat, gazing up at them, looking first to Lindsey, then to Jake, and back again. He put a paw on Lindsey's leg, hoping for a pat on the head or a scratch behind his ears—some kind of sign that everything was all right.

"Listen, Linds," Jake said, "I don't know what this emotional release is about. Maybe nothing, maybe everything. But I do know that you deserve that award. Look, your life has turned around, and you did it. You created all the greatness, all the goodness. It was there all the time. And the best is yet to come."

Still wrapped in the safety of his arms, Lindsey returned the whisper. "Thank you, Jake. You've always been there for me. Long before I even knew it."

He took her head in his hands and looked directly into her tired eyes, searching for something. But it was she who asked the question. Her voice trembled. "Why am I falling apart now?"

"I don't know, Lindsey. But for now, just breathe. Slowly ... Good ... You've been through a lot. Give yourself a break. Everything will be all right."

Jake's hand brushed back the stray hairs that had tumbled from her ponytail, partially covering her eyes. "Lindsey, I know this is none of my business, but now that Shawna and Anthony have broken up, will you let Anthony back into your life?"

"I don't mind you asking. It's okay, really. I've given that question a lot of thought. I know Anthony wants to come back to me. At least that's what his brief note said."

"Yeah. That's pretty much what I figured," Jake said, then he looked away as if he wasn't sure he wanted to hear her answer.

"There was a time," she said, "Well, most of the time, actually—when I would have jumped right back into his arms and tried to pick up where we left off. God, I wanted that so badly, and for so long." She gave him a weak smile and shook her head. "But not now. I could never be with him again. I have a new understanding of what is important in love and in life, and he doesn't fit the description. I'm certain of that. But what about you? What will you do now? Begin a new doctoral thesis?"

He smiled. "No. That's a definite no, at least for now. I've learned a thing or two about myself this year, and after all the snooping and sleuthing I've done, talking to all the players in your life and putting two and two together, so to speak, I've decided that I'm a better detective than a psychologist, though the two actually go together quite well. I do have a plan, and my time here in the mountains with you has helped me confirm it. So for now, I will enjoy great satisfaction through using my BS degree and my interest in plants, the earth, and any aspect of nature, to obtain a job at one of the local nurseries. And—" He grinned wickedly and wiggled his eyebrows. "You're gonna love this. I thought I might write a detective novel in my spare time. As a hobby, just for fun. What do you think of that?"

With his arm still around her shoulders, they strolled back and sat by the fire. "Sounds like a great plan for you," replied Lindsey. "It seems almost everyone I know is writing something: travel logs, architectural articles, fact and fiction about troubled or special needs children, and, of course, now, detective novels. So maybe I will, too. In addition to *Lindsey's Art Journaling with Children* teachers' book, I just might write—in *my* spare time—a romance novel."

Jake laughed out loud, and she was drawn into his sparkling eyes. He looked relaxed and happy, and so incredibly handsome, sitting by the light of the fire. So when he turned toward her and his smile was different, she knew something had changed. His eyes locked onto hers with such intensity it was as if she was able to see, really *see*, into his soul. And she sensed she wasn't the only one by the fire with these feelings.

He leaned in slowly, and their lips met for their first kiss, a kiss that produced spirals of ecstasy more intimate than any sexual encounter from her past.

"Lindsey?" he whispered.

Her eyes were still closed. "Jake."

"Is it just me or—?"

"Shh. It's us, Jake. Finally. It's us."

She didn't want either of them to move from that position, but the fire was dying, and the night was cool. Not wanting the evening to end, she suggested he keep the fire going. He not only split and added aromatic logs to the fire like a skilled woodsman, he also refilled their plastic cups with wine without spilling a drop. They held hands in comfortable silence, enjoying this final night in the Zuni Mountains under a star-filled sky. What would tomorrow bring? At this very moment, it didn't matter. She'd take it one day at a time.

Lindsey replayed their first kiss over and over in her mind. How could a kiss as tender and light as a treetop breeze send shivers of desire with the intensity of a hurricane through her entire body? An all-new physical and emotional experience unfolded, and she had a feeling that here, tonight, uncharted territory was about to be explored—map not included.

As pleasant shivers of anticipated passion tingled through her body, snapshots of annoying past kisses flickered around her brain. Anthony had been her first in every way, and she'd thought he was the sexiest man alive. He had the body and the technique. They had made love—no, they'd *had sex* often, but none of it had ever felt as good as this one kiss from Jake. Maybe Anthony had never really loved her. More shocking still, maybe she'd never really loved him. They'd had an initial attraction, but now she remembered all the red flags her friend Laura had brought up. She'd ignored them all, refused to see, because she wanted to be loved and have a family more than anything else.

Then there was Emmett. He'd never even kissed her lips. He'd lived in her house, taken her money, but he'd never—oh, well. Perhaps a blessing in disguise.

Martin had seemed nice enough, and their lovemaking was good, but there had never been sparks, nothing she could call chemistry. He'd taken care of her—at least he'd paid his own way and even purchased several thoughtful gifts for her.

In her life she'd encountered loveless kisses, ungiven kisses, and cardboard kisses. Not much to go on. She had no experience with true love, had no concept of the thrilling, dizzying chemistry it could bring ... until now.

Lindsey gazed at Jake and offered him a small, shy smile. "I'll need to conduct some research for my romance novel, and I've decided that you—if you're willing—will be my one and only subject," she said. He didn't pull away when she took his hand in hers and led him toward the tent. He would not be sleeping in his Jeep tonight.

Jake grabbed the birdcage with his other hand, and Lindsey called, "Come on, Wendell. You can come, too."

As she rearranged the items inside the tent to create more space, her thoughts drifted to Laura, then to one of her favorite fairy tales. She gave Jake a playful grin. "Hey, you mentioned you had a sister. I don't suppose you have a brother for Rose Red?"

She didn't wait for his reply. No answer was needed, but she took great pleasure in watching Jake's puzzled look. She'd explain some other day.

Once they were comfortably settled in the tent, Lindsey, unable to suppress either her joy or her natural kindergarten teacher tendencies, began to sing *When You Wish Upon A Star*. Soon Wendell and Malcolm joined in, each in his own way, and an owl even hooted a few times. Jake eventually joined in too, though it quickly became evident that carrying a tune was not one of his strengths. But it didn't matter. Their small choir produced the most magical, joyful noise Lindsey had ever heard. One she will never forget.

Jake leaned in and kissed her, his eyes warm and full of love. "Looks like I've found my Happily Ever After," he said.

Cricket Rohman earned her MA in Literature and Philosophy from California State University. She authored picture books and big book songbooks used by teachers before making the longed-for leap to writing adult fiction a few years ago. She finds inspiration and joy living with her husband and dog in both the Arizona desert and the Colorado mountains. *Kindergarten Baby* is her debut novel and Book 1 of the School Days-Grimm Nights series.

Cricket loves to hear from readers; connect with her online.

Website: http://www.cricketrohman.com

Facebook: https://www.facebook.com/CricketRohmanAuthor

Dear Readers:

One last thing . . .

I am honored that you took the time to read my debut novel, Kindergarten Baby. Thank you. The main characters, Jake and Lindsey, live in my head every day as I contemplate their future adventures. Of course, the dog, Wendell, is not only in my head, he's in my heart. And I must admit that I had a dog just like him years ago.

If you enjoyed this book, I would be forever grateful if you would post a review on one of the bookseller sites, Goodreads, or your own blog. And, I'd love it if you'd drop by my facebook author page, click on the red tab "Read My Book" and join my email list. It's true. I really do love to hear from readers.

All my best,

Cricket Rohman